The

BY THE SAME AUTHOR

TUPELO NIGHTS
(1988)

THE BEST THERE EVER WAS
(1990)

LOVE & OBITS
(1992)

John Ed Bradley

THE BILLIONAIRE

BLOOMSBURY

First published in Great Britain 1994

This paperback edition published 1995

Bloomsbury Publishing Plc, 2 Soho Square, London W1V 6HB

A CIP catalogue record for this book is
available from the British Library

ISBN 0 7475 2036 4

10 9 8 7 6 5 4 3 2 1

Printed and bound in Great Britain by Cox & Wyman Ltd, Reading, Berkshire

To my grandmother,
Mrs. Euna Labbé Fontenot,
who had a store

I

Where I come from, you hear a lot of stories—some of them actually true. There's one my mother likes to tell about the first time Carnihan and I met.

It's a day in early spring, 1959, and Pop's outside planting ligustrum hedges on the edge of their weedy, half-acre lot, his hands black with manure and potting soil, sweat dampening his Smoke High baseball cap. He's wearing a white V-neck T-shirt, khaki pants, and a pair of coaching shoes—in other words, what he always wears on his days off. My mother is watching at the utility room window when Deenie Carnihan walks over from her house next door and stands in front of him. Miss Deenie is a beautiful woman with a good shape and long, near-white hair reaching down to the middle of her back, and today she's cradling her newborn son—Carnihan, as it turns out. "Darned Dizzy Deenie," some people in town still call her—a name she acquired back in high school after fainting onstage during a talent show. She was doing an uncertain tap dance, my mother always seems to add, and of a sudden she slipped and fell to the floor, her face smashing against the polished tiles. Anemia, the doctors said later, and on top of that her period had started. And she was such a frail girl, remember . . . ?

(My mother tends to wander, and can go on forever about other women she's known with anemia, or the degrees of slipperiness of assorted floor tiles, or the problems she herself has experienced during menstruation . . .)

So while my father's tending to his plants, Miss Deenie proceeds to poke a breast through the cup of her nursing bra and stuff its ruddy peak into Carnihan's mouth. Carnihan immediately goes at the breast with the wild abandon that too often marked his days, his lips and hands working, pumping, his eyes all aflutter. In the hot little utility room my mother stands momentarily paralyzed, her mouth forming a perfect circle, a noise like rain coming from the back of her throat. Miss Deenie, though married to a man everyone considers a saint, has long had the reputation of being easy with men, and there she goes adding to it yet again. I'm back in the kitchen—down in my playpen swatting away at my favorite mobile of padded sea horses and conch shells—and in a flash my mother comes alive, takes me up in her arms, and runs screaming outside.

Pop looks up. He's alarmed, all right. "Shut the door there, Betty," he says. "You'll let the cool air out." But she ignores him, sprints up to Miss Deenie, and tells her she's an indecent primitive who belongs with the natives in darkest Africa. Tells her she's a disgrace to all cultured peoples, Southerners in general, and the Louisiana Cajun French in particular, and to the Roman Catholic church, of which Miss Deenie is supposed to be a member. Being a modern woman, my mother had tastefully declined to breast-feed my two older sisters and me, but of course this hardly explains her anger. What she says, when she tells this story, is that she is being challenged by Darned Dizzy Deenie, her very marriage is being threatened—*right there among the ligustrum hedges!*

Pop, meanwhile, is trying to look as though he doesn't have the slightest interest in anything Darned Dizzy Deenie has to say much less show him. My mother and Miss Deenie start shouting at each other, and I take a swipe at Carnihan with my knotted right hand. I hit his furry, tomato-shaped head, knock him away from his mother's breast, and lunge at the thing myself. Carnihan cries and screams and swings his hands at me, but my jaws have clamped down hard on the woman and I refuse to let go. The Voohries clan is having a barbecue just up the street, and they hear the racket and come running, and everybody tries to help, about twenty in all. Someone suggests calling the fire department, another using a crowbar to separate us.

Half an hour goes by before they can pull me away.

That's the story, anyway, the way Miss Betty always tells it. And I have to believe it's true, although I never dared ask Carnihan for his version of it. The reason was, Carnihan could be extraordinarily sensitive about his mother, and the mere mention of her name was often enough to choke him up. Cancer killed her when he was still just a boy, and his father, a storekeeper in town, raised him without any help except for a great-aunt who reported once a week to clean the house and cook a hot meal and remind them both what a woman was like. When Carnihan was a kid, he was always desperately trying to embrace any new experience. He said it was on account of missing his mother. He just felt he had to fill the void with whatever felt right at the time, or with "whatever worked," as I seem to recall him saying.

For a time there was a picture of Miss Deenie he carried in his wallet. It had been clipped from a larger photograph and showed her head topped with a foot-tall beehive hairdo, her fine blue eyes squinting from behind a pair of granny glasses. One day at school Carnihan lost the picture—or somebody stole it—and he went running down the hall, yelling like a madman, and it took two teachers and a janitor to subdue him. The principal called his father at work and asked him to report to the school immediately, and when Mr. Hank arrived sweating through his clothes and nervously chewing his lips, he and Carnihan stood by the front office and held each other for a long time —they just held each other with their faces pressed close and both of them sobbing. This happened between classes, when students were supposed to report to their next room and chaos reigned in the hallway. A few of the onlookers, myself among them, whispered about the dead parent, and some wept silently, and still others tittered and scuffled among themselves lest they appear to endorse behavior such as the Carnihans'.

Mr. Hank was wearing his work apron and carrying a feather duster, and he kept patting Carnihan on the back of the head and telling him everything would be okay. Nearly ten years had passed since Miss Deenie's death, but you'd have thought it had happened that same morning. "You'll be fine, boy," Mr. Hank was saying. "You'll be fine. Come now. Chin up. Up. Chin up."

Someone arrived with a camera and took a picture, and later it ran in *The Tiger,* our senior yearbook. "Henry Jackson Carnihan III Consoles Henry Jackson Carnihan IV," the caption said.

The only reason I mention this incident is to state at the outset that none of us, even those closest to him, could ever make good sense of Carnihan. People said, "Over a picture of Darned Dizzy Deenie, can you believe?" and cackled to show their dismay. Or they said, "Carnihan ain't long for this world." Or, "Watch. He'll do something really stupid one day."

In any event, we wondered how a person could love his mother *that much,* and secretly we envied his reputation as an eccentric. Carnihan was as wild a thing as there ever was in Smoke, and for that he deserved both our pity and our worship.

After high school he joined the Navy and was stationed for two years at a base in the Philippines before returning home and going to work at his father's general mercantile store. It wasn't hard for me to square my image of him as a romantic rebel with the person who reported to Hometown Family Goods each morning, a knee-length apron covering his suit of navy polyester, a red club tie hanging from his neck, and I took this as further proof of Carnihan's unpredictable nature. At age twenty-two he married a local girl named Marla Castle, but she left him after a few months and filed for divorce. The legal papers cited irreconcilable differences, but Carnihan told me she had ambition and just didn't want to waste her life on a guy who worked at a general store. After she left, Carnihan started to drink at the local bars and he gambled away most of his salary on football and basketball games, car races, beauty contests, anything. He quickly found himself in the hole, and, tired of dodging bookmakers, he sold his and Marla's little starter home on Court Street, paid his debts off, and moved in with Mr. Hank. This "period of abstinence," as he would later call it, lasted but a few years, and then he was reborn to the life he'd known earlier, which is to say to the life of a man bent on denying himself nothing. By now he was twenty-four years old, and I was living away and seldom saw him. The times I did return home, however, always on vacation, we sat amidst the clutter of the Hometown office and talked about women.

"Sit down, brother," he'd say. "Let me tell you a story. You're not gonna believe it." And he'd rattle off a tale about some woman he picked up and took to a hotel and went to bed with. I knew there was scant truth to his stories, but I found them fantastic and enjoyed hearing him talk. When he got excited he'd pace the floor, his hands flailing the air, his heels beating like drumsticks against the wood and linoleum. And he'd flash a smile that suggested there was more to his adventure—*oh, much, much more, Pacie boy!*—but he couldn't share it with me because he didn't want to besmirch his precious little harlot's reputation.

"You degrade yourself," I told him, not really meaning it.

"Maybe. But what's the point of getting some nookie if you can't tell your best pal about it?"

Carnihan really was my best pal, and he was the first person I called when I decided to quit my job in Washington, D.C., and move back to Louisiana. This was in February 1987, about six months after I sold my first novel for ten thousand dollars to a small New York publishing house that promised to promote me as a "stunning new voice in the Southern Gothic tradition." In retrospect, an advance of ten grand doesn't sound like much for a book destined to make millions, but I'd acquired an agent, the quixotic Cinda Lovey, and she envisioned a six-figure movie deal and a spot on the bestseller lists as soon as the book was launched in April. I was only twenty-eight years old, but I was going to be a major new voice on the literary landscape. Or so Cinda said. And all this for a slim volume of some one hundred and eighty pages that I'd managed to knock out while working full time as a newspaperman.

Carnihan agreed to fly up at my expense, and to help me load the truck I'd rented and drive it down south. I owned a car, a retooled '67 Mustang that happened to be my most cherished possession, and I planned to pull it in tow on a trailer. The night Carnihan flew in, we got in the car and went for a ride through the city with the top down. It was cold out, about thirty-five degrees, and the faster I drove the colder it felt. The alcohol helped anesthetize the pain, but the chill still cut deep. You could see the Mustang's mustard-yellow paint reflected in the huge windows of the office buildings we raced past. Carnihan was quiet until we got to the White House, when he sat up on top of the passenger seat and started to whoop it up. The wind blew his hair back and puffed his cheeks and he threw his arms over his head and just seemed to surrender to the moment. It's a little hard to explain, but when you come from a place like Smoke you never expect to see much of the world. While I could identify with how Carnihan was feeling, I also feared the reaction of the cops and Secret Service agents stationed around the building, and so I reached back and yanked him down to the floor. "This ain't back home," I told him. "Hey, Jay?" He nodded to let me know he understood, and we made the block a few times before finally returning to the street where I lived and fitting the car on the trailer.

We didn't go to bed that night, convinced that a few hours of sleep would make us more tired come morning than if we didn't get any rest at all. At around 6 A.M., when the early-bird traffic started to move outside, Carnihan and I hauled everything downstairs and lined it up on the sidewalk. We fitted what we could into the truck and decided to abandon the rest, leaving it for the bums who flopped in the neighborhood. When we left the sun was shining bright in the alleyways and coloring the trunks of the trees. Birds were singing and for a change you could hear them. The city was uncharacteristically quiet, absent the noise of traffic and building construction and airplanes tracing the path of the Potomac, bound for National Airport.

We'd cleared the city and were traveling a stretch of open highway when Carnihan nudged me on the shoulder. "Have you thought about your next book?" he asked, shouting to be heard above the engine. "What it's going to be about . . . ?"

"Best not to talk about it," I answered. "A writer shouldn't discuss his work. He kills the magic that way."

"He kills the what?"

"The *magic.*" I actually spat the word. "When a writer sits down to work something like magic happens. It's hard to explain and so it's best not to try to."

He didn't say anything for a few miles and I tried to recall what had been so damned magical about writing *Strange Weather.* I'd seen it through by getting up each day at 5 A.M. and drinking bitter black coffee until I nearly hallucinated, then by sitting at my computer and writing one bawdy sex scene after another. If there had been magic, I suppose, it was in composing such athletic prose at that hour of the day, or in getting out of bed at all. At the paper I'd been assigned to the cops beat, which meant I covered police activity in the D.C. metropolitan area. My day generally started at 10 A.M. and ended at 7 P.M., when I filed a thousand-word report about who'd murdered whom. The city's epidemic of crack-cocaine-related killings was setting records, and my job was to try to put a human face on all the ugly numbers. Even more magical than being able to write a novel while working cops was having survived for four years in a city which, as a reporter, I referred to each day as either the "nation's murder capital" or "the bloodiest place in the land."

I drove as far as Roanoke, Virginia, about five hours from Washington, before fatigue set in and I pulled into a rest area to eat some of the sandwiches we'd packed and to take a nap. It was noon, and although the weather had warmed considerably only a few travelers picnicked at the covered tables and under the trees. I parked in the sun and we climbed into the back of the truck, found nooks on top of my gear, and slept on padded blankets. When I awoke it was pitch-black inside, no light shone through the cracks in the closed door, and a long time passed before I could determine where I was. My mouth was dry and wine-tasting and my head ached. I figured I'd slept at least five hours. "Lord, take me now and get it over with," I grumbled, expecting a like response from Carnihan.

When he said nothing, I sat up and slipped down the mound of clothes and furniture. Outside I walked around the parking lot under the pale yellow lamps that hummed and buzzed like insects, and found Carnihan sitting with a woman at one of the picnic tables. They were pressed close together, shoulders touching, huddled against the breeze.

"This is my friend," he said, "the author I was telling you about." There was a hint of pride in his voice, and I gave the lady a smile.

She put her hand out and I shook it, limp, greasy thing that it was. "I never met no novel writer before," she announced. "Glad to make your acquaintance."

"Her name's Missy," Carnihan said. "She's hitching down to New Orleans for Mardi Gras and I offered to give her a lift. That okay with you, brother?"

"Fine," I muttered, "although there isn't much room in the cab. You mind riding in back, Missy?"

"Not at all. Any air get back there?"

"Cold air," I said.

"Sure there ain't room up front? I'm little. I won't be no bother." She stood up, to show how small she was. Her legs seemed too short for the rest of her body, and her face looked like that of an undernourished monkey. To complete the picture, her hair was a stringy mess hanging down to her shoulders.

Carnihan said, "How long a drive to New Orleans from here?"

"Eighteen hours if we push it."

"That's nothing," Missy said.

"Eighteen hours is nothing?"

"Not for Missy," Carnihan said. "She used to be a long-distance truck driver, hauling loads coast to coast. Isn't that right, Missy?"

She nodded and smiled her spooky monkey smile. "I can take over when you boys get tired," she said, then picked up the duffel bag at her feet and started for the truck.

Now that she'd turned her back to us, I was free to cut a reproving glance at Carnihan. "This is a mistake," I said through clenched teeth. "The woman could be a killer for all we know."

"A killer? Well, if she's a killer, Pace, then we're both dead meat. And if we're dead, we don't have a thing in this world to worry about, do we now?"

I was too tired to find fault with his line of reasoning, and too full of pity for Missy to leave her out on the road. "One day you're going to get us in some real trouble," I told him.

He took this as my consent, and punched a fist at the air to show his delight. I suppose he had some lurid picture of himself making love to the girl, because he threw an arm around me and whispered in my ear, "We have begun our adventure, Pacie boy."

Missy put her bag in back and we headed down the road. The cab had a bench seat and she sat in the middle, closer to Carnihan than me. She actually smelled rather nice, I thought, like pink cotton candy. I silently praised my powers of observation when she declared that just this morning she'd left a job with a traveling carnival that had taken her to every state in the continental U.S. She had a rich brother who lived in a twenty-room mansion in uptown New Orleans. He'd offered her a job as an assistant manager at one of the fried chicken franchises he owned, and said he'd provide her with room and board until she could secure a place of her own. "I want to make a success of my life," she said. "This is a new beginning for me."

"Hear that, Pace?" Carnihan said. "Missy, you, and me—three newborn babies for the world."

We stopped for gas and Carnihan bought Cokes and a family-size bag of fried pork rinds. As we continued along the interstate Missy crushed her empty can between her hands and said she was delighted to have met us because it was a hard time of year for hitchhiking and she'd known a guy who'd frozen to death standing by the roadside, his thumb up in the air. This was meant to be a joke, but it didn't go over very well. Only Missy laughed. "Yesterday," she declared, "I was shoveling elephant dirt at the zoo in Baltimore, and today I'm going to the Mardi Gras. Life does turn, don't it?"

I figured it turned, all right, especially so since I recalled her saying that she'd worked for a carnival, and also as a truck driver. "Know anybody in New Orleans?" I asked at the same time Carnihan inquired about elephant dirt. "Is it anything like elephant shit?" was the actual question he raised.

"No, I don't know anyone there," Missy was saying. "I always wanted to see it, though. I read where Bourbon Street has buildings with naked girls just standing in the windows. They get paid for standing. If nothing else, I could always do that."

Carnihan asked his elephant dirt question again.

"How would I know anything about *that*?" Missy replied. "I was a dancer, bub."

"A what?"

"An exotic dancer—at the Kit Kat Club in D.C., bub."

A few minutes later I said, "What does your brother think about you being a nude dancer, Missy?"

"Ain't got no brother," she answered.

Claiming to need the toilet, I pulled off at the next exit and stopped at a gas station. Carnihan hopped down from the cab and shambled behind me, murmuring a string of obscenities under his breath. We went into the bathroom and locked the door and stood in the dark laughing so hard that we had to lean on each other for support.

"What'll we do?" he said.

"Let's tell her the truth—that we think she's crazy."

"What do crazy people care about the truth?"

"Let's tell her our wives wouldn't appreciate the two of us riding around with an exotic dancer."

"But I already told her I wasn't married."

"Then we'll kill her. That's it. We'll kill her and hide her body somewhere and just head back down the road."

We finally decided to lure her away from the truck, then to speed off before she could get in the way and stop us. We left the bathroom and walked to the vehicle, and to our delight discovered that Missy wasn't there. The station attendant was filling up a car at one of the pumps, and I asked him if he'd seen our traveling companion. "She's in the ladies'," he said.

Carnihan and I got into the cab and fled for the interstate, depositing planks of rubber on the pavement. I drove ten miles over the limit, straining the big beat-up truck and making the Mustang swerve. By the time we reached Tennessee we'd managed to convince ourselves that Missy was a serial killer who liked to dismember her victims and collect their private parts. Her primary target was Louisiana Cajuns under the age of thirty.

I didn't remember her duffel bag until we reached the city of Knoxville. I stopped the truck on the shoulder and Carnihan and I got out. We were rough in handling the bag, and so whatever was inside yelped and whimpered.

Carnihan spun around on his heels. "What the . . . ?"

I knew it was a dog before he did. "It's a mutt, Jay. She kept her mutt in there."

Carnihan opened the bag and the animal poked its muzzle out. The eyes emerged, small and blue, followed by ears as big as banana leaves. Its body resembled a dachshund's, although the splotchy blue of its hide was identical to that of the catahoula hound indigenous to my home state. I'd never seen a more peculiar-looking thing in all my life, and was about to say as much when the animal leaped into my arms and commenced to lather my face with its tongue.

Carnihan crossed his arms and leaned against the bumper. He was sulking, and I figured it was because we were stuck with mad Missy's dog. But then he said, "He likes you more than me."

"No, he doesn't. He's just happy is all. He'd been stuck in that bag, bouncing around in the truck. It's a wonder he didn't suffocate. Here, Jay, take him."

The dog went crazy in Carnihan's arms, and for some reason I experienced a sharp pang of jealousy. I reached to take it back. "How old do you think it is?"

"Six, seven months at most." He wrenched the dog's mouth open and inspected the teeth and gums. "I'd say she fed him well. He looks healthy."

"Is he a boy, Jay? Are we sure about that?"

Carnihan held it up and we conducted a quick examination. "He's more man than boy," he remarked, admiring its credentials. "We need to name him."

Only now did it occur to me that he intended to keep the animal. "No, Jay. We can't."

"Missy. How 'bout Missy, Pace?"

"Hey, look. That dog doesn't belong to us."

"Mister, then. Mister's the opposite of Missy, ain't it?"

"Jay, it's not ours. We have to return it."

"How about Beatnik, then, since we found him on the road?"

He thrust the dog against my chest and it proceeded to lick the spots on my face that it had failed to dirty the first time. I admit to feeling a gush of affection for the odd blue thing, and to trying to justify driving off with it. Its mama was a truck-driving, elephant-dirt-shoveling, exotic-dancing schizophrenic with rotten teeth and hair, I reasoned, and it deserved a better life than the one she would give it. Its mama had abused it, leaving it tied up in a duffel bag packed with stinking clothes and tins of fruit and potted meat. I was beginning to tell myself more when Carnihan announced, "Beatnik just loves us too much," and supplied once and for all the reason why the dog should join us.

Driving through northern Alabama I decided to abandon use of the word *it* and refer to Beatnik as *he*. The dog's personality was too engaging to continue to refer to him so impersonally, and a vivid picture had begun to take shape in my mind of how he'd look ten years from now. I saw him lying at my feet in an oak-paneled study crowded with antique books and furniture, snoring away and oblivious to the noisy patter at his master's computer keyboard. As if suddenly aware of what I was thinking, Carnihan sat up tall in his seat and said, "We'll share him, Pace. He's half yours and half mine. Agreed?"

Apparently I didn't answer quickly enough, because Carnihan said again, "Agreed, Pace? Half yours, half mine?"

"Agreed," I said, and reached over and stroked Beatnik's ridiculous pear-shaped head.

That night we drove as far as Meridian, Mississippi, and stopped in the parking lot of a Monster Mart discount store. Carnihan opened the passenger door and used it to shield himself from the road as he urinated a busy white stream. Beatnik scurried over to the front tire, lifted his leg, and relieved himself as well. Although no one had passed us by, I hated the impression we were giving—that of white trash who use the roadside as their personal toilet.

"You should've told me you needed the bathroom," I said. "We could've stopped at a rest area."

"Oh, heavens no," he said, "this place is worse than any shithouse anyway." He zipped his pants back up. "I'd do the other thing here too if I had the urge. Maybe in the morning."

We fashioned nooks in back of the truck, and Beatnik, whimpering in bewilderment, needed only a moment to choose Carnihan as his bedmate. "I guess it is me he loves, after all," Carnihan said, pulling the animal close.

Despite my exhaustion it took a while for me to fall asleep, mainly because Carnihan kept babbling about the many sins of Monster Mart Inc. Last I recall, he was detailing his plot to assassinate Rayford Holly, founder of the nationwide chain of Discount Cities, as the stores were called.

"Holly's the richest man in America," Carnihan was saying, "with personal wealth of about twenty-eight billion dollars. And yet he chooses to live in Liberty, Arkansas. He drives a 'sixty-two GMC pickup truck and eats lunch at the same diner every day of the week. He pretends to be Mr. Everyman when the truth is he's not even human."

Carnihan snorted and beat his fist against the truck wall. When he spoke again you could tell he was addressing the dog. "I plan to hurt him. Yes, I do. Huh, boy. Huh, boy. Huh, boy."

I lifted my head and stared into the darkness. "Go to sleep, you dumb fool. We have a big day tomorrow."

But Carnihan started up again. "Holly's destroyed small towns like ours all across this country. What he does, he throws up a Monster Mart, sells below wholesale, and steals business from the mom-and-pop operations like Hometown Family Goods. Then when he's run everyone out of business, he jacks his prices up and really fucks the consumer. People have nowhere else to shop. It's like the old company store in a mining town—"

"Jay?"

He took in a deep breath. "The beast, my man. He walks this earth. And I can tell you his name."

Carnihan finally quieted down and I went back to sleep, only to be awakened a short time later. He was opening the door to the back of the truck, making too much noise. I lay with an arm under my head and watched him hop down to the pavement, shuffle over to a light standard, and lower his pants. Beatnik stood staring from atop the cargo. He seemed as astonished as I was.

When Carnihan finished he wiped himself with an athletic sock. Rather than return to his nook, however, he closed the back door and locked it, and I heard his feet slapping the asphalt as he hurried to the cab in front. Beatnik whimpered and clawed a padded blanket, then the engine coughed and roared and we were moving in a wide arc, heading, I assumed, back to the interstate.

It was too dark to read my watch, but I figured it was about three in the morning. Even if Carnihan drove the speed limit we'd make it home before Pop left for his morning golf game. I closed my eyes and ruminated on the writer's life. I imagined all the things that would soon be mine—the love of great women, the admiration of famous men, the endless flood of delicious green money. Beatnik came over and lay beside me, his tail kicking happily against my ribs. "Do you know how lucky you are that we found you?" I said. "Do you know who I am?"

I spent the rest of the drive plotting my immediate future, or at least wondering about it. My father had offered to let me stay at their house on Delmas Street, but I'd been on my own for several years and wanted to keep it that way. I was starting to build a fairly vivid picture of myself as a young artist, and it did not include the small bedroom where I'd dreamed away my childhood, staring at posters of professional football stars on the walls and listening to pop music. I saw myself as a haunted, soul-scarred fellow who lived in a dilapidated bayouside shack, or, even better, in an enormous Victorian boardinghouse run by a fat lady, formerly the town tramp. The fellow I saw kept late hours, toiling away at an ancient manual typewriter, a hand-rolled cigarette smoldering at his lips. His hair was long and badly cut and he often went days without bathing. Painfully thin, he took his daily meal of tomato soup and crackers at the Palace Cafe, and he was often heard mumbling to himself. Some mornings he walked the sunlit streets, shouting the number of words he'd written the night before. He was the most mysterious resident the town had ever known, and a legend had grown up around him.

I had a plan. I'd live in Smoke until about six months after *Strange Weather* was published, which also happened to be the time my first royalty check arrived. Then, weary of the demands that accompany celebrity, I'd retreat for a few years to Paris and live the life of a disillusioned expatriate. In a nondescript flat on the Left Bank I'd complete my second novel while gathering material for a third, this one to center on a new lost generation of American intellectuals like myself. While I had yet to choose a subject for the second book, I decided now that the third should depict my days abroad. I imagined the voice of my brilliant young novelist telling of his adventures with the city's most libidinous women. The narrator's sexual escapades, microscopically detailed, would make those in *Strange Weather* look like innocent teenage encounters.

Since these were the plans I had for myself, how, then, could I move in with Miss Betty and Pop? As much as I loved my parents, I figured my biographers would have too hard a time reconciling their ordinary lives with my extraordinary one. Also, and probably more accurately, I planned to do a lot of late-night carousing and didn't want my folks to know about it. Miss Betty was a retired schoolteacher who kept house, cooked two meals a day, played Po-ke-no with friends, and videotaped soap operas when she happened to be away for the afternoon. Pop, a retired high school football coach, shot golf each morning with his pals at the Indian Hills Country Club; at night, when he wasn't napping in his favorite recliner, he liked to stretch out on his bedroom floor, play solitaire, and watch whatever happened to be showing on ESPN. But if my parents were provincial, so was Smoke. To my knowledge its lone bookstore still offered little beyond Bibles, home-living magazines, and cookbooks. The library carried few new titles and none with language offensive to the head librarian, a Pentacostal of the tongues-speaking variety who reportedly drew the line at "goshdurn." *Strange Weather* probably would be denied a place on the shelves there, but I welcomed the controversy, figuring it would help boost sales. "Poor Smoke," you heard people say when discussing the place. They seemed to think of it as a lifelong friend fallen ill with some incurable disease. "Poor Smoke," they said, certain that death was near.

Heading in, we took old battered Highway 190 to a cloverleaf loop that swung us onto I-49, and drove the new stretch of pavement for about half a mile before exiting at Creswell Lane, a skinny concrete strip crowded with fast-food restaurants, clothing and video stores, insurance agencies, and satellite offices for area banks. I still couldn't see anything, so I closed my eyes and called the area up from memory. When we stopped at the end of the street I envisioned the fire station to the right, and, off to the left, as gray and imposing as a battleship, the football stadium where Pop had coached for thirty years and where Carnihan and I had played for him more than ten years before. In my mind's eye the rye grass was tall and swaying in the cold morning breeze, and blackbirds pecked for food in the end zones. Carnihan turned left and we were on Union Street, water and live oaks towering on either side of the road. We passed a butcher shop, a pizzeria, and, getting close now, turned right at a florist's with huge Valentine's Day hearts pasted to the windows and a lighted sign saying RED ROSES: $9.99 A DOZEN, C & C. This was Dunbar Street, and now we had less than a block to go. Beatnik, sensing something, began to bark, and I barked, too, happy to be home and happy to be young and happy that, being so prodigiously blessed, everything now seemed possible.

Carnihan backed the truck down the driveway, angling it toward the front door to facilitate the job of unloading. He threw the door open and a blast of spinning light came in, bright and warm, carrying the heady green scent of pine from the trees lining the lawn. I shielded my eyes with my hands and only after a moment could I focus on Carnihan, his jaw dark with stubble, his hair greasy and matted to his scalp.

I handed him the dog. "Well, let's go see if Miss Betty's decent."

We entered through the front door, and I was shouting, announcing our arrival, when a voice—Miss Betty's—came from the back of the house. "I'm not *dee-cent*!"

"What's that?" I called.

"I'm not . . ."—she paused to let us think about it—"*dee-cent*!" This was an old family joke, originating back when I was in grade school and a group of my pals, following me into her bedroom, spied her without a stitch of clothes on.

"I'm not *dee-cent*!" she said again.

"Well, neither are we!" Carnihan howled, rattling every bit of glass in the house. "But at least we're dressed!"

We walked into the kitchen and the lights flashed on and a terrific roar went up as about fifty people, all friends and family, descended upon Carnihan and me, saying, "Welcome home, Pacie boy." And: "Good to see you again, old buddy." And: "Never thought I'd live to see the day." I was too stunned to speak so I just stood there smiling, thrilled by the fuss. Red, white, and blue bunting streamed down from the ceiling, and there were posters, tacked to the walls, with Miss Betty's smart script saying hooray for the sale of *Strange Weather* and wishing me every success. I spotted Pop and he winked and raised a hand in greeting. He was wearing what he always wore, and he looked not a day older than the last time I was home, Christmas before last, some fourteen months ago. His hair, bristly as a porcupine's, was clipped close to the scalp, and his face was carved up with enough steep promontories and deep hollows to give a person vertigo. His eyes were green and smart, and in them I glimpsed what I'd always found there, which is to say, a great store of love for me, his only son. "I'm not *dee-cent*!" I said to him now. "Hey, Pop! Did you hear? I'm not . . ."

He laughed and shook his head and threw his arms around me. "No, you're not, boy. But you're home. And thank God for it. Just thank the good Lord for it."

I suddenly felt ashamed of myself for having thought my parents too provincial for my biographers. They had raised me, after all, and they knew how to throw one helluva party. "Thirsty, son?" I heard Pop say, then spotted Miss Betty crossing the kitchen floor with a magnum bottle of champagne. She gave it to Carnihan and he wrenched the plastic cork out, and foam spewed everywhere. Another roar went up, followed by more hugs and kisses. Somebody found a Cajun song on the radio, and we paired off and two-stepped to the fiddle-rich number, Pop with Miss Betty, and Carnihan with Beatnik, and me with my two beautiful sisters, neither of whom was having any problem articulating just how thrilled she was to have me back.

Claire said: "We're so lucky to have such a brother!"

And Abigail: "Why, we're the luckiest people alive!"

Since it was a workday, everybody cleared out by ten o'clock, returning to their vehicles parked out of view up the street. Miss Betty led Carnihan and me to the dinette table in the kitchen and served us each a plate piled high with the shrimp-and-artichoke salad and oyster dressing she'd prepared the night before. Pop took his chair at the head of the table and fanned the sports section of the local paper in front of him. The paper was called the *Daily World*, but we all knew it as the *Daily Lip*, a name that seemed infinitely more accurate considering how its editorial-page writers tended to squawk and moan.

"Want one, Daddy?" Miss Betty asked, offering him a cookie sheet crowded with homemade drop biscuits.

Pop looked up from the paper. "No," he said. "Two."

"Yesterday afternoon," Miss Betty said, "I sent your father to the store for the bunting and poster boards, and he surprised me with that big bottle of Cordon Negro. How much did you pay for that, anyway, Daddy?"

Pop was too busy eating to do much more than grunt.

"Hey, Pop," Carnihan said. "It wasn't Monster Mart where you bought all this, was it?"

"It was Hometown," Pop replied.

"But we don't sell champagne."

"I got that at a liquor store."

"The bunting and all, you got that from us, did you?"

"I can show you the receipt if you'd like."

"No, no," Carnihan said. "I trust you."

After the meal we sat outside on the back patio and had cups of hot chicory coffee and watched purple martins fly circles in the air above Pop's multilevel birdhouse. Beatnik parked himself on Miss Betty's lap and snored like an old man, his lips blubbering with each exhalation. The sun burned high in the sky and it had gotten too warm for a jacket. Two trees in the yard were bare—the pecan and the sycamore—but all the others were still green with leaves. A century-old live oak, heavy with Spanish moss and supporting dozens of squirrel nests, spread its massive limbs across the lawn, dropping pools of shade. Ligustrum hedges bordered the property—the same bushes Pop had been planting the day Carnihan and I first met. They now stood about twelve feet tall and fenced off Miss Betty and Pop from the neighbors. Mrs. Kuel, a perpetually sad-faced woman of about fifty who liked to water her lawn at all hours, lived alone in the big white house to the immediate north. And Gloria and Ronnie Thibodeaux occupied the sprawling redbrick house to the south. Carnihan had actually lived next door for only a few years after Miss Deenie's death. Mr. Hank, haunted by her memory, had sold the place and built a farm on a fifteen-acre tract of high, wooded ground off Worm Road, just north of town. Miss Betty and other friends had tried to get him to date and to at least consider remarrying, but he'd seemed content with what many regarded as a monastic life, raising goats and some of the finest tomatoes the parish had ever seen. "Who can compare with my Deenie?" he'd told my mother. "No. Thank you, Betty. But I prefer not to do that to a woman."

Carnihan excused himself and went inside for more coffee. And Pop, sitting up on his chaise longue, cleared his throat for what I reckoned to be an important announcement. "So this book of yours, Pace? Are you going to let your mother and I read it now or will we have to wait and buy a copy when it comes out?"

Although I'd anticipated this moment with dread, I was glad now that it had come so suddenly, and not a little relieved. "I brought a few copies down from Washington," I told him. "I'd hoped to surprise you with one."

"Am I in it?"

"No, you're not."

"And your mother?"

"It's fiction, Pop. I made it all up."

I walked to the front of the house and dug around in the back of the truck for the big cardboard box containing Xeroxes of *Strange Weather*. I gave a copy each to Miss Betty, Pop, and Carnihan, and they all found it necessary to hug me again. Carnihan studied the cover page for a while and said, "Does it rain a lot in your book, Pace? I'd been meaning to ask."

"Why would it rain, Jay?"

"Well, the title, brother. When I think of strange weather I think of hurricane season. Is there one in here?"

"I'm afraid not. The title is a metaphor for the storm brewing inside my protagonist."

"Your protagonist, did you say?" Carnihan had a funny look on his face. He seemed incredulous that I would find such a story worth telling, or, still more unbelievable, that a publisher would pay money to print it. "So this person—your protagonist, as you call him . . . is he the one who's strange?"

"You think I should've called it *Strange Protagonist*? It's not too late, you know. I can call my editor."

"Hey, come on, brother. I didn't mean to upset you."

"That's right, Pace," Miss Betty said. "We all can't think thoughts as deep as yours."

"What do I know anyway?" Carnihan said. "I'm just a guy who works in a general store. I saw *Strange Weather* and immediately figured that's what it was about."

Miss Betty and Pop lugged their books into the house, and Carnihan and I took the Mustang off the trailer and started for downtown. I was driving, and Carnihan sat holding Beatnik close to his chest, a glass of milk punch wedged between his legs. In minutes we came upon the courthouse square and I stared blankly at the darkened storefronts that only a decade ago had been bright with color. While some of the businesses had relocated next to the Monster Mart on Smoke's southern end, most of them had been forced into bankruptcy. Closed were a five-and-dime, a dress shop, a tailor, a printer, a sports emporium, a gunsmith, a beautician's, a furniture mart, a café, and a department store called Abdalla's, once the biggest retail business in the entire parish. The buildings were unoccupied, their entrances sealed with sheets of plywood. For Sale signs hung in the black windows. It all had the wind-scoured, tumbleweed look of a ghost town, and I'd have said as much had anyone but Carnihan been there.

"I know what you're thinking," he told me.

"No, you don't."

"You're thinking Hometown's next, I'll be out of work soon."

Our eyes met but I couldn't hold his for long.

"You're right, too. You're right about what you're thinking. Pretty soon now I'll be standing on the side of the road—me and Beatnik, both of us skin and bones, tired and hungry. 'Will work for food' is what the sign around my neck'll say."

Hometown Family Goods, as I recalled, was opened at the turn of the century by Carnihan's great-grandfather Henry, one of the first English merchants to set up shop in the predominantly French town. Because he was regarded as an outsider—descended from the same people who first persecuted then banished the Acadians from their Nova Scotia homeland little more than a century before—Henry Carnihan was forced to cater to a Negro clientele, which, though loyal, lacked the financial resources to give him the security and social status he'd desired. Not until he married a local French woman did his fortunes begin to change. He stopped calling Cajuns "Frogs" and they, in turn, quit referring to him as "Monsieur Yank." Business soared, and before long he built the largest mercantile around.

Hometown was located on the lower lip of the business district, a high-ceilinged, barnlike structure situated between the telephone company and a mobile home park. It had an old-time lunch counter where for as long as I could remember meals had been prepared by a woman named Ruby Dean Clark. Hometown's shelves were thick cypress planks that still smelled as if they'd been planed just yesterday, and they were stocked with items that were unavailable anywhere else. As a kid I loved to walk the aisles and memorize the names of the ancient remedies, and to play with tools that had no modern use. There were containers of Black Draught syrup and Nok of Dix throat tablets and Dier Kiss talcum and Eagle's toothache gel and Dr. Caldwell's senna laxative and Johnson's foot soap and 666 Preparation with quinine. Also, as Mr. Hank used to boast, Hometown was the first store in the entire state of Louisiana to sell toilet paper printed with a floral pattern.

On the wall behind the business counter, four poster-size portraits were hung: the first, a fuzzy black-and-white of Henry Carnihan; the second of his son H.J.; the third of Mr. Hank; and the fourth—an enlarged reproduction of a photograph taken while he was in the service—of Jay Carnihan himself.

We turned right on Market Street and passed another ruin, the Delta Theater. The huge marquee displayed but one word, CLOSED, and the poster windows were empty, dust caked on the splintered glass. This was where I'd spent my Saturday afternoons as a boy, watching cowboy and war movies, and, during those sweaty junior high school years, trying to sneak kisses from girls. Next to the theater the parish had constructed a new jailhouse of pale yellow brick, and in the windows of the upper floors I saw men in orange coveralls staring through the bars and wire mesh, looking as hangdog as everything around them.

Would *Strange Weather* help rejuvenate Smoke? I believed it would. Although the screen rights to the book had not yet been optioned, I was certain that the movie adaptation eventually would be filmed on these same streets, bringing in millions of dollars. A tourist trade would follow, and surely businesses would open to accommodate it. I gazed at the old Delta building in the rearview mirror and imagined how it would look a year or so from now when Hollywood money transformed it into the glittering palace it had once been, and people in expensive clothing lined the curb in front, and the marquee glowed like heavenly fire. PACE BURNETTE'S STRANGE WEATHER were the words I saw, trailed by the names of the biggest film stars of the day.

"Not counting Monster Mart," Carnihan said to me now, as I wheeled into the Hometown parking lot, "the only business that'd been making it in Smoke was Babylon out on the Lewisburg Road. But a few months ago sheriff's deputies stormed the place, arrested the owner, and padlocked the front door."

"They running poker tables or something?"

"No, man, it was a whorehouse."

I vaguely remembered the place, standing hard by a country lane: a simple beer garden and a lousy one at that, notorious for attracting people who wore tattoos on their flesh and clothes that reeked of oil and sweat, and who seemed to have a penchant for throwing up in public. Whenever local lawmen went out searching for suspects in theft and homicide cases, Babylon was always the first place they stopped.

"From the outside it still looks like any other roadside tavern," Carnihan was saying, "but inside, the way they've fixed it up, you'd think it was the lobby of some great hotel. Anita Billedeaux, she's the owner . . . Anita single-handedly kicked out all the riffraff and made it what might be called respectable, and she brought in girls from all over the South—from Beaumont and Biloxi and Jackson and Mobile. But then she started skimping on her payments to the sheriff, and he called for a raid to teach her a lesson. What's weird is that they were romantically linked—she and Sorel were lovers, if you can believe it." He gave a chuckle and shook his head. "Well, they later reconciled and Sorel let her reopen the place. The customers haven't come back around, though. They're afraid of another raid."

Carnihan stepped out of the car, dropping Beatnik to the ground.

"I like to go there after work," he said. "I like it a lot. The ambience is really nice."

I tried to give him a cool stare, but I couldn't keep from laughing. "You go for the ambience, do you? For the *ambience*, you say?"

He smiled in that remarkably stupid way of his, a way you couldn't help but find endearing. "The women, brother, I tell you, they've got so durned much ambience they'd strain even Daddy's limits of self-control."

We walked around to the front of the store and he pulled the screen door open. The door had a metal kickplate that said EVANGELINE MAID, and showed a bas-relief of Longfellow's fair maiden holding a loaf of bread. Carnihan bowed at the waist as I pushed past him and entered the enormous room, bright now in the early afternoon. Light came from the great plate-glass windows and from the rows of green-shaded lamps that traced the aisles. The air was thick and radiator-warm and smelled of oats and coffee beans and shredded tobacco, and of a time and a way of life that just weren't supposed to exist anymore.

"There's a girl at Babylon . . ." Carnihan said. "She reminds me of someone we went to school with."

I gave him a look.

"In fact, I'm certain it's her."

I wheeled back around and was about to press him for a name when his father came running from behind the lunch counter and wrapped me in a stubborn embrace. Mr. Hank was a small man closer to his seventieth birthday than to his sixtieth, but he was quick on his feet and I couldn't dodge him. He had a thin, clean-shaven face that seemed perpetually turned up in a smile, and short hair that never was out of place, even in the wind. I think he used some sort of styling gel, probably some ancient item he stocked there in the store. Mr. Hank didn't look like someone who could squeeze the air from your lungs, but there he went, emptying mine. "Well, look who's home," he said, nearly lifting me off the floor. "If it isn't Pace Burnette! Pace Burnette, of all people! It's Pace Burnette . . ."

I liked the way Mr. Hank said my name. He made it sound as though I had already made my mark on the world and that nothing I could accomplish in the future could match some of the moments he'd already been witness to. He'd seen me take my first steps, for example, and learn how to ride a bicycle, and play football against teams like the Warren Gators and Bayou Loup Acadians; and what, his big smile always seemed to say, could be more impressive than that?

"Pace Burnette. It's Pace Burnette, all right. It's Pace . . ."

Carnihan had walked the length of the store and come to a stop in front of what was known as the business counter. It was really just a beat-up little table with a cash register on top, but in the old days it was where they used to ring up customers when people still bothered to shop at Hometown.

"We just came to check on things," Carnihan told his father. "Anybody buy anything?" He didn't wait for an answer. He pressed the register's No Sale button and a cash drawer popped out, bumping against his hip. "Another slow day, huh, Daddy?"

"Not too bad."

"Nothing here that wasn't here last time I checked."

Mr. Hank slid his hands down deep in the pockets of his apron. "Leave it alone, Jay. Please. Just for today."

"Why for today?"

"Pacie's home, to start. The second reason, and by no means any less important . . . the second reason is that I said to."

The zinc top of the lunch counter was still wet from cleaning, and I could smell Ajax and grease: evidence that the world's best short-order cook had just been there.

"Ruby Dean left after lunch," Mr. Hank said. "Something about something, I didn't hear. I'm sure she'll be disappointed when I tell her you came by."

"Still big as a house, is she?"

"Two, three houses," Mr. Hank answered, although his mind seemed to be elsewhere. He'd spotted Beatnik and was watching him snoop around the store, sniffing at this and that. "What is it supposed to be?" Mr. Hank said. "It isn't . . . ? Tell me it isn't yours, son."

"Mine and his." Carnihan pointed a finger at me. "We found him on the road home. His name's Beatnik."

"But I don't like an animal in my store."

"He'll kill the rats."

"Hometown has no rats."

"He'll kill the roaches, then. We've got plenty of them."

"He's absolutely the ugliest thing I have ever seen in my life." But even as he spoke Mr. Hank was taking the dog up in his arms. "Hello there, Beatnik. How are you, boy? How are you?"

Let me give a picture of the store, as it was that day and as I would always remember it. Salt licks stood next to pallets loaded with huge bags of flour, beans, and sugar. Mason jars were stacked on the floor between aisles crowded with cane and chocolate syrups and marshmallow cream. Major appliances, some a hundred years old, some brand-new, lined the walls, which themselves were papered with calendars for years no one could remember having lived. There was a shelf no less than ten feet long devoted entirely to feminine napkins. Another, directly beneath it, bent under the weight of bicycle parts and plumbing fixtures. Next to that cowboy hats, pajamas, and enema bags were jumbled together, a layer of dust upon them. Hometown also sold leather saddles, thermometers, bolts of embroidered Chinese silk, metronomes, and high-fidelity stereos. Miss Deenie had been fond of gardening, and kiosks loaded with vegetable and fruit seeds remained as evidence of her passion.

"It's less a store than a shrine to everything American," I said as I walked along, hands clasped behind my back. "Hey, Jay, you should charge admission."

"Yeah, well . . . If things don't get any better."

"Take this swamp root syrup, for example." I held up the bottle. "I bet the Smithsonian would consider this a rare archaeological find."

"Either that or the Food and Drug Administration would arrest us for stocking it."

"Yours for a dollar-fifty," Mr. Hank called from where he stood staring out the front window.

". . . contains extractives of bucher leaves, peppermint herb, rhubarb root, mandrake root, cape aloes, scullcap leaves, colombo root, birch, balsam copaiba, and balsam tolu." I was reading from the back label, struggling to pronounce some of the words. "Golden seal root, valerian root, sassafras, cinnamon, and oils of juniper. It's made in Bethpage, New York, and it says here it's sold by druggists nationwide."

"Yeah?" Carnihan said. "And what does it do?"

The answer wasn't easy to find. "It promotes the flow of urine, thereby aiding the kidneys in their necessary work of eliminating waste matter."

"It's a diuretic," Mr. Hank said. "It makes the bathroom your home for the day."

Carnihan was standing behind the lunch counter, flipping through charge accounts. "We keep most of that stuff around for the newspaper boys," he said. "Every now and then when things are slow a photographer with the *Lip* comes by and takes a picture for the front page. It's good advertising, and it's cheap."

"It's free," Mr. Hank said.

"That's what I mean."

Of a sudden Carnihan remembered something. "Hey, Daddy. What about the office? Anyone answer the ad?"

"No."

"Not a single query?"

"Nope."

"Something I failed to mention," Carnihan said, handing me one of the many sections stacked next to the register. "It's all there in black and white. Page B2, down toward the bottom."

I immediately spotted what he was talking about: a red-ink circle around a listing for an unfurnished medical office adjacent to Hometown Family Goods.

"What's this?" I said.

"Dr. McDermott had a breakdown, and the medical board rescinded his license to practice."

"That's awful."

"He'd leased from us for forty years, Pace—that is, until a few months ago. He was diagnosed with Alzheimer's and he just finally lost it. Now he's eating lime Jell-O and singing campfire songs at the old folks home around the corner."

"He was a fine man," Mr. Hank said. "He dressed beautifully and he laughed a lot. Show some respect, boy."

"A lot of our business came from him," Carnihan said. "People trickled in, looking for Tylenol and antacids and leaving with milk pails and spring bonnets. Unless somebody rents the space, I'm afraid things will get even tighter around here."

The medical office stood between the stockroom and a parking lot, and you couldn't see it from Market Street out in front of the store. I hadn't been there since high school when I went to Dr. McDermott for a routine physical exam, but I remembered the cathedral ceiling in the waiting room and the satiny red oak floor of the hallway. And now I thought how splendid a place it would be for someone such as myself: an unconventional home for an unconventional man of letters. I imagined the National Historical Society placing a bronze plaque at its entrance a hundred years from now, officially recognizing the site where Pace Burnette, Nobel laureate, awaited publication of his classic first novel and commenced work on his second.

"I'll take it," I said, and slapped my hand a bit too enthusiastically against the countertop.

"You'll take what?" Carnihan asked. He looked baffled.

"Dr. McDermott's. I'll rent it and live there."

"Oh, Pace," Mr. Hank said. He lifted a hand to his forehead and made his eyes flutter. "It's a nice gesture, son, but you should find yourself a comfortable home. Have a flower garden and a lawn to mow. You'll want to entertain young ladies, and this just isn't the proper setting."

"If they don't like it, then they won't like me."

"He's a writer, Daddy. He's got an image to keep."

"Are writers foolish?" Mr. Hank asked. "Answer me that. Are they crazy? Are they dumb?"

Carnihan stood there smiling at me. I don't know why I expected him to answer; I'd already done that by insisting on renting the old doctor's place.

About half an hour later Carnihan and I drove back to the house on Delmas Street and found Miss Betty and Pop outside adding potting soil to the base of a plant, or pretending to. The thing was big and leafy and really didn't need their attention, and it came to me that they were using the plant as a prop to keep from looking as if they'd been waiting for me. *Strange Weather* was their problem, not the fig.

"Just found a place to rent," I announced without first bothering to say hello.

"Oh, Pace." Miss Betty raised a dirty hand to her face.

"We came for the truck. We're going to move my stuff over there now. I should be settled in by late this afternoon."

They both looked at the Mustang, idling by the curb. Carnihan was slumped behind the wheel, waiting to follow me back to the store. Beatnik watched from the window.

"You couldn't have found anything," Miss Betty said with a note of alarm. "Not this fast, anyway."

"Where is it, son?" Pop asked. He didn't look as upset as she did, but that didn't mean anything. Pop was a master when it came to hiding his feelings.

"Dr. McDermott's," I said.

"Behind Hometown?" Blood momentarily brightened Miss Betty's cheeks, then seemed to completely drain from them. "Why, Pace, you're no doctor. That's a doctor's office!"

"It's only temporary. The novel'll be out in a couple of months, and then I'll go to Paris. After that I'll buy a real nice spread somewhere here in Smoke."

"A real nice . . . ?" It was Pop.

"Spread," I answered. "Nothing too big. I want to avoid appearances. I'm only twenty-eight, remember?"

Of course I knew better than to ask what they thought of the book. No doubt they'd spent the last few hours reading it, and I figured they'd have said something had they liked it. As a rule my parents never offered a negative opinion except when it came to state politics or the New Orleans Saints football team. When they liked something, however, they were quick to praise it. A trip to the minimart might produce this response: "Golly, Pace, you must've found the coldest jug of milk in all of Louisiana." Theirs was a conscientious effort to shed a positive light on a world that wasn't falling apart as quickly as everyone seemed to think. But when something upset them, Pop generally fell silent, thrust his hands in his pockets, and stared at the ground, and Miss Betty got teary-eyed and sniffled as if from a head cold.

Now as I started the truck and let the engine warm, I tried to ignore my father's reticence and to disregard the streaked makeup on my mother's face. Pop was holding the plant in his arms, Miss Betty the bag of soil.

Speaking to my feelings of disappointment, I told myself that perhaps the fig did need work, after all.

I was backing down the drive when Miss Betty ran to catch up. "Will you and Jay join us for dinner tonight, Pace?" she said. "I can invite Abbie and Claire."

"We planned to go out on the town," I said. "To celebrate." This wasn't entirely true, but the alternative seemed awful. *Strange Weather* had turned Miss Betty into Strange Mother, and there wasn't a thing entertaining about that.

"I can make a gumbo."

"Some other time, okay, Miss Betty?"

"What kind? You want okra, seafood, or chicken and sausage?"

Who cares about that? I wanted to cry out. What about *Strange Weather*? Isn't it the best book you've ever read? Instead I said, "Chicken and sausage will be fine, Miss Betty. But later, all right? We've already got plans for tonight."

She nodded and I could see the tears again, making their way down her cheeks. Her wave was weak and tortured, her goodbye a whisper. "We love you, baby," I seemed to hear her say. "We love you. Love you . . ."

But she hated the book, I knew. She and Pop had found it repulsive, immoral, humiliating. Sex in hunting blinds, sex in churchyards, sex in mop closets. I reminded myself that I was an artist, a person with vision and a mandate to make sense of what it means to live a life in the latter half of the twentieth century, and that they were just two middle-aged people whose existence was vicarious at best, revolving around the accomplishments of others—their children—and thus entirely empty. I decided I would forgive them for being so simple, but they would have to forgive me for being so complex. I also decided that when the book was published to universal acclaim and mind-numbing sales, they would change their opinion and see genius where now they saw only perversity.

And no longer would Carnihan and I have to go out on the town for dinner. We could celebrate at home with them and gladly eat whatever she happened to serve—possum, gator, water moccasin, hoot owl, and nutria rat included.

Later that evening, after depositing my gear in the lobby of Dr. McDermott's and giving Mr. Hank permission to take Beatnik to Worm Road for the night, Carnihan and I drove to a place called Prudhomme's Cafe, some fifteen minutes from Smoke. The restaurant stood by a service road running parallel to I-49; a sign near the ditch in front promised good Cajun cooking.

The maître d' wasn't able to seat us right away, so Carnihan and I went into the bar and ordered Bloody Marys. The drink's high taste of Tabasco sauce made my nose trickle, and it also seemed to intensify my thirst. Carnihan had a similar reaction. "Do you serve this by the pitcher?" he said to the woman behind the bar. She smiled and he said, "Then give us each one."

Twenty minutes went by before our table was ready, but by then we were too full of tomato juice, celery sticks, and pickled string beans to want anything more. Carnihan gave the maître d' two bucks for his trouble, and I patted the man's shoulder. "We'll just stay in the bar," I said. "We like it here."

"Love it!" Carnihan yelled, then uncorked a belch as noisy as any drunk's.

I'd hoped to engage Carnihan in a conversation about Babylon and his unlikely encounter with our old schoolmate, but no matter how many attempts I made he was determined to talk about the year we were seniors at Smoke High and members of Pop's last team. Carnihan claimed to remember the scores of all ten games, then proceeded to name them. The only one I could recall was also the easiest: a 6–0 win over our biggest rival, the Warren Gators, and also our only victory. In the final contest of the season we had erased nine consecutive weeks of humiliating defeats, and Carnihan and I, lost in the moment, had tried to carry Pop on our shoulders to the middle of the churned-up field. He had refused the ride, however, finding it ostentatious and, in his words, "unsportsmanlike as everything." "Be gracious, boys," Pop had scolded us. "Be gracious." We'd looked up at him and noted the film of tears in his eyes. "Remember who you are," he'd said, doing his best to smile. The bleachers had emptied and all our boosters had crowded around, and it was the only time, Carnihan said, that he'd ever seen my father cry.

"Does Pop do that much?" he asked now, turning to look at me. The alcohol had inflamed his face and he was having trouble keeping his head still. "Does he cry, I should say?"

"That last game," I answered with a heavy tongue, "was the only time I'd ever seen him, too. He keeps everything inside." I held a couple of fingers up for the bartender, indicating we were ready for another round. "What about Mr. Hank, Jay? He cry much?"

"Daddy?"

Since I didn't think it needed repeating, I merely shrugged.

"I saw him only once, too," Carnihan said.

"I've never seen him."

"Who?"

"Mr. Hank. I've known him all my life, and I've never seen him cry. Not a tear. Not one . . . not a single drop."

"Well, once he did. Oh, yes."

"Not around me, he didn't."

Carnihan started to say something and got choked up.

"When your mother . . . ?" I asked.

His head bobbed again and his face turned even redder than before. He pulled at the collar of his shirt and gave me a beat-up smile. "God, it's gotten warm in here."

I paid the bill and we went outside in the cool, thin air, neither of us fit to descend the stairs, much less drive a car. We threw our arms around each other and staggered across the lot, groaning in pain and because we simply felt like it. A couple scuttled past, the man showing an unhappy face, the woman gripping her purse as if to protect it from us. Only then did it occur to me how terrifying Carnihan and I must've looked, and how truly regrettable our behavior was. We reached the car and lay back against the trunk, gazing up at a sky ablaze with stars.

"Give me the keys," Carnihan said, holding his hand out.

"I'm afraid I can't do that, brother."

"But you don't know where we're going."

"We're going to Dr. McDermott's," I said, "to sleep on the floor. Tomorrow I'll worry about setting the bed up."

"That's not where we're going," Carnihan said. He started to laugh and ribbons of hair fell over his eyes. "We're going to Babylon, brother." He leaned his face close to mine, and I saw how serious, how sober he suddenly was. He might not have had a drink all night.

I didn't trust his story about our old classmate, and yet the prospect of seeing her in the beer garden, working her way through a knot of lonely, depraved men, intrigued me almost as much as it repulsed me. Could one of the girls with whom we'd grown up now be engaged in such work? I hardly thought so. I remembered the hookers I'd seen in Washington, the ones I occasionally wrote about in my police reports. At dark they came to stand on the corners of the street where I worked, and inevitably they were flanked by a rough-looking character with a pencil-thin mustache, a mole on his cheek, a dragon tattoo on the side of his neck. On cold nights you'd have to lock your car doors because, stopped at a traffic light, there was really no other way to keep the girls from piling in, taking seats in front and back, and staying until they warmed up.

Imagine, then, my difficulty squaring that picture with the one I held of the young women of Smoke, most of whom had been raised to think of themselves as fine Southern ladies, or, as I'd once heard Carnihan himself say, "people to whom the world owes much." Some, we'd complained back in school, were so well bred they never had a pimple, bad breath, or a bowel movement. The prospect of finding one in a bordello was about as strong as finding one in any place but church come Sunday morning. We good citizens of Smoke knew who we were, and perhaps more positively we knew who we weren't, as well.

At the end of Dunbar Street we crossed some railroad tracks and drove down McCarthy Lane cutting potato and bean fields awash with moonlight. We turned right on the Lewisburg Road where small country houses and twisted chicken trees hugged the blacktop, and fields stretched flat and black toward far stands of hardwood trees. This was farm country, and even in a winter as mild as this one, it looked cold and uninviting. There was a lumber company standing close to the first bend in the road, and just past it Babylon A-Go-Go. A malfunctioning neon sign marked the entrance—"Go" was all it still managed to say. A saloon occupied the middle building, on either side of which stood runs of rooms with brightly painted doors and unscreened windows holding air-conditioning units.

We stumbled in and faced a woman with great, shivering blocks of fat at her neck: Anita, I presumed. She sipped a beer and her eyes rolled back; loose flesh danced along her upper arms. Carnihan waved and mumbled a sullen hello, but she didn't respond except to cup a hand around her mouth and belch quite loudly. Past the bar was a large sitting room crowded with furniture: Empire sofas, big stuffy chairs, café tables, floor and desk lamps, plastic trees in huge terra-cotta pots. There were pictures on the wall, to boot: men playing a Cajun card game called bourre, ducks on a rippled pond, a faded print of late-afternoon cotton fields. I liked the dark, quiet spirit of the place, and its smell of floor polish and perfume. The ceiling was a good twelve feet high; at its center, hanging above a dance floor, was an enormous chandelier that looked like an upside-down Christmas tree. At the moment an old jukebox decorated with colored tubes was playing a song I'd never heard before. It sounded like one of those zydeco numbers in which all the musicians beat their tubs and washboards at once and sing whatever little ditty comes to mind. Beneath the big light a cowboy in black, mud-caked boots was dancing alone, leading his imaginary partner through a dizzying run of dips and turns that no real woman could possibly have kept up with.

"Is it always like this?"

"What do you mean?"

"Hardly anyone's here."

"The raid, remember? Everyone's afraid to come back."

We sat at a table by the jukebox. A few feet away a woman was lying on a couch, talking on a telephone, her voice full of sighs and dirty promises. She held a belted throw pillow against her deep bosom, another between her legs. I noted the smudge of lipstick on the phone's mouthpiece. "She handles that thing like a marital aid," Carnihan said. And I knew he was talking about the receiver.

In a chair next to her sat another woman, this one a dewy brunette wearing a cardigan sweater unbuttoned to her navel. She watched Carnihan and me with an expression intended to suggest lust and longing. Recalling my own reaction this morning to Miss Betty's oyster dressing, I immediately knew where she was coming from. "You 'member me?" the woman called in a hoarse, strangely masculine voice. I blinked a few times, hoping to clear my eyes, or at least to draw more light from the darkness. And, yes, I did recognize her. There might've been prettier girls on this earth than Genine Monteleone, but none more desirable. I'd been crazy mad goofy in love with her going back to our days together in Miss Irene's kindergarten class, when she wore pigtails and charm bracelets and white patent-leather shoes, and I slipped crayon drawings of arrow-impaled hearts into her lunch pail.

"You mean to tell me . . ." she muttered now, strutting over and claiming the chair beside me.

Genine and I hadn't seen each other since the night of our high school graduation, but it was clear she'd forgotten that I had the uncanny ability to go without blinking for as long as two minutes at a time, and thus to deceive without much effort. Maintaining a bemused expression on my face, I said, "I beg your pardon, miss," and offered a bored half-smile to further confuse her. "I'm afraid you have me mixed up with someone else."

She'd grown up to be a trifle thin, Genine had, and to own a head of hair as big and involved as a globe of the world. Her eyes were huge and sleepy, and what little makeup she wore seemed hastily applied, or perhaps rubbed off. Her face was showing disappointment, her lips the most malevolent frown I'd ever seen. And yet she was as lovely as when we were children and blissfully smitten with each other.

"You're afraid, are you?" she said at last, doubling her hands into tight fists and waving one in my face. "You'd better be afraid, Pace Burnette."

"So you remember him," Carnihan said.

"Like yesterday," came her reply. She placed her chin in her hand and leaned forward, until our noses nearly touched. "Pace Burnette, if you don't tell me my name—"

"Give him a hint," Carnihan interrupted.

She thought for a moment and said, "Larry Chowder."

"Larry Chowder? Larry 'Peahead' Chowder? I'm sorry, miss, but you'll have to do better than that."

"Okay, then. How 'bout this? In homeroom, senior year, I sat two chairs behind you."

"And which one was I?"

"The one sitting two chairs in front. Come on, Pace. Tell me my name."

I stared at her, still without blinking. "At school, were you in any clubs? The home ec society? Pep squad? Anything of that nature?"

The question drew her to her feet, and she started to perform a cheerleading routine that brought back the year 1975, the autumnal scent of bonfires and spilled whiskey, and the warm, happy tears in my father's eyes. For some reason the dancing cowboy took this as his cue to take a break. While he hobbled dizzily off the floor in search of a chair, Anita and the telephone lady watched Genine as if they couldn't be less impressed. Genine finished with a split, and the familiar cry "Go Tigers!" filled the room.

As captain of the cheering squad, I recalled, Genine Monteleone had been as incompetent at her duties as Carnihan and I had been at ours as players. What she'd lacked in ability, however, she'd made up for with enthusiasm. Or so Miss Betty had said once.

"Good lord, how are you, Genny?" I finally shouted in mock surprise, rising to my feet and hugging her close. "Genny Monteleone! Hey, Jay, it's Genny. It's Genny, of all the . . ."

Carnihan sat laughing and drumming his knuckles against the table, and Genine pressed her mouth against the side of my face.

"Poor Pace," she said. "You're red as a beet."

"Am I?"

And then she pulled me tight and kissed me again.

"Did you really not remember me?"

I nodded my head yes, then decided to stop the charade, and shook it no. "Of course I remembered."

"Then you should be ashamed of yourself . . . playing me along like that." And, lo and behold, she kissed me a third time.

"You're the one who should be ashamed," I told her. "Not me."

She seemed to think I was admonishing her for working at a place like Babylon, and to help clear up any confusion I said, "You think I'd forget the girl I gave my first heart to?"

Behind the bar Anita coughed like a tuberculid horse, and the telephone lady sighed and whispered another dirty word. The cowboy, seeming lost and bewildered, returned to the floor and continued his solitary dance, his boots tracking a parabola of mud on the high-polished wood.

Was it possible, I wondered, that Genine had fallen this low? I remembered how she used to perform flips across the gym floor at our Friday afternoon pep rallies, and how she'd had a reputation for being a bit of a prude, rarely holding hands with boys let alone kissing them. She must've sensed my incredulity, because she raised another knuckled fist to my face. "I'm not one of them, Pace, if that's what you're thinking."

"Oh, no, Genny. Of course not." I laughed and shook my head with unnecessary vigor, and thus failed utterly to look convincing.

Carnihan was staring at Anita. "What's she doing here, anyway? I thought you said she had the night off."

"So says she got antsy and had some bookwork to do. It's a lie, though. She just wanted to make sure no one was stealing."

"Nice lady," I said.

Genine shrugged her shoulders. "First thing she does is check the book to see the number of customers went with girls. Then she counts the beer bottles in the trash and on the tables, and then she checks the till. If the numbers don't add up, she closes the door, turns the lights on, and threatens to beat it out of us. The girls and me all put up a few dollars to make up whatever's missing, because she means it. I saw her hit this boy the other day, this soldier from Fort Polk. She hit him in the nose, and he fell back unconscious with his eyes wide open and not even blinking. Blood flew everywhere. I spent half the night with a mop and bucket wiping the floor. I asked her if she really thought it was necessary to punch people out like that, and she called it her personal management style."

"Oh, sure," Carnihan said. "I know the strategy."

"And how would you know that?" I asked.

"Well, it's the same one Rayford Holly uses at his Monster Marts. Each spring—May, I think it is—he gets in his truck and rides from town to town, picking out stores at random and paying a little visit. He's been doing this the last few years, ever since his wife died. This white-haired old billionaire in a 'sixty-two GMC. No air-conditioning or radio. Nothing but a change of clothes and a sack of peanut butter sandwiches one of his servants packed for the trip. He likes to make out he's going on some big adventure, looking to find himself. They say he doesn't even bring a bodyguard along, although I seriously doubt this—I mean, can the man be that stupid? Anyway, he parks his truck in the fire lane and hurries in before anyone can recognize him, and he walks the aisles looking for trouble. Slurpees spilled on the floor, clothes off the racks, dead fish in the aquariums. From what I hear he's even got a name for this—"

"Jay," I said, "Genine was telling us about her work."

"The journey to self-discovery. He calls those trips that. Can you believe he's got the nerve to call them that?"

She grabbed his hand and folded her fingers into his. "He's tired of Monster Mart, too, baby. Give it a rest for once, all right? Just for tonight?"

"I plan on kidnapping him," Carnihan said. "When he comes through Smoke looking to discover himself, I'm going to show him who he is. I'll put a gun in his ribs, is what I'll do. Drive him around town and show him what he's done. 'Discover Abdalla's,' I plan on saying. 'Discover Low's Five-and-Dime.' Once he's seen it all, I'll take him on a journey you don't come back from."

Genine was shaking her head. You could tell she'd heard it all before. "You know how crazy you sound, Jay? It scares me, you get this way."

"I want an apology," he continued. "I want to hear him say the words. 'I am sorry, Mr. Carnihan.' After that, he's free to go. He can call in the cops and they can throw me behind bars for the rest of my life. At least I'll have the satisfaction."

"Satisfaction with what?" I asked.

"Hearing Rayford Holly say the words. That he's sorry for what he's done. To me and my daddy, in particular."

"Well, I'm just sorry we have to hear all this," Genine said. "Pace comes home after being away so long, and you have to start on Rayford Holly again."

"An apology," Carnihan said. "Just remember where you heard it first." He got up and wobbled over to the bar. "A g and t, please. Heavy on the g."

Genine turned to me with a look of immense sorrow. She seemed to be on the verge of tears, and I reacted as I always had whenever I saw her looking troubled and depressed: I got that way myself. "Genny, what's wrong?"

"Nothing." But by her tone of voice she might've said "Everything." She glanced back at Carnihan. "Did he tell you we were engaged, Pace?"

"I beg your pardon."

"Jay and me? Did he tell you we were getting married?"

"Did he tell me . . . *what*?" Even more than Carnihan's threat against Holly, I considered this the stuff of ridiculous fantasy. She was joking, I figured, testing me to see how I'd respond. But then she held her left hand up and showed me the ring: a small gold band adorned with a tiny diamond.

"Since last week," she said. "He proposed right here at Babylon . . . right where we're sitting."

I touched the little stone with the tip of my finger. "Looks like a mighty fine jewel you got there, Genny."

"Oh, it's not, really." And yet you could see how much she treasured it. A minute went by when neither of us said anything. I feigned interest in the ring, examining it from every angle. Something was wrong. Carnihan and Genine were getting married, and yet he hadn't told me a thing about it. Carnihan and Genine were getting married, and yet she was working as a barmaid in a whorehouse. Although I tried to disguise my confusion, I could feel my facial muscles begin to quiver, and I had trouble looking Genine in the eye. On top of that, she was asking questions about my days in Washington, and I was blurting out irrelevant answers. "The president lives there," I said at one point. "And the first lady, of course . . . their children." Then Carnihan returned to the table, toting drinks; and I was relieved beyond telling.

He plopped down in his chair and asked me somewhat distractedly, "You will be my best man, won't you, Pace?"

I gave him a smile and a playful pat on the back. "Sure, brother. Aren't I always?"

"We haven't set a date yet," he said. "But it'll be sometime this summer."

"Oh, yeah? In June, perhaps?"

"No, not June. June was when me and Marla got married. I swore I'd never get married then again."

"You two go ahead," Genine said. "Don't bother about me. I don't mind being reminded about Marla and June and all the hell else."

"Sometimes Genine forgets that she was married once too," Carnihan said. "And that about a week ago her ex-husband stopped by Babylon for a drink and a piece of pie."

"Not my piece," she said, squirming a bit in her chair.

"Tell Pace the story, Gen. He'll want to take notes. Maybe he'll put you in a book and make you famous."

She batted her eyes and forced a dramatic sigh. "I don't want to bore you. I'm not like somebody we know on the subject of Rayford Holly."

"I wouldn't be bored," I said. "I'd like to hear it."

She took in a deep breath. "You remember Larry Chowder, Pace? I mentioned him earlier?"

"Sure. Peahead played football with us. He was the biggest kid my father ever coached."

"Well, we get married then divorced. No big thing, right? Happens to a lot of people. He's living in Warren, and I'm in Smoke. And last weekend he comes in to visit his old daddy at the home, and he stops off here on his way out because I guess he's heard, and he takes a seat and I get him a drink, and it's like I was something from another life, an accident he had on the road. It's all a blur to him—it's like he's trying to place me. He sits at the bar and gets drunk, so drunk that he passes out and Anita's got to carry him to a room. He's gone by the time I come in to work the next day, but he hasn't paid his bill. So guess who gets stuck with it? Anita hands me the thing as soon as I walk through the door. A hundred and twenty bucks."

"Damn, Genny."

"Dumb monkey," Carnihan said. "Maybe that's why they called him Peahead. Who'd want to be married to that?"

But she hadn't finished telling her story. "I've been here about a month now, Pace, I started not long after the raid. I'm the official hostess—my job, in case you were wondering, is to keep everyone happy. Sometimes there aren't enough girls to go around, so I talk to the men and try to keep them from getting rowdy." She smiled at me and for a moment looked seventeen years old, like the high-jumping cheerleader I used to know.

"Okay," Carnihan said. "Tell him the part about Rayford Holly and Monster Mart."

"Nothing to tell, really. I put in an application and they turned me down. I guess I wasn't what they were looking for."

Carnihan said, "Rayford Holly, Pace. I'm telling you, brother, he's Beelzebub with a redneck accent."

"It had nothing to do with him," Genine said. "It's the economy. Jobs are filled as soon as they come open. It wasn't anything against me personally. It's just the times, is all." You could tell this was something she'd said countless times before in an attempt to convince herself that she wasn't to blame for her problems, and it might've worked had she put a little more into it. "Some kind of a career I've got going, huh, Pace?"

"Of course it's not selling hundred-year-old enema bags and tittie-growth serum like I do," Carnihan said, "but it does pay the bills, doesn't it, Gen?"

I smiled to let Genine know I was on her side, or maybe I did it because there was nothing to say.

"One thing I've learned about living," she said, "is that if you planned on things going one way, count on them going the other."

I was beginning to wonder if anyone in the world was happy tonight when a group of fraternity boys from the university in Warren burst through the door screaming with laughter and managed, in a matter of seconds, to replace the gloom with a general cheerfulness. The telephone lady got off the couch and took turns dancing with the boys, and when she tired of them the boys danced with themselves.

Carnihan arm-wrestled with the biggest of the bunch and lost after a brief struggle, and to show what a good sport he was he bought everyone a drink. Then the noisiest of the group stumbled over to our table and asked Genine if she was available. "Wanna do sum'pin . . . ?" were the actual words he used.

Carnihan jumped to his feet in defense of Genine's honor. "What are you saying there, son?" he bellowed.

The boy blanched, stammered an apology, and reported to Anita his intention to pick up our tab. Although both Genine and I objected, Carnihan argued that it was the right thing for the kid to do. "His old man's probably rich. And it'll make him feel like a high-roller. Oh, let him have his fun."

We didn't leave until after midnight. Genine walked us out to the car, and she and Carnihan embraced for a long time, the neon "Go" flashing, painting them pink. They declared their undying love for each other, and then she put her arms around me, and we hugged and swayed and patted each other on the back. "I'm glad you're home," she said.

It felt good to hold a woman. I didn't want to let go.

Carnihan said, "Maybe it's you two who should get married. What in hell're you trying to do with my woman, Burnette?"

As Carnihan and I were driving out of the parking lot, one of the fraternity boys stepped from a room shoving his shirt in his pants. When he spotted Carnihan he let out a shrill bird whistle and pumped a fist in the air. You might've thought he'd just done something heroic, like scored a touchdown giving his team a victory. I waved goodbye, and Carnihan blew a fat-lipped kiss.

"I love you," Genine said.

"I love you, too," Carnihan told her.

Once we'd pulled onto the Lewisburg Road, Carnihan turned the radio off and placed a hand on my shoulder. "I guess I should explain about me and Genny." He gave me a cigarette and I punched the lighter in. We were halfway through our smokes before he said anything more. "We aren't getting married, Pace. It's just a game we play."

I sat quietly, waiting for the rest.

"Yep, just a game. The bastard Peahead left her not long after he found out she couldn't have babies." He waited for this to sink in, and actually repeated the word "babies" a couple of times. "Genny's got something called an infantile uterus. It's where the woman doesn't mature enough to carry a baby. Her womb never develops—it stays how it was when she was just a kid."

"Never heard of it," I said.

He nodded as if to suggest I'd somehow doubted him. "Well, it's real, all right."

I looked out at the dark fields rushing past. My ears were still ringing from the music in the bar. "Maybe we should talk about something else," I said.

"Hometown's about done its dance. And Genine, poor baby—Genine's no hostess, Pace."

"Yeah?"

"Didn't you see how fidgety she got when those college boys came in? She didn't want you to know." He rolled his window down and, although it was only half-spent, flicked his cigarette outside. "It's like she said. It's the times, is all. It really has nothing to do with the kind of person she is."

"But the engagement ring you gave her . . . I saw it. She showed me the diamond."

"Ruby Dean was sweeping the floor the other day and found that ugly thing. She gave it to me for safekeeping, and I put it in the register. One afternoon Genny happens to drop by for a cup of coffee, and Ruby Dean asks her if she isn't in need of something pretty. Genny just sat there and cried."

We drove on for a while without saying anything. I kept seeing Genine as I knew her little more than a decade ago. I remembered her in a pleated orange-and-black skirt and a sweater with a big furry *S* in the center, and her legs lean and tanned, and her hair, long and straight then, gleaming under the stadium lights. I remembered running through the goalposts minutes before the opening kickoff, racing out onto the field, and Genine and the five or six other cheerleaders leading the way to the sideline, holding hands like a string of paper dolls. People cheered and jumped to their feet, and the band played, and it seemed we would always be that way: young and seventeen and whooping it up on Friday night.

"She doesn't worry about catching something?"

Carnihan looked at me. I seemed to have pulled him from a dream similar to the one I'd been having.

"Well, does she?"

"She says if it's like everything else in Smoke, it'll be ten years late in getting here. And by then they'll already have found a cure."

He started another cigarette burning, the smoke boiling like a cloud. And I pushed even harder on the accelerator.

II

Too tired to put my bed together, I retired for the night on a cold, steel table in one of Dr. McDermott's examination rooms. The overhead plumbing got fussy every half hour or so, but I slept hard and well until Ruby Dean Clark woke me up at eight o'clock the next morning. She stood hovering over me, her face big and round and glistening with sweat, the top of her head covered with a hair net. Her smell of biscuits and fried eggs was as strong and willful as I remembered it, and my immediate urge, which I resisted, was to press my face against her grease-splotched uniform and inhale until my lungs filled and burned. "Time to eat," she said. "Come 'n' get it, boy."

As she left the room her nylon-encased thighs, rubbing together, sounded like hamsters turning an exercise wheel in a cage.

I was stiff and sore and a bit hung over, but I managed to dress hurriedly in the same clothes I'd worn the night before, maneuver through the junk that crowded the hall, and make my way through the maze of shelving units in Hometown's stockroom. I proceeded through a red velvet curtain and shambled into the store, careful, since I was still half blind with sleep, not to trip over anything. At the counter six or seven people were seated, all of them hunched over breakfast plates, saying nothing. I took the City section of the morning *Lip* from the extras stacked next to the cash register and claimed a stool between two women studying their faces in oval-shaped compact mirrors. These were tellers at one of the downtown banks, wearing identical uniforms, and I presumed eight hours of imprisonment in a drive-thru booth was enough companionship for both of them, and that to get them to acknowledge each other now would cost you.

At the moment Ruby Dean was transferring a mound of eggs from the sputtering grill to a plate, while simultaneously pouring someone a cup of coffee. Behind the counter she was as vital to the world as a brain surgeon, and she carried herself as if she knew it and expected everyone else to know it as well. There was a chalkboard over by the register listing today's specials: RICE BISCUITS, GRIT BISCUITS, PLAIN YEAST BISCUITS . . . BROWN-EGG PANCAKES, PORK SAUSAGE, SHORTENING BREAD (LO-FAT) . . . BUTTERMILK MILK . . . WHITE MILK . . .

She held the plate with a wet hand towel and deposited it in front of a man who sat reading the ingredients listed on a small breakfast box of raisin bran cereal. He was a fellow of middle age who today was wearing a white linen suit and a fat polyester necktie that didn't reach but halfway down his shirtfront. The top of his head was absent a ring of hair the size of a lady's bracelet, and, as I recalled, he was alternately fat and thin, depending on a stomach condition. This was Silas Poe, senior officer in the accounting department at the Homestead Bank, and the most devoted customer the Hometown lunch counter had ever known. Over the last twenty-odd years Silas had missed only twenty-odd weeks of meals at the store, that time being spent in Las Vegas, where he traveled each fall to play craps and video poker and to send home to Hometown a stream of picture postcards all addressed to Ruby Dean:

> *. . . wishing you were here saw Robert Goulet last night and ate the buffet all you can eat but nothing like you . . .*

> *. . . walked in the desert in the morning with the sun just up wondering about the meaning of life and why all this sand . . .*

. . . be home in three days can't wait for a cup of coffee and news from poor Smoke . . .

Silas didn't see me walk up; otherwise he'd have gone out of his way to make an embarrassing fuss. He was emptying half a bottle of Tabasco on his eggs and grits, and Ruby Dean was watching him with a pained expression on her face. She might've been looking at the desecration of a great work of art, the way her eyes turned wet and glassy and her mouth twitched.

"Now you know better than that," she said when it finally got to be too much for her.

"Know better that what?"

"And right—" She wagged a finger at him. "Right while I stand here and watch! What about your intestines, man?"

"What intestines?" Silas said, positioning his face a few inches from the food. "It's my stomach that's the problem." And then he began to eat in such a hurry that it was hard to tell which was moving faster, his fork or his mouth.

"Hey, there, Ruby Dean."

"Why, Pace."

"Pace?" It was Silas again, flashing an energetic wave.

Ruby Dean picked her towel up and started cleaning the place in front of me. "What can I get for you, boy? Pancakes okay?"

"Sure."

"Eggs?"

"I'll take a few."

"How many exactly?"

"Four."

"How 'bout I give you eight? Life in the big city has gone and made you skinny, boy."

"Then if that's the case," I said, "would you mind adding some bacon and a glass of orange juice? And maybe put one or two of those eggs on top of the pancakes. Over easy."

"Yes, your highness. Anything else?"

"No, my queen. Thank you."

As I noted now, Ruby Dean still kept a picture of her son Hayward on the counter, right next to the one of Martin Luther King, Jr., leading a march through the streets of Birmingham, Alabama. Hayward had been the only truly gifted athlete on my father's last team, and, if my numbers were right, he'd just completed his sixth season with the Miami Dolphins of the National Football League. A first-round draft choice out of Grambling in 1980, Hayward was a swift and tenacious defensive back who last season had been a unanimous selection to the All-Pro team, his third such honor. As Mr. Hank liked to boast, Hayward's salary was ten times that of the wealthiest banker in Smoke, and he'd married the most beautiful woman in Miami, one LaShonda Gordy, a lawyer specializing in personal injury cases. After receiving a half-million-dollar bonus for signing his rookie contract, Hayward had bought a big brick house for Ruby Dean in one of our older neighborhoods and opened a trust in her name. Although he'd tried to get her to retire from the lunch counter, Ruby Dean had refused to quit, and often had been heard to wonder what Mr. Hank would do if ever she left. As a result of Hayward's generosity, she was far better off than most of the people she served, and yet she continued to work with humility and grace, suffering their occasional complaints without a rude or defensive word in exchange. Hayward's picture showed him in uniform, celebrating after an interception, and he had signed it across the bottom: "To Mama, from an admirer—Your loving son, Hayward Jeffrey."

Carnihan and Mr. Hank arrived in the Hometown delivery truck just as I was finishing up breakfast. Beatnik's nails came clicking on the floor, followed by Mr. Hank's gentle instructions: "Have yourself a good old time. Entertain yourself and sleep all you like. But if you need the toilet, young fella, please let one of us know."

Mr. Hank said hello to everyone then removed the feather duster from his apron pocket and started cleaning the shelves, beginning with the area crowded with bottles of HadAcol, Howell's Castoria, Wampole's Preparation, and Porter's Pain King, which, if I recalled correctly, aided "muscular aches for people, cows, and horses." The duster was a gray-black plume of ostrich and pigeon feathers, and Mr. Hank was rarely seen without it, inside as well as outside the store. For years I'd heard stories about how, a day or two after Miss Deenie died, he was discovered dusting objects along Delmas Street. Horrified neighbors had watched from their windows as he cleaned mailboxes, trees, bushes, water faucets, and fire hydrants.

"Is he yours?" Silas Poe asked.

"Yes, he is," Mr. Hank said. "He's mine and my boy's, and I guess he's Pace's too."

"Has anybody told him he was ugly yet?"

"I don't think so. No one's been near that insensitive."

"Then don't y'all tell him," Silas said. "I want to see his reaction when he finally gets a look at himself in a mirror."

I gave Beatnik a piece of pancake and he scurried with it to the other side of the store. He was hidden from view and you couldn't tell what he was doing, but then came the sound of his nails frantically clawing at the floor, and I figured he was trying to bury his treasure for some later day.

"Jay, bring him to me, please." It was Mr. Hank, dusting now at the front of the store.

Carnihan did as he was told and Mr. Hank, holding the dog with one arm, continued his work with the other, his bouquet of feathers whisking over the shelves. Ever since I was old enough to entertain some understanding of the meaning of loss, I'd never been able to look at this man without feeling a mix of pity and wonder, and without a deep, hard ache coming to my chest. I had only a dim recollection of Miss Deenie, but it was plain to me that some days she was all Mr. Hank could see or think about. You might speak to him, tell him something of vast importance, and he wouldn't hear a word. "Hometown's on fire!" I recall Carnihan telling him once, using a voice filled with alarm. Mr. Hank had simply stood there with his eyes glazed over and a peculiar smile at his lips. *Fire?* Who could worry about such a thing when anyone as sweet and fine as his Deenie was dead and gone?

"See here," Mr. Hank was saying, pointing to a spot over in Tools. "This is your place. This is where I'd like you to spend most of your time. On that strip of carpet there."

"He doesn't understand a word you're saying," Silas said.

"He understands. He's smart, this dog."

Carnihan said, "He understands enough not to put Tabasco on everything when he's got a trick stomach."

"Just wait till he gets a look at himself," Silas said. "We'll see about trick stomachs. I bet he loses his from the shock of it all."

The bank clerks left at nine sharp, and Carnihan took the open seat to my right. He made a figure eight in the shallow lake of syrup at the bottom of my plate and licked the stuff clean with his tongue. I said something about sleeping well but he didn't comment. He didn't look at me, either, and I couldn't figure out why until he said, "I read maybe a quarter of your book last night. I was up past midnight."

He made another figure eight, and this time wiped his finger on a napkin. He crossed his arms and started to shake his head in a wearisome manner. "Tell me, Pace, how on earth could you do it?"

"Do what, brother?"

"Write those things. Everybody having sex. Everybody talking the worst kind of trash. In one scene you have this protagonist, as you called him, thinking about going to bed with his mother. His own mother, for crying out loud!"

I didn't mean to be defensive, and yet I asked nonetheless, "Ever hear of Oedipus, Jay? Oedipus Rex?"

Carnihan thought about it. "Is he from Cankton?"

"No, I'm afraid he was from Greece."

"How would I know anyone from Greece?" He was staring at me, and I had a tough time staring back. "I can tell you who I do know, Pace, and that's Miss Betty and Pop. All I kept thinking about was how humiliated they're going to be."

"It's just a story, Jay, it isn't even true. None of it."

"I know that, and they'll know that. But anyone who reads it'll think this is who you are, Pace, and who they are, and what poor Smoke is like. The protagonist, this Peter Burn, he even has your initials and part of your last name."

Turning away, I caught a glimpse of myself in the mirror behind the grill and noted the volcanic redness of the cheeks, the involuntary squint of the eyes, the lips clamped shut. Shame was what filled my face, and I didn't like the look of it. "I guess I wanted to make the reader think," I said at last.

"Well, you make him think plenty. You make him think you're some kind of peckerwood or something."

I'd prepared myself for such criticism, but it still stung. I reminded myself that *Strange Weather* was one of no more than a handful of books Carnihan had read in his lifetime, and I might have said as much had Mr. Hank not called me over to the phone. "Hey, Pace. It's your mother."

The walk from the lunch counter to where Mr. Hank was standing seemed longer than it actually was, about twenty feet. I reckoned Carnihan was watching me, as were Ruby Dean and the few remaining diners who'd overheard his remarks about my book. But when I reached the phone and wheeled back around I saw that only Beatnik seemed to be interested, and he was happily occupied between a couple of bales of hay twine with the crust of pancake I'd given him earlier.

"Hello, baby," Miss Betty said. "Sleep well?"

"Fine, thank you. And you?"

"Never better," she replied, and seemed to mean it, which came as a surprise. I'd expected a reprimand, but her voice was as dear and gentle as ever. "I'm calling to tell you that your agent called. Cindy is her name?"

"Cinda."

"Cinder?"

"No, Miss Betty. Cinda. Cin-*da*!" And I spelled it.

Then, for no reason that made sense, I scribbled this onto a scratch pad: *Call Cinda Lovey in New York*. "Did she leave a message? Anything happening with the book?"

"Only that there's news. And to call her sometime this morning. She says you two need to chat."

I put the phone down and returned to the counter and what was left of breakfast. I felt better because my mother had not scolded me, and because Cinda Lovey was finally delivering on her promise to help make me rich and famous. I figured the book either had sold to publishers abroad or to a movie studio at home, and that Cinda was calling with numbers for me to contemplate. Not wanting to appear eager, I decided to wait a while, at least a few hours, before calling her back. Also, waiting might give Hollywood the impression that I was hesitant to sell my story, and this might drive the price up.

Ruby Dean came over to where I was sitting, leaving a clever pattern of circles with her washrag as she wiped the counter. "Want anything else, Pace? More juice or coffee?"

"Coffee'd be nice, thank you."

She held the glass pot at a height of three feet above my cup and started to pour, lowering it as the cup filled. Her timing was perfect because as the coffee reached the rim of the cup, so did the pinched mouth of her pot. Not an ounce was spilled. "You're a pro, aren't you, Ruby Dean?"

"Yes, I am," she said. "You got that right. Uh-huh."

"You're the greatest cook that ever lived."

"And ever will live."

"Would you also say you're the all-time best?"

"Yes, I would. You see those pictures, Pace—all those Carnihan men up on that wall there? I keep waiting for the day when they put old Ruby Dean in line."

"Lord knows she deserves it," I said.

"Ain't that the truth. Oh, yeah. Uh-huh. Ain't it, though! Yes sir!" And off she went making more perfect circles.

I spent the rest of the morning unpacking in Dr. McDermott's office—and answering a certain call that comes when one's diet suddenly shifts from bland Yankee cooking to some of the spiciest known to man. By noon I'd succeeded in placing everything where it seemed to belong, including my bed, which I crammed into what previously had been an X-ray lab. I covered the windows with a dark blue sheet and napped until a little after noon, when a trash truck made a nasty hydraulic fuss depositing the contents of the Hometown bin into its open back.

Cinda Lovey, when I awoke, was foremost on my mind. I pictured her seated at an antique cherry desk in her Manhattan office, high above the city, wearing a telephone headset and juggling calls from the world's literary and theatrical kingpins. A sufficient amount of time had passed since her call, so I figured I could go ahead and check in now. I used the phone in the Hometown office, having received permission from Carnihan to dial long-distance. I could feel the beat of my heart accelerate and my breath begin to thin, for calling Cinda was always a high-speed adventure. Any number of life-altering events were likely to have occurred while you were going dumbly about the business of living your life. While you were eating breakfast, for example, a movie producer was checking the balance of his bank account to make sure he could spring half a million for the rights to your novel. And while you were sitting resolutely on the commode, a publisher in Moscow was assigning your book to his best translator, with instructions to get it right, to get it absolutely right, for such a tale as Pace Burnette's was a singular joy, and one for all the world to cherish.

"It ain't gonna happen," Cinda said when she got on the line. "I'm sorry, Pace."

"I beg your pardon?"

She started to cough and spit one smoky, obscene word after another. "Look, we sent your manuscript to a number of studios. And their readers . . . well, they say it's too dark, won't work, and shouldn't be done. They didn't like it. It's as simple as that."

"Okay."

"Our sister agency in London, I think I told you about them . . . they said the response from the European publishers was just as disappointing." The line beeped, signaling a call waiting. "Hang on," she said, and put me on hold. When she came back it was to utter another string of profanities.

"So you start work on a new novel—okay?—and forget about this one."

"But it isn't even out yet, Cinda. How can you say I should forget about something that hasn't even been published yet?"

"How can I? Because it's my business to tell you the truth."

"But suppose it becomes a bestseller . . . a *runaway* bestseller? Wouldn't public demand alone . . . ?"

"Public demand?" She laughed and the line beeped again. And then she was gone.

I put my face in my hands and fought an urge to cry. Baubles of fire appeared before my eyes, and a liquid echo sounded in my ears, the words of Cinda Lovey saying "It ain't gonna happen" over and over again. I got up from the chair and staggered toward the door just as Carnihan stepped from the bathroom wiping his hands on a paper towel. "What happened?" he said. "What's wrong, brother?" I brushed by him and made my way through the stockroom. By the time I reached Dr. McDermott's I was battling simultaneous urges to faint and to throw up breakfast. Steadying myself with both hands on the walls, I reached the examination room, lay on the steel table, and curled up like a desiccated old man on his deathbed. I wasn't going to be rich and famous; I wouldn't enjoy the company of the world's great women. The cold steel made my skin crawl and seemed to wrap itself around my heart. Unable to resist any longer, I let myself weep. I convulsed violently and cursed myself for being so stupid and naive. I had begun to lift a knotted hand and shake it at the heavens when the familiar clicking of Beatnik's nails sounded in the room. I looked down and there he stood, tail wagging, tongue hanging out. He looked happy, ready for more pancake, more anything. He whimpered, then barked, and, as I watched, he stepped up to a chair, lifted one of his back legs, and urinated a lazy stream onto the floor.

"Dumb dog," I muttered. "Get the hell outa here."

I heard footsteps and figured Carnihan was coming to find out what was wrong. "Go away," I shouted. "Please!"

Beatnik became frightened and ran from the room, but the footsteps sounded closer and I sat up and turned to face the door, intent on letting Carnihan know that not only was he unwelcome but that I wished him an instant, unutterably painful death as well. "I said go away, leave me alone! Please!"

But it was Pop, dressed in his drab khakis and too-tight T-shirt. He was carrying a couple of brown paper bags filled with groceries, and the effort had reddened his face.

"Didn't mean to intrude," he said.

"Oh, no. Sorry, Pop. I thought you were Jay."

"Your mother and I figured you'd need some provisions."

"Sure," I said, scrambling to give him a hand. "Thank you. Please. Come in."

Without commenting, he stepped over the puddle of urine and put the bags on the table. He looked around the room before finally settling his eyes on me. "What's wrong, son?"

"Nothing."

"You want to talk about it?"

"It's nothing, Pop. Trust me."

He chuckled and pointed to my face, to the tears that stained my cheeks. "It's nothing?"

"It's allergies. I always have sinus problems this time of year. You know that."

He gazed back down at the floor, Beatnik's accident. "Let me clean this up."

"I'll do it."

"No. Let me. I want to. You just lay back and take it easy."

I did as I was told. He left the room and returned carrying a bucket filled with soapy water, a mop plunked down in it. "Watch closely," he said. "You might learn something."

He soaked the urine up, dunked the mop into the suds, and wrung it out. I could smell the sappy essence of pine, sharp and clean, and I could smell his cologne, the same drugstore kind he'd worn all his life. "Can we talk about your book, Pace?"

He didn't look up, so it was hard for me to tell what he was thinking. "Sure, Pop. But if it upset you—"

"I really enjoyed it. I thought it showed a lot of feeling and imagination. I could see how much hard work you put into it."

"You liked it?"

"Where did you learn all those words, son?"

"Which ones?"

"All of them. There were so many."

"Oh, I don't know, Pop. From reading, I guess, and from school. I always liked words."

He straightened up and I could see how he was having trouble breathing. His face was even redder than before, and he'd begun to sweat. "Well, you have to figure a person really knows a thing or two about language to write a book. It's a talent you have, Pace . . . a gift, if I say so myself." He looked back down at the floor, inspecting the wide wet circle. "I'm proud of you, Pace. And so is your mother. I just wanted you to know how much."

I lay back on the tabletop and let myself feel good again. A few moments ago, after the call to Cinda, I was cursing the heavens for having denied me, and now I couldn't have been more relieved, sensing an even greater victory. I recalled what Genine had told me the night before: "One thing I've learned about living, is that if you planned on things going one way, count on them going the other." And I thought I should write it down somewhere and never let myself forget it.

"The sex," I said, "it didn't upset you?"

"Not me, son. Sex is an important part of life—and one of the most fun." He laughed from deep within his chest, still pushing the mop around. "Now your mother, I admit she thought it was racy, maybe a little *too* for her tastes, but she's smart enough to differentiate between what's real and what isn't. We admire what you've done, Pace . . . your accomplishment."

I gave him a smile but what I really felt like doing was holding him in my arms and crying again. "Thank you," I said. "Thank you, Pop. And when you get back home, will you tell Miss Betty I said the same?"

"I'll tell her."

He finished the job and placed the mop and bucket in the corner, the worn, red-painted handle propped against the wall. "Does this place have a kitchen?" he said. "I've got a few things in those bags that need to be refrigerated."

"There's no kitchen, no. But there's a cooler in what used to be a blood lab. Jay said it was for holding plasma and medicine bottles, but I checked and it looks pretty clean."

It was clear that Pop wasn't much impressed by this proposition, but nevertheless he took the bags up in his arms and started down the hall. "What about a stove, Pace?"

"I can always buy a hot plate."

"Oh, no, you don't want one of those. What you need is a microwave oven. It cooks better and faster and it's much more efficient. A hot plate's a fire hazard."

In the blood lab he put the bags down and looked around to make sure we were alone. "Don't let Jay know I'm telling you this. But Monster Mart's running a sale on them this week—on microwaves. I saw the ad yesterday in the *Lip*. You can get one cheap, about a hundred bucks."

"I thought I'd just open an account at the lunch counter and eat Ruby Dean's specials every day."

"But what about supper? She's not open then, is she?"

"Well, at night I'll go to the Palace Cafe."

"Or Delmas Street. You can always come home to eat."

"That's right," I said. "And I will."

He took his wallet out and laid two freshly printed one-hundred-dollar bills on the table. "I want you to have this," he said, sliding the money toward me.

"I don't need it, Pop. I'm a rich author now, remember?"

"It's for that oven. I insist."

"But, Pop, I wanted an old-time hot plate like Hemingway used in his garret in Paris. I've got no need for anything better. No hungry artist worth his salt ever nuked something in a microwave when he could burn it over a good hot flame."

"Well, I want you to have one whether you think you need it or not." He looked around again to make sure no one was eavesdropping. "Go this afternoon, Pace. Buy one with a turntable—your mother says they're best."

"It's sacrilegious, you know . . . talking about Monster Mart anywhere within a five-mile radius of this place?"

"Yeah. I'll probably fry in hell for it."

I took the cash and put it in my pocket. After my talk with Cinda, I figured I'd be needing this and more to get by. I thanked Pop and insisted the money be considered a loan, but he laughed and waved the notion away. "What? I can't buy my son a present anymore? The world's not that old yet, mister."

We unloaded the groceries and household goods and I followed him out into the parking lot. He took a couple of imaginary golf swings and shielded his eyes watching the imaginary balls sail away. Finally he got in his car and rolled the window down. As he had earlier in the blood lab, he looked around to make sure no one was listening. "You're a wonderful writer, Pace. And you'll go far." He paused and waited again until he was certain he had my complete attention. "And I don't give a good goddamn what that Cinda Lovey had to tell you."

He patted me on the arm and left before I could say anything. Only after the red blush of his taillights disappeared did I start feeling sorry for myself again.

I turned in early that night hoping to sleep off my depression, but I dreamed about Cinda Lovey, her husky Manhattan voice saying "It ain't gonna happen" over and over again, her cruel laugh coming whenever I brought up *Strange Weather.*

I got out of bed and shuffled to the window and saw the Hometown delivery truck parked outside. It was a little dinked-up Toyota with a magnetic sign on each door advertising the store as "the last of a breed" and listing a telephone number to call. If the truck was there, I knew Carnihan would be as well, since he used the thing as his personal vehicle during off-hours. I found him sitting at the lunch counter with his head positioned beneath a desk lamp, taking the full brunt of a high-wattage bulb. He appeared to be lost in thought, as if contemplating an exam question. An enormous ledger in red leather binding was spread out before him, and he held a pencil in one hand and a drink of some kind in the other. It was a Bloody Mary: you could see the dense tomato red, the pale green of a celery stick. I stepped heavily across the floor to let him know he had company, but he gave no sign of having noticed. He was scribbling on a scratch pad, his lips moving though issuing no sound, his eyes bright with the single blossom of lamplight.

"Working late?"

"Always."

"Want a break?"

"Sure, brother. Grab yourself a chair."

I sat on the stool next to him and waited. His eyes were shot red at the corners, and his lips were dry and chapped. "I was trying to balance the books," he said, glancing down at his notations. "Impossible. Absolutely impossible. At the rate the store's going . . . well, it's really not worth repeating, is it?" I was close enough to smell his breath, a fruity sweetness. "I'll go ahead and put this away now," he said, closing the ledger. "You want to talk? You feel up to it?"

"Sure, Jay. Let's talk."

He was staring at the contents of his glass. "Ruby Dean lets me keep a bottle of Absolut in her icebox, so it's there if ever you need a little pick-me-up. There's tomato juice, Tabasco, string beans, lime wedges, celery . . . I love Mary as Bloody as I can get her." He opened the refrigerator door and pointed to a tray inside.

"Thanks," I said.

"I was hoping you'd wake up. I was thinking about taking a drive out to Babylon. I called Genny a while ago. She says there's a new girl on board, starting just tonight." He sipped his drink and added, wincing a bit, "From New York."

"I don't know if I'm up for Babylon."

"What in the world would a girl from New York be doing in a town like Smoke, Pace, working at a place like Babylon? You'd think she could do better—a dress shop, say, or, at the very worst, Monster Mart."

"People from New York are no different from all us Cajuns. They're from New York, is all."

"I'd like to meet her, nonetheless. Hear how she talks. You think she has an accent?"

"Not everyone in New York talks funny, you know."

"Well, everyone down here does. They talk like 'dat.' So even if she does talk normal it'll be different." He opened the refrigerator again and removed a bottle. "Absolut Peppar. You like 'em hot, Pace?"

"It's kind of late."

"I'll go light on the Tabasco, I promise."

I watched as he mixed a couple of drinks. You could tell he'd done this countless times before, he was as expert with Bloody Marys as Ruby Dean was with biscuits.

"You missed your calling," I told him. "You should've been a bartender. You'd've made quite a name for yourself."

"Never too late, you know . . . maybe after Hometown closes."

Carnihan was in one of his Rayford-Holly-Must-Die moods, saying things like "Him with his tired old brogans and tiepins and oily white hair" and "Thinking he can ruin this country, thinking he can own every last little piece of it." He probably could tell I wasn't paying much attention, because after a while, in the middle of one of his declarations, he stopped short and said, "Just speak up when you change your mind about Babylon."

It took only four drinks for that to happen, and I found myself seated on the vinyl bench in the Hometown delivery truck, sucking on a cigarette as he sped toward the Lewisburg Road. We took a shortcut through the run-down neighborhood where Ruby Dean had lived before Hayward put her in an uptown manse, and I watched the shanties flash by, each looking more decrepit than the one before it. The road changed from blacktop to gravel and finally to dirt, and skinny dogs lay in it, not bothering to lift their heads as we blew past them kicking dust.

We reached Babylon in record time, and Carnihan skidded to a stop on the shell lot, parking between the same two pickup trucks that had been there last time. He hopped out, removed the magnetic signs from the doors, and placed them facedown on the seat. "Don't want to give ourselves away," he said. "Not here, anyway." He slapped me on the back and led me to the door. "Not exactly the kind of advertisement Daddy would go for, is it now?"

As before, Anita didn't acknowledge us when we entered the lounge, although her eyes, tiny blue pools in a glittery field of silver, did fix on us and follow us past the bar. The telephone lady was talking it up on the couch; I happened to hear the word "tasty" mentioned as we walked past her. Over on the dance floor the cowboy was holding his imaginary partner and laughing as if from the pleasure of her company. Observing this man, it struck me how alcohol helped a person make sense of what otherwise might seem odd, almost insane behavior. Still heady with Absolut, I found myself admiring the cowboy's athletic step, his daring dips and turns, and wondering if, a little later on, he might be willing to share his invisible friend.

"Where's Genine?" I asked Carnihan.

He didn't answer. He pointed instead to a young woman sitting by herself near the jukebox. "That must be her. The one I was telling you about."

"Who?"

"The girl from New York. The one just starting."

I followed him to her table and stood waiting with my hands in my pockets. For some reason I was nervous; the buildup had been so great, it was a little like meeting a celebrity. "So you're the new person from New York?" he finally said, flashing that stupid smile of his. "From New York City, right?"

"New York, New York," she answered, giving a dumb smile of her own. "A city so great they named it twice."

She couldn't have been more than eighteen, wearing what looked like a business suit, this one of an expensive wool fabric dressed with pinstripes. It was the kind of clothes that better suited a lawyer for the state or an advertising executive with an important presentation to give. Her hair was short, black, and neatly combed, and her nails, painted fire-engine red, were filed to narrow points. You could tell she spent a lot of time on those nails: she drummed them against the tabletop to make sure you gave them their due.

"I heard about you from Genine," Carnihan said.

"Genine?"

"Genine Monteleone. She works here."

"Oh, sure. Genny. The one with all the hair."

He leaned back and punched me on the arm. "Did you hear that, brother? She's got one. You can hear it in every word."

"It's there," I told him. "An accent, by God."

"This is Pace Burnette," he said to the girl. "You ever hear of him?" When she said she hadn't, he told her I was going to be rich and famous, a novelist of world renown. "You should hear the name of his book," he said. "Go on, Pace. Tell her."

"It's *Strange Weather*," I replied. I never thought I'd be ashamed to tell anyone the title of my book, least of all a person who probably struggled with a first-grade reader, but I could feel the blood rush to my face and scald my ears.

"How interesting," she said, nodding her head. "*Strange Weather*." She took her cigarette and tapped it against a glass ashtray. "It's wonderfully atmospheric, Pace, and romantic as well. If I say so myself, it portends riveting suspense and harrowing conclusions. A wicked plot, too, I'd bet."

"Wicked's too nice a word," Carnihan said. "You never read anything quite like it."

"Would you bring it by, Pace? I'd truly love to read it."

"Truly," Carnihan said. "Don't you love that word, 'truly'?"

I didn't answer and he said, "Pace just came back to Smoke from Washington."

"From Washington? From Washington, D.C., is that?"

"Truly," Carnihan said. "He truly lived there."

We sat at her table, and Carnihan took out his package of cigarettes. "After I graduated," I explained, "a college journalism professor of mine helped me get a job as a copy aide at the paper up there. He knew the managing editor. After a year I was made a staff writer and assigned to the cops beat."

"Cops?"

"I wrote about homicides, drug busts, bank robberies, killer traffic accidents, that sort of thing."

She started to speak but Carnihan cut her off. "Guess what they call people who drowned?"

She glanced at me and lifted her shoulders, a feeble attempt at a shrug. "I couldn't begin to."

"Floaters," he said. "They called them floaters."

This apparently fascinated her as much as it did him. "These floaters, Pace, did you see many of them?"

"More than I would've liked."

"That word 'truly,' " Carnihan said. "You said it earlier. Not many people in this part of the country say that. Down here we get a lot of 'reallys,' isn't that right, Pace?"

"That's right," I said. "It's always quite an event when someone in South Louisiana uses the word 'truly.' "

Her name was Bethany Bixler, she told us, and please don't make the mistake of calling her Beth; she didn't like it. Her father had been "in stocks and bonds, a Wall Street type," her mother an "interior decorator and horseback-riding enthusiast." They had died in a plane crash in 1983, and her inheritance, which she described as "astronomical," had been squandered before her twenty-first birthday. She lost their twelve-room apartment on the Upper East Side, along with an eleven-seater airplane, a Lamborghini Diablo, and a Jaguar XJRS coupe. When Carnihan asked how she'd managed to spend so much money in so short a time, she replied simply, "Oh, I wrote a bunch of checks." After several years of profligate living, she had accompanied a boyfriend, Rupert, down to New Orleans with the intention of getting married, but a few days after their arrival he disappeared and had not been heard from since. Rupert, she suspected, had been aligned with the Dixie Mafia, a drug courier perhaps, although she didn't want Carnihan and me to quote her on that. One morning he'd gone out for beignets and never returned, and she'd spent the next several weeks looking for him. Distraught and uncertain as to where to turn next, she'd ventured into the Louisiana hinterland, at once disturbed and enthralled by the vast swampy terrain. She had hoped to find adventure in it, and to gradually erase the memory of her loss. She'd arrived in Smoke on the day of a parade. Up and down the main thoroughfare, everyone was cheering a large, square-jawed, black man who had hands as big as cinder blocks. He wore a suit with a white carnation on the lapel, the tips of which had been browned by the sun.

"That would be Hayward," Carnihan said. "Hayward Jeffrey Clark. He's a friend of ours."

I'd noticed, during the telling of her story, that Bethany had focused almost solely on me, and I found her eyes on me still. "Pace Burnette," she said quietly. She smiled and brought the cigarette to her face, and I watched as her lips embraced it.

"This Rupert," Carnihan said, "does he have a last name?"

For whatever reason, the question upset her. She stared at Carnihan and her eyes became tight and small, her mouth a muscled snail. "Hey, Jay, let me ask you something. Did your mother ever tell you it's impolite to speak when you're not being spoken to?"

"What . . . ?" He swallowed hard, and his eyelids began to flutter. "What do you mean . . . 'my mother'?"

"You need to learn some manners, my friend."

"Yeah? And what would you know about manners?"

She blew a stream of smoke at his face. "Enough to keep my mouth shut when I have nothing in this world to say."

Carnihan got up from the table and walked over to the bar. You could hear him muttering under his breath, saying "Mother" over and over again. He affected a limp, although I couldn't recall any recent complaint about his having hurt a leg.

"Your buddy asked for it," Bethany said. As if to remind me that she was qualified to judge, she added, "Truly."

I began to say something, but then changed my mind. She seemed to know what it was anyway, because, tamping her cigarette out, she said, "You're right, I was out of line." And she walked over to where he was standing. She nudged him playfully on the shoulder, using her pointed fingernails, and pressed her mouth against his cheek as she whispered in his ear. He wheeled around, and his face was bright and happy.

They came back and sat at the table. "I just get depressed whenever I talk about the past," she said.

"You're not alone," Carnihan said. "The past or the future. Either one'll get me down."

"And what about the present?" I asked.

"It doesn't do much for me, either," he said.

The door opened and a blast of cold air blew in. "Close that thing," Anita commanded, the first words I'd ever heard her speak. "*Now,* Genny. Hurry."

Genine Monteleone entered stamping her feet and hugging her arms close to her chest. "Must've dropped ten degrees in the last ten minutes," she said, trailing behind a man with a ring of keys bouncing against his hip. He was short and heavyset, his belly so outsize that he couldn't keep the tail of his shirt tucked in. To cover himself, he kept tugging at his belt loops.

"It was an hour in the room," Genine told Anita, handing some money over. "Can I have a beer now?"

She began writing in a ledger, her tongue tracing over her lips. "No," she said. "Make that a g and t."

I could not say what tipped her off to our presence, but of a sudden she seemed to know we were there. And she looked embarrassed, deeply so. As she began to walk toward us I was reminded of an unwilling participant in a beauty contest. She held herself straight and upright as if corseted, and her mouth twitched nervously at the corners. Her big globe of hair had been flattened, and she tried in vain to fluff it back into shape.

She and Carnihan made an elaborate pretense of being the fresh young couple: she thumbed a fleck of something off his chin and kissed the spot, and he brushed back an errant lock of hair that had fallen in her face. He whispered in her ear, and she leaned her head against his shoulder. I glanced back at the fellow with whom she'd entered the lounge. He was watching from across the room as if deeply wounded, the gaze of a jilted lover. I felt vaguely sorry for him.

"Your g and t," Anita called. "Hey, Genny!" And Carnihan raced over to retrieve it.

"Have you learned all about Rupert?" Genine said, smiling.

"Yes, we have," I answered. "Poor man. I was wondering whether there was something we might do to help you find him, Bethany."

"Oh, just that . . . just hearing how much you care."

Carnihan returned with a tray full of drinks and passed it around. "Gin and tonics," he said. "Or is it gins and tonic?"

The girls turned to me for the answer, and, when I didn't come up with it, Genine said, "But you're supposed to be the big writer."

I considered telling her I no longer claimed that title, and of my afternoon telephone call with Cinda Lovey. But this would've killed the good time we were having and might've encouraged confessions from the others. I didn't want Genine to have to embarrass herself any more, and God knows Carnihan had enough troubles. Also, Bethany was under no obligation to come clean about who she was. Rupert didn't exist, after all, and New York had never been her home. She was from the small bayou town of Port Bess, fewer than ten miles east of Smoke, a place famous for nothing but the speed trap that greeted visitors passing through. As Bethany lifted her cocktail to drink, I noted the inscription encircling the crimson stone at the center of her graduation ring. PORT BESS HIGH SCHOOL, it said. CLASS OF 1985.

However the drinks were called, we put enough of them away in the next hour to empty two one-liter bottles of Tanqueray and as many of Schweppe's. Anita kept busy behind the bar, tallying our tab when she wasn't filling orders, and for this reason, I presumed, she chose not to chide Genine and Bethany for their neglect of the dancing cowboy, the fat man, and the two or three other sad sacks who'd gathered there today. Carnihan told a story about his time in the Navy, and it so amused Bethany that she patted his hand and held his upper arm as she had mine earlier. "You're very interesting," she said.

By the way he stammered and swooned it might've been a declaration of love. "Am I really, Beth . . . I mean, Bethany."

For no reason that was clear I suddenly stood on wobbly legs and announced that I'd had my fill and could take no more. Or at least that's what I think I said. Both Genine and Bethany tugged at my shirt, insisting I sit down, and at the bar Anita spoke for the second time tonight: "More g and t's coming up."

My tongue was soaked with the bitter green taste of lime, and my innards had all come to rest in my throat, waiting for their cue to leap to the floor.

"Pace?" I recall one of the girls saying. "Pace, are you okay, honey? Don't you want to sit down now?"

And Carnihan: "Oh, he's fine. The man's skinny but he's like a tank, for God's sake. He has an iron constitution."

"But he looks so bad, he looks . . ."

Their voices followed me all the way to the floor, whereupon they diminished to a whisper before finally vanishing altogether. When I awoke, it was in a room totally unfamiliar to me. It wasn't the X-ray lab or any of the examination rooms at Dr. McDermott's. A narrow shaft of light was coming through a part in a bank of water-stained curtains. Beneath the window a radiator, clanking and coughing, emitted a spit of steam shaped like a corkscrew, and a cold draft blew from the same direction, defeating the little heater's efforts. I was vaguely aware of a dream I'd had of my father. It was nighttime and we were at Delmas Street playing basketball outside. Pop, standing about thirty feet from the goal, made a trick shot with his eyes closed, and I ran over to congratulate him. I attempted to hike him up on my shoulders and take him on a victory lap, but he pushed me away and told me to be gracious. He reminded me of his age, then he said, "Remember who you are."

At the moment it was distressing to remember who I was—and where I was. I lay under a moth-eaten, Army-issue blanket staring at a ceiling decorated with silver sparkles. The mattress beneath me, dressed with gritty gray sheets, dipped at its middle, forming a hollow from which I was having trouble extricating myself. I'd spent the night in one of Babylon's cinder block cells, but what I couldn't be certain of were the circumstances under which I had stayed there. Was I sleeping off too many g and t's? Or there as a customer of a different sort, the first business ever scored by Bethany Bixler, or, perhaps, yet another mark of Genine Monteleone's?

I was also discouraged to note that my clothes lay piled on a chair in the corner, my underwear resting on top.

I got up at last and pulled the blanket back, exposing the sheets to the light. Cloud shapes suggested an interesting history, but none looked fresh. Clutching my head to keep my brains in place, I staggered to the bathroom and nudged the door open. I lifted the toilet seat and spied brown silt stains in the basin. Under the lavatory a plastic trash can held a single object: a wadded-up plug of tissue paper. I wondered what this was. I picked it up and sniffed, and then unrolled the wad until the dimpled head of a condom appeared.

"Oh lord," I muttered. "Oh sweet precious lord."

I stumbled back into the room, collapsed on the bed, and pulled the blanket up over my head. I supposed the condom was proof of how I'd spent the rest of the night, and, since a woman's perfume seemed to be in evidence on the bedsheets, that I had not been alone. I was lying there with my eyes closed, trying to recall at least a fragment of what had happened, when the door rattled open and someone entered. I kept still, and waited a moment before daring to crack my eyes open and look. It was Bethany, dressed differently now than she had been earlier. She wore tight, straight-leg jeans and a plain white shirt. Sunglasses were perched on top of her head, and she was carrying a brown leather purse the size of a gym bag. I watched as she sat in front of the vanity directly across from the bed and began writing on a slip of paper. In the mirror her face looked freshly powdered, her cheeks as sweetly pink as a newborn's. She wrote for a while, then shredded the paper, stuffing the scraps into her pants pocket. She started again, taking her time—too much time, in my opinion, about five minutes.

When she was finished she stood and gazed down at me, but by now I had clamped my eyes shut again. I felt her hard stare, and was tempted to stop pretending and ask her a question or two. To begin, I wondered about my wallet: had she taken everything in it, how little there was? Second, had that discarded object in the bathroom once been a possession of mine, or had it belonged to someone else?

She took her purse and opened the door; I felt more cold come in, and thought again of the dream I'd had of my father. "Remember who you are," his voice repeated in my ear. After checking to make sure she was gone, I got up and walked to the vanity. You could see your breath in the air, and, in my case, smell it, like something dead in the woods. I picked up the note and was beginning to read when the door rattled open. She had pulled her sunglasses down, hiding her eyes, and her smile, under the circumstances, was more enthusiastic than seemed either polite or necessary. "Hey, Pace, I hope you and Jay don't think I'm a whore." And then the door closed and she was gone again.

I checked my wallet and was thrilled to find a few bucks still in the fold. My wristwatch said it was noon, a day in February; it took me a moment to remember the year. I suddenly became aware of the cold, and dressed in such a hurry that I left my socks turned inside out. This was what her letter said:

Hello Sleepyhead,

First off, nothing happened, so don't worry.

After you passed out, Jay sat you up in your chair then proceeded to pass out himself. First me and Genine carried you to this room, then him to the one right next door. You owe $10 an hour for 10 hours, and I told Anita a handjob although one never took place. (I had to tell her something, and that was cheapest on the list.) The total for you is $120, and the same for Jay. Anita lives in the room closest to the lounge—#1—and you can pay her cash, check, Visa, or American Express.

In closing, let me say that next time you mumble in your sleep, and I'm in the room, don't keep saying remember who you are. It ain't a lot of fun.

Also, as for that item in the toilet, it was there when we brought you in. So better wash your hands . . .

Bethany Bixler

Since he didn't have a credit card, and was yet to surrender the notion that I'd soon be a millionaire, Carnihan didn't object when I offered to charge our bill to one of my accounts. "You know I'd do the same if I were in your shoes," he said.

I gently rapped on the orange door with the number 1 painted unevenly at its center. Anita answered before I'd finished knocking. "You think my ears don't work?" she asked.

The light of day was not at all kind to her. Pink sponge rollers formed furrows in her white-blond hair, and the meaty folds of flesh beneath her chin were running with sweat. Her eyes, unpainted, showed more red than blue, and they looked too narrow to accommodate the width of a razor blade. She quoted the bar tab, then the so-called service charges, and I nodded and handed over what was needed. "Be right back," she said.

From behind me, leaning against the front of the truck, Carnihan said, "Three-forty sounds high, brother. Negotiate with the woman." But I had no idea how to. Through a crack in the door I could see someone who wasn't Anita walking around. It was a man dressed all in khaki, his jackboots making a leathery squeak. He turned a television on and stood in front of it, knotting his sand-colored tie. It was the sheriff, Gilbert Sorel. I recognized him from the billboards he'd put up during the last election, some of which were still standing. A VOTE FOR GILBERT SOREL IS A VOTE FOR THE CHILDREN, they all said, and showed the man with his family. It didn't surprise me to see him there with Anita, for the big-bellied, tobacco-chewing Southern sheriff and his concubine the town madam are the star-crossed lovers of our time, a cliché that even a place as original as Smoke couldn't escape.

Anita returned and pushed the door open. She handed me a charge slip to sign. "Put your work and home telephone numbers, too. In case there's a problem."

"I just moved back to town. I don't have a phone yet."

"Well, I need one in case. So put your friend's number."

I did just that, and when Anita gave me the receipt the tips of our fingers touched—accidentally, as it were. I apologized, and she stared at me and started to laugh. She said, "Ah, you ain't done shit." And then she slammed the door shut in my face.

We were in the thick of Ruby Dean's former neighborhood when Carnihan, braking fast, pulled the truck over to the side of the road. He stepped out and put the magnetic signs back on the doors. "You never know," he said, "who might see us between here and the store and decide to come in with a big order."

When the ride wasn't rough and bumpy, it was filled with corners to negotiate, and all the excited movement nearly made me sick. Carnihan had enjoyed as high a time as I had, but you never would've known it. He looked fresh and cheerful, and he whistled tunes I hadn't heard in years. One of them, "Do the Hustle," had been a hit during the disco era, and it brought to mind rayon shirts, platform shoes, and Plexiglas dance floors throbbing with colored lights. As we drove by the Smoke Lumber Company, its Victorian facade sporting dozens of rusty signs advertising paint and tool manufacturers, Carnihan honked his horn at a lady inching her way upstreet with the aid of a walker. "Hey, Mrs. Mistrot," he called. "How the hell are you today!" And he laughed so hard that it seemed I could feel my skull crack, the fissure originating at a point between my eyes and running north and south.

"I guess you saw her ring," he said. "She's a Coonass, old man. Like you and me."

"Hey, Jay? Not so loud, all right?"

"She must've practiced real hard to get that accent down. Man, could she talk. And from right down the road—from Port Bess of all places."

"Don't talk. Please. I just can't bear it."

"What a dream," he said. "What a fabulous dream."

He started whistling "Do the Hustle" again, and I tried to shut him out by covering my ears with my hands. I could hear him, though, all the way until we reached Market Street and Hometown. He parked in back, which is to say in front of Dr. McDermott's, and I followed him in. Mr. Hank was adding boxes of feminine napkins to his already prodigious collection, and behind the counter Ruby Dean was kneading a mound of bread dough, flour reaching all the way up to her elbows. Carnihan ignored them both, positioned himself behind the business register, and pressed the No Sale button. The drawer popped out, and only then, seeing that nothing had changed since the last time he checked, did he stop whistling.

III

The next day I unpacked my computer and set it up on a table in what had been Dr. McDermott's private office. I turned it on and watched the amber-colored cursor beating at the upper left-hand corner of the screen. Having just finished my sixth cup of coffee, I was beginning to feel my heart beat in places which for my previous twenty-eight years had been conspicuously silent, such as my toenails and teeth. I put my hands on the keyboard and let the words come: "The woman, who called herself Saleena, sat drinking a cup of iron-black coffee." It was a good sentence, I thought, clean and uncomplicated, and it seemed to flow right out of me, just as I recalled having told Carnihan it would. In particular the name Saleena suggested magic at work. I pictured a woman who looked like Genine Monteleone, and whose life was as tragic, and whose spirit was as big and irrepressible. The second sentence was harder to come up with, however—in fact, so hard that I couldn't come up with it at all.

After staring at the screen for almost an hour, I assigned a name to the document, filed it away, and turned the computer off.

I had started my second novel, and, although it wasn't a start that would set any speed records, I believed I deserved a reward for the effort.

"Wanna go to Babylon?" I asked Carnihan a few minutes later. He was sitting on a stool at the business counter, facing the front of the store. His eyelids sagged heavily and he seemed to be in a trance. His mouth was open.

"Hey, Jay," I said, speaking directly into his ear. "Wake up, pal. What do you say we go to Babylon?"

"Whah . . . ?" He blinked and turned to look at me. "Oh, hey, there, brother. Nice to see you."

"Were you asleep?"

He shook his head. "Resting."

"Didn't you get enough last night?"

"No. Well . . . I got detoured. Driving home after work."

It struck me that he wasn't wearing his starched blue suit, red club tie, and apron, but everyday clothes with wrinkles on every last inch of them. His hair was greasy and hanging in clumps, and his stubble was thick and black, particularly around the mouth. "Tell me, Jay. Were you a bad boy again last night? Is there something you'd like to share with Father Burnette?"

He cracked an eye open. "Bless me, Father, for I have sinned. I've engaged in self-abuse four thousand times since my last confession."

"Anything else, my son?"

"Well, yes. There is something. I went to meet Bethany Bixler last night, only she never showed up. Genine said she was scheduled to work, but she didn't make it. I waited until the bar closed at daybreak, then I drove here." He sighed and I could smell his tired breath. "I slept in the stockroom, Father. On a blanket on the floor."

"You could've slept with me in the office."

"I knocked but you didn't answer, Father."

"You have a key, don't you?"

"Yes, I have one. And I don't know why I didn't use it. Maybe I was too tired to. I don't remember much."

"G and t's again?"

"That and a few Bloody Marys, maybe a beer or two, maybe a screwdriver. Were there Manhattans? Yes, as I recall . . . oh, yes, five or six." He nodded in the direction of Mr. Hank, who was dusting a giant nail bin. "Daddy called me a slacker this morning. 'Two days in a row,' he says, holding up two bitten-off little fingers. 'Well,' I tell him, 'except to eat at the lunch counter, nobody comes to Hometown anymore anyway. What the hell difference does it make?' "

Mr. Hank must've heard him, because he stuffed his duster in his apron pocket and came striding up the aisle, his arms swinging at his sides. His face was peeled back as if by a bad wind. "You are a slacker, boy," he said, "and a drunk one at that. You smell drunk and you look drunk and if I were half the man my poor dead papa was I'd have you out in the street."

"Fine, then," Carnihan said. "Throw me out."

"Go!"

"Okay. Watch me."

Carnihan took his time getting off the stool. He squeezed between Mr. Hank and me, shambled down the center aisle, and let himself out. When the screen door closed behind him, dust rained down from the ceiling, a powdery trickle. He walked all the way to the middle of Market Street before coming to a stop, and there he dropped to a seat and wrapped his arms around his legs.

"People have always liked our suits and ties," Mr. Hank said. "They like a clean apron, crisply starched." He glanced back at the pictures of his forebears on the wall, seeming to search for confirmation.

Out in the street a taxicab came screaming to a stop mere inches from Carnihan, and I saw Ace Boudreaux at the wheel and a familiar face in the seat behind him: it was Genine, looking hot and bewildered. She and Carnihan exchanged a few words and then she helped him up off the ground. "Are you happy now?" Carnihan shouted as he stumbled back in the store. "I almost got run over out there, and it would've been your fault."

"I'm not," Mr. Hank answered quietly. "I'm not happy at all." He was shaking, and his eyes were wild and trembling; his breath came in gasps.

Genine took a seat at the counter. Her hair was teased out and starched in place, the shade of red on her lips perfectly matching that of her nails, shoes, and belt. You couldn't help but look at her. She was like a red drop of paint on a snow-white canvas—somehow it was the only thing your eyes bothered to fix upon. Mimicking the motion of a windshield wiper, she gave the room a wave.

"You missed the big fight," Silas Poe said. He was sitting to her immediate right, holding the Sports section of the morning *Lip* in one hand, a Tabasco-wet biscuit in the other. "Yeah, old Hank there nearly branded Jay to death with his duster."

"Now I bet that would hurt," she said.

Carnihan had shuffled over to where Mr. Hank was cleaning a collection of ladies' dress hats. His face was filled with defeat and it seemed he was about to cry. "I want to say I'm sorry," he said. "I apologize, Daddy."

Mr. Hank wheeled around and swept his ostrich feathers over Carnihan's back. It was more a reflexive response than a deliberate one, and I was glad when Carnihan didn't take offense.

"I'm sorry," he said again. "I apologize."

This time Mr. Hank dusted Carnihan's neck and chest. "I forgive you, boy," he said. "I'll always forgive you."

At the counter Silas stood up and dropped some cash next to his plate. He winked and waved goodbye to Ruby Dean, the *Daily Lip* tucked under his arm. You could see, underlined in red, those ponies he liked at the track tonight. He pushed through the screen door and a gust of wind caught his ample clothes and blew them back like a sail.

"I want you to remember something," Mr. Hank was telling Carnihan. "You're a *Carnihan*, Jay. A *Carnihan*, do you hear?"

"Yes," Carnihan said.

"A *Carnihan,*" Mr. Hank said again, and then he spelled it for him, his voice powerful enough to rattle the glass shades of the lights overhead.

At last Mr. Hank went back to his hats and Carnihan came over and sat beside me. "Aren't you glad we cleared that up?" he said, no longer sounding so apologetic.

"Cleared what up?"

"This business about who I goddamn am."

I reached over and brushed away some of the lint Mr. Hank's

duster had left on his shirt. "Well," I said, "sometimes it's just nice to be reminded."

Down the counter Ruby Dean was cleaning Silas Poe's place. She took his plate and coffee cup and deposited them in the sink, and with her spatula she swung his money over the mouth of a garbage can. "You think I'm stupid?" she said to no one in particular. "No, I ain't stupid. I know where this comes from." And she dropped it in the trash.

"It comes from his paycheck," Carnihan said, hurrying over and letting himself behind the counter. "From his job at the bank. And before that the federal mint."

"No, it doesn't," Ruby Dean said. "He won at the track last night, he showed me."

Carnihan picked the money out of the trash; some of it, I noted, was colored red from where it had come to rest on a bolus of fancy ketchup. He cleaned it off with a bundle of napkins and brought it over to the business register. "Green used to be my favorite color until it got to be so damned scarce around here." He pressed the No Sale button and lay the money in the proper slot. "Even the grass in Smoke has all turned brown."

"Not my grass," Ruby Dean said.

"Still green, is it?" Carnihan said. "Why, I'd've thought it would be gold by now for all the money Hayward's been making."

Although I wasn't feeling very inspired, I told everyone goodbye and went back to Dr. McDermott's for Round 2 of my bout with the new book. I sat at my desk and turned the computer on, and Saleena and her coffee came back to me in all their iron-black glory. But was iron really colored black? I wondered. And why had I written, "who called herself Saleena"? Did her friends call her by a different name?

Then the sound of heels tapping the parquet came from behind me. It was Genine, I knew; her step was as unique as her movie star voice and mad beautician's hairdo.

"Are you avoiding me?" she said, suddenly appearing in the open doorway.

"I didn't think I was."

"Well, I know you are. And I know why."

I stood and led her into the room, and she sat in a chair with her legs crossed at the knee. It was true, of course: I had been avoiding her. I lay a hand on top of my computer terminal and said, "The bad thing about one of these, Gen, is that you don't get the feel of the paper. The feel of the paper—you ask any writer, he'll tell you how important that is."

She didn't respond, not that I'd expected her to.

"You're not wearing your ring today," I said.

She glanced at her hand as if just discovering this fact herself. "No," she said.

I could feel the heat rise in my face. I thought I'd tell her about Saleena, but she cut me off as I was about to begin. "Be honest with me, Pace. The sonofabitch told you, didn't he?"

"The sonofabitch?"

"Jay. He told you about me and Babylon, and about the ring . . . how Mrs. Clark found it when she was cleaning up?" I started to answer, but she pressed on, sounding as if she, too, would've liked to brand him with a feather duster. "And that we never really had any plan to get married? I bet he told you about that, too, didn't he?"

I waited until I was certain she was finished, and then I gave a nod. "He told me," I said.

"And so now you think I'm a whore?"

I stared at her, trying to decide what might be appropriate to say next. "No" seemed hardly to cover it. She probably needed to hear that none of it mattered, that somebody had loved her since Miss Irene's and always would. But I'm a coward, and just as cowardice had kept me from dialing her up ten years ago and inviting her out on a date, cowardice kept me quiet now.

"It's the times, is all," she said. "Have I mentioned that?"

"Yes, you have, Genny. You have mentioned about the times."

"I love him, Pace, I really do love him." She was nodding her head as if to convince herself, and a shadowy brown tear traced along her cheek. "Ever since high school it was Jay I thought about. He was always wild and shy at the same time, and I guess a girl just goes for that." She reached up and rubbed her face with the back of her hand. "Didn't he get Most Popular Boy our senior year?"

"Yes, he did," I replied, although I didn't remember.

"It's this Bethany person," she said. "It's this hot little actress he wants. And she's not even from New York, Pace, she made all that up. She's from Port Bess, can you believe!"

Genine cried a while longer, some of it coming hard and violent, some soft and not so deep. I had a feeling she too was acting, but I didn't dare say it. I also doubted that she'd ever loved Carnihan, but at the moment I could think of no reason why she'd want to lie about such a thing.

When she was finished, she took my hands in hers and moved back to get a more complete picture of me. Having seen enough, she stepped forward again, filling the space between us, and then she put her mouth on mine. It was different from how she'd kissed me the other night at Babylon. Her mouth was open, and I could taste her morning coffee and cigarettes. I could feel where the tears had run and spoiled her makeup, and I could smell the quiet scent of toilet water, like something green and fresh from a garden. Another way the kiss was different was how I felt about it. I put my arms around her and held her until it was nearly uncomfortable, and then, in my mind's eye, I saw a heavyset man walking through the door at Babylon. He had a fist of keys on his hip, and his shirttail wouldn't stay tucked in his trousers. *Must've dropped ten degrees in the last ten minutes*, I heard a voice say. And that was when I pushed her away.

"We can't, Genny. It'd be great to, but we just can't."

Ignoring me, she stepped forward with a loopy smile on her face, and this time when we kissed she was the one who had to push me away.

"Awful, isn't it?" she said.

I didn't know how to answer. I wondered if she meant the way I kissed.

"I meant about sex, Pace. About how sex is awful."

"Sex? Oh, sure, Genny. Sex is awful, isn't it? It's an awful damned thing. I've always maintained . . . just ask Carnihan if you don't believe me. He'll tell you how awful I think it is."

"And it's silly, that's another thing. People say it's proof that God has a sense of humor, since He's the one who invented it. But what it makes me wonder, I wonder how *smart* He must be. I ask myself, couldn't He have come up with something more interesting? Why didn't He make it something we could do alone?"

"Alone?"

"Right. Such as standing still for a few minutes with your eyes closed—that was all it took to satisfy yourself? Instead, we have to look at each other, and then reach for each other, and then do what we do. What fools He's gone and made of us, Pace. What fools."

"I guess so, Genny."

"Don't ever kiss me again, all right?"

"All right," I said. "Trust me on that. I never will."

But she was coming back for another, and I was rushing toward her, and both of us making sounds as if we were about to drown.

She left and I stayed there a while smelling her toilet water and tasting her coffee and cigarettes. I kept thinking about her mouth, and how, being rather large, it had seemed to fit perfectly with mine. You don't find that every day, I told myself, someone whose mouth is an exact match for yours.

Saleena was still waiting for me on the computer screen, but I had no use for her now, what with Genine Monteleone to worry about.

That night after closing Carnihan made Bloody Marys at the lunch counter, mixing the drinks by the light of the open refrigerator door. They'd become his specialty, and along with Vienna sausages and potted meat, they were about the only thing I ever saw him put in his mouth anymore.

"The funny thing is," he was saying, "at first I thought she didn't like me. She kept staring at you, remember?"

"Who's that, Jay?"

"Bethany. Come on, brother." He smiled and took a long, noisy swallow. "And if that wasn't enough she jumped my case about speaking when I wasn't being spoken to, and said whatever it was she said about my mother—" He stopped short, unable to finish; only after knocking back another drink did he start up again. "Well, after I walked over to the bar and she came to apologize . . . only then did I know that she truly did care." He paused to make sure I'd noted his use of the word "truly." "Did you see how she whispered something?" He pointed to his ear.

"Yeah, I did notice that."

"Did you wonder what she said?"

"I don't remember what I thought."

"She said that from the moment we walked in the door, she'd been trying to decide who it was I looked like. She said it was killing her, and she started to get angry. Finally she just blew up and took it out on me."

"So the way she treated you was nothing personal?"

"Oh, no. Not personal to me, it wasn't."

He put his ingredients back in the refrigerator, and added nothing more to the conversation. Then he locked the store and we started for Babylon. The radio was playing and for a while neither of us spoke. At a stoplight he put his hand on my arm and said, "Wait here a second. I want to show you something." I put the car in neutral and he pulled his wallet out and removed a small slip of paper identical to the one Bethany had left me in Anita's room. He handed it over and I held it up to the dashboard and read a message similar to the one she'd written me. The biggest difference between his and mine was the postscript. "Like the one I've been waiting for," his said. "The man. That's who."

"I don't get it, Jay. Especially that last part."

"The person she said I looked like? The one who made her crazy trying to remember?"

I pointed a finger at him. "Not you? *Rupert*?"

"Rupert," he said, nodding his head as if he himself was having a hard time believing it.

At Babylon we sat by the jukebox and played Johnny Rivers and watched the dancing cowboy entertain himself beneath the giant chandelier. We drank tonic water spiked with lime and ate fried pork rinds, pickled quail eggs, and beer nuts. Genine had the night off, and Bethany didn't show up, and for all Carnihan had to say he might not have been there either. For most of the evening he watched the door, his eyes widening each time it opened. "Is it . . . ? Ah, hell."

The telephone lady sat on the green couch with her legs crossed, balancing a drink on her kneecap. She must've understood that we belonged to the other girls, because she didn't bother to waste any conversation on us. At around midnight Anita tramped over and hovered there with both hands clenched at her sides. A deep shadow, shaped like a giant recreational vehicle, fell across the table, and although I angled my chair back, I found myself totally eclipsed. I knew that in a fight she could take me, pound me to a pulp; thinking it wise, I kept my mouth shut.

Carnihan leaned back and put a pork rind in his mouth. I recognized the look in his eyes: it said he welcomed a beating as much as he did giving one.

"We're just waiting for someone," he said.

Anita seemed to understand. She nodded. "It happens. It happens a lot in this business."

"What happens?"

She laughed in her mean way and I found it hard to see her eyes through all the fat. "They sit down to supper, pick up the fork and knife, and find they just don't have the appetite."

"Appetite for what?" Carnihan said. But you could tell he knew the answer.

I didn't start to fade until around 3 A.M., when "Poor Side of Town" was playing for the hundredth time. I asked Carnihan if he was ready to go, and he said, "But we just got here."

We'd come over in the Mustang, and I reminded him of this, adding, "I'm really awfully tired. And I need to do some work in the morning."

"Well, go ahead without me, then. If she doesn't show up, I'll call Ace or thumb a ride. Don't worry about me."

On the road home I got to thinking about my new book and decided the second sentence would be as follows: "The coffee burned the back of Saleena's throat and made her nose run, but she drank it anyway, knowing this would be a long night."

I said the sentence over and over, memorizing it. I didn't want to forget it before I got home. I had no idea what the long night held for Saleena, but I figured that come morning—my own morning, after getting some rest—I'd be able to summon enough magic to provide an answer.

In the office I sat at my computer, intent on recording the sentence and filing it away, but I found that my mind was in revolt and I couldn't remember a word. Staring at the screen, I began to wonder about the woman's name. Was Saleena a Gypsy name? Was it Cajun? I didn't know any Saleenas, not a one. And I despaired that it was even a person's name at all, seeming to recall that it was a place in California, John Steinbeck country. And spelled differently. *Salinas.*

I turned the machine off but not without first cursing and raising a fist to its flat, black face. It was nearly four in the morning before I retired to the X-ray lab, feeling worthless and defeated. "It ain't gonna happen," I said over and over, trying to mimic Cinda Lovey's big-city voice.

A little later I was awakened by car doors slamming. I pushed myself out of bed, stumbled over to the window, and saw Carnihan standing in the parking lot with Genine supporting him. He was saying something about Bethany, and he sounded drunk.

I put some shorts and a T-shirt on and met them at the door. "Let's take him to the examination room," I said, pointing. "There, Gen. On your right."

I went back into the X-ray lab and got a blanket and a pillow from the closet, and a vomit pan just in case things got ugly. In the examination room I helped Genine strip him down to his underwear and lift him up on the steel table. "How bad is he?" I said. But by then I could smell the alcohol.

"He started hitting it real hard after you left. That's what Anita said." Genine took the pillow and placed it under his head, then drew the blanket over him. She ran her fingers through his hair, pushing it back out of his face. "He called and begged me to come," she said. "He was blabbering and not making sense. I told him to settle down and not to worry about it, that I wasn't even asleep. Dumb me, I thought he felt bad about waking me up. But that wasn't why." She looked up at me with a smile. "Bethany. He was upset that she didn't show up at work again."

"Well, I know. I stayed there until around three."

"Poor baby," she said to Carnihan. "You poor baby." And she stroked his arm, her nails leaving traces along his pale, muscled flesh. "I meant to tell you, Pace, that I sort of exaggerated something this afternoon. That business about always being in love with him?"

"Sure, Genny. I understand."

She was staring at him, and so was I, waiting for him to do something. "Earlier in the day when you and I were back here, I kept thinking you'd stop me and tell me I didn't really love him. I couldn't figure out why you let me ramble on."

"I was nervous, I suppose."

"Well, so was I. But what started it, I remembered giving you a hug that night under the Go sign at Babylon? It was just a little thing, and lasted just a second, but I'd wanted to kiss you then. I felt something, it's hard to explain."

"I felt it, too."

"It was nothing to be ashamed about. It's been I don't know how long since I felt something like that."

"It was innocent," I said.

"That's it, that's the word." She glanced up, and we stared at each other across the comatose form of Jay Carnihan.

"Innocent," she said with a snort of laughter. "Who'd've thought I'd ever use a word like that on myself again?"

For a minute neither of us said anything. It struck me that her hair wasn't as starched and puffy as it had been earlier in the day, and that without makeup she looked young—young enough, I'd say, to get carded at a bar. It was also true that she was beautiful if you took the time to examine each of her facial features individually: taken all together, though, they seemed an odd trick of nature, since none of them matched. Her nose was small and delicately formed, but it looked spare and pitiful above the wide, fleshy mouth. Likewise, Genine's ears weren't quite right for the shape of her skull, and her forehead . . . well, she simply didn't have much of one. And that also posed a problem, considering the enormous, rose-colored blooms that were her cheeks. It followed that her chest did not match her hips, nor her feet, her hands, nor—and I was letting myself extend this conceit as far as possible—her true, inviolate self and the one who took men into the rooms at Babylon.

"What's wrong? Is it my hair?"

"You're a looker, Gen. A real looker."

She stepped around the table and stood a few inches away from me, the light from the streetlamp outside swimming through her hair. I kept staring at her face, seeing all the parts that didn't quite go together. It wouldn't have surprised me to discover one eye brown and the other blue, but tonight they were the same—thin, green irises flecked with hazel, pupils deep enough as to seem never ending.

"I can't ever have babies," she said. "I have a female problem that can't be fixed. Everything looks normal, and it feels normal, only deep inside it isn't."

I was quiet, knowing this was something she'd been struggling to find the courage to tell me. It also was the reason she'd exaggerated her feelings for Carnihan: she was frightened of me and wanted to protect herself.

"There's always an excuse, right? For every girl like me you meet, you'll hear it eventually. What was it Bethany was telling everyone? Oh, yeah. Rupert got kidnapped by the mob." She laughed and fingered Carnihan's hair. "I should've told Peahead in the beginning. But I thought I'd lose him. I was scared of how he'd react, and so I waited, all the way until after we were married. It was why he hit me the first time. I can't blame him, not for that one. But the second one, when I had to get my jaw wired . . ."

She swallowed hard, unable to finish. I reached out and put my hand on her face.

"When I leave tonight," she said, "I want you to take a few minutes and think about what you want for yourself—the kind of life. Do you want somebody who's been the places I have and who'll remind you of that every time you lie down with her? And then think about babies and whether you want to have some."

"All we did today was kiss, Gen."

She held a hand up, stopping me. "This is another thing I don't understand about God and His sense of humor. When you're young and want a baby, and for some reason can't, none that you can think of has a dirty diaper or colic or stays up all night crying because a shadow went across the wall or a clock chimed. Those you remember all have these precious little butterflies chasing after them, and short fat arms like raw biscuit dough you want to bite, and some small, quiet sound to make when you reach down and play motorboat on their belly."

Coward. I should've thrown my arms around her and held her

close. What agony she was putting herself through. I should've kissed her again, felt her mouth, our lips exactly right.

Finally she reached up and brushed my hair back as she had Carnihan's. "Isn't it funny how many things there are you just have to have when you yourself can't have them?"

She gave her head a weary shake, and looked around the room as if just now remembering where she was. "I'd better get going."

After she left I sat there a long time watching Carnihan. A blush of scarlet came across the window and I heard her brakes squeak and knock. This was how she'd left me the day before, after we'd kissed and she'd first ragged God for His lack of humor. Taking her time, waiting to see if I'd run out after her.

Five minutes passed before I was certain she was gone, and I shambled down the hall to the X-ray lab and went to bed, whispering her name over and over into the mattress until I was able to sleep.

Over the next three days Carnihan rarely left the stool at the business counter. His hair stayed dirty and his stubble grew heavier and there was a feral stink about him that made Mr. Hank dust the shelves at a pace even faster than usual.

Carnihan was wearing the Hometown uniform again, but his apron was wrinkled, his trousers stained with greasy droppings from the corn chips he sat flicking into his mouth for hours on end. His socks went unchanged and his shoes lost their shine. Saddest of all, not once did he press the No Sale button and check the money tray.

On several different occasions I tried to engage him in conversation, but he wasn't inclined to make the effort. "Wonder what happened to her," was all he said.

One morning during this benighted period of his, I was eating breakfast at the lunch counter when Genine Monteleone came into the store. She'd just left a beautician, and her hair was colored pumpkin-orange except in a few spots where traces of brown still showed. Bangs reached about halfway down her forehead, and a clever curl, shaped like an upside-down question mark, dangled in front of each ear. To date it was the strangest head of hair I'd ever seen, and I was surprised that she was able to fit it through the door.

"Audubon," she announced, without first saying hello. "I went and got myself one of them audubon haircuts."

Silas Poe laid his red pen and sports page down. "Audubon? Did you say audubon, Genny?"

"Yeah," she answered. "Oughta been on a monkey's ass."

Even though it was warm out, she was wearing a Smoke High letterman's jacket and a tight-fitting dress made of crushed velvet. The jacket was black with leather sleeves, Larry Chowder's number 67 high up on each shoulder, a big orange *S* on the left breast. Her makeup was as thick as a Halloween mask, and she smelled of fancy perfume mixed oddly with mothballs.

As she started for the counter, some of the diners laughed and whispered among themselves, and Beatnik erupted with a fit of angry yapping, his ears drawn back and flattened against his head. Baring his teeth, he chased Genine all the way to where I was sitting. "Oh, glory," she cried, and slid onto the stool next to me. She raised her feet, barely sparing her new pair of pumps.

Carnihan cracked his eyes open; you could see webbed blood in the whites. "Hey, there, Genny." But he didn't move to help her. It was Mr. Hank who finally came to her rescue. He whisked Beatnik up in his arms and ran with him to the other side of the store. "I want to apologize personally for what just happened," he said. "He won't do it again, I can assure you."

"Can you? How can you predict what he's going to do?"

"I just told him to behave. One time. That's all it takes." He dropped Beatnik to the ground and pointed at Carnihan. "It's tragic to see, but Beatnik has displaced his anger with Jay."

"A dog has done this?"

"Smart as he is, he doesn't understand what's gotten into the boy. He took his frustrations out on you."

Genine touched her new hair. "Well, that's good to know. I thought it had something to do with my rinse."

I was miserable and shy about seeing Genine again, and so I did my best to appear terrifically occupied with breakfast. She, on the other hand, was so composed she might never have known the passion and confusion that marked our meeting the other day in Dr. McDermott's. She applied a cool, gratuitous peck to my cheek, and gave me one of her windshield-wiper waves. "Good old Pace Burnette," she said.

"Good old me," I replied, still chewing.

"Yep. Good old you."

I'd dreaded seeing her again because I was afraid of more confessions and turmoil, but, funny thing, now that she'd decided to treat me as if nothing had happened, I found myself battling disappointment.

"I left a smudge," she said.

"Huh . . . ?"

She removed a handkerchief from her pocket and dampened a corner with her tongue. I watched her do this, how she took her time, and it worked to put a fire in my belly and one other place. She placed her left hand against my face, to steady it, and with her right she wiped off the lipstick.

"Better," she said.

I was wondering how to ask her about the jacket when Ruby Dean walked up with a cup balanced on a saucer, her big legs making noise. She placed the cup in front of Genine and poured without looking, stopping when there was just enough room for cream and sugar. "Eatin', honey?"

"Eggs and ham like Pace, Mrs. Clark."

"Any biscuits?"

"No, thank you. Biscuits go right to my hips."

Ruby Dean cracked a couple of eggs onto the flat, black grill and placed two big chunks of country ham next to them. The egg whites bubbled and spit, and their edges turned crispy brown, and the yolks bounced up and down without breaking. The ham steamed and sizzled and blackened in spots, and the thin rim of fat around each piece melted and pooled beneath the meat. It was all such great theater that I resisted an urge to hop to my feet and offer wild, unrestrained applause.

As soon as Genine was served, I stepped down from the stool and brushed the crumbs off my shirt. "Well, I guess it's time to go open up a vein and bleed."

She looked at me with a curious expression on her face, and I said, "I'm going to write."

"Then why didn't you say that? If you're going to write, say you're going to write."

"Ever wonder why so many novelists end up drunks and suicides, Genny? It's because of the darkness they're forced to confront each day of their miserable lives. It's because they're asked to toe the lip of the abyss and to make sense of what they've seen." I glared at her and pretended to be struck with a violent tremor. "The horror, Genny, the horror."

She reached over, put her hand in mine, and gave it a shake. "I wish you luck, but before you go get drunk and kill yourself, there's something we need to talk about."

I was reluctant to say anything, recalling the other day. So I waited, the two of us still holding hands.

"It's about Jay. I was wondering what we might do to help the boy along."

"To help him along?" I glanced back at him. "Would you like for me to wake him up?"

"He keeps coming to Babylon, Pace, every night. In the beginning he just sat there watching the door for Bethany. But the last few nights he's been getting out of control. He won't stop talking, for one. Rayford Holly this, Rayford Holly that. And he's taken to dancing alone. Him and of course that other fellow . . . that cowboy."

"Carnihan dances?"

"He just moves around, holding himself. But it scares me, two crazies like that. Anita wanted to beat him up but I said no law was being broken. She said if he and the cowboy got to touching, to look out. It's a crime to be a homosexual in the state of Louisiana. And she figures she'd be within her rights."

"I'll talk to him," I said. "Soon as he wakes up."

She looked at her food and poked it with her fork. "There was one other thing we needed to discuss."

"All right, Genny."

"I was wondering why you hadn't said anything about me wearing Peahead's jacket."

"Well, I thought maybe you had it on to keep warm."

"You think I don't know better than to wear a coat when it's eighty degrees outside, or that I don't have a nicer one than this?"

"I guess I figured you might, since that one's ten years old and ain't too dressy."

She nodded and played with her food again. "You feeling jealous, Pace . . . that I'm wearing Larry's jacket?"

"Sure, Gen. It's killing me."

I started to leave and she gave me another quiet peck on the cheek, this time making sure to smudge my face. "Don't bleed too much in there, you hear?"

Back in Dr. McDermott's, I turned my computer on and killed the file holding the sentence about Saleena. I'd decided it wasn't so clean and uncomplicated a piece of writing after all, and that there was nothing magical about it. I didn't like Saleena, besides: to my way of thinking she was starting to show every sign of being a major-league bitch. I didn't know anything about her except how she liked her coffee, but I still couldn't stand the woman.

I was straightening things up in the X-ray lab when a gentle knocking came from down the hall. I knew it was Mr. Hank: soft and without urgency, this one—a womanly knock, I daresay. Unlike Carnihan and Beatnik, he was respectful of my privacy and as a rule never went past the waiting room without my permission. I walked over to meet him.

"I wouldn't disturb you, Pace, but I think it's important." He took a letter from his apron pocket. "This just came in the mail. Not two minutes ago."

"Yes sir?"

"It's from New York."

He left and I peeled the envelope open. It was a letter from Cinda Lovey, or, rather, a note typed onto a small card with her name stamped in bold black type across the top. THE CINDA LOVEY LITERARY AGENCY. Mimeographed copies of the first two reviews of *Strange Weather* accompanied it. "You're in my thoughts and prayers at this time," Cinda wrote. "Remember we all have to start somewhere. Don't be discouraged."

The reviews were appearing this month in two widely circulated trade magazines for the publishing industry, and neither was more than a hundred words long. What impressed me immediately was how hard someone could hit in such a short space, and how viciously.

My dialogue was flat and uninspired, the notices said, my characterizations insufficiently drawn, and my insights callow. I had a mannered, angular prose style that reminded one critic of nails on a chalkboard and the other of a dentist's drill. Did these two know each other? I wondered. Their criticisms were remarkably similar. Sometimes critics throw in a line or two of tepid praise to soften the impact of a merciless review, particularly when it concerns a first novel, but none could be found here. The closest they came to praise was in misspelling my name. I was "Pace Burdette" to both of them.

It took me about an hour to quell the flow of bile that kept flooding my mouth. I tore the mimeographed copies up and threw them outside in the Dumpster, slamming the heavy steel door as hard as I could. "Wouldn't know good writing if it reared up and bit you on the ass," I said out loud, then lifted and slammed the door down a second time.

I went back to the X-ray lab and lay in bed for a while, but then I thought about the reviews lying in pieces in the Dumpster and decided I'd want them one day. I'd want them as proof of where I came from: to quote during my Nobel Prize acceptance speech, or to explain to my grandkids why I wrote only one book.

I spent about fifteen minutes taping the pieces back together. My hands were shaking and it wasn't easy work. I finally figured out why the reviewers had been so tough on me: they were jealous, both of them. When I was done I put the reviews in the top drawer of Dr. McDermott's desk and left the room, locking the door behind me. I thought about those horror movies in which parents, after losing a child, close his room off forever. Fifty years pass and some unsuspecting stranger comes along and opens the door and sees dust and cobwebs covering toy dolls and Little League trophies and pictures of Dear One before he chased a fly ball into the street and met his fate beneath a speeding truck. This was my plan for the office: I would never go in there again. Never.

"Wouldn't know good writing . . ." I said again, but found myself unable to finish.

In the X-ray lab I retrieved the two hundred dollars my father had given me. I'd hidden it in a roll of athletic socks, and it took a while, about ten pairs, before I found the right one. Carnihan would probably sleep past noon, and I figured this was as good a time as any to get out and buy that microwave oven Miss Betty and Pop had decided I needed. Since I was feeling so mean and nasty, so shat-upon, I figured buying myself a present would work to pick me up. I walked down the hall and registered a hot pain in my gut as I passed the office. I looked at the door and considered putting a fist through it, but then good sense prevailed and I wept instead. I pressed my head against the wood and released the pain in sobs and heaves. "Burdette," I said to myself. "You're way too proud, man."

In the car on my way to Monster Mart, I studied the passing scenery: the empty buildings, the blackened storefronts, the Delta marquee displaying the word CLOSED. Everything seemed darker and more depressed than before. I remembered having thought that I alone could resurrect the place, bring it back to life. Its savior, I'd hoped to be.

To reach Monster Mart, you took a newly poured concrete road cutting between a cinema fourplex and a half-dozen specialty shops that had migrated there after downtown Smoke started to go under. One building joined another and they were all made of cinder blocks, painted plantation white, and shaped like cigar boxes tipped over. Monster Mart stood at the far end of this shopping center, its huge, square form covering two hundred thousand square feet of retail space. Red, white, and blue streamers crisscrossed the parking lot in front, and an enormous, oval-shaped picture of Rayford Holly filled the space between the words MONSTER and MART on the store's facade.

Holly was seen gazing out from a pair of granny glasses, a black bow tie at his neck. He was smiling, and a cartoon bubble at his lips said "God Bless the U.S. of A.!"

To the left of the building, situated next to the children's carousel rides and bucking horses, stood a fifty-foot-tall balloon in the shape and likeness of the old man. It was an advertising gimmick that seemed to have the same winning effect on people as the giant balloons seen in New York City holiday parades. You couldn't help but gawk at the thing or want to climb its pillowy body and see the world from atop its big, happy head. Ropes extended down from the balloon's shoulders and were staked to the pavement, anchors to keep it from blowing away. This afternoon the balloon appeared to be overinflated somewhat, since Holly looked heftier than he did in newspaper photographs.

The balloon presented him waving his right hand and giving the okay sign with his left. A white banner on his chest, worn like that of a beauty pageant contestant, said AMERICA'S BEST FRIEND: RAYFORD HOLLY.

Since there were so many cars in the lot, I had to park about half a mile from the entrance. As I walked into the store a woman handed me a sheet of green paper listing the day's special sale items. "Rayford Holly welcomes you to Monster Mart," she said. "We hope you have a pleasant shopping experience."

I was still brooding over the reviews, and could think of nothing to tell her. She was wearing a light blue smock over a white shirt and stretch jeans—the same clothes every other employee was wearing, including the male ones. Over her right breast pocket was an oval-shaped picture of Rayford Holly, and over her left a name tag that said MARGE COONS.

"Where are the microwave ovens?" I asked.

"Appliances." So many people were filing through the doors that she had a hard time keeping up. She seemed frazzled. "It's back by Furniture."

"And where is Furniture?"

"Rayford Holly welcomes you to Monster Mart," she said again. "We hope you have a pleasant shopping experience."

"You already said that," I told her.

"Four times a minute," she said. "That's how often we have to say it." And she repeated the greeting and handed out more fliers. Most of the customers simply glanced at the paper, crushed it in a ball, and tossed it on the floor, but Marge Coons was not deterred. "That-a-way," she finally said to me, nodding her head in no true direction I could make out. She said her words again and I felt them penetrate my skull like a knife. Everyone was taking a shopping buggy, even the children. I rounded one up and followed the ugly human mass into the store.

As I was cruising through Candy, awed by the wealth of goodies crowding the shelves, a voice came on the intercom overhead. It was deep and distinctly Southern, full of corn bread and grits, and reminiscent of the overbaked country drawl often practiced by bad television actors. "How y'all are?" it said. "This here is Rayford Holly of Liberty, Arkansas, speaking. I say welcome, and thank you. Y'all have fun, now!"

A sputtering was heard, followed by a drum-heavy rendition of "The Star-Spangled Banner." A minute passed and Rayford Holly's voice returned, and the music began to fade. "God Bless the U.S. of A.!" he said, and unleashed a loud, ear-splitting whoop that any good shopper immediately recognized as a hog call.

For every customer with a buggy, there was a Monster Mart employee with a big, phony smile, a price gun, and a picture of Rayford Holly on his chest. Scores of dirty, screaming children crowded the aisles, their parents nowhere near. I wondered who the kids belonged to, and figured the store baby-sat them. People dropped their children off with instructions to behave. Some conveniently forgot to return for them at closing time and the kids sought out hiding places behind stacks of tractor tires and pallets of dog food. Late at night after the store closed, they roamed the dark interior, playing Army and Hide-and-Seek and eating from the giant cartons of chocolate-covered malted milk balls that seemed to be everywhere. American children weren't being raised on TV anymore, I decided, but on Monster Mart. I was trying to determine which was worse when Rayford Holly's hog call came over the intercom again, providing me with the answer.

It was in Personal Hygiene, driving my buggy hard, that I encountered Bethany Bixler again. Perched atop an aluminum stepladder, she was building a pyramid of red and green mouthwash on a display platform, her face colored a pasty white by the fluorescent lights overhead. The pyramid was about eight feet high and, at its base, as many feet across. I was in such a hurry to find Appliances that I zoomed right past her, seeing only another blue smock and stretch jeans, the bow-tied picture of her boss. If not for her perfume I probably wouldn't have noticed her at all. "Babylon," I thought upon inhaling the scent, then muttered her name.

I was lucky. She was too intensely occupied with her work to bother looking at anything else, so I passed her by without being noticed. I stopped at the end of the aisle and hid behind another giant display, this one of assorted shaving gels. She looked plain and simple, up there on the ladder, no different from any other Monster Mart employee. It wasn't easy reconciling my memory of the saucy femme fatale with the person in front of me, and an intense feeling of pity washed through me.

A shopper stopped next to the enormous triangle of mouthwash, her cart nudging the table on which it was being built. "I need some Scope. The cinnamon kind."

Bethany glanced down at her and gave a fake smile.

"It won't fall if I take one?"

"It shouldn't."

The woman removed a bottle from the lowest tier and put it in her basket. The triangle had about ten levels and each was crammed tight with bottles. As soon as one tier started to empty, employees restocked it, and this kept the pyramid from toppling. Or at least that's how I figured the thing worked.

"It didn't fall."

"No ma'am. It's not supposed to."

I considered taking my own bottle from the pyramid, and, like the woman, pretending to be surprised when all the bottles didn't come tumbling down. It would be a good way of reintroducing myself. "Oh, I know you! You're that girl from the other night!" But then as I emerged from hiding and walked toward her again, I got a glimpse of her name tag. EULAINE DUVALL, it said, and I knew it was time for me to leave.

I started for the front of the store, or what I thought was the front. In seconds, though, I was lost and had to ask for directions. A dirty-faced kid, his mouth brown with chocolate stains, pointed the way.

Last thing I heard, Rayford Holly was squealing and grunting like a hog while "The Star-Spangled Banner" played in the background.

Carnihan woke up feeling cross, and reached over for the register's No Sale button. He stopped for some reason and brought his hand up to his face. He glared at me and wiped the sleep from his eyes. "Say that again? I don't think I heard you right."

"Bethany works at Monster Mart. I saw her there."

It was five o'clock in the afternoon, and I'd finally grown tired of trying to figure out how to break the news to him. He got up from the stool and walked in a circle before coming to stand in front of me. He reeked of odors I could provide no names for. Was that horse sweat? I wondered. But when would he have rubbed against a horse?

"I don't believe you," he said. "First that she works there, and second that you would betray me by stepping foot in there."

"Her name is Eulaine Duvall. Her real one."

"Another lie," he said, and laughed in that wild, openmouthed way of his. He put his hands on my shoulders, and I could see him become serious again.

"I was looking for a microwave oven," I said, "and you don't sell them here." He leaned against me, his breath warm on my face. "I had some money saved. Two hundred dollars. I would've bought a hot plate, but they're a fire hazard."

"I could've ordered you one from my wholesaler."

"A microwave?"

He gave a solemn nod and his hair fell down over his eyes. "I could've sold it to you at cost. Would Rayford Holly sell you anything at cost?"

"Then order it, order me one. I still have the money."

I removed the cash from my wallet and held it out to him. He snapped it up and thrust it back down into my shirt pocket. "Too late."

"Ah, come on, brother."

"Too late," he said again. "And don't call me 'brother.' Not after what you did today."

He hobbled over to the front of the store and locked the door and flipped the sign over in the window so that the word CLOSED could be seen from the street. Mr. Hank and Ruby Dean had gone for the day, and now it was only the two of us. He went behind the counter and started mixing what he always mixed when he went back there. "What did you say her name was?" he finally said. He was adding a celery stalk to his glass. "Eulia something?"

"Eulaine Duvall."

He drank the drink and smacked his lips, and then with his apron wiped the red scum off his mouth. "Sounds like a Port Bess name to me. Sounds like the bayou runs through it every night." He considered this a moment and shouted at the top of his lungs, " 'Eulaine! Oh, Eulaine! You climb down from that haystack right this minute, child, and come feed them pigs!' " He let loose with a shout of laughter and took another long swallow. " 'But Mama, I done be getting poked, Mama!' 'I said come feed them pigs, child! You can always poke little cousin Leroy later! Them pigs be hungry!' "

He smoked and drank and continued his conversation between Mama and Eulaine until he started to lose his voice and a foggy whisper marked his speech. When he finally stopped screaming my ears rang in the silence.

"Eulaine, you say it was?"

"That's what her name tag said."

He cut through the stockroom and Dr. McDermott's on his way outside. A couple of teenagers were walking down North Street and they stopped to watch him. He cupped his hands around his mouth and started shouting again. " 'Eulaine? Where are you, Eulaine?' 'But it ain't cousin Leroy, Mama! It's Daddy I got up in the hay!' 'All right, then, child! You poke Daddy good now! Mama'll feed them pigs! Here, pigs! Here, pigs!' "

The kids ran away, and Carnihan waved a fist at them. "Run, you little demons! Run!"

He peeled the magnetic signs off both doors and stashed them in the cab of the truck. I stood waiting by the Dumpster to find out whether he wanted me along. He started the engine, pumped the gas, and dropped planks of rubber as he left the parking lot. I watched as he wheeled left onto North Street and steered through the stop sign at Market without braking. He sped in front of the store and turned back into the lot again, shifted up a gear for greater acceleration, and came hurtling toward me. I didn't move because I knew he'd stop, which he finally did with only a few inches to spare.

"Do you apologize?" he asked through the window.

"I do."

"Now if I can only get Bethany to apologize."

"Eulaine."

"I'll get her, too. And after the two of them, Rayford Holly." He laughed to himself, shifted into neutral, and nudged the gas. "I want to hear him say the words."

"I'm sorry?"

"Just like that. But with meaning."

When we got to Monster Mart he parked in the emergency vehicle zone next to the building, left the engine running, and marched into the store swinging his knobby elbows. Marge Coons offered him one of her green fliers but he pushed right past it, bumping her arm. She said her words and I covered my head with my hands to keep them from penetrating. "Rayford Holly this," Carnihan said to Marge. He grabbed his crotch and gave it a lift. To me he said, "Where are we going?"

"Personal Hygiene."

"Tell me when we get close. I want to sneak up on her and knock her off her ladder and kick her smack in the face."

He started in the wrong direction, so I got in front of him and led the way, tracing the path I'd gone before. I turned back every now and then to see how he was getting along. His eyes were big and filled with tears and he kept shaking his head and biting his lower lip. It reminded me of how he used to look back in high school before a ball game, when he knew he was going to get his head handed to him but was willing to do battle anyway.

"What does a lousy, lying hick from Port Bess, Louisiana, know about personal hygiene?" he grumbled.

We reached the place and stood behind the pyramid of shaving gels. The only employee in the area was a man strutting up the aisle, his feet slapping the floor harder than seemed necessary. He held his hands behind his back and he was wearing a bow tie like Rayford Holly's. You knew he was a manager of some sort, to dress and carry himself that way. He had dry, thin hair and a skinny neck with a giant Adam's apple that seemed to serve as his own personal compass: it pointed the way and he just naturally followed. The man also had a forest of cheap plastic pens in his breast pocket, each a different color, and each with a picture of Rayford Holly on the cap. "God Bless the U.S. of A.!" the intercom said. "God bless us, every one!"

The man stopped and pretended to consider the gels, but what he was really doing was getting a bead on Carnihan and me. "Finding everything you need?" he asked.

Carnihan looked as if he'd been caught committing a crime. He hunched his shoulders in and shook his head with perhaps too much vigor. His eyes became shifty and he started chewing his lip again, and I knew I'd have to say something.

"Eulaine Duvall. Is she still here?"

He checked his watch. "Lanie punches out at six."

"Where is she now?"

"Checkout, last I saw. We get busy . . . always get busy after five o'clock." He was watching Carnihan and you could tell he was wondering whether to call Security. "Is it important?"

"Oh, no," I said. "We'll wait till she gets off."

"Very well," the man said. He removed one of the pens from his pocket and handed it to Carnihan. "Rayford Holly thanks you for shopping Monster Mart," he said, and his Adam's apple gave a nod and a quiver. He started back on his way.

As soon as the man was out of sight, Carnihan dropped the pen to the floor and stamped down hard on it with the heel of his shoe. The plastic cracked and splintered and blue ink spurted onto the tiles. Carnihan left a trail of shoeprints as he walked toward the exit: small, rectangular stamps with CAT'S PAW printed at the center of each.

When we got back outside a crowd of children was standing around the Hometown delivery truck, watching it run. "Beat it," Carnihan said. "Get lost."

One of them, a girl no more than ten years old, wiped her blistered lips against the sleeve of her shirt. When she opened her mouth you could see the rot between her teeth. "Are you the billionaire?" she asked.

"That old geezer . . . ?"

"They say he's coming, they say soon."

"Who says he's coming?"

"They do. Them in the store." She shot a thumb at the building. "This is where he parks. That's what they say."

"Well, I ain't him," Carnihan said. "And he ain't, either." He poked my chest with a finger.

"They say he drives a truck."

"He drives a 'sixty-two GMC," Carnihan said. "Does this look like a GMC?" He got in and so did I. "This is a Toyota, for your information. Made five years ago. Its shift is on the floor, his is up here on the wheel well." Carnihan revved the engine, scattering the kids, then made a quick U-turn and parked in a slot for the handicapped. "Do I look like Rayford Holly?" he said to me. "Am I as ugly as all that? Be honest, now."

Some of the children went back in the store, and others congregated around the Rayford Holly balloon. They tugged at the ropes that kept it grounded and argued among themselves about how to make it fly. They seemed to think it was a hot-air balloon that could take them places.

"Helium," Carnihan mumbled. "I bet that's what keeps it up."

When I didn't say anything, he said, "How the hell else would it stand straight up like that without a wrinkle?"

He left the truck and walked over to the thing, and stood there a long time simply gazing up at it. His mouth was open as though he were waiting for raindrops, and his hands were tight and fisted. After a while he took out his pocketknife and opened the blade. He said something to the kids and they slowly backed away, mesmerized by the instrument in his hand. I couldn't hear much of what he was saying. He cut one of the ropes where it was staked, and the balloon drew up taller, as if taking a breath. He cut the other ropes and the balloon started to lilt. I could hear him counting backward now, and the kids joined in. "Ten, nine, eight, seven . . ." When the countdown finished and the balloon still had failed to take off, he gave it a nudge, pushing with both hands. One of the kids, the biggest of the bunch, also gave it a shove, and the others joined in. But it was clear the balloon wasn't going anywhere: Rayford Holly, as a matter of fact, looked even fatter than before.

Carnihan motioned for the kids to move back. He held the knife high over his head and drove it deep into the base of the balloon, striking a spot between Holly's gigantic feet. Carnihan grimaced, and a loud grunt followed. He jabbed it again and I could hear the sound of the balloon ripping, trailed closely by a violent rush of wind. You figured it would just fly off like a party balloon after you blow it up and release the nipple, but this thing was staying put. Its lilting motion became more exaggerated, exciting the children. They started to run in circles, yelling and clapping. Carnihan seemed energized by the attention. He began to drive the knife in harder, and the strange, animal noise came louder now. I kept expecting someone to run up and stop him, but the usual crunch of customers continued to enter and exit the store, few giving Carnihan more than a glance. Monster Mart often staged shows for children, and I supposed everyone thought Carnihan's stabbing of the Rayford Holly balloon was just another.

The kids were still screaming when Carnihan came back to the truck, running with his feet close to the ground and his head aswivel. Putting the knife back in his pocket, he took a last look in the direction of the store. The balloon had lost a lot of air, and its middle was creased with rolls of flab. In real life Rayford Holly was a tall, hard-angled fellow, but in this form he looked squat and fat.

Carnihan backed slowly out of the space and took his time driving to the service road. I thought he'd have enough sense to go back to Hometown, but he braked suddenly and wheeled back around, headed in the direction of Monster Mart. He coasted through the lot and parked between a family van and a Cadillac, some one hundred feet from the collapsed balloon.

"So I guess it wasn't helium," he said, leaning his head against the headrest. "Helium and it'd be somewhere over New Orleans by now."

The balloon looked like the hide of a skinned whale. The only part still holding air was the top half of the head, and you could see the billionaire's bespectacled gaze fixed on some point at the rear of the lot. Several men were standing beside the balloon, staring with their hands held behind their backs. They all wore little black bow ties, and even from a distance you could see the forest of colored pens in their shirt pockets.

"They could throw you in jail a long time for that," I said to Carnihan. "Willful destruction of private property, to start."

"Who could?" He was watching the store managers with a big, greasy smile on his face. "Those buffoons? Come on, Pace. Get real, my man."

"Well, the cops could."

He laughed and slapped the top of the steering wheel. "Cops this," he said, and gave his crotch another lift.

Bethany emerged from the store a few minutes later, carrying her smock in one hand, a plastic bag in the other. Except for a quick look, she showed no interest in the balloon.

"She seems different," Carnihan said. "I think I liked her better at the go-go."

"How's that?"

His eyes came to a squint. "She seemed less a whore."

We followed her car to I-49 and stayed a safe distance behind until the exit ramp at 190, when Carnihan momentarily lapsed and sped right up close to her tail. I thought he'd ram her, but then he seemed to come awake, letting a cushion grow between them.

Port Bess was only about ten minutes away, but the drive seemed longer because neither of us said anything. All you could hear was the engine running and the wind buffeting against the truck. I kept seeing Carnihan at the instant when he first stabbed the balloon, and hearing the awful noise he made. I wished I'd left him alone on his stool, back at Hometown, guarding the register. I wished I was back in Washington, writing about floaters and other assorted dead.

We followed her through Port Bess and its dismal strip of filling stations and convenience stores, and out onto another stretch of road where the land was wide and desolate, and lonely farmhouses stood under groves of pecan trees shining like skeletons in the silvery darkness.

Bethany didn't turn off until reaching Bayou Blanc, a muddy, slow-moving body of water with a grassy levee skirting its near side. To keep from being spotted, Carnihan pulled over on the shoulder of the highway, and we watched as she veered off the levee road and drove along a rutted path that crossed under twin bridges spanning the bayou. This same road led back up to the levee on the other side of the highway, where it joined the shell road on top. There was a run of vacation camps down at the foot of the levee—shacks, mostly, jacked up on stilts, with weather-beaten piers jutting out into the water.

A few minutes passed and Bethany appeared on the far side of the levee road, her taillights a pretty bloom in the riot of dust. Carnihan took this as his cue to follow, and we drove down to the water and under the bridges, the echo of traffic beating overhead. When we reached the road on top there was no sign of Bethany, but then I spotted her taillights down by one of the bayouside camps, this one a dilapidated shanty hiked up on brick pilings, a thin ribbon of smoke issuing from its chimney.

Carnihan turned the headlights off and we stopped at a safe distance from the camp entrance, about fifty yards away. Bethany's car door flung open and an interior light came on, and you could see her looking at herself in the rearview mirror. She rubbed her eyes and ran a comb through her hair.

"She's primping," Carnihan said. "Look at that." He seemed disgusted, the way he kept shaking his head. "Wait till I get my hands on this Rupert person."

She went in the house through a back door, and Carnihan and I walked down the slope, moving with care through the tall, damp grass. There were three windows on this side of the house and we trudged back to the last one, where Carnihan positioned himself at one corner and I took the other. This was a small kitchen papered lime-green and crowded with pictures of Jesus and the Blessed Virgin, and you could see Bethany at the sink rinsing out a cup. Coffee was bubbling in the little glass cap at the top of a percolator and you could smell it brewing. From the rear Bethany resembled a boy, that lean and straight up and down, her bristly black hair boxed square at her neck.

She seemed to be staring out the window over the sink, but then it came to me that she was studying her reflection in the flat panels of glass. She brought her hands up to her face and pulled them all the way down to her chin, stretching the skin. It was something I'd often seen Miss Betty do, whenever she was feeling old and tired and thought it might show in her face. After a while Bethany seemed to decide there was nothing she could do about how she looked, not tonight anyway, and she left the kitchen, taking with her the plastic bag she'd brought from Monster Mart.

Carnihan and I bent down low and moved over to a middle room where another light had come on. This window had curtains pulled tight and only a thin crack to see through. Carnihan got there first and put his face close to the glass, and I stood behind him, straining to see over the top of his head.

Bethany was standing next to a hospital bed in the center of the room, gazing down at a woman covered with white sheets and a thermal blanket. The woman had badly cut hair and gnarled, spastic hands, and there was a look in her eyes that told you she wasn't aware of anyone's presence, not even her own. Bethany kissed her on the forehead. "Sorry I'm late." She unfolded a metal chair and sat beside the bed. "Did you have to wait long? I hope you weren't scared." She leaned forward and kissed the woman again and started stroking her hair. "I hope you weren't, I hope you weren't scared, Mama."

Carnihan spun around and glared at me. His eyes were wild with surprise and he'd started to tremble. I shook my head and whispered, "Save it."

"Mama, I see Dorie made a fire. It isn't too warm for you?"

The woman didn't answer and Bethany opened the bag and took out several paperback novels with covers depicting beautiful, deep-bosomed women swooning in the arms of beautiful, deep-chested men. "Look, Mama. Look what I brought." She'd raised her voice and was almost shouting. "Did Dorie say anything about me being late, Mama? Did she complain?" She leaned over the bed and put her hands under the sheets at the woman's middle. "No accidents today? Or did Dorie change you before she left?"

The woman didn't answer and Bethany spent a long time just looking at her. There was nothing in the woman's face to tell how she was feeling, nor in Bethany's; and it was terrible, this silence. Finally Bethany opened one of the books. "Dorie didn't mention anything about not getting paid, did she, Mama?"

She stared at the page a minute before beginning to read out loud. Her face held the same weary expression it had when she'd looked at herself in the kitchen window, and I could've cried for what that meant. Bethany was a good reader because she was very expressive and didn't stumble over any pronunciations. When she got to parts with dialogue it sounded as if the characters were really talking. Another thing that impressed me was her accent, which no longer had the Yankee inflections we'd heard at Babylon. Now it sounded more like Carnihan's and mine, which is to say flat and clipped and decidedly Cajun.

Five minutes passed before she put the book down.

"What do you think of these two, Mama? Will Rupert ever come back? Will Bethany ever get him back?" She laughed at this and hugged herself and started rocking in the small metal chair. "Oh, Mama, will he ever come back?"

On the ride home Carnihan got sick and had to pull off the highway. He stood in front of the truck, washed by headlights. Figuring it best to leave him alone, I stayed inside and rolled the window down and breathed the muggy swamp air. I tried not to look at him, I didn't want to see. He finished and climbed behind the wheel, and we started back down the road.

In downtown Smoke, waiting out a traffic light, he turned to me and said, "There ain't no fairness in this world, Pace. None."

I was quiet, not sure how to respond. We looked at each other and I nodded and the green light splashed across his face.

IV

That night after he dropped me off I lay in bed trying to sort out the troubles I'd come home to. Carnihan, Genine, Bethany. I also tried to sort out myself.

I smoked with an ashtray resting on the covers stretched tight between my legs, and I watched the light from outside play across the ceiling. I went through an entire pack and the better part of a second, stopping when it began to feel as if I'd taken a hot charcoal in my mouth.

I finally got to sleep as dawn was breaking, and I had the weirdest dream. Carnihan and I were billionaires. Somehow or another we'd hit it rich, and all our troubles had disappeared. The sky was blue except for where the turrets of our castles blocked it. Our automobiles were ones-of-a-kind and they never ran low on gas. We wore new clothes every day and every night there was a new girl to take to bed. We had so much money we were different from everybody else. We didn't have a care, is the thing. Being billionaires had set us free.

After a few hours of this I woke with a huge smile on my face. I woke expecting to find myself in silk pajamas, a centerfold type with makeup on her face lying there beside me. But then I got a good look around and saw that nothing had changed. The X-ray lab still smelled of rubbing alcohol, the window addressed a giant trash bin. I'd been dreaming. A blinding headache hit me and the indefatigable taste of carbon filled my mouth, and I said what I always say when I can't stand the way I feel: "Lord, take me now and get it over with."

By the time I got dressed and left Dr. McDermott's it was half past ten. I pushed through the curtain at the back of the store, fully expecting to encounter Carnihan on his stool; but I was surprised to find him dusting the shelves with an intensity of purpose that frankly shamed Mr. Hank's previous efforts. He was smiling, his hair had a fussy blow-dried look, and his clothes and apron were clean and neatly pressed.

"Hiya, brother! Top of the day to you."

Without daring to return the greeting, I eased upon a stool and drained a cup of coffee in a single gulp. As soon as I finished, Ruby Dean gave me a refill, which I dispensed with as quickly as the first. "Go slow," she said. "You'll burn your mouth. You'll hurt yourself."

"I'm already hurt."

"Okay, then. Go fast." And she left the pot and went to turn the strips of bacon she had frying on the grill.

Today's sign said in green chalk: BEIGNETS, CALAS TOUT CHAUD, CRAB OMELETTE, PAIN PERDU, BASIC CAKES AND CANE SYRUP.

"What is that?"

"What is what?" She looked at the blackboard.

"That second to last thing."

"Lost bread."

There were no customers at the counter, and, as always, none shopping the shelves. Carnihan's reckless cleaning, however, gave the illusion of a crowd, as he seemed to be in so many places at once. After a while he came and sat beside me and draped his arm over my shoulders. "I went back. After dropping you off. I went back to see her." He was nodding his head with great excitement, as if I'd somehow suggested that he wasn't telling the truth. I didn't say anything and he took a paper napkin and wiped the corner of my mouth. "You had a little something there."

Although I hadn't placed an order, Ruby Dean seemed to know what I needed: fresh-squeezed orange juice, the cakes, and about a dozen sausage wheels.

"We come from the same places," Carnihan said. "The same, exact ones."

I forked some pancake and a wedge of meat. "Yeah. Delmas Street, it's called. We both come from Delmas Street."

This amused him. "Delmas Street? I meant Bethany, brother. Me and Bethany come from the same places." He fished his wallet out of his back pocket and opened it to an accordion of photographs. "You remember this?" And he placed a picture of his mother down on the countertop. It was the one that had gotten him in trouble back in high school—the one showing Miss Deenie with a stack of hair sticking up out of the frame, eyes squinting from behind a pair of glasses.

"I thought somebody stole that."

"Turns out I'd misplaced it."

"You disrupted the entire school. You had the principals searching everyone, opening lockers. 'Round up the usual suspects,' you kept saying."

He shrugged and, careful to handle it by the edge, put the picture back in a transparent glove. "My mistake," he said. "I'd accidentally misplaced it."

"Where?"

"Here." And he patted the spot: his shirt pocket. "I'd felt lonely that morning in homeroom. The bell rang. I didn't have time to put it back in my billfold."

I ate more pancake and washed it down with juice. Carnihan took up the napkin and wiped my mouth again. "There it is," he said. "A little fleck of something. Keeps coming back."

While I ate he told me about his return trip to Bayou Blanc. He described scrambling down the levee and going back to the window at the side of the house. Bethany, he said, was still reading in the middle room, her mother staring up at the ceiling. "Advanced Alzheimer's," he said. "That's what she has."

"Say again?"

"Alzheimer's. My aunt had it. Remember the lady used to come clean house and cook after Mama died?"

It took a moment but her name did come back. "Aunt Rose," I said. "Nice lady. Always had a smile."

"The disease attacks the nervous system. You lose control of your bodily functions, and your mind gets so bad you don't remember a day of your life." He paused and reflected upon this. "Of course it's a lot different from what my mother had. But what's happening in that house down by the bayou is pretty much the same."

"And how is that?"

"Bethany's watching her mother die. Just like I had to watch mine."

He said this without a hint of sadness, and in fact seemed as cheerful as when I first entered the store. I found this extraordinary considering how in the past he'd always become upset at the mention of Miss Deenie.

"I take back any hard words I might've said about Miss Bethany Bixler, a.k.a. Eulaine Duvall. She's been elevated to sainthood in my book. Canonized. I got her all figured out."

"Then tell me. Please."

"She saw she couldn't stomach being a hostess at Babylon, she was too pure for that, too good. But she needed the money—a job, anything to help support her poor, afflicted mama. Finally Monster Mart, of all places, comes to the rescue. They give her a job in Personal Hygiene since she's the picture of health herself. Now I don't forgive her for working there, because to me it's equal to sharing a bed with Rayford Holly. But I can understand it."

As it happened, Carnihan had lacked the nerve to knock on Bethany's door and talk to her. After she went to bed he left the house and drove way down the levee road, stopping where the bayou fanned out wide and drained into a basin. He stood on the bank counting stars and skipping rocks, and before he knew it the sun was lifting and coloring the trees, and snowy egrets were floating overhead in clouds.

It was 7 A.M. when he returned to Worm Road and found his father feeding the goats in the pasture behind the house. Mr. Hank was throwing hands of corn on the ground, talking to them as you might a human being. Since he didn't approve of Carnihan's late hours, Mr. Hank refused to speak, his mouth set hard, his eyes cast downward. But then Carnihan climbed over the fence and helped him with the goats. He got his own bucket of grain and let the tame ones eat from his open hand, and he asked his father their names. Mr. Hank watched in disbelief, unable to speak. He seemed on the verge of tears; never had Carnihan shown any interest in the animals before. When they were finished they walked up to the house, Mr. Hank's boots squeaking in the dew-wet grass. They had just reached the porch when Carnihan, stamping his heavy brogans against a welcome mat, turned to his father and said, "I've been wondering about Mama. What she was like."

I put my fork down and stopped eating because I knew what an important moment this must've been for Carnihan—after all, it had taken him twenty years to get there. "Go on," I said.

He took a sip of my juice. "You sure you want to hear it? I can stop now."

"No. Go on. Please."

They'd gone in the living room and settled on the couch, and he and Mr. Hank had spent the next two hours poring over family photo albums and sharing stories, the first of which was about how Miss Deenie and Mr. Hank had actually met. She'd been sitting on the square by the statue to the Confederate dead, and he was taking a break from the store, just out getting some air. She'd called him over and asked whether he knew he had an apron on. "Well, at least you don't keep it wrinkled," she'd said upon learning that it was part of his uniform.

Their courtship was brief—two weeks, in all. A judge married them in his courthouse chambers, then they drove to Biloxi and rented a room by the beach. Their first day there, his mother had waded out into the dark Gulf water and been stung by jellyfish, and Mr. Hank had rushed her to a nearby infirmary. The attending doctor had recommended she spend the night there, and Mr. Hank had slept on a bench in the waiting room outside the women's ward until around two in the morning, when, after making certain the nurses were out of sight, he'd slipped through the doors and crawled into Miss Deenie's bed. Their marriage was consummated there, and Carnihan conceived, with about a dozen patients sleeping all around. Or at least Mr. Hank had thought they were sleeping.

"I really doubt he'd tell you about their first time."

Carnihan held his hand up as if to take an oath. "But there's more. Just wait."

I swiveled on the stool and looked around the store, and only now did it occur to me that Mr. Hank and Beatnik weren't there. I asked Carnihan about them, and he replied, "Daddy was feeling pretty beat after the morning we had. He asked if I wouldn't mind running things by myself here today."

"That's quite a compliment," I said.

"Yes. I'd never had a better one."

He began to tell more of the story but a customer pushed through the front door and drifted along the length of the counter. She was about forty years old and dressed like a schoolmarm: she carried herself hunched over, her bony shoulders protruding beneath the woolly fabric of her shawl. When after a moment's hesitation she stepped toward the shelves, it struck me what an unprecedented occasion this was. Since returning home, had I seen a visitor to Hometown do anything but sit at the counter and take a meal? I honestly couldn't recall one.

Carnihan hopped off his stool and strode toward the woman, his apron flapping between his legs and inhibiting his step. "Welcome to Hometown," he called, opening his arms wide as if to embrace her. "Can I help you, ma'am?"

The woman shuffled over to the shelf where Mr. Hank kept his expansive collection of feminine napkins and, after some deliberation, selected a box. She handed it to Carnihan.

"Anything else?"

She shook her head and started digging in her handbag for money. It was plain how nervous she was, and that she wanted to hurry up, pay for the item, and leave as quickly as possible.

"No douche, ma'am? Nothing like that?" I thought I'd heard him wrong—I must've heard him wrong!—but then he said, "We carry all variety, some in fruit flavors as I recall."

The woman's head kicked back and a bright red blush came to her face. Her mouth fell open and a trembling hand went up to cover it; she also started backpedaling toward the door.

Carnihan, in the meantime, was striding up to the business

counter, playing catch with the box of napkins. "Maxi pads," he said. "Extra absorbent. New and improved."

The door jingled as the woman left, and the register jingled when Carnihan punched the three-dollar button. It was a different jingle than the one for No Sale. It sounded happier, I thought.

"You ran her off," Ruby Dean said. "No lady wants to hear about no douche, Jay."

"I was trying to be helpful."

"You ring it up and keep your mouth shut. This lady is very fine. A church woman. She don't want to hear about no maxi pads being no new and improved."

"People are too sensitive," he said.

"For your information, your daddy keeps all them different kinds on account of her . . . on account of that one lady there."

Carnihan spun around and poked a thumb at the door. "Who is she to get such consideration?"

"Just a woman. But he don't want to be short of the one she might be looking for. Last time she came—this was some months ago—he didn't have it." Ruby Dean was cleaning the counter, making much bigger circles than usual. "Last time she walked up to him and had to ask for the kind she liked. It embarrassed him, I tell you. No woman wants to ask about no Kotex, Jay. And no man—no *real* man—wants to stand there and have to hear her ask for it."

Ruby Dean wiped right past me, her circles edging up to my flatware. " 'No douche?' " she grumbled to herself. "Whoever heard of asking a church woman, a lady, 'No douche?' You oughta be ashamed of yourself, boy."

"Oughta be?" he asked.

She threw her rag down and stared at him.

Carnihan hipped the register drawer back in place. "Oughta be on a monkey's ass," he said. "You hear me, Ruby Dean?"

She went back to cleaning, and he played catch with the box a few minutes longer before returning it to the shelf.

He finished telling me about his morning and I went back to Dr. McDermott's and tried to clear the stink of smoke from the X-ray lab. I washed out the ashtray and sprayed half a bottle of disinfectant in the air. The disinfectant had a breezy, country scent which actually smelled worse than the stale smoke and ash. I kept feeling as if I needed to sneeze. After I'd gone to bed Carnihan came into the room and stood hovering over me, waiting to see if I was really sleeping. It took some effort to keep from flinching or opening my eyes and to affect a regular, musical rate of snores. When he left I turned over and covered my head with a pillow. I was vaguely aware of a couple of sentences trying to nudge their way into my consciousness—the critics again—but by force of will I was able to keep them out. Mainly I pictured Genine cutting somersaults across a football field, her legs flashing gold under the banks of lights.

When I came to, about two hours later, Carnihan was there again. I looked up and he smiled and said, "Top of the day to you," just as he had earlier in the morning.

"Bottom of it to you," I grumbled.

He put the keys to the Mustang on my chest and announced that he'd loaded a sack of feed in the trunk. "It's for the goats. Deliver it to Worm Road, if you don't mind. Daddy told me to tell you not to eat. He'll barbecue something."

I heard his shoes make it as far as the door. "I'm going to Monster Mart and wait for Bethany," he said.

Less than half an hour later I was driving, as ordered, in the direction of North Smoke. The windows were rolled down and the radio blared, but I was still only semiconscious. I knew it was vital for me to wake up fully before reaching Worm Road: a person needed total command of his faculties to drive that dreadful stretch. Worm Road's name seemed inspired, since it was so long and skinny and filled with unpredictable turns, but in fact its name had nothing to do with how it looked. The fellow who owned the land at the head of the road raised fish bait, and to attract customers he'd tacked a hand-painted sign up in his trees. WORMS FOR SALE, it said.

The first mile was rutted blacktop; the second, rutted gravel. Carnihan and Mr. Hank lived midway into the third mile, which was, I observed, rutted rut. I put my seat belt on and gritted my teeth, and tried to avoid those potholes leading straight to hell.

The house stood on a hill, and it was a much simpler affair than their former place on Delmas Street. Made of cypress and shaped like a big, square box with a single wing for the garage, it might've passed as the dwelling of an eighteenth-century frontiersman had Carnihan's satellite dish not stood out front.

When I arrived Mr. Hank was standing beside an open barbecue pit, Beatnik sitting between his feet on the pavement. A tumbling cloud of smoke momentarily obscured them from view, but then Mr. Hank stepped forward holding a double-tined fork and a sauce mop. He was wearing faded jeans and a camouflage hunting jacket, and work boots with slashes carved in the sides from where he'd gotten careless with a Weed Eater. Even more strange than seeing him out of uniform was seeing him with something other than his feather duster in hand. He was glad to see me, and said my name over and over in that fine, famous way of his.

"Bring the feed?" he asked.

"Yes sir."

I removed the sack from the trunk and he showed me where to put it. "I love my goats," he said, more to himself than to me.

I gave him an appreciative nod and looked off to where they were grazing in a pasture behind the house. The lot was rimmed with hardwood trees, and some of the animals were huddled in the late-afternoon shade, eating from bales of hay. The wind was blowing from the south and you could smell a musky stink.

"I love them and they love me," he said.

"Sir?"

"The goats. They're my absolute best friends." He reached down and gave Beatnik's head a shake. "Next to this little fella, of course."

He flipped the half-dozen steaks sizzling on the grill, and sprinkled water on the coals to keep the fire down. "How were things at the store today, Pace?"

"Busy in the morning from what I saw."

"Was it Ruby Dean who was busy?"

"Well, she was . . . and then somebody came in."

His face lit up with surprise, and he turned to look at me. "Somebody lost, come in asking for directions?"

"It was a lady."

He looked back at the meat, and you could see the red coals

reflected in his eyes. The sauce was in a small aluminum pan, and he soaked some up with the mop and brushed each steak, the fire below spitting as the grease dripped. "Was she looking for anything in particular?"

"I really don't know, sir."

He didn't speak for a while. He seemed to know I was lying, and he was careful not to embarrass me. "Well, even if it was the maxi pads she wanted, I hope she wasn't too bashful to ask Jay for some."

We stood watching the smoke pour from the chimneystack, saying nothing. A few minutes passed and he figured I should meet his goats. As he led me through the gate to the pasture, a few of them bleated and pushed up next to him, lipping his pockets. As soon as they figured out he didn't have anything, they grouped around me and started nudging my thighs and groin with their weird faces. It spooked me a little, since they seemed angry that I didn't have anything. I recalled stories about animals biting certain essential parts off people—off men, I should say.

"What do they want?"

"Usually I bring some grapes or candy or something. A little treat. I hide it in my pockets."

Over on the grass Mr. Hank had set up a picnic table, lawn chairs, and a cluster of oil lamps that burned yellow in the early dark. He removed the steaks from the grill and put them on a cookie sheet, then he went inside the house and brought out a bowl of green salad and a platter piled high with boiled potatoes and corn. While I took my time with the meal, Mr. Hank ate with wild, athletic hunger, rarely looking up from his plate. I tried to get him to talk about life in the country, but he was too busy to answer.

"I'd hoped to speak with you about Jay," he finally said, once all the food had been eaten. "It's why I schemed to have you drive out here tonight."

"Schemed?"

"That sack of feed was just a ruse." He got up from the table and walked over to the back porch. "I wanted to get you alone, here at the house. I needed to ask your considered opinion about something." This startled me, and, when I didn't say anything, he said, "I've decided to retire, son. Do you think Jay's ready to run the store alone?"

There was a quick thudding at my rib cage, and I found it hard to speak. "He can handle it," was all I could manage.

"The two of us had quite a morning. He stumbled in at dawn and asked about his mother. You might've thought he was experiencing some kind of religious conversion, the way he carried on. I didn't tell him the whole truth, of course. No son's ever ready for the whole truth about his mother." He paused and traced a hand over the back of Beatnik's head. "I won't be going to Hometown tomorrow. Or the day after that. Look at me, Pace. I'm getting old, for crying out loud."

"You're not old," I said.

"Old enough."

It was dark now except for the lanterns and what light came through the windows of the house. The goats were watching us from the fence, dark forms through whitewashed planks that glowed with an eerie phosphorescence.

"Let me tell you what I'm worried about, Pace. I'm worried Hometown won't be able to sustain him once Ruby Dean leaves."

He let this hang in the air for a moment, and I found myself too stupefied to ask anything but the obvious: "Is Ruby Dean leaving, Mr. Hank?"

He gave a solemn nod. "Yeah, boy."

I didn't know what to tell him, so I didn't speak at all. I pictured Ruby Dean holding her coffeepot, her nylon hose squeaking as she walked from one empty cup to another. It was so vibrant an image as to seem eternal.

"Ever catch her sneaking money into the register, Pace?"

"The lunch counter register?"

"No," he said. "The other one."

I shook my head.

"Well, I have. Several times, as a matter of fact. It's why Jay keeps pressing the No Sale button. He knows every penny we take in and give out, and yet he can't account for the extra twenty or thirty dollars we've been generating each day. Once he pulled me aside and asked if I believed in ghosts. He seemed to think his great-granddaddy Henry had come back to help us along."

"And it was Ruby Dean?"

He nodded and an uneasy smile came to his face. "She's also tried to surrender her salary, claiming she doesn't need it anymore. She tore up her checks, and I personally had to write out others and deposit them in her bank account. That woman . . ." He grew quiet and started shaking his head as if to release himself of a sadness. "A few weeks after Jay's mama died this young black gal comes into the store looking for work. She's twenty-two years old, has a son Jay's age, and is also caring for her mother and a baby sister. I ask what she can do, and she tells me, 'I can do whatever it takes, and you won't hear me complain about it.' " Mr. Hank chuckled quietly to himself. "I knew right off she was my kind of woman."

"How long before she leaves?"

"Two months."

"Two months," I repeated.

"Hayward and LaShonda have invited her to move in with them in Miami. They have the room, and they could use her help with the children."

A minute went by and neither of us spoke. Finally I said, "I suppose you'll have to find a replacement?"

"Not me, boy. That's up to Jay. As of today I'm retired, remember? But I'd find a replacement, all right—and a good one. Otherwise, Hometown Family Goods hasn't a chance."

I felt bad for not being able to come up with anything to say. He'd had a load to get off his chest and he'd needed someone to help him. We exchanged unhappy smiles, and he said, "The downstairs toilet doesn't work. You'll have to go to the one upstairs. Down at the end of the hall."

"I beg your pardon?"

"You don't need the bathroom?"

"Oh, yeah. Okay. I suppose I could go."

He stood and followed me to the door. I went in the house and glanced back at him. "Pace Burnette," he said, his voice suddenly coming big and strong. "Why if it isn't Pace Burnette. It's Pace Burnette, of all the . . ."

I really didn't need the bathroom. But I went upstairs, anyway, and stood over the toilet without doing anything. I flushed the toilet and washed my hands, then I walked toward the closed door that led to Carnihan's room. I flipped the light on and saw a mattress and box spring set up on a warped aluminum frame, dirty sheets hanging to the floor. Over the bed was a picture of the 1975 Smoke High football team, Carnihan's face encircled with red ink, mine with blue, and Pop's with green. Next door was Mr. Hank's room, and I went there now, poking my head in. The air had a familiar odor—Beatnik's, it came to me. Something on the dresser caught my eye, the only object there: it was a framed photograph of Miss Deenie at about eighteen. Her hair was yellow and hung like a sheet over her shoulders, and she seemed to be trying to imitate one of the more dramatic movie star poses of that era.

A fit of angry yapping erupted outside as I was descending the stairs. I spun around and ran to the end of the hall and stood before a great picture window addressing the back pasture. The picnic lanterns had been extinguished, and passing clouds blocked the night sky, but clearly I could see Mr. Hank standing in the middle of his herd, wheeling round and round with his arms stretched out. "Hiya! Hiya! Hiya!" he called. Some of the goats were bumping their mouths against his pockets front and back, and others were trying to run circles around him. Beatnik raced up and joined the fracas. "Hiya! Hiya! Hiya!" Mr. Hank called again.

The faster he moved, the more it seemed he was performing a dance. He kept spinning around until he started to lose his balance and stumble about. I couldn't figure out what he was doing. Was he putting on a show, suspecting that I was watching from above? Then it came to me that he was in trouble and trying to get away from the animals. Something was wrong and he couldn't escape them: they were pushing in closer, striking his pockets harder and harder. At last he stopped spinning altogether and dropped to a knee. He brought a hand up to his chest and slumped to the ground, and the goats converged on him, tearing at his jacket and pants, pulling at his boots.

I ran down the stairs and through the den and out toward the pasture. I was screaming his name and cursing the goats, but even before I reached the fence I knew he was dead. It seemed I heard a voice tell me so, Mr. Hank's, I'm certain it was. "I'm dead, Pace. Hey, Pace. I'm dead."

The goats scattered as I approached, and Beatnik took off running for the trees.

Mr. Hank was hot to the touch, and sweat ran down his face and dampened his neck. His eyes were open, his lips slightly parted. I pressed my mouth against his and breathed hard to fill his lungs. His chest rose and I raised a fist and struck his sternum. I blew into his mouth again and started to apply pressure with my hands. I pushed several times, then gave him another sharp blast of air. I don't know how long I did this, alternating the air with the pressure on his chest. A few minutes, maybe. After a while I started to cry and the crying sapped my strength and there was no air left to give.

I ran to the house and dialed 911 on the phone in the den. An operator came on and I told her to send help. I was screaming. I gave her the address, but she'd never heard of Worm Road and it took me a while to come up with directions. I threw the phone down and hurried back outside. The goats were surrounding him now, forming a circle. They watched without moving or making a sound. I yelled and screamed pushing through them and I took him in my arms and carried him up to the house. He wasn't hot anymore and his eyes were empty, and there just wasn't anything you could do.

I'd never seen anyone die before, or touched a dead person, or talked to one as I ended up doing.

"But you can't leave!" I was saying. "He's not ready yet! He's just not ready yet!"

I didn't call anyone until after the medics had carried him away. I dialed the house on Delmas Street and over the line you could hear the hyperbolic roar of a TV fight in the background. Pop's voice came hoarse and low, a whisper, and I knew I'd awakened him. He seemed to think I was in Washington; he asked about my work at the paper. "Come on, wake up, Pop. I'm on Worm Road, for heaven's sake."

"God, son. What time is it?"

I waited a while before telling him what happened. I was surprised that I was able to do it. "He fell in the pasture," I said. "He never got up." On the other end the television was muted. I could hear a lamp being switched on.

"What? . . . Tell me again."

I did what he asked, then I said, "You and Miss Betty come out here. I've got to go find Jay."

Pop shouted Miss Betty's name and she picked up on the kitchen phone. "It's Hank," he said. "Hank's died, Mama." And she began to cry. It came soft over the phone. Pop was crying too.

There were no streetlamps along Worm Road and great oaks blocked any light from above, making the way so dark as to seem impenetrable. I navigated the ruts as best I could, despite shaking hands and a shortness of breath that made me faint. By the time I reached the main road I had to stop to compose myself. I could feel the old man's lips all over again and taste the peppered meat on his tongue. I rolled the window down and spat outside, and when that wasn't enough I spat again.

I drove 190 at speeds never less than eighty miles an hour. When I reached Bayou Blanc I started shaking all over and felt as if I needed to throw up. I stopped under the twin bridges and staggered down to the bayou's edge and splashed water on my face. It stank of mud and oil but it revived me and the hurt went away. I drove back up the levee and spotted the Hometown delivery truck parked on the road, same place as last time. From the top of the slope I looked for Carnihan, watching for movement in the shadows. There was nothing so I scrambled down to the bottom of the levee, the weeds pulling like chains, and stooped down low as I closed in on the house. Lights shone in all the windows and I could hear music, something from a radio. It came soft and low, a country ballad. At the kitchen window in back I could hear movement in the house, a practiced shuffling. I scanned the room and after a minute Bethany appeared. She was dancing alone to what I knew was Wayne Toups, a Cajun song more slow than fast. Happiness showed in her face as she swept across the floor, turning in circles, and it came to me how she resembled Mr. Hank when he'd gone out to the pasture and shouted "Hiya! Hiya! Hiya!" It gave me the shakes, seeing her move like that. I raised a fist to rap on the glass but then I stopped myself: it was none of her business, and it wasn't right to intrude on her now. A commercial came on and she danced through that, too, spinning round and round, her face bright and happy. I backed away from the window and was walking toward the other side of the house when I spotted something moving at the end of the dock. It was Carnihan, lying on his back on the wind-scoured boards, gazing up at the sky. There was a cigarette in his mouth, the red tip flaring each time he took a drag. I wondered how to tell him, what words to use. I walked slowly toward him, careful not to rock the pier and frighten him.

When I got close enough I could see that his pants were unzipped and his boxer shorts unbuttoned. The dark line of his pubic hair was visible and he manipulated himself in a hard, mechanical way, the cords in his neck tightened by the effort. I spoke his name and he turned over to his side and looked up at me, his face dark with surprise. I crouched down beside him and he pulled his hand out of his pants and held it out to me as if to show there was nothing.

"Just enjoying the night," he said, and spat his cigarette into the water. He sat up and began to put himself back together.

"How 'bout this country air, Pace."

Poor fool. He was still wearing his red club tie and blue jacket, and I mentioned this before telling him about his father.

Three days later, in a hot misty drizzle, we buried Mr. Hank next to Miss Deenie in a cemetery just south of Smoke. Pop and I served as pallbearers, along with Carnihan, Silas Poe, another Hometown regular named Ol' Fontenot, and Ruby Dean's son, Hayward. Because of the weather most everyone stayed in their cars, watching the grave from where they'd parked on a shell road nearby. The funeral home had set a tent over the plot, and Ruby Dean and Carnihan sat under it on the row of chairs reserved for family. The rest of us stood directly behind them, pressed in tight to keep from getting wet.

During the ceremony Carnihan sat with his legs crossed and his hands folded in his lap. He seemed to find the whole affair curious, and traced his eyes over the crowd of mourners, not even blinking when one of them gave him a nod or a word of consolation. When it was over the priest handed him a metal crucifix with an effigy of Christ. Carnihan held the object flat in his open palms, as if it were something he'd prefer not to get to know personally. He offered the crucifix to Ruby Dean, but she seemed confused and refused to take it.

As the gathering was starting to break up, Genine Monteleone threw her arms around me and wept against my shoulder. Her grief was so deep and powerful that I could think of no words to soothe her. I caught a glimpse of Miss Betty and Pop standing nearby and gestured for them to come over. They hadn't slept much over the last few days, and it showed in their faces.

"Miss Betty, Pop, you remember Genny, don't you?"

My father offered his hand and my mother responded with a polite hello, but I could tell that neither of them recognized her. "Genine Monteleone," I said. "She was a cheerleader at the high school when I was there."

A spark of recognition came to Miss Betty's eyes, and her mouth fell open. "You can't be," she said.

"Yes ma'am."

The two of them embraced briefly and broke apart, only to embrace a second time. "Will you send your mother my love, Gen?"

"I will, thank you, Mrs. Burnette."

Pop said, "We should be getting to the reception, Mama." But instead of guiding her to the car he inched up closer to Genine. He seemed to be inspecting her for proof that she really was the girl he knew from ten years ago. "Genny who used to do those flip-flops?" He sounded unconvinced.

"That's me, Coach Burnette."

"Genny with hair way down her back?"

"Yes sir. Only I cut it. About five years ago."

"Genny Monteleone, you say?"

"It's me, Coach Burnette. I swear."

As he examined her, I decided I must've been crazy to entertain thoughts of pairing with this woman. Today she had taken great care to mute her appearance, but she still looked like the kind of woman who steps from a cheap hotel room at five o'clock in the morning readjusting the straps on her stiletto heels and looking for wet stains on her clothing.

"Well, I'll be darned," Pop said. "It is you. And all grown up. Wonderful to see you again, Genny."

"And you, Coach Burnette."

"Mama?" Pop spun around, his hand reaching for Miss Betty.

They started for their car and Genine threw her arms around me again. She was wearing a black outfit with blousy pants cut to resemble a dress. I noted the hole in the sleeve of her jacket where some careless patron of Babylon had deposited cigarette ash, and I wondered whether Pop, during his inspection, had observed the same.

"Jay won't talk to me," she said. "I was wondering if you knew why."

"No, Genny. He hasn't said much to me either."

"I thought maybe he was mad at me about something."

"I don't think so. If that's the case, then he's upset with everyone. He hasn't said much lately."

Carnihan was sitting across from us. Several people were talking to him, but he hardly seemed aware of their presence.

"Do you think he's in shock?" Genine asked. "Someone was saying at the funeral home that he hasn't even cried yet."

"That's true. He hasn't. At least not that I've seen."

"I've tried to talk to him. I ask him questions, but he won't answer. I don't know what to do."

"Give him some time."

"It'll hit him later. It's always hardest when it hits you later. It hurts more then."

The rain had stopped altogether now. She kissed me goodbye and headed toward the shell road, picking her feet up high to keep her heels from sticking in the sod. How odd she looked in this place, I thought. At the church earlier I'd almost laughed seeing her among the plastic statues and stained glass. Now for some reason I wanted to cry instead.

"Can you believe how many people turned out?" someone said. I spun around and it was Carnihan, smiling happily. He removed the boutonniere from his lapel and tossed it in the grave, then he put his hand on my back and guided me toward the delivery truck. His stride was strong, and I had to quicken my pace to keep up.

"You never would've thought Daddy was so popular," he said a few minutes later, as we were driving through Smoke, headed back to the store. "If only they'd come to Hometown like they came to this. Fair-weather friends, they are. All of them."

"Genny and I were just talking, brother. Maybe you're still in shock."

"I'm in something."

He didn't say anything more until we were almost there. Then he straightened his tie and asked, "I know this is supposed to be a reception, Pace, but do you think I should open the store for business?"

I felt my heart go cold and it took a while for me to answer. "Do you mean today? Right now?"

"Might be some money in the crowd. People who are grieving . . . you can sell them anything."

"I don't think that's a very good idea, Jay. Just be nice to everyone, all right? You want to show respect. Your father deserves that." I glanced over at him and he was staring straight ahead. "Are you gonna be okay?"

"I'm gonna be just fine," he answered.

We parked at Dr. McDermott's and went into the store. Earlier that morning Hayward and I had arranged several dozen folding chairs in the aisles, and covered the zinc countertop with white tablecloths, and placed a wreath on the screen door out front. Now as Carnihan strode past the business counter everyone stared at him with a mix of pity and sorrow. He smiled, offered the crowd a politician's exaggerated double-handed wave, and marched toward some old friends from high school. He entertained the group for a minute, then moseyed over to the business register and pressed the No Sale button. The money tray popped out, and I saw his lips curl in anger the instant before he hipped it back in place.

"You're not acting right," I told him. "People need you to act right."

"None of this is real," he said, and punched me on the shoulder on his way to talk to someone else.

I ladled myself a glass of punch and settled in the crowd gathered around the platters of food on the lunch counter. Many of the guests were staring up at the giant pictures on the wall, Mr. Hank's in particular. The photo showed his mouth clamped shut and frowning, and I thought this unfortunate since his broad, toothy smile would endure for me as his most memorable physical characteristic. His jawline showed a grainy shadow and his hair wasn't properly combed and the knot of his tie was lumpy and asymmetrical. He looked about as loony a creature as you'd ever hope to encounter, and I wondered why he'd chosen this picture to display to the world, unless he considered it an accurate reflection of himself.

"A handsome man," I heard Mrs. Kuel of Delmas Street remark. She was holding a goblet of punch in one hand and, in the other, a small paper saucer filled with party food. Another woman repeated this observation and soon most all of the women in attendance were commenting about his good looks.

"Yes, he was," one of the veterans from the American Legion post concurred. "A handsome man."

This gave the rest of the men an opportunity to agree, and one, Silas Poe, to nudge me with an elbow when I remained silent. "Don't you think Hank was a handsome man, Pace?"

I bit into a finger sandwich and gazed yet again at the portrait. "I think he was better than handsome," I said. "Mr. Hank was pretty goddamned beautiful."

A minute or two later Carnihan grabbed me by the arm and led me back to the stockroom. He stood at the crease in the curtain and looked around to make sure we were alone. Certain that all was safe, he gave me a wink and his lips turned up in a lascivious grin. "Girls, Pace. Isn't it amazing how they grow up?" He took another peek through the curtain. "Their breasts come out and their fuzzy little hormones kick in and they get to smelling so pretty you just want to o.d. on the stuff."

It was a pair of fourteen-year-olds who'd attracted his attention now. They were standing in the Tool department, running their fingers over an antique crowbar.

"You thought you caught me beating off, didn't you? The other night at Bethany's? I know you thought you caught me. I wasn't, though. I was only straightening it out." He leaned in close and I could smell his breath: Swedish meatballs, no less. "Don't you hate it when it gets crooked, old man?"

I reached to hold him, to make physical contact, but he pushed through the curtain and promptly found another gang of compatriots to embrace.

The odd thing was, I kept searching the crowd for Mr. Hank, knowing that he alone could make sense of Carnihan's behavior. I finally walked to the rear of the store where Hayward and LaShonda sat reading the morning *Lip*. I was pulling up a chair when, from the corner of my eye, I saw Ruby Dean squeeze through the lunch counter gate and put an apron on over her dress. "Taking orders," she announced, a rough, melancholy edge to her voice. On the chalkboard she wrote: ANYTHING ON THIS EARTH . . .

"Better do something," LaShonda said to Hayward. "Baby?"

He got up and walked over to the counter. "Come on, Mama. You can cook tomorrow."

"Taking orders," she said again, her voice now suggesting defiance. "Who in here's hungry?"

"Mama, you come sit down and rest yourself. Look at all this food. Look at all we've got."

Starting at the other end of the counter, Ruby Dean yanked off the tablecloths and dropped them to the floor. The only one she let remain was underneath the party food, and I knew she'd have pulled it off too had it not meant spilling everything. "Mama?" Hayward said again, but she'd turned her back to him and was running water in the sink. She wet a rag, wrung it out, and used it with a sprinkle of Ajax to make circles on the zinc, her arms pumping hard.

"Mama, you know better than that. I'm asking you to sit down. Mama? Come on, now."

Ruby Dean was almost finished cleaning when Silas Poe brushed past Hayward and sat on his favorite stool, down by the register. He took up a section of the *Lip* and ordered a chicken salad sandwich even though there were dozens of them already available. "Heavy on the Tabasco," he told her.

Ruby Dean gave him a tired look and opened the refrigerator door, jerking the handle hard and rattling Carnihan's Absolut and condiment tray inside. She removed her bowl of chicken salad and went to work, and in minutes every stool at the counter was taken. People were ordering items they'd already had their fill of, Hayward among them. He asked for a BLT. "Your black veil over there, Mama," he said. "You wouldn't consider moving it?"

As I saw from where I was sitting, the veil was blocking the pictures of Hayward and Martin Luther King, Jr.

"Sure, baby. I'll move it."

A short time later Carnihan joined the group of mourners to which I'd attached myself and stood sipping from a Bloody Mary he'd mixed himself, his eyes focused on one man in particular who after a while became uncomfortable and slipped off to another part of the store. Carnihan then fixed his unblinking gaze on a second fellow, and in minutes this man grew jittery and shuffled away. The next two people were as easily dismissed, and that left only Carnihan and me.

"Why'd you do that?" I asked.

He rocked his head back and glared at me as if astonished that I'd need to ask. "Do what, brother?"

"You chased your guests away."

"*My* guests?" he asked wearily, placing a hand on his chest. "Were these all *my* guests? I don't recall inviting them here. I would say they were *your* guests, Mr. Burnette."

"Whoever they belong to, Jay, you ran them off."

"They ran themselves off. I simply introduced them to the notion that they no longer were welcome." He consulted his watch. "I've got an appointment in about half an hour, Pace. They're going to have to leave, all of them. Can I count on you to show the last of the stragglers out?"

When I didn't respond, he pressed in closer. "You're welcome to join me . . . would you like to join me?"

"Join you where?"

"Don't be coy, brother. You know exactly."

And it came to me that this was the time of day Carnihan journeyed to Monster Mart, parked in its vast asphalt lake, and waited for Bethany Bixler to get off work.

"Last night she didn't dance," he said. "Imagine my disappointment."

I started to say something, but he abruptly spun around and strode away, taking his weird act elsewhere.

The crowd was starting to thin when I spotted Genine standing by herself in Appliances, far removed from everyone. I greeted her with a kiss and sat on the nearest surface available, which happened to be atop a turn-of-the-century washing machine with a burnished copper tub and a high-fangled wringer system. I smiled at Genine, hoping to dent her stony facade. I knew I'd failed when she said, "I never felt like such a whore in all my life. No one talks to me. Pariah, Pace. Isn't that a word?" I didn't answer, and she said, "And I don't mean the fish, either."

"Piranha?" I shook my head as if to dismiss the notion. "Of course you're no piranha."

My condescending tone seemed to rankle her, and she stared at me without blinking. "I don't know why I ever kissed you," she said at last, taking up her purse and heading for the door.

She was outside, striding up the sidewalk, before I decided to chase after her. I borrowed one of several umbrellas hanging on the hall tree next to the door and staggered out into the rain, finally catching up to her in front of the telephone office. "Genny? Wait a second. Please."

"Wait for what? To be insulted again?"

I held the umbrella up over her head but she was already soaked. Her hair, always so tediously coiffed, hung wet and curly to her shoulders, a disheveled mop. "He would've talked to me," she said. "He wouldn't've let me just stand there."

"Who wouldn't've?"

"Mr. Hank. He never judged me, Pace. Never. Not when I got on at Babylon." She darted forward, moving in the direction of the Delta Theater. I hustled up alongside her, endeavoring to cover her with the umbrella again. "He came there once," she said. "I never told anyone."

"To the go-go?"

"Durn right, to the go-go. Where else?"

The thought of Mr. Hank among the hookers and parlor furniture struck me as wildly funny, and I uncorked a scream of laughter that stopped Genine dead in her tracks. She wheeled around and I could see the anger in her eyes.

"That was awfully insensitive of me, Gen. Sorry."

She walked on with her hands in her jacket, not seeming to care about how wet she got. "This was several months ago," she said, keeping her head down. "I'd stopped by Hometown for a coffee and a doughnut, and I told him I'd finally found a job. He was happy for me and Mrs. Clark cooked up something special and they didn't charge me anything. That night was my first and he came with a long-stem red rose and sat on the green couch and ordered hot tea, which we don't even serve. Anyway, he gives me the flower and says he wants to be my first customer, it's why he came. He seemed to think the place was still a beer garden and that I'd be his waitress. Well, he sees one of the girls leave with a fellow, and it comes to him what Babylon is and he starts to get nervous. I order some whiskey and he drinks it up and after a while he seems to feel better. He asks me if I think I'll be okay. And I tell him yes, I'm just a hostess, and he smiles in his sad way and nods his head. He knows what my job really was. He just never judged me."

We had walked as far as the Palace Cafe on the corner of Market and Landry. Through the glass you could see people sitting at the booths and the waitresses mixing fried chicken salads behind the counter.

"We went into a room," Genine said. "Me and him."

I stopped and reached to touch her sleeve. For whatever reason, I needed to hear her say it again. "I don't believe you."

She gave a shrug and murmured, "You think I care what you believe, Pace Burnette," and she hurried across the street. She was walking faster now and I quit trying to keep up. At least one of us deserved to be spared the weather, I figured, and abandoned any attempt to cover her.

"It was that same night," she said, still a full stride ahead of me. "He put the television on and some crummy old picture was playing and we watched it, two hours' worth. *Pillow Talk,* the movie was. I remember now. Whenever a commercial came on he'd say, 'That Doris Day is a fine girl, Genny, really fine.' Or, 'Rock Hudson's a handsome fella, isn't he, now?' Anyway, when the movie's over he gives me enough money to satisfy Anita and I walk with him out to his car. We shake hands in the lot and he says, 'God, that was fun, Genny. It's been since my Deenie died I had such a time.' "

Genine, standing now in front of her little rented house, removed a knot of keys from her purse and opened the door. I followed her in and she took the umbrella, jiggled it a few times, spraying water, and propped it open on the floor.

"Don't you know that's bad luck," I said, "leaving it open like that."

She blew her nose into a wad of tissue. "My luck can't get no worse."

We were standing in her living room, a miscellany of cheap chairs and sofas all around. The furniture was the stuff of Salvation Army dreams, as were the pictures on the walls, a variety of faded cardboard prints showing sea, plains, and mountains. No people. The air was warm and smelled of gas.

I removed my coat and draped it over a battered BarcaLounger with lace doilies on the arms.

"Can I get you something to drink?" She was walking toward the back of the house, and I was trailing. "You want some coffee or Coke or something?"

"Coffee'd be nice."

The kitchen floor was checked with black and white tiles, an antique butcher's block occupying the middle. I sat at the small dinette table in the corner, choosing what appeared to be the sturdiest of the four mismatched chairs. Genine got the Mr. Coffee going, then removed a couple of dish towels from a drawer next to the sink and started patting her hair dry. "I need to blow-dry this mess," she said. "And get out of these clothes. I'll be back in a minute." She put a jar of creamer and a bowl of sugar on the table and instructed me to help myself. "Guess where the cups are?"

"In the cupboard?"

She was laughing as she left the room. "You always did make good grades, didn't you, Pace?"

I heard a blow-dryer start in the back of the house, and the overhead light blinked and fluttered for a while before going off completely. The power had shut off. Genine spit a single curse word and then her feet were heavy on the wood floor, coming toward me. She stood in the kitchen doorway wearing a tattered robe over green hospital scrub pants with the drawstring untied. The robe was loosely gathered at the middle, exposing the top half of her chest.

"Where's your fuse box?" I said.

"I don't know, I never looked." She carried a couple of cups to the table and filled them. Since the power failure had come before the coffee maker had run its course, half an inch of coffee was all that remained in the glass pot.

"Good thing I got this started before I decided to dry my hair," she said. "But it's kind of nice without electricity. You can hear the rain. Hear it up on the roof, Pace?"

"Is that a tin roof?"

"I don't know." A bemused expression came to her face. "I never bothered to look, and no one ever told me."

"Sounds like tin."

She gazed up at the ceiling, listening intently. "I rented this place to get out from under Mama. Once I got work at Babylon, I didn't want her asking questions about why I came in so late. She's getting on, you know. She doesn't need that."

In all she added four spoons of sugar; I counted.

"You know what I like best about living here?"

I shook my head.

"The view." She sat in the chair next to me. "I look out my window and I see the Pavy mansion and parts of a couple others. . . . Silas Poe's down the way. But when they look out of theirs what do they see but my little shack? They've paid all that money to live in Old Smoke, and yet this is all they've got to look at. I pay a hundred and twenty-five a month, and it's castles when I look outside."

"I'd say you're doing pretty well for yourself."

"Long time ago when I was a kid, I used to have this feeling I'd be rich. I'd stare at myself in the mirror and say, 'Only a matter of time, Gen. Be patient.' I was a dreamer, I tell you."

Before the power outage she'd managed to dry only the right side of her head, leaving the left side wet and tousled. She took up another dish towel and started patting it again. "You don't mind drinking your coffee in the dark, do you, Pace?"

"It's nice like this."

"Then let's not bother fooling with that fuse box until later. We can sit and listen to the rain."

And that was what we did for about fifteen minutes. The weather got worse, battering the house with gusts and sheets of rain, but then finally it broke and the wind died down and a slow, gray drizzle began to fall. Although since morning I had consumed as many as a dozen cups of coffee, the caffeine was having little effect on me. If anything I was feeling weary and desperate for rest, and I welcomed a return to Dr. McDermott's and the black quiet of the X-ray lab.

I finished the coffee and put the cup in the sink and rinsed it out with cold water. Genine stepped up behind me and placed her cup next to mine, pulling her robe tight to make sure she was covered. "Thanks for escorting me home," she said. "I wasn't very nice to you earlier. I'm sorry about that."

"It was nothing."

"What I said about not knowing why I kissed you . . . I didn't mean it. I'm the sort of person, I always know exactly why I do the things I do."

"You know everything?"

She nodded. "Just about."

I finished cleaning the cups and she took the towel she'd used to dry her hair and held it against my hands. Through the soft cotton she massaged each of my fingers and worked quickly and somewhat fussily down to my palms. I watched her face grow strong and resolute, the sinew of her neck showing, a moist redness at her cheeks. This was a new experience for me, having someone rub my hands dry, and I thought how nice it was with the rain on the roof and the dark so full and complete. I could feel a tingle come to my spine and chase across my arms, and my legs were ready to go, the knees to buckle beneath me. I closed my eyes and started to sway, not intentionally. When I opened them again she had put the towel away, and we were holding hands, our fingers entwined.

"I kissed you because I felt like it," she said.

"Huh?"

"I just wanted to, is why."

I leaned in to find her mouth but she moved away, taking my hand with her. She led me to the bedroom, pointed to the place on the bed where she wanted me to sit, and without my help she began to remove my clothes. "Here," she said, kneeling in front of me and taking my shoes off. After they were resting side by side under the footboard, she peeled my socks off and turned them into a clever roll. "Here," she said again, clapping her hands. And she unknotted my tie, the tail of it making a pretty silken sound when she pulled it from around my collar. She didn't stop until everything was off and then she stepped out of her scrub pants, letting them fall in a pile at her feet. She picked the pants up, folded them, and lay them on an ironing board in the corner, and when she turned back around the robe pulled open.

Clothes in transparent garment bags littered the bed—dresses she'd taken out trying to decide what to wear to the funeral—and she gathered them up now and hung them in the closet. When she returned to the bed she lit a green, pine-scented candle on the nightstand. I could smell the burning wax and see her face in the soft, warm light, which threw shadows against the walls. It was a pretty scent and one I recalled having smelled on her before. "What I was wearing today," she said. "It's the only thing black I own. If ever I'm rich I'll own more black dresses than I could ever wear."

I reached over and took her hand. "I thought it was mighty nice . . . . mighty fine."

"What?"

"What you had on today."

Her face grew wide in disbelief, and she shook her head. "The jacket has a hole in the sleeve. About so big." She held her thumb and forefinger less than an inch apart. "You had to notice it, Pace. I know you did."

I moved over and made room for her on the bed. "You're wrong. I didn't notice a thing."

"No? But I thought you just said it was nice."

"Except that. That it was nice was all I noticed."

The truth was, I'd never been with a girl before—not like this, anyway. But I figured it was a bad idea to say anything. I was twenty-eight years old, after all, and I'd written a book on the subject, pretending to be an expert. I might've found the situation comic had I not been so nervous. I might've seen a story there, something to write later on. "The Hooker and the Virgin." See there, I said to myself. You've already got your title.

"Don't you like it with a candle, Pace?"

"Oh, sure. I've always liked it that way."

But she seemed as timid and careful and uncertain as I was. I kept seeing Mr. Hank turning circles in his field, the goats bumping up against him. I wanted to cry but not for that reason.

I doubt that I was the most emphatic fellow she'd ever encountered, or the most sensitive and creative. I remember how her hair did not feel right in my hands: the one side dry, the other damp. And how she kissed with the slightest part in her mouth, not letting me in as deep as I hoped to go. I remember wanting, as soon as we were done, to start all over again, to have that first time forever, or at least to repeat it.

"Oh, wait, Genny," I called out. But by then it was over.

This much I can tell you from experience: No love ever began between two people that wasn't a mistake. Love in the beginning is meant to be wrong.

V

The next day Carnihan put a hand-lettered sign in the window that said, HOMETOWN OPEN, COUNTER CLOSED. It was the first thing I saw when I returned to the store in the morning. He was sitting by the business register, his arms crossed at his chest, his head bent low in a posture of sleep. The place had been cleaned, the folding chairs and tables stacked in the stockroom. Someone had polished the floor and scrubbed the zinc, leaving patterns of circles as telling as any signature. When it came to wiping things down, Ruby Dean Clark was an artist of the abstract expressionist school, and as gifted a one as ever lived.

"There's coffee," he said. "And some leftovers from the reception. I won't charge you anything. Eat all you like."

The leftovers happened to be soggy pimento-and-cheese sandwiches and a stubborn bean dip far along on its way to becoming a brick; I settled, instead, on a couple of candy bars, a bag of corn chips, and a glass of lemonade.

"Those weren't part of the deal last night," he said. "Sorry, brother."

"Just charge my account."

He nodded. "Will do."

I sat at my usual place and perused the morning *Lip;* and Carnihan said, "It still doesn't seem real to me, Pace."

"Well, of course it doesn't. You've lost your father—the person you were closest to in the world."

"I don't mean that. I mean what happened last night at Bayou Blanc. Bethany took a bath, and I caught her rubbing herself in the tub. She was rubbing that thing between her legs, that little beady thing with a name I could never pronounce."

"Her clitoris?"

"That's not how I would say it, so I guess that's right."

How do you tell your best pal that he needs time on a psychiatrist's couch? That he's lost his damned head? I was trying to answer these questions when he complained about Beatnik having urinated in the delivery truck. This had happened while Carnihan was down peeping on Bethany. "You think he really needed to go like that," he asked, "or was he trying to punish me?"

I chose not to answer, and he continued, "I think he did it on purpose. It was his way of getting back at me for who can say what. For Daddy having to die, I suppose."

The sign in the window worked to keep everyone but Silas Poe away. He came at his favorite time and occupied his favorite stool, and he read the *Lip* sports page and grumbled about just missing the Daily Double. He did eat breakfast, as I recall, one he prepared himself: a wash of Tabasco and some bean dip spread over a four-day-old biscuit. As he got up to leave, dropping coins on the counter, he tried to console Carnihan. "You'll get over it," he said, using a preacher's voice. "It might not seem possible now, but a person always gets over it."

"Gets over what?"

"The pain," he said. "It really does go away eventually. But you have to let it." Silas looked down at his newspaper and the names of the horses he planned to bet, and, as if suddenly struck by a notion, he circled a few more.

"You'll only lose," Carnihan told him.

Silas peered over the top of the paper and shook his head. "That may be true, son, but at least I'll lose trying."

"And what's that supposed to mean?" Carnihan shot back.

Silas didn't answer. He put his hat on, tucked the *Lip* under his arm, and walked outside.

"What's that supposed to mean?" Carnihan asked again.

I didn't respond, and he hobbled over to the door and shouted through the screen: "Hey, Silas, what is that supposed to mean! That crap about losing? Don't talk to me about losing, big man! You haven't the right! You haven't the right, do you hear?"

He was still carrying on when an overnight delivery man pulled up in front of the store and came in carrying a package.

"You Pace Burnette?" the fellow asked Carnihan.

"Lord, no," Carnihan replied, and pointed in my direction.

"That would be me," I told the man.

"Sign here." He handed me a clipboard with a receipt on it.

The package contained a copy of *Strange Weather,* the first to arrive from the publisher. My hands were trembling as I removed it from the envelope, and a splash of blood came to my cheeks and seemed to scald them. The book itself was small and thin, with inexpensive binding and print so heavy with ink that some of the words ran together and were hard to read. Despite its low production values, however, I thought I'd never seen a finer-looking thing in all my life. A sharp tremor shook my body and I resisted an urge to weep with joy and run screaming down Market Street, holding the book aloft. Critics be damned, I told myself. And Cinda Lovey, too. The cover showed the picture of a young man standing under a tree, the wind billowing his clothes, part of his face obscured by his dark, flowing hair. I opened the book and saw my name on top of every page: PACE on the left, BURNETTE on the right. My photograph on the dust jacket showed me with chapped, brooding lips and eyes shot red from a long night of drinking. The picture didn't carry a credit because I'd had it done in one of those arcade booths where you pay two bucks in change and pose for four snapshots that invariably distort the dimensions of your face, giving each feature a thinness or a roundness decidedly more ape than human. My editor had refused to contract a professional photographer to shoot me, so this was what I'd sent him.

"You look like somebody in serious need of a B_{12} shot," Carnihan said. He'd slipped up behind me and was peering over my shoulder. I wheeled around and he repeated his assessment, adding, "Yes sir. A B_{12} shot, a hairbrush, and a Chap Stick."

He took the book from my hands and, holding it up to his nose, rustled the pages and inhaled deeply with his eyes closed and a deeply satisfied smile on his face. "Some of the scenes in here," he said, "some of those where everybody's having sex . . . they should be scratch 'n' sniff, brother. You'd really move some copies then."

He gave me the book and I smelled it again, wondering how long its scent would last, knowing it never again would smell as glorious as it did at that moment.

"Write your next one about me," Carnihan said. "Tell the truth, though. Tell it exactly how it was."

As he was walking toward the business register I called after him, "Tell what how it was? Seems to me all you do is spy on Bethany Bixler and bitch about Rayford Holly. You haven't lived enough to rate a short story let alone a book."

"Just check with me later this week and see if you still think that. I'll have a masterpiece for you to tell."

His eyes were filled with conviction, and I knew he meant it. He sat on his stool and pressed the No Sale button—out of habit, I presumed, because when the drawer popped out he didn't even bother to look at it.

"You must be planning on covering a heckuva lot of ground, to have a masterpiece for me to tell after only one week."

He gave a smart laugh and stamped his feet on the floor. For a minute everything in the store was shaking. "You can't begin to imagine, brother, you just can't imagine. . . ."

My parents reacted to the sight of *Strange Weather* as I'd long dreamed they would. Miss Betty wept tears of joy into a dishrag and Pop danced a little jig in the living room.

"You really are marvelous," she said, examining the author photo at arm's length. "And I'm being objective here."

"Am I marvelous, Miss Betty? You really think so?"

"I really do."

It is quite a thing to be told you are marvelous, even by your mother, who can't help but think such a thing, and I spent some time counting the ways I made the world a better place.

"What about you, Pop? Do you think I'm marvelous?"

"If not that," he said, "then pretty incredibly close." And off he went hip-hopping around the room again.

It was of vast importance to me that one other person see the book, but she wasn't home when I went to show it to her. As I drove the Mustang out toward the Lewisburg Road, I called to mind my time with Genine in her little rented house. I remembered the smell of her green candle, the creak of her big, soft bed, her voice a whisper in the dark. I recalled the dry and damp sides of her hair, and a kind of fever came over me. By the time I reached Babylon I was so compromised by desire that I was forced to wait a while before leaving the car.

Although it was early afternoon the go-go was open, this being a Saturday, and I entered carrying the copy of *Strange Weather.* Anita scowled at me from behind the bar, and I scowled right back before ordering a g and t.

"Your friend's in number three," she said.

"Huh?" I'd been pretending to read, hoping that someone would see my name on the book.

"Genny. She went with a guy."

Anita drew a fair amount of pleasure from telling me this, I assumed, because she began to bellow with laughter and to snort in her fat, pimp way. There were only two other people in the lounge: the telephone lady who sat on the green couch, and next to her a handsome, well-dressed man who at the moment was whispering in her ear while pawing playfully at her knee. I tried to ignore Anita, and to appear involved with the book, but her laughter swelled again and I glanced up to find that she was pointing at me as if I were the butt of some joke.

"What's funny?"

"Nothing." She shook her head.

"Is it funny to you that I know how to read? I bet you don't get many people in here who can do that, do you, Anita?"

Her finger seemed to grow even more rigid as she stabbed the air, all the while uttering a stream of obscenities through tightly clenched teeth. I considered saying more but knew that nothing would serve me well against a mind as small and shit-filled as Anita's. When a man enters a place like Babylon he does so with the understanding that his dignity waits outside in the car, and so I bowed my head and turned the page and tried to pretend that what I was reading had any meaning at all. Trying to pretend, I discovered, is a little like pretending twice, and few things in this world are harder to do.

My agony lasted all of an hour, and then Genine walked through the door with her business associate in tow, a man as nicely put together as the one sitting with the telephone lady. Genine was wearing a satin party dress, fishnet stockings, and high heels; her hair looked like red ants after you poke their mound with a stick. She saw me and rushed over and applied a kiss to my cheek. It was one of those quick, dutiful jobs generally reserved for Uncle Bubba, who appears only at Christmas and always with the fatal smell of garlic and bourbon whiskey on his breath. I didn't like the kiss, perfunctory as it was, and so I brushed the back of my hand over where it still felt wet on my face.

"What's with the attitude?" she said.

"No attitude."

"You shouldn't come here anymore, Pace. Why would you want to go and hurt yourself like that?"

It was a good question, but one I knew better than to try to answer honestly. "Ah, you know the Burnettes, Genny. I come from a long line of masochists."

"How's that?"

"Just look at Pop, the poor guy. Twenty-something years he coached, and he hardly ever won a game."

"Last night never should've happened," she said. "Maybe we should just forget about it."

I wanted to be angry with her, and to some degree I was. But I knew she was right. It was the duty of someone less fortunate and well raised than myself to pursue the affections of a fallen woman such as Genine Monteleone. Young men without prospects belonged with hookers, not the clean-cut, all-American types like myself destined for great things. I glanced over at the man she'd been with. His suit was a fancy gray pinstripe, just like the fellow's next to him. And they both were reclining with their legs crossed and arms draped over the back of the couch. They resembled, I thought, athletes who'd scored some titanic victory, and who were relaxing afterward in the locker room.

"Pace, we shouldn't try to take this anywhere. Trust me. It would be a mistake to."

"I'm a full-grown man, Genny. I can take it wherever I damn well want to take it."

"Not without me, you can't. And I ain't budging." She placed her hand against the side of my face and looked at me as if I were an innocent, too young and dumb to understand what I was feeling. It was the way she'd looked at Carnihan that night she'd laid him out drunk in the examination room and whispered, "Poor Jay. Poor baby."

"Let's go somewhere," I said. "Let's go to Dr. McDermott's . . . to the X-ray lab."

"I've got work to do."

"Genny?"

"No, Pace. We'll both be better off."

"But I love you, Gen, I've loved you since Miss Irene's."

"Is that . . . ?" Only now did she see the book. She reached for it and after a brief struggle I let her have it, recalling that this was why I'd come, after all.

"It is! It's *Strange Weather,* Pace! Oh, God, look at this! Would you just look at this!"

She kissed me again, less like a drunk uncle than a girl with fire in her gut. I called for her to sit down, but she rushed over to the two men and waved the book at them. "This is that guy over there. This is my friend. This is Pace Burnette, the very one! It's Pace . . . !" All the while she was pointing to my picture on the back of the jacket, stabbing it with the sharpest of her phony Press-On nails.

The two men leaned forward to get a better look at me. They seemed at least mildly impressed, and I gave a nod to let them know that I, too, was pretty impressed with myself as well.

Then the telephone lady stood and curtsied before me, careful to keep the hem of her skirt down lest she show something for free. "I didn't know we had a famous author come to Babylon," she said, her voice light and squeaky and vastly different from the dark, sultry one I was used to hearing.

I felt an appreciative flutter at my chest. "Ah, it's nothing, really. But thanks."

Genine sat beside me and began to flip through the book. She ran her fingers over the print and pointed to my name on each page. "That's you. That's your name. Look at this, Pace! Your name!"

I looked at it and said, "Yep, it's mine, sure enough."

She saw that I'd drained my g and t and called to Anita for another, and when the drinks were ready we lifted a toast to the success of *Strange Weather* and to the long, happy life of its creator. Had a fireplace been handy, I'm sure we'd have thrown our glasses into the flames. The men on the couch roared, "Hear, hear, Pace! Hear, hear!"

In salute I raised my drink in their direction, and this brought more cheers and fists to the furniture.

Genine and I called for another round and one of the men walked over and asked if I might entertain the lounge with a reading. At first I thought he was joking, but to show his sincerity he clapped me on the back and turned to the others to see if they too might like to hear me.

"Oh, that'd be wonderful, Pace," Genine said. "Read for us. I'd love to hear you."

Even Anita seemed interested. Or, I should say, she didn't seem uninterested. In any case, she was no longer pointing at me, and my most recent g and t tasted more of gin than of tonic, in itself a remarkable development.

"Okay," I mumbled, suddenly feeling emboldened. "I'll read."

Light applause could be heard as I stood and addressed the room, the faces aglow with anticipation. I selected one of the novel's sexier passages and read by the strange colored light of the jukebox, which Anita had managed to mute with a switch behind the bar. The scene depicts Peter Burn in the bathtub at his home, candles burning all around him. He's lathering his groin with soap when his young, voluptuous mother, whom I refer to as Miss Louise, enters the room toting a pitcher of cold milk for him to drink. As Miss Louise lowers her rump to the lip of the tub, she jostles the pitcher and spills milk all over her blouse, which she promptly removes, exposing her breasts. Her nipples contract and her flesh pimples, and Peter, a freakishly endowed eighteen-year-old, grows aroused, his thing climbing up above the surface of hot, sudsy water. Miss Louise has removed her skirt and panties and is preparing to join her son in the tub when the telephone rings and awakens her to the awful sin which she is about to commit. They exchange a quiet kiss, ending the scene.

When I finished reading I looked up to find everyone staring at me with equal parts shock and incredulity. Anita, who probably thought she'd seen and heard everything up until now, raised her hand, pointed at me again, and unleashed a rowdy snort of yellow-toothed laughter that struck me with the force of a clenched fist. The two men flashed a pair of patronizing smiles and leaned deeper into the couch, assuming once again their mindless athletic chatter and poses. The telephone lady placed a call, her voice coming loud and fast.

I sat back down at the table, too humiliated to breathe let alone speak. Genine pried her lips into the shape of a smile and patted me reassuringly on the hand. Although the gesture was meant to be sympathetic, I took it as an insult and pulled away to let her know I didn't appreciate it.

"Usually it's the father doing ugly things to the daughter," she said quietly. "I think I like yours better."

"What?"

She made a circle with her hand. "It's the other way around. It's the father who abuses the daughter."

"Oh, is it? Is it really? And what would you know about that, Genny?" I glared at her and saw tears come to her eyes. She shook her head and looked away. Suddenly the jukebox kicked back on, and I was shouting to be heard above the music. "Who are they?" I said. "Are they from Smoke? Those men over there?"

"I didn't ask who they are," she said, an impatient edge to her voice. "I didn't care."

It was clear that, having successfully suppressed the urge to cry, she now was prepared to fight.

"You didn't ask their names?"

"Why would I want to know their names?"

The men were sitting close together, whispering. One of them rocked his head back and laughed and I heard the other say the word "milk," and then the name "Miss Louise." I was struck dumb with shame and felt my breath go shallow again. I wanted to hit somebody, and to get hit in return. Had I been thinking more clearly, I might've taken my complaint to the two men. But instead I turned back to Genine. "Did you go with the other guy, too, Genny? Did you do him, too?"

"I don't *do* anybody."

"Come on. You can tell me. We're old pals, remember? You went with both of them, didn't you?"

She rose to her feet and stared at me with hurt and confusion. She looked as if she'd just discovered something dreadful about me which she'd never suspected before, and she didn't know whether to despise or to pity me for it. "Let's go, Pace," she said finally. "It's time you were leaving."

She took my hand and started yanking me toward the door. She was pulling hard, pulling with all that was in her, and I didn't resist. Her nails dug deep into my palm, cutting the flesh, and although it sent pain shooting up my arm I didn't say anything.

"It was nice of you to come, Pace. I loved seeing your book. I can't tell you how proud I am of you."

"But I haven't paid my bill yet."

"It's already been taken care of," she said.

"But I don't want to leave, Genny."

"Yes, you do." She was breathing hard and her big bowl of hair had come undone and was hanging loose in her face. "Maybe we can have lunch sometime and take in a movie. Wouldn't that be fun, Pace?" She yanked again, nearly jerking my arm out of its socket. "You remember what fun is, don't you? It's what people like to do when one of them isn't bitching at the other."

She hipped the door open and pulled me out into the parking lot. The sun was hot and blinding; I closed my eyes against it and let her lead me.

She pulled me all the way to the Mustang and opened the door. When I didn't get in right away, she pushed me in.

"I can't take this," I said. "I can't take you doing this."

"I'm sorry, Pace. I'm sorry you're having such a hard time with me today, really I am."

I lifted a hand to shield the sun, but then her hair and face seemed to fill the sky and I could see the tears running down her cheeks. "Genny. I'm sorry. I'm sorry." I needed to know that she forgave me, but she turned sharply on her heels and started for the door. I punched the horn, thinking she'd turn around, but she kept walking, her head held down, her shoes on the gravel sounding fainter with each step.

I'd driven to within half a mile of Hometown before it came to me that I'd left my copy of *Strange Weather* behind. I wheeled the car around and headed back to Babylon, and when I walked inside Anita greeted me as if I'd never left but simply had visited the men's room or gone outside for some air.

The book was still on the table by the jukebox, but Genine was nowhere to be found.

"Back in number three again," Anita said from the bar. "Another customer. I let him have it cheap on account the sheets were all a mess from that other fellow."

I stood for a long time in the doorway. I didn't speak and I didn't fix my eyes on anything in particular. I kept thinking about Genine last night in her rented house. For whatever reason it seemed like years ago, another life. The green candle, the weather beating against the windows, the way she'd talked to me. I took the book and walked back out to the car. As I was driving away I looked in the rearview mirror and saw the bright orange door with the crooked number on it. The 3 was actually turned upside down, the fatter part of the body on top instead of bottom. I wheeled slowly onto the Lewisburg Road and pressed hard on the accelerator, depositing more rubber than my tires could honestly afford.

"It's the times, is all," I said aloud, looking up and finding my own eyes in the mirror.

When I got back to Hometown there were two cars parked in front with trunks cocked open. One was a rental, the other a new

Mercedes-Benz Ruby Dean had bought with Hayward's money. I drove slowly through the lot and parked at the entrance to Dr. McDermott's, then shuffled flatfooted through the stockroom, careful not to make any noise. I didn't want to give myself away. At the curtain I stopped and looked through the crack to see what was going on inside. Carnihan was standing over by the front door with his arms crossed, his feet about shoulder-width apart and planted firmly as if to bar anyone from coming in or out. LaShonda and Ruby Dean, both wearing dressy clothes, were cleaning up behind the counter, and Hayward was sitting on a stool with a big cardboard box on his lap. The box was filled with the million details of his mother's that had brought so much color to the store, including, I noted, the photograph of Martin Luther King, Jr., and the one of Hayward himself in uniform. I thought my arrival had gone unnoticed, but then Ruby Dean threw her rag down and called, "You come here and stop that hiding, Pace Burnette. Come talk sense to this boy."

I didn't move for a minute and she said again, "Pace? You stop that now. Get on out here."

I could see her waving for me to come in, and so I pressed through the curtain, feeling ashamed of myself for having spied, and embarrassed about being caught. "Hey, get this, brother," Carnihan said. "She thinks she's leaving, she actually thinks she's going with them."

Both LaShonda and Hayward were smiling at me. Ruby Dean raised a frilly white handkerchief and daubed at her cheeks and blew her nose. I was only a few feet away from her, and I could see how old and run-down she looked. Her eyes were red and puffy and the tip of her nose was rimmed with dry, flaky skin from where she'd rubbed the spot too hard and often. She seemed smaller than ever before, too.

"Can you believe this, Pace? Taking her from Hometown . . . *Stealing her!*" His voice broke off and he repositioned his feet. No one had moved toward the door, but by the way he braced himself you might've thought he'd just been challenged. "You ain't going anywhere," he said to Ruby Dean. "No ma'am. I won't let you." There was a sharp edge to his voice, and it was plain he was daring anyone to buck him.

"Why're you leaving so early?" I asked. "Mr. Hank had told me two months."

Carnihan said, "You mean you knew about this?"

"Things won't be any different in two months," LaShonda said. "In fact, they might even be worse. No, Pace, this is for the best."

Hayward started to speak but Carnihan cut him off. "You were always overrated," he said. "I don't care how much they pay you or how many times you make All-Pro. You'll always be the skinny little kid who used to come by the store begging for Moon Pies and R.C. Cola and all the hell else my poor old daddy gave you free." Carnihan hooted with laughter but it actually sounded more like a person crying. "You ain't taking her anywhere, Hayward. I'm serious, brother."

Hayward took the picture of Dr. King from the box and looked at it with his eyes set in a narrow squint. I thought he might throw the picture at Carnihan, but a minute passed and you could tell he'd overcome any violent impulse. He cleaned the glass window with his shirtsleeve and placed the picture back upright on the countertop. A smile came to his face and he seemed to be reminded of something. I wondered if maybe in the picture he had found an answer.

"Coming over here in your raggedy hand-me-downs," Carnihan said. "The very same clothes I'd worn myself not a year before when they were new—"

"I'll have to ask you not to talk to my husband that way," LaShonda said. She stepped from behind the counter and walked to within a few feet of Carnihan.

He seemed to shrink a little, staring at her.

"You ready to go, Mama?" Hayward stood up, still holding the box. "We got things at home yet to pack."

"All right," Ruby Dean said, sniffling. "All right." The handkerchief was still up at her face and her eyes were roaming around the store, taking in everything. She seemed to be trying to memorize the place, the whole vast mess of it, the old and the new. I wondered if maybe I should climb up on the stool and reach across the counter and hold her until she quieted, until her hurt went away. But then, knowing her pride, I figured it best to keep still and my mouth shut.

"We can always come back," LaShonda said to Ruby Dean. "You can cook again. See all your old friends."

"Everything'll be like it was," Hayward said.

Ruby Dean nodded but you could tell she didn't really believe them. There was something in her face I'd never seen before, a resignation, an impenetrableness. At last her eyes came to rest on the pictures up above the business counter. In particular she settled on Mr. Hank. "We'll be back. Won't be long." And she lifted a hand and waved.

At the door Carnihan took in a deep breath and pulled his arms in tighter. "Hey, LaShonda. Hey, Miss Ambulance Chaser. You never fooled me, baby. Not for a minute."

"Come on, Mama." It was Hayward, leading her from behind the counter. "It's time we were getting along now."

"Your nails are fake," Carnihan said, "and your speech is affected and your head's too big for your body. You wear too much makeup and too much perfume and sometimes I wonder if you're as plastic on the inside as you are on the out."

I got up and walked over to where Carnihan stood and slipped between him and the door. He didn't try to stop me. He was talking to Ruby Dean now, insulting her as he had LaShonda and Hayward. "You think I didn't know it was you putting money in my register, old woman? I knew it was you, I knew it all along. Every last dollar bill in that drawer had the stain of grease from your fingertips."

LaShonda stepped forward, wrapped her arms around Carnihan, and flattened her mouth against his face. "You be good, Jay," she said. "You be real good." His eyes closed and he had a difficult time opening them again. I saw his Adam's apple bob up and down, and a sob shake his chest, and his knees go limp. He remained standing, though, his arms still crossed, defiance showing in his face. "Bye, Jay," LaShonda said. "Bye, boy. Bye, baby."

After she went through the door, Hayward moved the box to his left arm and balanced it against his hip, then he put his right arm around Carnihan and pulled him close. He whispered something I couldn't hear, and slapped Carnihan once on the shoulder, not hard. Carnihan closed his eyes again and this time didn't open them back up. I could see a single tear trailing down his face, cutting a path, and after it reached his jaw Hayward wiped it away with his open hand.

"By the way," Hayward said, his voice coming strong now. "It wasn't R.C. Cola I drank, it was Chocolate Soldier soda. I thought of all the things you'd've remember that, big brother."

And then he kissed Carnihan on the same spot as LaShonda.

I held the screen door open and waited for Ruby Dean. I thought she might want a word alone with Carnihan, and so I took a few steps back, to give them room. She was slow moving across the store, as slow as I ever saw her move. Her feet dragged the wood and her legs, rubbing together, made their familiar noise. When she reached Carnihan she stared at him a long time. In the light streaming through the door she looked a hundred years old, so different from the lady I liked to remember. I wondered if she was memorizing Carnihan's face as she had everything else in Hometown. I waited for her to speak, but nothing came. A good minute went by. Finally she put her head down and walked past Carnihan, bumping him just slightly. She walked through the open door and out to her car.

"Pace," she said, putting her hand in mine, "when Silas Poe comes around will you tell him something for me?"

"Yes ma'am."

"Tell him to go easy on that red sauce. That Tabasco. Tell him Ruby Dean said so, y'hear?"

I helped her get in the car. "I'll tell him."

She patted my arm and started the engine, looking straight ahead through the windshield and nowhere else.

Hayward placed his box in the trunk of the rental and he and LaShonda hugged me and promised to be in touch.

"Maybe when things get back to normal," Hayward said, but something stopped him and he didn't finish.

They had just started up Market Street when Carnihan came crashing through the door and took off chasing after them. He ran with everything that was in him, and although it was far faster than he'd probably ever run in his lifetime, it wasn't fast enough to overtake them. I shouted his name a couple of times, and then I started running, too. I could tell Carnihan was screaming, I could hear it, but with the wind in my ears and the sound of my own crying it was a few minutes before I could make out what he was saying.

"Don't go, Mama! Please, please, please, Mama, don't go!" He ran past a bustle of lawyers' offices, down by the jailhouse, across the sleeping square.

"Oh, Mama!" he kept calling. "For heaven's sake! Don't go! Don't go . . . !"

Carnihan didn't return to the store until about two hours later, and even then he didn't come inside. I was sitting at the lunch counter, waiting in the dark with my head resting on the zinc, when I heard the Hometown delivery truck start up and the tires squeal. I caught only a glimpse of his tail end as he was leaving the lot, driving at about twice the posted limit.

Toward midnight I went to bed with a package of cigarettes and the bottle of Absolut Peppar Carnihan kept in Ruby Dean's refrigerator. I smoked and drank and cried, I cursed and I threw things, and then I got on my knees and said a prayer, there in the middle of the X-ray lab. I was still on the floor when his headlights came through the window, coloring everything. Hoping not to look as if I'd been up waiting for him, I crawled back under the sheets and closed my eyes, feigning sleep. The booze, ashtray, and cigarettes were all there with me, cluttering the top of the bed, and smoke was still thick in the room.

I don't know why I thought I could fool him.

A door opened and closed and footsteps sounded in the hall. You could tell he was not alone. Not that there was much noise, but you knew it was two people. One of them bumped against the wall, and then they both grumbled at the same time. I figured Carnihan had finally gotten up the courage to reveal himself at Bethany's door. He would need that sort of company tonight, and he was bringing her to Hometown to keep from having to spend another lonely night on Worm Road. Then I decided Genine was with him. He'd stopped by Babylon, gotten drunk, and she was dropping him off as she had last time.

I listened and distinctly heard Carnihan say: "Say it."

After a silence he said, "Apologize, goddammit. Say you're sorry. Say it like you mean it."

"Sorry for what?" came a voice, a man's. It was deep and loud and brave, that voice, and not a bit amused. And it seemed familiar to me. But how did I know it? Someone from town, maybe? A regular at the counter?

"Sorry for what?" said the voice. "What have I done? Explain that and maybe then I'll tell you whether I'm sorry."

No, now that I listened, there wasn't anything local about it. Nothing of the bayou or the swamp, nothing of Smoke. It was Southern, though, redneck most likely.

"Apologize and I let you go," Carnihan demanded. "Tell me you didn't mean it. Tell me you were wrong."

The voice replied, "Wrong about what?"

"You killed my town!" Carnihan shouted. "You killed it!"

I sat up like a shot in bed and started kicking the sheets, sending things flying in every direction. I scrambled against the mattress, driving my legs. I suppose I was digging for a crack in which to insert myself, a fissure in which to hide. More than anything I wanted to escape, to be out of there. For a minute the only sound was of my thrashing about, but then I became aware of a noise coming up from my throat, the low, mad groan of an animal in fear for its life.

"Say it, say you're sorry!"

The man just laughed. He laughed and let go with one of his famous hog calls. And of course by then I knew who it was.

VI

The first thing he ever said to me came in a whisper, so low that I had to strain to hear. He was sitting on the floor with his wrists and ankles bound with rope, peering down into the top drawer of Dr. McDermott's desk, reading by the overhead light Carnihan had decided to leave on. There were grass stains on his trousers from where Carnihan had tackled him, and one sleeve of his shirt was ripped at the shoulder seam, not badly.

He looked like anyone else, I thought.

"You Burdette? The one who wrote the book?"

"It's Burnette."

He stared up at me. "Too bad about these reviews."

I had just entered the office after struggling for a few hours to summon the courage to walk in, show myself, and check up on him. We were quiet for a minute and I could tell he meant what he said. Something in his face let on the same depth of understanding I'd seen in Pop's eyes when he'd told me to pay no mind to Cinda Lovey. It was how you looked at an animal after it'd been struck in the road and was dying and there was nothing you could do to bring it back. If you talked to it, trying to ease its pain, this was how you sounded.

"Get away from there. Come on now. *Get!*"

"Critics," Rayford Holly said. "What the hell do they know anyway? What makes them so qualified?"

I figured he'd had to grasp the handle of the drawer with his teeth to pull it open. He'd sat up to see what was inside, what tool might aid in his escape. And the two clippings, patched together with Miracle Glue and tape, were lying right there for anyone to see.

"Just don't tell Carnihan, all right? I don't want him to know what a lousy writer everyone says I am."

"Carnihan the one ran me off the road?"

I was quiet: he knew our names now, both of them. "He just wants you to apologize," I said. "That's not asking so much."

"I won't."

"It has nothing to do with money. There won't be a ransom demand or a death threat or anything like that. Just say you regret what you did and you'll be on your way again."

"Nope, not me. Rayford Holly has nothing in this world to be sorry about." He gave his head an angry shake and a current of pain lit his face. He rearranged his feet where Carnihan had tied him to a leg of the desk, and after a while his eyes cleared and he no longer looked so hurt and uncomfortable.

"I got no regrets at all, Burnette. None. It's not every man can say that. Can you say that?"

"What kind of person," I asked, "would choose to stay tied up, his life endangered, rather than say I'm sorry?"

"This kind," he said, and flipped his head back to show that he was talking about himself.

It struck me that he wasn't afraid at all, that I was the one who couldn't stop shaking.

Dawn was about an hour away, and Carnihan had gone to pick up the old man's truck and drive it to Worm Road, where he planned to hide it in the trees skirting the goat pasture—a place you couldn't see from the house. If he left the doors open, Carnihan had told me, the goats would climb inside and eat everything they could get their lips on. The old man's peanut butter sandwiches, the paper sack he carried them in. His single change of clothes. They'd eat the steering wheel, the little metal knobs on the dashboard. The dashboard.

If he didn't apologize, Carnihan had said, we could bring him out to the farm and tie him up in what remained of the truck. See if goats ate billionaire.

I was still holding the twelve-gauge automatic shotgun he'd handed me before walking out the door.

"You hunt, Burnette?"

"Not since I was a kid."

"You hold that gun like someone taught you what it means. You think you know what it means?"

I didn't say anything, and he continued, "You ran out of patience with hunting, didn't you, son? You went out one day, expecting to bag your limit, and you didn't get a shot off; so you got disgusted and quit. You had more important things to do. Your time was too valuable to waste walking around a field with the barrel of a gun stuck up on your shoulder." He gave me a wink, figuring we'd just shared a secret about myself. "Tell me I'm wrong, boy."

"You're wrong."

He laughed until something caught in his throat and he started to cough. "Do you want me to apologize for that, too? For being wrong about why you quit hunting?"

"You can if you want. I'm not the one who kidnapped you."

"Well, then, I tell you, Burnette, I'm sorry. Yes sir, I'm sorry. But for that only. Not the other thing."

It was plain he was trying to make a connection with me, to show how meaningless a thing such as an apology really was. And it was also plain that he'd succeeded. Already I'd decided he was not so bad a fellow for the one who single-handedly had killed off small-town America, as Carnihan liked to say. You could see in his face that he'd been through hard things before and would surely get through this one.

In a moment of clarity, perhaps the only real one I'd had since moving back home, I recognized my life as being over.

"I didn't like the killing," I told him at last.

"What's that?"

We looked at each other. "Why I finally quit hunting."

The old man seemed to consider this. His eyes roamed to the ceiling and he appeared to chew something. "It's the dogs I always enjoyed," he said, his voice coming in a whisper again, "more than the shooting part. The sweat smell of the dogs after a run, and the proud look on their faces, like they really accomplished something. I like to hear how quiet they can be out in the goat weed and buffalo grass, working some bird. Then afterward you put them in a kennel in back of the truck and they huddle together and sleep with their tails flipping every few minutes to get at a fly. They're sort of like children, that way . . . the way they need you."

How do you speak to such a rumination? I was starting to leave the room when he said, "I never had any children myself. What about you, Burnette?"

I should've told him that I'd never been married, or that I'd had only one real opportunity with a woman, but something else came out. "I'm not even thirty yet, Mr. Holly."

"That's what I mean," he said, suddenly regaining that big backwoods voice of his—the same voice I'd heard the other day over the intercom at Monster Mart.

I shuffled back to the X-ray lab and sat on the edge of the bed, holding the shotgun on my lap, fingering the oil-wet barrel. So, Pace, I said to myself, you've grown up to be a kidnapper. Or someone said it. When I listened it sounded like Miss Betty and Pop and my two beautiful sisters speaking as one, a chorus. Behind them came the voices of everyone I'd ever loved even halfway. A hot, busy pain came to my chest and it seemed I couldn't get enough air, would drown unless someone reached a hand out to help me. I kept waiting for Carnihan's headlights to wash over the window and lend a silver glow to the walls. I needed that glow and I needed his voice making sense of America's richest man tied to the desk in Dr. McDermott's office.

There was a plan. Carnihan would return in an hour or two, after the sun came up and Ace started running his cab. Ace would pick him up at Worm Road and drive him back to the place where he'd exchanged the Hometown truck for the old man's. That was somewhere on the service road between Smoke and Warren, which was where the old man had been headed when, sometime around eight o'clock yesterday evening, a wild, black-haired hoodlum had rammed his back end, forced him off the road, and bound and gagged him. Carnihan would tell Ace that his battery needed a jump start. Ace would help him. After that Carnihan would come back to the store and get the old man to apologize.

"Mr. Holly, I'm going to untie you now."

I'd left the shotgun out in the hall, leaning against the door frame. There weren't any shells in it anyway.

"But I didn't say I was sorry yet."

"It doesn't matter, I'm letting you go."

"Do what you have to. See if I care. But I still ain't sorry. No one can make me be what I'm not."

"Fine," I told him.

I squatted beside him and started to pull at the knots. His hands were blue from lack of circulation and his nails were splintered and dirty, more like a plumber's than those you'd expect to see on a billionaire. His hair was white and silky-fine in texture, parted evenly above the left ear and swept over to the other side, hardly disguising his baldness. He was a tall man who packed little weight, and yet there was something hard and solid about his physique, a rawness of bone that suggested time spent in the gym. His eyes were blue and almost perfectly round and they never seemed to blink. His clothes were cheap polyester and I wondered if they came straight off the rack at his hometown Monster Mart. You could build a case against him for that: for trying to show that he was no different from everybody else, that a ten-dollar pair of trousers and a seven-fifty shirt were good enough for him, when he could afford to wear anything he liked. To my thinking it mocked the people who'd made him rich and who dreamed of having what would always be just beyond their reach.

"You know that big lighted sign in front of all your stores? It has you wearing granny glasses and a bow tie."

"That's just for show, son."

"For show?"

"People like a country billionaire just like they like a country lawyer or a country doctor or a country singer. They see them as one of their own, and that makes them more apt to open up their pocketbooks. It's all part of the psychology of retail. First, make them think you're one of them."

I looked in his eyes and slightly hated him. And although I wondered if maybe he deserved these ropes, I was still determined to set him free.

"I rarely wear a tie. A buttoned-up collar chafes my neck."

"Huh?"

"Plus, I don't see the meaning of a tie. What purpose does it serve but decoration? Is it there to hide the fact that your shirt has buttons? There's little poetry in a tie, Burnette—you're a writer, you should know that."

It took me about ten minutes to get the rope off. When I was done he sat rubbing his wrists, feeling the welts. His eyes never left me. It occurred to me that he didn't seem any different than before, when he was bound, and I wondered why that would be. Shouldn't he be happy? He had his freedom, after all.

"We could go one of these days," he said, whispering again. "Just you and me, Burdette. Maybe the other boy. Carnihan."

He'd mispronounced my name again, but I was more interested in his proposition. "Where's that we could go?"

"You know anything about bobwhite quail? They're a sweet bird. You won't be disappointed this time."

I couldn't believe what he was saying. I'd thought he'd have gone for the gun by now, or run outside, crying for help. Instead he sat there, looking perfectly content.

"You can leave, Mr. Holly. No one's stopping you."

"A quail is like a woman, son. You have to creep up on it, be slow and graceful to move, show it your respect. If you're too loud or too aggressive you never get close enough to see it much less raise your sights and pull the trigger. If you hunt it right, you get your shot off before it can even guess what you've come for."

What the hell was he getting at? I wondered. "The sheriff's department, Mr. Holly . . . it's right up the street, if you'd like to bring them in on this. It wouldn't be hard to prove you were kidnapped. Of course I'd prefer you pretended this never happened, and just walked from here. But I wouldn't blame you if you wanted to do something about it. I know I would."

"I'd rather take you hunting," he said. There was a note of sadness in his words, as if I'd rejected him.

"I'll tell Carnihan you were sorry, is why I let you go. He won't believe me, but I'll tell him that."

"Don't speak for me, son. Don't tell him anything of the kind. He could have all my money, every dime I ever collected, but I'd die before giving him the satisfaction."

He rose to his feet and did a couple of deep kneebends: hands on hips, shoulders pulled back, chest pushed out. He jogged in place until sweat started to form on his face and then he performed a few dozen jumping jacks, counting off each one. ". . . hut five hut six hut seven hut eight . . ." When he finished he lowered himself back down to the floor and did ten ladies'-style push-ups, which is to say he didn't stretch out all the way but used his knees as an anchor. He exhaled as he pushed himself up, inhaled as he let himself down. It was hard to tell whether he was exercising to feel better after being tied up for so long or to prove something to me.

He was in the middle of a set of sit-ups when headlights splashed across the window and lent a pale brightness to the room. It was early yet for Carnihan's return, but from outside the window came the irregular humming of the Hometown delivery truck, the engine seeming to mimic the sound of a sewing machine.

"Daddy's home!" the old man said, straining to speak the words for his routine. He'd reached thirty-some repetitions and was still going strong.

"Did he say it yet?" Carnihan asked as soon as he came through the door. He was carrying a snub-nosed pistol with a pearl handle. "He better have said it. Did he?"

I shook my head. "He won't. I asked him to. He absolutely refuses. He says he'd rather die than give you the satisfaction."

"Then he'll just have to die," Carnihan said, standing beside me now. I could smell his odor like old athletic socks you can't launder the stink out of. His hair was in bad shape, too, greasy black and sticking in clumps to his head; a rim of stubble added to the overall rudeness of his appearance.

"I decided it would take too long to wait for Ace," he said. "I remembered the lady who delivers the *Lip* comes by early, so I hitched a ride with her out to the service road. It took all there was in me to keep from telling her I had the richest man in America staying over at the store."

I stepped back, to clear my head of his stink and to let him better see how surprised I was. "Is 'staying over' really what you mean, Jay?"

"I admit it excited me," he said, "holding such a secret. At one point, riding with that woman, I actually got aroused. I mean, I could feel myself getting . . . well, you're a writer. You can imagine it." He held the pistol up to let me get a closer look, and flashed its soft, polished finish under the lights. "Found this in his truck."

"He had this with him?"

"He could've used it on me, back when I ran him off the road. It was right there under the floor mat. It's loaded, too." The gun was just big enough to fit in his palm. "Why do you think he didn't shoot me?"

"Fifty!" I heard the old man shout from the office.

"Fifty what?" Carnihan said, starting to walk in that direction. "Fifty what, Pace?" He reached the doorway and immediately jumped back, lifting the gun and pointing it inside. "He's out of his ropes! He's busted loose from his ropes!"

You could hear the old man counting again as he started another set of exercises, the numbers coming in between bursts of laughter. I reached the door, bumping against Carnihan, and there the old man went, doing more ladies'-style push-ups, moving even faster than before. The vein and sinew of his neck throbbed with each repetition, and his face was colored purple with blood.

Carnihan lowered the gun and turned to glare at me, his upper lip twitching.

"You untied him, didn't you?"

"He won't apologize, Jay. It's no use."

Carnihan stood unmoving in his place. You could actually see his eyes wobble, the whole of his fury concentrated there. "He'll apologize as long as I've got the gun."

"I don't think so."

"Sonofa . . ." He lurched forward at last, strode across the room, and plopped himself on the old man's back, pinning him to the floor. "Go get me the ropes, Pace! And hurry, goddammit!"

I looked at where I'd thrown them in the corner. I knew it didn't make sense, tying him up again, when the old man had no intention of either escaping or turning us in.

"Know where you can start?" the old man asked.

Carnihan didn't answer.

"You can start with the name of the store. It's probably the worst I've ever heard in all my years in general mercantile." The weight on his shoulders and back hardly seemed to bother him. "Hometown Family Goods. It sounds like something from the stagecoach days . . . a place with hitching posts out front." He laughed as best he could, and scratched his nose against the floor. "Blame yourself, Mr. Carnihan. Or whoever it was who came up with that one. Boy, is it a stinker."

"The name has nothing to do with it," Carnihan said. He was staring down at the back of the old man's head. "It's Monster Mart that's the problem."

"Hometown Family Goods," the old man said in something of a whisper. "Let me hear you say it."

"Suppose I don't feel like it."

"Come on, boy. Is it asking so much to have you speak the name of a place you love?" Carnihan didn't answer and the old man said, "You can't bear to, can you?"

"I can say anything I feel like saying. In case you haven't noticed, I'm the one holding the gun."

"You should apologize to me—for offending me with a name such as that. Come on, boy. Say it. I want to hear the name."

"It's better than Monster Mart," Carnihan mumbled. "At least it means something."

"What name're we talking about now?"

"This one," Carnihan said, and pressed the pistol against the old man's head. "This is the name I mean."

The old man still wasn't afraid. If anything he was more emboldened. There was a smile on his face and it wasn't from fear. "I wonder how you can live with yourself," he said. "Lying like you do. Not only to me, but to Burdette here. And, not to mention, to yourself." Then in one easy motion the old man pushed himself up off the floor, with Carnihan still on his back. It was an extraordinary thing to see, since Carnihan weighed about a hundred and eighty pounds.

His chest touched the floor and he was starting to push up again when Carnihan hopped off and limped over to where I was standing. "You think our name sounds better than Monster Mart, don't you, Pace?" He was staring at me, and there was pain in his voice, not a little.

"You're not dragging me into this, Jay. I won't let you."

"We need an impartial judge," he said.

"Then you'll have to go get somebody else."

"Ruby Dean," he muttered. "She'd tell him."

"Ruby Dean's an honest person," I said. "You'd lose."

The old man had stopped exercising. He rolled over on his back and stared up at the ceiling with his hands folded behind his head. "May I speak?" he asked. Neither Carnihan nor I said anything, and he continued, "It's just too dull a name, son—there's nothing interesting about it, nothing to entertain the eye when you look at it from a ways up the street. I really don't mean to hurt your feelings, I can see you're attached to it. But some things need to be said."

"It's worked just fine for eighty-some years now, I'll have you know. No one's complained about it yet."

"Oh, they've complained, all right. They've complained every time they chose to shop at my place over yours. It hasn't been in anything they've said that they've complained—they wouldn't do that to you, Jay, they like you and they like your family—but in the one of cash registers ringing."

Carnihan tightened his grip on the gun. He seemed to be trying to come up with a rebuttal, and having a time of it. "I'll come sit on you again," he said finally. "I'm not kidding, either. I'll sit . . ."

He'd meant to be threatening, but he sounded so beaten and pathetic that neither the old man nor I could bear to look at him. The old man got off the floor and sat at the desk. He put his hands on his knees and inhaled deeply, and his eyes fluttered closed. His face regained its normal color as the skin slowly faded to pink. When finally he spoke it was with an attitude of broad experience: the old wizened grandpappy explaining the eternal acts of nature to an idiot child. "Just for the sake of argument," he began, "and I'm only playing devil's advocate here, Jay—this is nothing personal . . . let's just say you're driving down the road one evening and see two signs up ahead. One says 'Monster Mart,' the other 'Hometown Family Goods.' " He paused and held the names between his open hands, demonstrating. "They're both the same size, these signs, lit up bright with the same number and color of lights. The question I pose to you is this: Which promises the greater adventure?"

The old man waited for a reply, and when none came, he said, "When I was a boy, Jay, everyone called me Rayf. My whole name is Winston Rayford Holly, and back then I didn't much care for the middle part. Rayford sounded far too uncivilized to my ears, since I fancied myself a fellow of some refinement. By the time I was sixteen I'd read from cover to cover the Great Books of the Western World, after all. And I had plans for myself. So when I went off to college I let on that I was Winston and nothing else. I was still Winston when I moved back home four years later."

"Well, ain't that interesting," Carnihan said.

The old man ignored him. "I had this notion, you see. I intended to sell the big-city fashions of the day, and I figured I'd get rich on account it was time someone introduced Liberty to the twentieth century—for men, to hiking and riding suits and breeches, and, for the ladies, to togs and frocks and whatever French millinery happened to be the rage. The bank gave me a loan, and I called the store Fascinating Fashions. Each day I reported with a 'Winston Holly' name tag, talking my slippery words and flaunting my liberal education, putting on my expensive ways. Somebody came in the store, said, 'How's it hanging, there, Rayf?' I'd tell him, 'It's Winston now, thank you very much.' I sold a few girdles and a hat or two. But not much else. After six months I was finished, or Fascinating Fashions was. I look back now and see the only thing fascinating about it was how long it managed to last."

The old man opened his eyes and stared across the room. Unable to match his gaze, Carnihan turned and looked at me. "Do you find this at all interesting, Pace, what he's saying?"

"It's pretty good," I said.

Carnihan seemed to think about it. "Go ahead," he said.

"Had an old uncle . . ." the old man started up again, smiling a big smile now, "an old uncle by the name of Ben who'd been in the beauty shop business, with parlors in Little Rock and Texarkana, a few other towns. Ben is in the rich, full swing of retirement when Fascinating Fashions goes under. Old Ben, he learns of my troubles and comes to me and offers help. There's a department store in town having problems, about to close, and he wants to buy it out and put me in it. Ben's got no family but his one brother, my father, and he decides he'd like to do this for me while he's still alive. And of course I'm more than willing to let him since about this time my future looks about as exciting as a pile of paper clips."

Carnihan raised his hand, like a kid in class. "I hate to interrupt, but how long is this going to take?"

"You got an appointment?"

"Well, I wanted to take a nap before it was tomorrow night and time to go to bed anyway."

"Give me another minute," the old man said, fluttering his eyelids shut again. He took another deep breath before continuing. "We called it Monster Mart for no reason but the poetry of those two words placed side by side. People now don't like to believe that, they want some other story, but I tell you this is true. At the grand opening we hired a bunch of kids to dress up like zombies and vampires and such, and we put them standing out by the road, waving customers in. And we're out by the front door greeting them, me and Ben, both of us dressed in white linen and skinny bow ties that drooped like a cowboy's mustache, and shoes of such a quality you just can't buy anymore. 'Meet my nephew and business partner, Rayford,' Ben'd say to those he knew, mostly country folk, simple people. And I noted the shimmy of his accent, how just since the doors opened it'd seemed to have grown more complicated in its meanderings, and how well everyone responded to it. From Uncle Ben's mouth the name 'Rayford' sounded more winsome a word than any other in the English language, and I found I liked it, and wished to be it."

"So you quit on Winston, started talking like a hick, and overnight became the richest S.O.B. in all America."

"I resent that remark, I really do—my mother, for your information, was no bitch. She was a saint with every credential but the halo."

Carnihan said, "If you resent it so much then do something about it." He showed his stupid gun again. "I'm waiting."

"Well, I didn't wait," the old man said. "I scooped dried shrimp and candy into bags and I put bikes together when they came in a box and I cleaned out the aquarium and I mopped the floor and saved the pennies I found. I gave the people what they needed and after that I gave them what they wanted. The store took off because I willed it to, and then the second one did, and the third, and the fourth. Now I'm so rich when I urinate it comes out a sort of grass-green." He paused to make sure he still had our attention. "There are several messages you might've gathered from this story. Anybody?"

"We kidnap him," Carnihan said, "and then he gives us a frickin' pop quiz."

"Number one," the old man said, "don't try to sell 'em ivory-headed shoehorns and tailor-made dress suits when they want claw hammers and overalls. Second, be who you are, not somebody else. And third, poetry is the key to man's existence."

"Poetry?" Carnihan spoke as if he hated the word. "I always thought it was something else . . . like food."

Except for what Carnihan had told me, I knew practically nothing about Rayford Holly, since so little of what I'd ever read about him included glimpses of his personal life. As a rule he didn't grant interviews, and although in the past he hadn't seemed to mind being questioned about his business dealings, he was always evasive and less than forthcoming, his responses oblique. That early morning, though, holed up in Dr. McDermott's office, I learned more about him than I really cared to, some of the information being so particular that I wondered what motivated him to reveal it.

He told us the names of his hunting dogs, then went on a tear about how the town of Liberty had an ordinance outlawing drains in dog runs. Without a connection to the main sewer line, his men had to hose the crap right out into the yard, and this had caused a problem with flies and other insects. The flies had got into his house, and on and on.

Somehow he returned to the subject of poetry, and he wondered whether we knew the name Walt Whitman, who happened to be his all-time favorite writer. He then quoted a line from something called "Song of the Open Road": "Afoot and light-hearted I take to the open road, healthy, free, the world before me, the long brown path before me, leading wherever I choose."

He was standing as he recited this, his right hand over his heart in the fashion of one saying the pledge. Tears welled in his eyes, and his lips trembled. I liked the poem well enough, it spoke to me, but I could've done without the emotion.

Carnihan was sitting on the floor with his back against the wall, looking defeated, half asleep. His mouth was hanging open as if he couldn't bear the stress and strain of keeping it closed, and spots of drool were collecting at the corners.

The sun was up before Carnihan and I finally left the room; the old man was still standing by the desk, his hands building pictures in the air as he told one story after another. I laughed and shook my head, and Carnihan, holding a piece of paper to his face, pretended to sob. You'd think it would be energizing to be harangued by the world's most famous billionaire, but nothing in my experience had ever been as exhausting. I retired to the X-ray lab, Carnihan to an examination room, and we both found flat surfaces on which to rest and cover our heads. I was whipped and rattled, and I slept easily, although a voice in my subconscious kept telling me that soon enough I'd be awakened to the end of my life. Sheriff Sorel and his SWAT team (sounded like a Cajun zyedeco band, if you asked me) would storm Dr. McDermott's, and some uniformed misfit with crooked teeth and too much Wild Root Hair Tonic would bark into a bullhorn and order us to come out with our hands up.

Then other voices began to speak to me. Winston Rayford Holly's had joined those of my friends and family, and everyone was saying, "So, Pace, you've grown up to be a kidnapper."

When I awoke it was half past noon and rain was falling outside, coming in big fat drops. A few hurricanes notwithstanding, I'd never seen such a storm, and I was simultaneously frightened and soothed. Part of me wanted to run outside and declare war against it, to raise fists to the sky and dare things to fall any harder. But the other part, and the more persuasive one, sought only to be sucked up by the storm's ferocious rhythms and to go back to sleep. Choosing the part that was less messy and dangerous, I slept for another four or five hours and woke to the familiar aroma of fried eggs, ham, and fresh-brewed coffee—or, as memory served, to the aroma of Ruby Dean. It followed that since her warm smell was in the room so she would be, but when I opened my eyes it was to the sight of the old man, standing at the foot of the bed. He was wearing a ribbed stovepipe chef's hat he'd found somewhere on the shelves and plain white clothes still papered with manufacturer's tags. "Time to eat. Come 'n' get it, boy."

As I recalled, only a few weeks ago these had been Ruby Dean's words, welcoming me home. And I felt my flesh goose as it struck me that a transference of souls had taken place. Out in Florida, I wondered, had Ruby Dean Clark taken to running bird dogs, shooting at bobwhite quail, and speaking with a drawl more common to the wooded hills of northern Arkansas than to the alligator swamps of southern Louisiana? At this moment, were LaShonda and Hayward being held hostage by that voice, terrorized by its willfulness, devoured by its appetite?

I was slow to get up, not wishing for more surprises, and ventured down the hall to the examination room, which was empty. Padding through the stockroom, I noticed that it wasn't as disorderly as usual, that in fact it had been swept and tidied, its collection of boxes either stacked along the wall or flattened into single panels, its walkways cleared of debris. Even the red curtain in the doorway had been laundered, decades of dust, spiderwebs, and roach droppings beaten out of it.

Likewise, when I entered the store I saw a different place, or, rather, one better dressed than it had been in years. The wood floors shone red with peppermint oil, the front windows had been washed and polished to a sea-blue gleam, and the shelves and pallets looked like a jigsaw puzzle that had finally been put together. Something about the store's atmosphere was more relaxed and inviting, and, gazing up at the ceiling, it occurred to me that the difference involved light. The old man had replaced the burnt-out bulbs in the hanging lamps, and a battalion of glass shades glowed the finest, darkest green.

One thing, however, did look more slatternly than before, and that was the lunch counter. Dirty dinner plates were stacked along the zinc top, a paper egg carton was open down by the register, with several cracked shells sticking up out of it, and rings of milk and juice formed chaotic patterns on the surface. I wondered what Ruby Dean might've said, seeing this mess, and eased onto the stool with the plate of steaming food in front of it. This seat happened to be right next to the one where Carnihan quietly sat reading a folded section of yesterday's *Lip* and chewing a too-dark strip of bacon.

"G'morning," I mumbled, although it was nearly nighttime. Having provoked no response, I punched him on the arm and said, "Okay, then, Jay. G'evening."

Still, Carnihan didn't say anything.

The old man was standing at the opposite end of the counter, his back to us, talking to Silas Poe. Next to them stood Ruby Dean's blackboard, which neatly read: NO FRESH BREAD FOR SANDWICHES, BUT ANYTHING CANNED, REFRIGERATED OR FROZEN I CAN MAKE, INCLUDING PANCAKES, MY SPECIALTY. Both men were talking in lively, animated tones, and I wondered whether Silas, himself a banker, had recognized the old man. It seemed unlikely: he'd never be this relaxed in the presence of someone so monied.

I pointed to the clock on the wall, determined to try again. "Kind of late for ham and eggs, ain't it, Jay?"

When Carnihan didn't answer I became alarmed and swiveled in my seat to get a closer look at him. At first glance he seemed to be transfixed by a story in the paper, but at second you saw he was only pretending to read. His eyes stared without focus, and the paper was just the object he'd chosen to stick in front of his face. Also, he was gnashing his teeth at such a rate as to cause me some concern. Tapping his shoulder, I asked if he wasn't well, and got the same answer as before, which is to say none.

I yanked the paper from his hands, and, in response, his eyes swirled around before settling on a wire basket filled with individual packets of Sweet'n Low.

"Hey, brother, kind of late for breakfast, wouldn't you say? Isn't six-thirty more toward the supper hour?"

"How many times're you gonna ask me that?" His voice seemed spat rather than spoken from his mouth.

"As many as it takes to get an answer."

"God, Pace, look who he's talking to. He's talking to Silas, for heaven's sake! They're over. Our lives. We're finished."

We both stared down at the end of the counter, the two of them bellowing. They might've been engaged in a contest: who could laugh louder without shattering the windowpanes.

"How long have you been here?" I asked.

"I dunno . . . maybe five minutes—I came in early enough to watch Ol' Fontenot leave. He'd come to eat, too. Him and all the others from the bank." Carnihan waved a hand at the trash on the counter. "Look at this. I bet he's fed half the town."

"I'd say more, I'd say three-quarters."

Carnihan put his face in his hands and pretended to weep. Or at least I thought he was pretending. He made a racket, in any case. "Over," he said. "Finished."

Finally Silas Poe got up from his stool and came staggering over. On his way he popped half a roll of antacids in his mouth. "Don't be sad there, young man," he said. "I know you miss him—we all do—but he'd be glad . . . he'd be right proud of you."

I waited for Carnihan to reply, but like me he was too busy trying to understand Silas's point. Would Mr. Hank have been happy to know that his son had kidnapped America's richest man? Silas's face revealed little except perhaps that he was experiencing another one of his Tabasco stomachs.

"Your new cook," he said at last. "I approve of him, son, I heartily approve." And he belched, the sulfuric stink of medicine coming up with it.

As soon as he was gone the old man started cleaning up. He treated us as you would any young punks who claimed seats at your counter—in other words, he totally ignored us.

"Silas Poe," the old man finally said after a while, more to himself than to the two of us. "I wonder if he's any relation to the poet."

"Silas ain't related to nobody," Carnihan said. "He's all alone in this world, is why he likes to come here."

"Edgar Allan Poe, I'm speaking of."

"Sorry, partner. Nobody in Smoke by that name."

"Nobody in Smoke . . ." the old man muttered, pausing when it came to him that Carnihan had been serious.

He stood in front of us. "Anything else I can help you with, gentlemen? How about more biscuits?"

I was trying to figure out where to go to get sick, and thus was unable to summon the spirit to reply. Carnihan, on the other hand, leaned forward, extending himself over the counter, and grabbed the old man by his shirt.

"Did I ask you to open my store for business? Did I ask you to be my cook?"

Clearly these were rhetorical questions, but the old man didn't take them that way. He stood there thinking for a while, then answered simply, "No, boss, you didn't."

Carnihan nodded. He seemed to agree. "Something else. Who's kidnapped who here? Is it us who's kidnapped you, Winston, or you who's kidnapped us? I'm a little confused."

"It's you who's kidnapped me."

Carnihan let go of the old man and rubbed his hands on his pants, as if to clean them of something. "Just as long as we understand each other, Winston."

The old man had arranged the dirty glasses and plates in the left compartment of the basin, flatware and cups in the right. So as not to show favoritism with either category, he took a turn with each, spending more time sudsing and rinsing than was necessary. It was clear to me that he knew next to nothing about washing dishes, but the task seemed to give him a lot of pleasure. He started whistling and shuffling his feet, the bottom half of his body dancing while the upper half kept busy at work. He was only about halfway done when Carnihan called him over and asked for a moment's indulgence. "I've got a few questions for you," he said. "It shouldn't take but a minute and then you can go back to your sink."

The old man was drying his hands on the apron. He nodded but at the same time seemed suspicious.

"Why didn't you leave when you had a chance, Winston? Any normal person would have."

The old man stood there chewing his lower lip, quiet for too long a time. And I knew that whatever he said would bear the weight of all this thinking—in other words, that it would fall short of the truth.

"Ever hear of the Stockholm syndrome? It's a psychological condition in which the victim of a kidnapping empathizes with his captors. Something in him cracks, and he comes to understand their reasons for holding him. He believes in and supports them, and, in some cases, he falls in love with them." He picked up Carnihan's plate and walked with it back to the sink. "I think that's what's happened to me."

Carnihan was staring at the spot where his plate had been. "What's this now? Where'd you catch this thing?"

"Stockholm," the old man answered, his hands and forearms once again white with suds. "But you don't catch it there. This ain't no virus. It's a syndrome. Syndromes aren't contagious."

"I wouldn't be so sure," Carnihan said. "So many of them going around these days, you know. . . ."

"Well, then," the old man said, putting a match in his mouth, "I suppose in that case I caught it here, right here at Hometown. Your old store gave it to me, boy. Right over there—" He indicated an area at the far end of the counter. "Right over there is where it happened. You see there, son. You should've sprayed last week."

"Sprayed for what?"

"Bugs, my boy. Spiders, wasps, roaches, mites . . . *syndromes!* God almighty, you kidnap me less than twenty-four hours and already I've come down with something."

When the old man was finished with the dishes, Carnihan said, "You ever been kidnapped before, Winston? You seem to know a lot about it."

The old man shook his head.

"Maybe I put that wrong. I should've said *I*'ve never kidnapped anyone before, and *I* didn't know anything about it. I'm not very good at it, I'm afraid."

The old man's eyes came alive with a kind of pity. The look he gave Carnihan reminded me of how he'd looked at me after reading my bad reviews. "You're doing fine, boy. Don't you worry. You're doing just fine."

"Am I really?"

"Yes, you are, boy. Keep it up." Then, as if to shatter the gloom, he said, "I collected forty-eight dollars today."

"Forty-eight?"

"And that doesn't include tips. Got over twelve in them." He patted his pocket, jingling change. "That's just at the lunch counter here. I sold a hammer, some ten-penny nails, a Bonnie B hair net, and a bolt of gingham. It didn't come to much, but I put the money over there." He pointed to the business register.

In an instant Carnihan rose from his haze and scrambled across the room. He pressed the No Sale button, opening the cash drawer. The sound it made was louder than ever, and I felt a heavy pounding come to my chest.

"My lord," Carnihan muttered, as tears of gratitude filled his eyes. "My sweet, precious lord." He fingered the day's earnings and glanced back at the old man. "How'd you do it? How'd you get them in here? How'd you make them buy?"

"It wasn't hard. I stood outside in the rain and waved them in. For a while there every chair was taken." He nodded at Carnihan. "A couple people even asked for you, boy."

"That was nice."

"I said I was your new man, your cook."

Carnihan swallowed hard. "They believe that?"

"Well, why wouldn't they? Do I look to you like the sort of person who'd intentionally deceive anyone?"

"I thought maybe they'd recognize you. Smoke has a newspaper, you know? It's lousy, but at least it's a paper. We have television, too. I just thought maybe they'd seen your face before . . . in the business reports or somewhere."

The old man unleashed a snipped-off version of his hog call. Apparently he'd already thought this out. "I could be a famous Hollywood actor and as long as I was in Smoke it wouldn't register on anybody who I was. Oh, they might wonder at the resemblance, but they wouldn't dare make the leap of thinking I was him. Small towns are peculiar like that. They run on the notion that nothing changes, and that only by mistake are they part of the world around them. Besides, study me real good for a minute. Do I look like anyone?"

He was right, of course. The floppy stovepipe hat, the grease-stained shirt, the pants still for sale. He was a clever parody of anyone who ever served grits for a living, and it wouldn't've surprised me to discover faded blue tattoos of naked Polynesian girls showing through the patches of hair on his arms.

"See there," he said. "I look like no one. And like everyone. Both at the same time."

"I bet I know some people who'd recognize you," Carnihan said. "They'd know you at Monster Mart, for instance."

"Well, sure they'd know me there, I just visited, after all. But let me tell you this. I've walked into stores of mine when I wasn't expected, on stops on my journey to self-discovery. I've stumbled in with the crowd, and no one's known who in damnation I was—*in my own stores!* Once in a town I won't now mention I even bought a basketful and paid with a check. They asked for an I.D., and I showed them my driver's license and still it didn't register. There my face was stitched to their smocks, and beaming in a hundred million kilowatts of electrical firepower up on the sign outside, and I might as well've been some old boy who'd come in just to get outa the heat."

He was staring at himself in the mirror behind the counter, seeming delighted by what he saw.

"You can learn a lot about yourself," he continued, "being treated like the average fellow. You can discover things. And I don't mean what it feels like to open a door by yourself, or to hold your own umbrella in the rain, or to carve up your own food. I'm talking about the things which give meaning to a life—yes, by golly, the little poetic moments that define us all." He was staring at Carnihan. "You want a for-instance, son?"

"Okay."

"Suppose you get lost one day out on the road—out on Mr. Whitman's long brown path—and pull over on the shoulder feeling confused and scared and wondering if you'll ever reach the place you need to go. You flag down the first car to show and it stops and the driver gets out and of course you don't know this person. You're thinking he could be a killer or a thief and he's thinking the same. You ask for directions, and you're relieved when he lifts a finger and points the way. Or what he thinks is the way. But then, wait a second . . . he tells you he isn't sure. 'Does the sun set in the West?' he wants to know. He actually says that, and you consider getting smart. 'If it doesn't,' you want to tell him, 'the newspaper boys sure will have a story to write.' He's pointing this way and that, confusing you blind. Finally he gets back in his car and tells you to follow, that he'll lead you there. You tail him for miles and miles, until he pulls into the very place you'd been looking for. Will he accept payment for his troubles? Of course he won't. He rolls his window down and takes your hand. And he shakes it harder than he probably should, so that you won't forget him. And then he leaves trailing mountains of dust and thinking to himself that he did a good thing today, and that it could've been him lost out on the road. Or his wife or daughter lost, or some other loved one. And he understands something deep and eternal. He understands that times like this are what make us human, and that it was worth the trouble if only to feel as he does."

Carnihan, by now, was supporting his head with his hand. He looked mesmerized, struck dumb. "I think I understand," he said.

The old man squeezed through the counter gate, walked over to the front of the store, and stared out the window. It was the same pose as Mr. Hank's, but it seemed to be one facing the future rather than the past. Four or five Smokies sauntered by, still wearing raincoats. The weather had passed, and now the evening light, given puddles of water to reflect against and the rain-wet green of the trees, was about as beautiful as it ever gets in our piece of the world. Behind all the pretty green, I noticed a blueness in the air: it would be dark soon.

"I'd bet Bethany would know who you are," Carnihan said of a sudden. He spun around on his stool. "Hey, Winston, I know somebody who'd know who you are."

"Bethany?"

"She's a girl, works at your store here in Smoke. She's a clerk there, just started a few weeks ago."

"And you'd bet she knows me? How much would you bet?"

Carnihan didn't need much time to reply: "A million dollars would do."

"A million dollars? Tell me something, boy, do you have that kind of money? You can't, can you?"

"If I win, a million. If you win . . . well let's discuss it."

"If *I* win . . ." The old man seemed to give the subject more attention than it deserved. He went back behind the counter and picked up a spatula. "If she recognizes me within a space of ten minutes after we meet," he said, "then I'll see to it that a million dollars are placed in your personal bank account. But if she doesn't . . ." He paused to think about what he wanted, or maybe just to let the tension build. "If she doesn't, son, you change the name of the store."

"I don't know," Carnihan said. You could see he didn't like it, which seemed incredible to me. It was a million dollars, after all. *A million!* He shook his head. "It's not worth it, giving up the name."

"But you said whatever I wanted. And that's it. You scrap the name Hometown Family Goods, and we put our heads together and come up with something else."

"I still say it's too high a price."

"Two million, then. We'll make it two million dollars."

Carnihan refitted his face into the cup of his hand and blubbered his lips with a quick exhalation. Was he bluffing, hoping to up the ante? I really couldn't tell. At last he said, "The answer is no. No amount of money—"

"Five, then, boy. Let's make it five."

By this time I was beginning to feel faint, and a coffee burn started in my stomach. I grabbed the counter to steady myself. "Good God, man. Five million dollars! Do it, Jay!"

"But it's Hometown, Pace! I like the name. It was Daddy's name and his daddy's name and his daddy's daddy's name. It was all our name . . . all of Smoke's."

"To hell with it," I said. "For five million dollars you could call it any damned thing he likes. Who cares, anyway, brother? You really think anyone cares?"

"I do."

"See there," the old man said. "The boy has pride. I admire that. The boy knows some things just aren't for sale."

A light came to Carnihan's eyes as if something had suddenly been revealed to him. He held his hand out to the old man. "All right," he said. "You pay five million if she recognizes you. If she doesn't, I get rid of the name."

They gave each other a shake and the bet was sealed. When they broke hands both of them punched fists at the air and started hopping around as if they'd already won.

"You went cheap, boy. I'd have gone as high as ten. Ten million dollars! Ten million dollars for the name!"

Carnihan took this better than I'd expected. He walked back behind the counter, opened the refrigerator door, and removed his bottle of Absolut. "Yeah, well," he said, "that's too bad, Winston. I could've used the money. But I'll tell you something . . ." And here he paused and lifted the vodka up to his mouth. "You went high, partner. Four million dollars too high. Because, the way I was thinking, I'd've settled for one."

Carnihan mixed a pitcher of Bloody Marys and we drank from giant milk shake tumblers. The alcohol fired a part of my brain that apparently had lain dormant until now, and I felt myself growing giddy at the thought that I was actually drinking cocktails with America's richest man. "It's Rayford Holly," I told myself. "It's Rayford Holly you're drinking with."

The old man was too busily occupied with his tumbler to notice my sudden infatuation. Or maybe, having inspired this reaction in people before, he was as comfortable with it as he was with the well-traveled brand of clodhoppers he wore.

Only when I failed to respond to the proposition of another round did he presume that something was wrong.

"What's'a matter, Burdette?"

I didn't answer, I couldn't.

Carnihan was pouring three more tumblers full. "You got a problem, Pace? Let us hear it. Speak up."

"He's Rayford Holly." And I pointed to the one I meant. "Rayford Holly's drinking with us, Jay."

"You want an autograph?" I shook my head and the old man said, "Good, because I don't give them out—not even to sweet things like yourself." He puckered his lips and blew me a kiss.

We were nicely loosened up when the old man asked whether, sometime soon, real soon, we'd permit him to make a telephone call. "Need to check in with HQ," he said, wiping his Bloody Mary mustache onto the sleeve of his shirt.

"That the little woman?" Carnihan asked.

The old man smiled and his eyes narrowed to a squint. It was a sad smile, though, and the squint was the kind that comes involuntarily, when something hurts. "Since my wife died it has been," he said. He was looking at the tumbler in his hands. "HQ means headquarters, son. Up in Liberty. They go twenty-four hours without hearing from me and everyone panics. That's another thing about these little journeys of mine. One thing you learn is how chickenshit all your hired hands are."

"No phone calls," Carnihan said. "Not until you do it."

"Are we still on that?" I asked.

"I won't," the old man said. "Not me."

"Then you can forget about making that call."

The old man shrugged. "In the long run, son, it'll only bring the heat down faster on you. I'm just trying to help. You don't want my people filing a missing-person report, do you?"

"No. But we haven't kept you long enough to make anyone suspicious. We only got you late last night. So don't play games, Winston. I'm on to you, man. I'm really on to you."

"That may be so," the old man said, "but it'd already been a few days since my last call. I should phone them without any more delay. I'm telling you it's important."

Carnihan watched him from across the counter. You could tell he didn't believe him. "I'll let you call, Winston. But you've got to apologize."

"I won't."

"Then shut up about it, all right? You'll go and give yourself a stroke. Or me one."

Carnihan left the guns and rope behind when at last we took off for Bayou Blanc. We went in the Mustang because the old man said he'd never ridden in a convertible before, and because the night was cool after the rain, the air bright with the smell of flowers and grass. Before leaving Hometown I put the top down and plugged a Hadley Castille tape in the stereo, turning the volume up so we could hear the music above the buffeting wind.

The old man was sitting in the backseat, leaning forward and hugging the headrest. "Hadley who?" he asked.

"Castille," I answered, having to shout for the noise. "He plays the accordion. He sings."

"And this is what kind of music?"

"Chank-a-chank. You never heard of chank-a-chank?"

He cupped an ear. "Is that French they're singing?"

"Cajun French," I told him. "A little different from what you'd hear in France." I turned the volume up another notch, and in the rearview saw his smile climb a notch as well.

This was another new experience for him, I reckoned, and it was clear to me now why he wasn't desperate to leave us. The old man's journey to self-discovery was just that. And he'd found plenty in Smoke. We were just getting started and already he'd popped his cherry on a list of things. He'd been kidnapped, cooked for a bunch of strangers, cleaned a heap of dirty dishes, rode in a topless automobile, and listened to Cajun music. By some trick of fate he'd landed in an amusement park where Jay Carnihan and Pace Burnette were the guides. The great thing about this park, if you were the old man, was that you possessed complimentary tickets to any and all rides as long as you remembered not to apologize.

"Winston?" Carnihan said. "You still got that tip money in your pocket?"

"I got it."

"You want to buy us something to drink? Before we go to Bayou Blanc and I win my five mil?"

"Sure. I'll buy whatever you want."

"Driver," Carnihan said. "What'say we stop by Babylon, introduce our hostage to Anita and the telephone lady?"

"I don't think that's a good idea," I said. "Maybe later."

"When later?"

"I'd rather not see Genny tonight, if you don't mind, Jay." I knew better than to get any more specific, but he kept staring at me as if an explanation were due. I needed a minute to come up with one: "Last time I went there something happened. Something I'd rather not talk about."

He seemed to understand. He turned back in his bucket seat and said to the old man, "Genine Monteleone, Winston, that's his HQ." In the rearview, the old man puckered his lips and blew another kiss. "Tall girl with big hair," Carnihan said, demonstrating, with his arms, just how big. "She works at this club I want to take you to."

"Just as long as you know I'm not sorry," the old man said with a cocky grin.

By now we were cruising through downtown, driving past abandoned buildings showing lease and sale signs in almost every window. As he always did when we went this way, Carnihan shut his eyes to avoid having to see it. The old man, no longer displaying such a proud face, dropped down in his seat and swiveled his head from side to side. He mumbled something, too softly for me to hear. Carnihan couldn't make it out, either.

"Are you apologizing back there?" he said. "God, that was easy. Last billionaire we kidnapped took years to break down."

The old man threw his arm over the seat and glanced back at the Abdalla building. "What was that? Anything?"

"A department store," Carnihan said. "A nice one. No one was ever a stranger there."

The old man didn't say anything, not until we made the block and passed another vacant building. "And there? What was that?"

"A five-and-dime. Run by the same family for about fifty years. At Christmas they'd give free toys to kids."

I slowed down to let the old man get a longer look at what had been J. W. Low's. And I remembered the place: parakeets in big wire cages, model airplanes hanging by fishing line from the ceiling, Disney music piped in over the sound system.

"What about the family?" the old man asked, his eyes tracing over the building. "Where'd they go? They didn't die, did they?"

"They went out of business, Winston, and then seemed to scatter with the wind. Oh, they told everyone they were retiring, not wanting people to feel sorry for them, but we all knew what the score was." He waited a second, then said: "Monster Mart."

We were passing another empty building, this one formerly Garbo's Barbershop. The glass pole next to the door was so caked with dirt you couldn't see the red, white, and blue ribbon inside. The front window was *X*ed over with masking tape, and someone had scribbled FOR ANYTHING on the door in heavy white chalk.

"You don't cut hair at Monster Mart, do you, Winston?"

The old man didn't answer.

"Is there no money in that? Too hard to find good help willing to shave a neck?"

The old man took the twelve dollars cash from his pocket and placed it between Carnihan and me. "What about that drink? Don't you boys still want that drink?" He was trying to sound chipper. "It's on me. Whatever on this earth you want."

"Aren't you sorry, Winston? Aren't you the least bit sorry?"

Ever true to himself, he didn't speak. I watched in the mirror for the words to find his lips, but all he did was rip the tags off his pants and toss them in the street. "Do you always drive like this?" he finally asked.

"Only when we're trying to get away from something," Carnihan answered.

To reach the nearest convenience store, I cut through a neighborhood which had started to slide of late, fast becoming one of those areas where you'd better not enter without a prayerbook and a police escort. Wood-frame houses sat next to the road, some of them a hundred years old but in such a state as to look twice that. Burglar bars crossed the windows of even the smallest shanties. I didn't drive there intending to show the old man any more of what Monster Mart had done to Smoke, but he took it that way. "Did you really have to take me here?"

I caught his eye in the mirror. "It's the quickest route."

"I didn't know we were in such a hurry."

"I thought you wanted a drink. This is how you go to get one." I pointed to the quick-stop up ahead. "Shopkeep keeps his cooler so cold you can hardly stand to hold the bottle."

"I'd've taken a warm one, a hot one even, to keep from having to see this neighborhood."

Carnihan laughed. "No one'll hurt you here, Winston." He reached back and tapped the old man on the shoulder. "Long as they don't find out who you are."

When we reached Bayou Blanc the old man asked if I wouldn't mind slowing down so he could have a better look at the place. It was night and the youngest possible moonlight washed over everything green and silver and other colors not yet named. The old man seemed to like looking at the bayou, and you couldn't blame him after what he'd been made to see in town.

I parked where we always parked and when we walked down the levee the weeds grabbed at us as they always did. Bethany's mother was in the same room as last time, lying on the same bed and gazing up at the same ceiling, the same colored tongue hanging limp and fat from the same contorted mouth. At her window a billionaire poet on a journey to self-discovery was standing between Carnihan and me, and that really was the only difference worth mentioning.

"Is this Bethany?" the old man whispered. "Does she really work for me?"

Carnihan put a finger to his mouth to shush him and we duckwalked to the back window, where Bethany was cooking at the kitchen stove. "She's the one," Carnihan said, and gave a smile both proud and possessive.

"Lovely," the old man said. "Really. A lovely, radiant child. In what department does she work?"

"Caught her stacking mouthwash once," I said. "Personal Hygiene, the area was called."

This didn't sit well with the old man. He shook his head: her obvious talents were being wasted. "She should be up front greeting people at the door. Why, look at her."

The kitchen radio was playing Cajun music, and Bethany, too busy at the stove, couldn't dance but to rock her hips and to kick a foot up every now and then. Her left hand was stirring a spoon in a pot of white beans, her right clasping the handle of a skillet crowded with slabs of French bread frying in oil.

"How're we gonna do this?" I asked.

Carnihan put another finger to his lips and motioned for us to follow him. We duckwalked to the dock and took seats on the dry, brown boards at the end, our legs hanging over, feet just touching the water.

"We can't go up there all together," I said. "Mr. Holly, you'll have to do it alone."

"I was thinking the same," Carnihan said. "He'll have to act like someone, otherwise she'll know we've been trailing her."

"But if I act like someone," the old man said, "I give you the advantage. No, she mustn't be influenced by thinking of me as anyone. If she does then she's not likely to guess at who I am."

We were sitting with our shoulders touching, the old man in the middle getting it from both sides. The night roared as the swamp seemed to welcome the darkness: fish hitting bugs in the shallows, the incessant whine of tires from the highway, wild dogs howling at the moon. It was a big, mad symphony, and, being from the town, I wasn't all that comfortable with it. I kept recalling stories about gators supping on the legs of people foolish enough to dangle their feet in the water. Just to be safe, I raised mine up and tucked them under me. And the old man and Carnihan followed in turn.

"Tell her you got lost on the road," I said. "Tell her you were out looking for the home of a friend . . . going to a dinner or the like. A poker game."

"I won't even be that specific. I'm in need of some direction. I've lost my way."

"Yes, and haven't we all, Winston." Carnihan hopped back up to his feet. "Now haven't we just about all."

The house was up on stilts—brick pilings, actually, each about three feet square—and this gave Carnihan and me just enough room to slide under the porch and hide in the dirt and monkey grass. There were discarded paint cans and lard buckets to compete with for space, and it was a wonder Bethany didn't hear us for all the noise we made. The old man stood at the foot of the steps slicking his hair down with his hands. When he reckoned himself presentable, he whispered, "Start timing me now, boys," and bounded up the steps, striding across the boards with so much weight and fury that dust came raining down on Carnihan and me. It was practically impossible not to cough, but I managed with the help of Carnihan, who whispered a reminder of what was on the line: "Five million dollars, brother. Five million . . ." I saw the figure in my head, the run of zeros trailing the lonely digit. It was lovely.

Bethany opened the door only as far as the chain lock allowed. "Yes sir?" Just like that: *"Yes sir?"*

I strained to see through a crack in the boards. The old man seemed immense from this perspective.

"I think I've lost my way. I apologize for disturbing you at such an hour."

"That's all right. I was just in the kitchen."

There was light on him, and plenty of it. Why didn't she say something, see him for who he was? I checked my watch. Not fifteen seconds had gone by.

"Do you have something on the stove, ma'am? 'Cause if you're cooking I wouldn't want to—"

"Oh, no. It's cooked. I wasn't that hungry anyway. Mainly it's for my mother."

The old man reset his feet and the boards groaned and more dust fell. I took the stuff in the mouth this time. "Well, I was wondering if I might use your telephone."

She was long in answering, and I thought that maybe it had come to her. "I don't think so, mister. Nothing against you personally, but I don't think it'd be very smart."

The old man didn't say anything.

"They raped a girl in the camp two down from this one back when I was in high school."

The old man put his hands in his pants. He shook his head as if he either couldn't stand or believe the thought.

"We could hear her screaming but we thought it was just another party. They scream a lot at their parties, those down that way. People don't know how to hold their liquor anymore."

"Well, they never really did, did they? It's not only nowadays that's a problem."

She considered this, and seemed to give the remark a profundity it didn't deserve. "Every so often," Bethany said, "a body turns up in the water, floating on its belly. They think they can dump it in the swamp and it'll stay put, but a body never does. I saw one once. Dumb me, I thought it was one of those floats you blow up on the beach . . . one of those rafts everybody likes? It was traveling about half a mile an hour, so slow, right about thirty yards from the bank. I've never been in that water again, and I never will, either."

"I'm just a traveler," the old man said, "who's lost his way on the road. I never killed anyone or raped a woman, and I don't intend to start tonight." He backpedaled toward the steps. "You're right it ain't very smart to answer your door to a stranger, and a man at that. Men aren't to be trusted. Your mama and whoever, they taught you right, ma'am, absolutely right."

He was completely off the porch now, standing in the weeds. And I could see Bethany cleanly through the crack, one half of her face in shadow, the other bright with an electric splash of yellow. She was still wearing her Monster Mart uniform—the stretch jeans, the white shirt, the smock with the oval patch showing the face of Rayford Holly.

"Is that beans you cooked?" The old man inhaled deeply, smelling the air. "Beans with a touch of cayenne pepper and small chunks of pork fat for flavor."

"You got a sharp nose, mister. An intelligent nose."

"Well . . ." The old man slapped his hands together and started up the drive to the top of the levee. He was taking it slow because he knew what I knew: he'd hooked her hard and fast and any moment now she'd call him back with permission to use the phone and probably to eat whatever he desired. The old man had seduced Carnihan and me and he'd seduced Silas Poe and now he was seducing Bethany Bixler. I thought of the birds he liked to hunt, of the bobwhite quail, and how you crept up on them, careful not to make much noise, and then shot them before they could figure out what you'd come for. I looked at my watch, moving the face to catch some light. Only two minutes had gone by, but already I knew there was no hope, not for Carnihan anyway. In my head the number five and the run of zeros started to blink and sputter like a neon sign going out. Finally everything went dark except for a few thin traces of gas making their way around the tubes.

I tried to think of a name to replace Hometown Family Goods. All things taken together, Hometown Family Fools sounded appropriate, and I made a mental note to bring it up with Carnihan as soon as we got out from under the house.

"Hey, where is it you're going?"

"What's that?"

"I said, where is it you're going?"

I wanted to turn and crane my neck and see his reaction, but any movement now would give us away. I imagined him turning slowly enough to show that he didn't have the strength to walk back and chase after her even if his intention was to violate.

"Where? Well, that's a long story, ma'am. Too long."

He was so clever, this guy. He knew the moves, every one. He'd started back up the road again, I figured, but she wouldn't let him go very far. She couldn't.

"Just so it isn't long-distance! Or if it is, just as long as you reverse the charges!"

Suddenly I felt sorry for Bethany Bixler. I knew she was a good person and meant to do right, but I also knew that someone so vulnerable would only be hurt in the end.

"What time is it?" the old man said. He was up on the porch now, and Bethany was unfastening the lock. "I got here, what? . . . four, five minutes ago?"

She glanced back at a clock on the wall. "It's about four after eight. You got here at eight."

"Tell me when it's eight-ten, will you, ma'am?"

"You turn into a pumpkin then or what?" And she shoved the door closed behind him, keeping me from hearing his reply.

Carnihan and I scrambled out from under the house and perched ourselves at the window to watch. There wasn't much to see but the two of them talking. Since he hadn't attacked yet, she probably figured he wasn't inclined to. He'd have tried something by now . . . as soon as she opened the door. They shook hands, his reaching out first, hers coming with some hesitation. He shuffled his feet like a bashful child with a burning urge to pee and she pointed to the telephone. He walked past her and she said something and he stopped and patted his stomach. She was offering him a plate of food. He shook his head and shrugged his skinny shoulders, he didn't want to inconvenience her. She shook her head, of course it wouldn't be an inconvenience! She wouldn't've offered if it were any trouble! They both laughed, relieved for some reason, and he trailed after her to the kitchen. Bethany had her back turned to him now; he wheeled around, faced the window, and stuck his tongue out.

"Why that sonofabitch," Carnihan grumbled.

We duckwalked over to the next window, where Bethany was introducing him to her mother. She hesitated, not having gotten his name. "Winston," his lips said.

"Mama, this is Mr. Winston," said hers. You could hear some of it. "Mr. Winston is lost on the road, Mama." The woman's tongue moved, her fat, wet eyes traced an uneven path across the ceiling. "I'm feeding him some supper, Mama."

The old man was standing at the foot of the bed with his hands folded together in front of him. It was a posture of supplication, I thought. Or defeat. Or deep, unfathomable sorrow. His head was down as if it hurt him to look at what lay in front of him. He said something, the words a whisper, sounding less like a question than an answer. Bethany's face seemed to grow darker. She nodded sadly. "Alzheimer's," she replied. "You know what that is, Winston?"

He walked over to the corner and sat on a metal chair. A wash of color came to his face and left again, that quickly. He shook his head and started to speak. "My wife . . ." He was stuttering. "My darling, my loving, my . . ."

Since he was so close, no more than ten feet away, I could hear him through the glass, the words heavy, weighted down; he seemed to be pushing them up through mud. I knew he was being honest, that this of all things was true. When he couldn't finish, Bethany gave him her hand. He took it and she pulled him up to his feet and led him away.

Not much had happened, but suddenly I felt as though I had a fix on the old man, or at least understood him better. He was alone in the world as we are all alone and even twenty-eight billion dollars hadn't been able to save him from that.

"Are you fooling with me, Winston?" Bethany was saying now. "Have you really heard it before?"

"Sure, I've heard it. I once had a friend named Eulaine. And we called her Lanie, too."

"Please don't do this to me. It isn't fair."

"Wonderful girl, this Eulaine was. Just wonderful. Used to like to dance, I recall. Saturday nights we'd go to this club called the Satin. She'd dance until her legs failed or the band stopped, whichever came first. I'd've married her but she fell for some other boy. Big boy. Name of Hennisey."

"Your Eulaine liked to dance? Why, I like to dance!" Bethany brought a hand up to her face and lightly touched her mouth. "Whatever happened to her, Winston? Have the two of you stayed in touch all these years?"

He was slow to answer. "We might've, but we couldn't."

"You couldn't? Why couldn't you, Winston?"

"She died. Eulaine died . . . now what year was that?" And he started fingering his chin, pondering the question.

"It wasn't 1969, was it?"

He lowered his hand to the tabletop, his face flushed with wonder. His smile had a tic to it. "Well, yes, it was. It most certainly was 1969. She died in the . . ." And he started rubbing his face again, searching for the answer.

"The spring? The spring of 'sixty-nine?" She reached over and grabbed his hand. "It wasn't April, was it, Winston?"

"Well, yes, now that I think about it, it was in the month of April my friend Eulaine died. How could you have known that?"

Bethany seemed on the verge of tears. She kept shaking her head and mumbling the word "April" under her breath. I wasn't much at reading lips, but this one was easy.

"Answer me, child. How could you know that?"

Bethany emerged from her trance and said, "Tell me the exact date of her death, Winston? The exact . . . the date?"

"I think it was . . . well, let me see here, Miss Lanie." He spent about thirty seconds trying to come up with the answer, and only now did it occur to me that he was stalling, chewing up time. Several minutes had lapsed since he knocked on the door, and she was so caught up in his subterfuge that she wouldn't recognize him now if he spelled his name out in rice and beans right there on the tabletop.

"Could it've been the tenth?" the old man asked, hesitating before speaking the date. When she didn't respond as he'd hoped, he said, "No, that wasn't it, that wasn't it at all. The tenth of April was when my Aunt Pearl Chessum died. I think it was the seventeenth, yep, it was the . . ." Bethany was beginning to look disappointed, and so the old man was forced to reconsider. "No, no, no. What am I thinking of? The seventeenth of April was when my folks were united in holy matrimony. It was . . . well, let me think. Oh, yes, it was the twenty-third—"

"The twenty-third?" Bethany leaped from her chair and placed her hands against either side of her head, covering the tops of her ears. She squeezed as if to keep something from spilling out.

"It was the twenty-third," the old man said. "I remember it like yesterday. Poor Eulaine. Having to die like that."

"I was born the twenty-fourth of April," she said. "The day after, Winston. The very one. Doesn't that strike you as odd?"

"One day one Eulaine dies," he answered, "the next day another

Eulaine is born. I'd say that's odd, all right, I'd say that's more than odd." Seeming bewildered, he put a hand to his chest to settle his beating heart. "Did I mention earlier how much you two look alike? Did I mention that? I might even venture to say you could pass as sisters . . . as twin sisters. When you opened your door to me tonight I thought, I said to myself, 'God, you've given her back to me.' I've been lonely, you understand."

"Do you believe in reincarnation, Winston?"

"The word sounds familiar."

"Well, then, let me tell you about it. . . ." And off she went describing the process.

The patch on her smock was no more than a foot from her eyeballs, and the real live Rayford Holly sat just across the table. And the bet was all but over.

"These beans," the old man said, cutting her off, "whatever is your recipe, if you don't mind sharing."

She stopped rambling and stared off into space.

"Miss Lanie?"

"Oh, Winston." She reached over and patted the top of his hand. "What on earth has come over me?" He lifted his head up from the plate of food, and she said, "It's how you season them is all, it's how us Cajuns do it. When you think you've put in too much red pepper, put in twice as much more and turn the fire up underneath. Mama . . . now Mama was the one. Mama could open a can of Spam and turn it into the best thing you ever put in your mouth. I so miss that about her: seeing her in the kitchen, how happy it made her. You know how some people walk around with a pocketknife or a rabbit's foot in their pocket? Mama'd walk around with this little shaker of red pepper, sprinkling it on whatever you put in front of her." Bethany started to pick at her own plate of beans. She was lifting a forkful to her mouth when she paused suddenly and said, "You aren't from here, are you, Winston? From Louisiana, I mean."

"I'm from Liberty, Arkansas, Miss Lanie."

"Liberty? How do I know Liberty?" She looked at her food, concentrating. You might've thought the answer was there on her plate, hiding beneath the slop. "Liberty! Why, Liberty's corporate headquarters for the place where I work!" She put her fork down and clapped her hands together. "Do you really live in Liberty, Winston? In Monster Mart's Liberty?"

"Lived there all my life," he answered, still eating. "Thought I wouldn't live anywhere else, but then I got this job. It's why I'm heading so far down south."

Carnihan was looking at his watch, studying the slow sweep of the second hand. Less than a minute remained before the time was up, but it seemed something was close to happening. If she recalled Liberty, perhaps she'd also remember the name of its most famous resident. The old man had mentioned Liberty to intensify things, I figured, and to show that as a gambler he could play it fast and loose even when victory was close at hand.

"I've never been out of the state of Louisiana," Bethany said. "Farthest north I ever got was Russell, about an hour from here. I almost went to Florida for my senior trip but Mama got really bad and I had to stay and look after her. She collapsed was what happened. I suppose I could've left her with the girl who comes to sit, but it's like I said at the time, Florida ain't going nowhere. I can always go later."

The old man stared outside the window. You couldn't tell what he was looking for, but he squinted as if to see better. Carnihan booted the face of his watch with a finger. "It's over, Pace. He won, he beat us."

He was starting to say something else when I grabbed him by the shirt and pulled him down to the ground. The old man was opening the window.

"What's wrong?" Bethany said. "Something there?"

"I thought I saw a Peeping Tom."

"A what . . . ?"

"I thought I saw someone."

Carnihan and I crawled back under the house, making such a racket that it was a miracle she didn't hear. On top of that, we'd left footprints in the sod next to the house, and our sweaty stink lingered, as well.

"If you're out there," the old man called, "you've got no class! You've got no class, do you hear?"

He spat a curse word and slammed the window shut, sending more dust upon us.

All told, the old man spent forty-five minutes in the house. He ate another plate of beans and bread and for dessert a soup bowl filled with ice cream and chocolate syrup. Their conversation covered religion, politics, popular romance novels, movies, movie stars, travel, family, and yet more details about the life and death of the first Eulaine, who, as it turned out, also had lived by a slow-moving body of water. Well, the old man actually said it was a lake, although, by the end of their visit, Bethany had converted it into a muddy bayou overrun with snakes and gators and the gnawed-upon bodies of murder victims.

They were walking toward the front of the house, passing through her mother's room, when Bethany remembered why the old man had stopped by in the first place. "Oh, the phone! You needed to make a call, didn't you, Winston?"

She led him to the living room.

"Too late to call anyone now," he said. "Maybe you can direct me." They moved out to the porch and stood at the top of the steps. Carnihan and I were still hiding, careful not to show any small part of ourselves.

"The town of Smoke is where I'm headed," the old man said.

"Smoke's just up ahead, Winston—on 190. You keep going till you hit this ramp and cloverleaf. Take it and drive to the Creswell Lane exit. That's pretty much the main drag these days. Rest of the town's good as dead. What is it you do, anyway?"

"I'm a short-order chef. A cook. That's why I was so curious about your bean recipe." He stepped down to the ground and turned back to face her. "Ever hear of a place called Hometown Family Goods? They've hired me on there."

"Hometown Family . . . ?"

"Goods. I'll be running their lunch counter."

She gazed off toward the highway, her face revealing nothing. I tried to recall whether we'd told her about the store that night at Babylon, and wondered if maybe it'd come up during that period of drunkenness which still was hugely unclear to me. "Hometown?" Bethany said. "Nope. Never heard of it."

"Well, that's what they used to call it. From what I understand, though, they're changing the name to something with a little more poetry in it . . . changing it soon." The old man tipped the brim of an imaginary hat. "Thank you for a lovely evening, Miss Lanie. I won't soon forget it."

"Maybe I'll come see you . . . over at the store?"

"Please do. My plates can always use a little extra spice." He started back up the levee. Bethany stayed outside until he'd reached the road, then she turned off the porch lights and the ones in the living room and headed to the back of the house. You could hear her walking, her steps heavier than when the old man had been inside. Her mother's bedroom window went black and so did the one in the kitchen. Music came from the radio, and with it a practiced shuffling that I recognized as the sound of her dancing alone.

VII

"I wish I had some rope. I'd tie you back up and never let you loose. To hell with hearing you apologize."

That was what Carnihan said as we started on our way toward Smoke, leaving behind the bayou and the swamp and a girl who'd just been shot through the heart and bagged like a bobwhite quail. Carnihan was furious, though with good reason, I reckoned. Rayford Holly had just shared a plate with Bethany Bixler and kissed the top of her delicate hand. He'd also won a bet that would've made Carnihan the richest man the town of Smoke had ever known, and now he was entitled to do what probably hurt Carnihan more than anything else: change the name of Hometown Family Goods to one with a touch of Arkansas poetry.

Although he had every reason to gloat, the old man to my surprise was extraordinarily gracious in victory—far more so than Carnihan would've been. He sat in the backseat with cartons of beer on either side of him, and he held his head back and let the wind rush over and whistle around him. He looked, from where I sat, like the two well-dressed fellows at Babylon who were privileged to witness the one reading of *Strange Weather* I'd ever given and would ever give. In fact, the more I studied the old man in my rectangle of glass the more I understood just how profoundly sexual his triumph was. For tonight at least he was endowed with the manliest set of credentials in the car, and also the only ones put to use of late.

"What about Fascinating Fashions, boys? Whaddaya'll think of that?" He held his hands up about a foot apart, helping us to imagine it in lights. "I like it. Yes. I like it a lot."

"Forget that," Carnihan said. He raised a fist and might've punched the dashboard had it not been the Mustang's.

I gave him a look that let him know he could hit the car, as long as he understood he'd have to walk the rest of the way home.

"I'm proof of how fascinating your fashions are," the old man said. "Just look at what I have on. Just look at this."

Maybe I was wrong about him not gloating. A nasty smirk had found his lips and it didn't seem inclined to leave.

"I absolutely refuse to call it Fascinating Fashions," Carnihan said. "We've been running low on clothes for the last twenty years, and besides . . ." He stopped short of completing the sentence and turned around in his seat to better see the old man. "It just isn't right, Winston. It just isn't."

"Right? Who cares about right? I'm interested in poetry, boy." The old man erupted with one of those snorts of laughter I knew I'd never get used to, not in a lifetime, and then he drummed his hands on Carnihan's headrest. He didn't drum hard, though, otherwise I'd've thrown him out, too.

"Do you boys dance?" the old man asked as we were closing in on Smoke. He'd folded his hands and was holding them behind his head. "Because if you do, I wouldn't mind tagging along—that is, if you can handle the competition."

"Sure, we dance," Carnihan said. "We dance like nobody you ever saw, me and Pace."

"Like nobody you ever saw," I mused, scratching my scalp. "Is that good or bad, Jay?"

"You'd never know it to look at me," the old man said in his dreamiest voice yet, "but I used to be quite a hoofer. Matter of fact, me and Louella won a trophy for it once—about six-foot tall, it was. That's ballroom dancing I'm talking about."

"This at the Satin?" Carnihan asked. "The place you took Eulaine, right?"

"Well, to be truthful, boys, there was no Eulaine. I said that to give the girl a lift. She needed it."

"You said it to stall," Carnihan said. "You were killing time, is what. You were manipulating her feelings for your own selfish desires. You used her, Winston."

"I'm afraid I did, son. But it was business, after all."

The old man could talk like nobody else. He was still talking when we got back to the store and Carnihan inserted himself behind the lunch counter and mixed a batch of Bloody Marys. He didn't stop until Carnihan put a drink in front of him and said, "Louella? What kind of name is that, anyway, Winston?"

"It's like Eulaine, son—a poetic one. A name for somebody with legs like they don't make anymore, and hair as soft as eiderdown, and a heart so big you wonder how it fits in her chest. A name for the ages, in other words."

As he spoke he stared down at his Bloody Mary with a defeated smile on his face, and I imagined him pulling the sheets back on some hospital bed and exposing her legs to a panel of fluorescent lights overhead. All the muscle was gone and the flesh was hanging loose and dry and patches of age spots showed around her knees and ankles. I imagined him breaking down at that sight: those legs they broke the mold for, those perfect ones, Louella's. And I liked him more than ever and wished we'd met under different circumstances.

"You really want to go dancing, Winston? I'll take you." Carnihan refilled the old man's glass. "But only if you give me an opportunity to redeem myself. I'm talking about the bet."

"You do like money, don't you, son?"

"This isn't about money, it's about Hometown Family Goods, or Fascinating Fashions, as you seem determined to call it. The truth is, sir, I like the name, the old one."

"Tell me what you've got in mind."

"I wager that somebody recognizes you. If they do, I keep my name. If they don't, then you can name your price. Anything." Carnihan took a sip of his drink and this, along with the thought of victory, brought a rusty gleam to his eyes. That gleam had been missing for a few hours now, and I thought how nice it was to see it again. "We went ten minutes at Bethany's, whaddaya say we go ten days on this one?"

"Ten?"

"After ten days if no one knows who you are, I hereby promise to do anything you like, whatever you decide. But if someone does know you, the name of the store stays as it is."

"Anything? I sincerely doubt you mean anything." But already the old man was extending his hand across the counter, waiting for Carnihan's.

"I don't have to decide what I want right now, do I, boy? I can wait until I win, can't I?"

"You can wait."

"Can I still work as your cook?"

"You can cook. As a matter of fact, I've got some deliveries scheduled for early tomorrow morning."

"Pancake mix?"

"Yeah, plenty of mix. Boxes and boxes of mix."

"Good," the old man said, toasting his own image in the mirror behind the counter. "I built my reputation on pancakes."

It was a little after 9 P.M. when they left for Babylon in the delivery truck. I was watching through the window of the X-ray lab as Carnihan braked suddenly and the old man jumped out and peeled the magnetic signs off the doors.

I left Dr. McDermott's and went into the store and strolled the aisles, memorizing names of medicines for ills which I hadn't known existed. Magic Mint was an artificially sweetened pill for "general and profound malaise," or so claimed the label on its glass jar. I nearly took one but decided that no medicine known to man could cure my problem. What I needed was a time machine to whisk me back a distance, and from what I could see in the dark of the store Mr.

Hank hadn't stocked any. As I scanned the crowded shelves the voices of Carnihan and the old man seemed to follow me, and I figured the only way to run them off was to welcome new ones. As best as I could recall, Miss Betty and Pop had pleasant voices which didn't require constant exercise: I returned the jar of Magic Mint to its rightful place and headed out in the Mustang.

It was bedtime at the house on Delmas Street, and my parents were wearing their nightclothes—"jammies," Miss Betty still called them. "Change to Rachel Wayne, baby," she was saying now, patting her hands together and waving Pop to action. "It's time for the news and time for you to get up off that floor. Put your cards away. Let's go, put them up. Come on, Pop. Pop? Fight's over, buster. Fight's over. Time for bed. . . ."

As Pop got off the floor he punched the remote control and Rachel Wayne came on, her slightly bloated and heavily made-up face reading from a stack of yellow paper. The lead story involved a peaceful gathering of farmers on the steps of the federal building on Union Street. The farmers were unhappy about the cost of living and they'd banded together as a show of "solidarity," just as certain Eastern Europeans were known to do. They might be nobodies from Smoke, Louisiana, one of the farmers was heard to say, but they intended to send a message to Washington. What impressed me most about the report was not their struggle to make ends meet but that all the farmers looked extraordinarily well-fed and several of them were sporting diamond-encrusted Rolex watches and pinkie rings. No doubt Pop registered the same. Lying in bed with Miss Betty, he issued a low whistle and said, "And I bet they all drive German cars and run half-million-dollar combines in their fields."

Miss Betty looked up from her knitting. "They do have it rough, don't they?" she said.

"And send their kids to private school." Pop whistled again. "Did you go to private school, Pace?"

"No sir. I went to public school."

"And did your old Pop stand his fat, bejeweled self on the steps of the federal courthouse and make a blubbering idiot of himself, talking about respect?"

"No sir, he didn't."

"Durn right, he didn't. Solidarity be damned. And may God bless the individual."

Watching TV on Delmas Street was always interesting. The spectators were often heard to speak to the television screen, and if the television screen gave the slightest suggestion of talking back, Pop raised his remote and changed the channel.

The second story was about the disappearance of Rayford Holly, America's richest man. Rachel read with perhaps too much enthusiasm but this was to be excused since the "eccentric billionaire," as she called him, had last been seen in southern Louisiana. According to a spokesperson with Monster Mart Inc., Holly missed appointments at three of his stores and had not been heard from in several days. Holly, from Liberty, Arkansas, was on his annual publicity junket in the southeastern United States. He had spent an hour at his store in Smoke and left after drinking coffee with the store's manager and a few selected employees and shoppers. The spokesperson refused to comment when asked if an official investigation had been initiated into his disappearance; a missing-person's report had been filed, however.

A boxed photograph of the old man flashed on the blue screen behind Rachel. Taken several years ago, it showed him wearing a tuxedo several sizes too big. His hair was swept back off the forehead and locked in place with oil, and his sideburns needed a trim. He had on a tie and granny glasses; and next to him stood a woman: his wife, Louella, I presumed. Her hair lay in a barbed pile on top of her head and she had a thick nose and chin and was a trifle jowly. Her eyes had been colored pink by the camera flash, as had the gaudy costume necklace she was wearing.

As a sidebar, Rachel reported that Monster Mart earnings had risen twenty-six percent in first-quarter sales. The company, America's largest retailer, had moved over twelve billion dollars in merchandise, up from nine billion. In light of the old man's disappearance, I questioned the timing of releasing this information, but then I reckoned HQ was just sending him a message: that even without him business was booming, and that, closer to the point, he had lots of new money to spend as soon as he got back home.

"Somebody's gonna get rich," Miss Betty said, not bothering to look up from her knitting.

"I doubt it," Pop said. "They'll catch whoever did this, they usually do. It's recovering the victim that's always hardest. Rayford Holly's probably dead in a ditch somewhere, poor man. When they find him it'll be long after the buzzards do."

"Now isn't that a nice thought?" Miss Betty said. She poked Pop playfully with her needles. "I'll have to dream about buzzards now. Why couldn't you have mentioned . . . I dunno, parakeets or lovebirds or something?"

"Parakeets, Mother? Never in my life have I seen a parakeet in the wilds of southern Louisiana. And, the day I do, I surely doubt it'll be dining on the flesh of a dead man, let alone a dead billionaire."

"I just hope they didn't torture him," Miss Betty said. "They do that, you know? They torture them with battery cables hooked up to automobile engines. I've read about it. They attach the metal grips to their—"

"Okay, okay," Pop said. "We can just about imagine."

I might've screamed in terror had their dialogue not struck me as deliriously funny. I imagined people all across the country having the same bedtime conversation. I imagined prayers being offered for the safety of America's richest man, who, if you listened to my mother, had already had his testicles electrocuted. I myself was about to ask God to intercede on his behalf when it occurred to me that the only torture Rayford Holly was being made to endure was at the hands of Anita the pimp. For all I knew he'd taken a room with an upside-down number on the door and was preparing to get his money's worth from none other than Genine Monteleone.

The humor I'd found in my parents' response to Rachel Wayne's report escaped me now and a spinning whiteness filled the space in front of my eyes. I rose carefully to my feet, made my proper farewells, and left the room. Pop followed me outside, the heels of his leather slippers padding the floor.

On the front porch we stood side by side gazing at the basketball goal awash with starlight.

"Too bad it's so late," he said. "We could shoot a game."

It seemed to me a wonderful idea. "Great. I'll run to the shed and get the ball."

"Whoa, there, son. It's almost ten-thirty at night, for heaven's sake." He seemed to have come awake at last. He gave me one of those penetrating gazes which somehow examine parts of your body you yourself have never seen. "You want to tell me what's wrong, son?"

"I'm just restless, is all. I was lying in bed at Dr. McDermott's and I couldn't sleep and so I decided to get up and come by and see how real people live."

"Real people go to bed at a real hour. Or a reasonable one. And they don't sweat as much as you seem to be doing."

I wasn't listening very attentively. I was still staring at the elegant form of the basketball goal and trying to recall what had brought me to this place. "I guess I just needed some action," I heard myself say.

"So you came to Delmas Street?"

"Let's do something, Pop."

"Do something? Okay. Let's do something, Pace. Let's call it a night." And he closed the door behind him. I stood out in the gloom and listened as he engaged the dead bolt and chain lock and started for bed, his slippers making music as he went.

They finally came back at three o'clock in the morning, as I was asleep and dreaming of Paris, a place I'd never seen except on such occasions. "Fascinating Hometown Fashions," I heard the old man say out in the lot. "Now that's poetry, boss . . . *poetry*!"

Carnihan had parked his little sewing machine of a truck next to the Dumpster, and they piled out of the front and back and marched in single file through Dr. McDermott's and into the store. They flipped the green lamps on and warmed the stove and started a radio full of music. They cooked up some grub and dirtied as many dishes as possible. They drank the Absolut and tomato juice and they ate every last celery stick, string bean, and lemon wedge on the cocktail tray. They danced ballroom-style across the store, bumping into shelves and seed racks and nail bins. Later I would learn that they made love, or that the dancing cowboy and the telephone lady did, there among the feminine napkins, just barely hidden from view. I could never dream of Paris without becoming sexually aroused, and so I needed a minute before leaving the X-ray lab and finding my way to them. Ostensibly I was there to tell Carnihan about Rachel Wayne's story, but the truth was I felt desperate to be a part of the festivities—and to see Genine again.

As it happened, I entered the store as the one in the group with whom I thought I might be in love was pressing her beautiful, full lips to the proffered forehead of the one with all the money, and I left before she removed them. They were standing on top of Ruby Dean's lunch counter, once a sacred place, and although I figured they had climbed up there to dance and to show off for the others, they were doing neither. I have seen pairs of lovers in crowds who are entirely oblivious to everyone else around them, and who seem to exist not in the actual, many-peopled world but in one they've designed and built and populated only with themselves. That was the state in which I discovered the old man and Genine, and that was why I didn't stick around.

I slept until half past seven in the morning, when the garbage truck bellied up to my window and commenced its hydraulic madness. I was in no rush getting dressed, and, to prove to myself that the absolute worst hadn't happened, I even put on fresh clothes. I pushed through the back curtain expecting to see the detritus of last night's carnival, but instead I discovered as orderly a scene as any Ruby Dean had ever inspired. Every stool was taken but one, and each of the diners was happily occupied with coffee, a breakfast plate, and a section of the morning *Lip*. For the most part they were the same bunch I'd joined on my first morning at the store—the regulars, back again after stints at the Palace and the Little Chef and their own kitchen nooks. A couple of delivery men were unloading hand trucks stacked with crates of cured and fresh meat, and outside more waited with egg cartons. I sat and examined the chalkboard, which in a rather uncertain hand announced a temporary outage of juice and suggested Tang as an alternative. YOU'LL LOVE IT! read the last line.

I had not had Tang in twenty years, and considered ordering a glass until it came to me that the stuff was probably that old, having sat all this time under cobwebs and insect dung, home to any and all microscopic organisms industrious enough to squeeze past the lid. The old man handed me a menu and wiped down my place. A package of generic cigarettes was twisted into the right sleeve of his T-shirt, absent the slightly crinkled one he'd lodged over an ear. He was wearing a white paper hat cut to resemble an overturned canoe, and a pair of reading glasses which magnified his eyes twice their normal size. You wouldn't think that a few stage props and a subservient attitude could successfully conceal his identity, but there people sat reading about the disappearance of America's richest man and not one of them connected the out-of-focus picture in the *Lip* with the fellow behind the counter mixing too-tart glasses of instant breakfast drink.

"Don't you ever get tired?" I asked him.

He shook his head. "Don't have time to."

I ordered a stack of pancakes and a cup of coffee. He reached for the wrong ear and came down with the cigarette instead of his pencil, and pretended to write my order with it. The two lady bank tellers sitting on either side of me shook with laughter. I wondered if he'd seduced them, too. The last time I'd seen faces as star-struck as theirs was about five hours earlier, when Genine was leaving tiny round prints from her high heels on the countertop.

"Where's Carnihan?" I asked, taking a sip of the coffee.

"He had some errands to run, said he'd be back in an hour or two. He had to drive everyone across town and then stop by Worm Road. Something about a dog and some goats?"

"Yep."

"Well, he went to feed them."

The pancake batter was in a tall plastic pitcher, and the old man poured from it now onto the grill, depositing four football-shaped cakes that sputtered against the flat black surface. The aroma, while being nice enough to bring a throbbing lump to my throat, fell short of doing what last night's dream of Paris had. I watched the old man tease the cakes with a spatula, lifting the corners to make sure they didn't burn.

"Your friend asked me to ask you a couple of things," the old man said, glancing back over his shoulder.

I nodded and smiled.

"Number one, to keep an eye on me while he's gone. And number two, to call and ask your mother if she wouldn't mind having us over for dinner sometime within the next couple of days. He mentioned barbecue. I told him it wasn't polite to invite yourself, let alone to dictate the meal you wanted served, but he insisted."

"The first part's easy. But the second . . . you're right about it being impolite. I'll have to think about it."

Silas Poe got up from his stool and moseyed over to the register, holding his bill and cash in one hand, the "A" section of the *Daily Lip* in the other. It was rare to see him reading a page other than sports, but at the moment he seemed transfixed by the lead story about the missing billionaire. My heartbeat quickened in anticipation of his most certain discovery, but, no, he turned the page and started reading something else. "I'll just leave this here," he said, balancing his payment on top of the register. "Many thanks for another delightful repast, Winston."

He removed some antacids from his pocket and, still reading, backed through the door and out into the street.

I sat feeling pissy toward the old man and wondering what had really happened last night. Had he told her who he was and promised a fortune for her affections? Although this seemed unlikely considering his desire to remain anonymous, I figured she'd taken to him about as well as everyone else had, especially so since, having been kicked around so much in her life, she was vulnerable to any kindness. I felt tortured and stupid, picturing Genine's parade of lovers, which now included the old man, and wondering whether he rated better than I.

I framed a picture of the two of them in bed together, and I put words in their mouths which in fact they wouldn't have dared to say. And by the time he served my pancakes I was ready to lay into him, to really punch him one. But then he topped the stack with spoons of creamy honey butter and half a can of cane syrup, and warmed my coffee with some from a fresh pot.

He was a kind old fart, I decided, a bit randy but kind. And I was embarrassed for letting my imagination run wild and for casting him in bed with as pure and fine a girl as Genine.

The heat had almost completely left my face when he took up my knife and fork and started to cut the pancakes up, making clever designs a perfect fit for your mouth, and pretty to look at, to boot. His hands completed their magic and I looked up at him. "I just got that one kiss," he said, "the one you saw."

"Oh? Which one was that?"

"I'm ashamed, Burdette, deeply ashamed. We drank too much, all of us . . . we just got carried away."

"Listen here, Winston, you don't have to explain anything to me. I've been there myself, I know how it goes."

"Been where?"

Since I couldn't rightly say, I didn't speak. After a minute he continued, "You've probably thought things—distasteful ones. I know the confusion. I've experienced it myself with Louella."

"I'm not Genine's keeper, Winston. I'm really no different from you, all right? Or from any other fellow she knows." I should've left it at that, but for some reason I was compelled to add, "We're just two of . . . I dunno, Winston—two of hundreds, I suppose. So there's not a thing for you to be ashamed of."

"God, you count high," he said. "Hundreds, has she?"

He speared some of the pancake and was holding the fork up for me to eat, waiting with the syrup dripping and painting the zinc. When I reached for the fork he pulled it away and held it just out of reach. "You don't know much, do you?" he said.

This came as a surprise, and I needed a moment to respond. "I think I know some things."

"I thought writers had to be smart. I thought they had to have been a few places and collected a few experiences. You can't just make things up, right? You've got to have lived them!"

I couldn't figure why he'd want to speak so loudly. Everyone was staring at him. He winked at the bank tellers and they laughed and daubed their lips with paper napkins.

"What you need . . ." he said, "you need to learn more about women. Not to be upsetting, son, but you don't seem to know the first thing about them. And you know nothing about love, either."

He gazed into the eyes of the bank tellers and spoke softly: "No love ever began between two people that wasn't a mistake. Love in the beginning is meant to be wrong."

At first they appeared to be taken off guard. But then they nodded in full agreement and started patting their mouths again. This seemed to be a universal truth, this business about love, and I seemed to be the only one who'd never heard it before. Did it make sense? I spent a long time trying to decide, knowing better than to ask him for an explanation.

"Do I need to spell it out for you?" he finally asked. He pressed his elbows against the counter and leaned forward, the forked pancake only inches from my mouth.

I considered slapping his hand away and sending the food flying, or else covering my ears and closing my eyes until the sound and sight of him went away. But I lingered too long and his voice came again. "Love can't be right, boy, not at the start. And do you know why it can't?" He waited until I shook my head. "Because love is the impossible thing we spend our lives trying to decide of. You know what else love is, Burdette?"

I tried to answer, but he cut me off.

"Love is a pancake," he said, then raised the fork to his mouth, opened wide, and filched what should've been my first bite of breakfast.

I looked at him for a minute, trying to stare him down. And when I could no longer bear the weight of his gaze I lurched for the empty fork. He stepped back and I clutched two full fists of air. He began to eat busily, moving the fat bolus from one side of his jaw to the other, making a big show. The women laughed and I laughed too lest I look like a fool. He finished eating and dropped the fork in my plate and returned to the clutter of sausage he had frying on the grill. He was saying the word "Love" over and over, softly, as to annoy. "Love is a woman," he was saying. "Love is a bed. Love is a road. . . ."

I didn't dare to look at the two captivated bank tellers, nor at anything but my stack of pancakes cut to resemble a tic-tac-toe grid. Blood burned the width and breadth of my heart, and, like Carnihan, I wished we'd never let him out of the ropes.

As the old man was removing the sausages and placing them on a platter covered with paper towel, Silas Poe pushed back through the door and walked over to the register. He'd bought a copy of the *New*

Orleans Times Picayune, and he was reading something on the front page: another account about Rayford Holly's disappearance.

"More coffee?" the old man called.

Silas grunted and shook his head. He was too busy speeding through the newspaper story, his lips moving over every word. He paused briefly and mumbled, "Just some Tums, please," then he set his mouth in motion again.

The old man came over and took a roll of antacids from the candy tray. "My mistake," he said. "Next time I'll have to remember to go easy on the Tabasco."

Silas blinked a few times and finally looked up from his paper. "Blasphemy, Winston." He tore the Tums open and popped half a dozen in his mouth, then he staggered out the door, still reading closely. As he crossed Market Street, he paid so little attention to where he was going that he barely avoided the path of a truck speeding past.

"What about you, ladies? Get you something?" The old man was talking to the bank tellers, and they both pointed somewhat timidly to the plate loaded high with crispy black sausage wheels. The old man gave them each a few and, for good measure, added scoops of scrambled eggs. If that wasn't enough, he deposited sugar-glazed doughnuts on their plates, and peppermints wrapped in cellophane.

"Remember us to your friends," he said. "Remember Hometown."

I sat in silence as the women ate and drank and, leaning way back on their stools, spoke around me.

"We're late," one said.

The other checked her watch and gave a sigh. "Oh, my!" she muttered, taking some money from her purse and placing it beside her flatware.

"Remember us," the old man said again. "To your friends."

They paid at the register and walked out together, taking the same path Silas had and stealing occasional glances back at the old man. I watched them until they disappeared among the trees and statues of the square, the blue and green of their uniforms blending in with the colors of the garden.

"First you made them laugh," I told the old man when he came to retrieve his tip, "and then they talked to each other."

He shrugged and counted his coins.

"Those two women haven't given each other the time of day for as long as I've known them."

He put the change in his apron pocket and started collecting dirty dishes in a plastic tub. "Is that something else I should apologize for?" he asked.

He was wiping a glass with a dishrag, scrubbing it, making it shine like it probably hadn't in years. "I keep thinking about your situation, Burdette. And I've figured something out. I know what your problem is. You're too close-minded, is it. That's what's wrong. And I also know the reason. It's really rather simple. You haven't lived enough."

"I've lived plenty."

"No, son, you haven't. You haven't lived at all."

"For your information, Winston, I happen to have lived in the nation's capital for four years. Did you know that? I wrote for one of the best newspapers in the country, covering the police beat. I saw everything you can ever hope to see."

"That's right. You saw it. You didn't live it, though. You saw it and then you sat down at your desk and wrote about it." He started cleaning another glass. "If that's living, boy, I'd rather choose dying."

"Can I have my check, please?"

He didn't answer, and I let the conversation die. I just wanted him to shut up and leave me alone. I took a bite of the pancake but found that I could neither chew nor swallow it.

"If something isn't right, Burdette, then it's wrong."

"I'm not listening anymore, Winston."

"And you know what they say to do when something's wrong."

What felt like an eternity went by and he still failed to provide an answer. Unable to take it any longer, I lowered a fist to the counter. "Okay, then, Winston. Speak to me. What do they say to do when something's wrong?"

I was waiting for him to hoot and laugh at me again, or maybe eat more pancake and come with another moronic declamation about love. Instead he leaned in close and covered my clenched fist with his hand. "You fix it," he said.

For the last few minutes people had been waiting at the register, and of a sudden the old man became aware of them. He limped over to the other end of the counter and went to work checking them out. After ringing one up, he said, "Remember us to your friends." And to the next: "Remember Hometown."

It was true that he was the richest man in America, but he was no good counting change. He was slow and he fumbled with the coins in the money tray. His thick, blunt hands, his fingers like pipe, weren't right for the job, and it took him about ten minutes to clear everybody out.

As he was finishing up, Carnihan came through the door with Beatnik trailing close behind. It had been days since I'd last seen the mutt, and I was happy to find him looking so well. "Oh, Beatnik," I called, patting my hands together. "How are you, boy! How are you!"

I anticipated a grand reunion. But, wouldn't you know, he looked at me for only a second before scrambling behind the counter and leaping into Rayford Holly's outstretched arms.

That was the beginning of one of those romances the bards used to write sonnets about: quilled pens to parchment paper in the glow of burning whale oil. While it had occurred to me that Carnihan might unconsciously be clinging to the old man as a surrogate father, I never imagined that Beatnik might be in need of filling a similar void. I felt a little silly applying pop psychology to the behavior of a dog, but Mr. Hank had always boasted of Beatnik's superior intelligence and this worked for me as additional proof of that: Beatnik had rejected a person who was so uneasy with canines that he washed his hands after petting them, and embraced another whose appreciation of them was such that he found beauty in the sound of their tails swatting at flies. Beatnik had grown a lot since the day we rescued him from mad Missy's duffel bag. His coat of hair, thick and shiny now, had responded well to life on the farm, and his color blue was richer than ever. Seeing him again made me lonesome for Mr. Hank, and I found myself slipping into the kind of funk that can ruin a day if not addressed promptly.

"Let's go to Babylon," I said, surprised by my own enthusiasm.

"They're not even open yet," Carnihan said. "It's only ten in the morning."

I'd revealed more of myself than I would've liked, and, to try to cover up, I pointed to the clock on the wall as if just now discovering the time. "Yeah, you're right. I don't know what I'm thinking of."

"Whatever it's of," the old man said from behind the counter, "it's finally starting to make some sense." He reached over and tapped my shoulder, harder than seemed appropriate. "You fix it, boy," he said.

Carnihan sat next to me and watched as I devoured more breakfast. Since the counter had emptied the air seemed lighter and sweeter to breathe, maybe because I no longer had to worry about someone like Silas discovering who the old man was. You could tell, though, that the old man didn't like the quiet. He was holding Beatnik in his arms, watching the door with sad-eyed longing. He seemed to be willing it to open and more hungry callers to make their way to his counter.

"We've got to do better," he said.

A funny smile came to Carnihan's face and it stayed there a minute, twitching at the corners. Finally he said, "Whaddaya mean *we*, kemosabe?"

"I mean Hometown," the old man answered. "We've got to get more people in here. We've got to pick things up."

Carnihan eased off his stool and started walking among the shelves. He kept his hands folded behind his back and he held his head on his shoulders in a somewhat professorial air. "I don't mean to question your loyalty," he said, "but you have to admit, it is kind of strange hearing you talk about this place as if it were your own, while across town the doors to your Monster Mart have been open for only about an hour and already you've done more business than we've seen in years."

"Must be that syndrome he was telling you about," I said. "That Swedish one."

"Well, it'd better be," Carnihan said. "Because otherwise I'd wonder if I was finally getting through to him."

He picked up a copy of the *Lip* and scanned the front page. There was a photograph of the old man spread above the fold, the same one that had appeared last night on Rachel Wayne's news show. It was in black and white, however, and you couldn't see the pink of Louella's eyes and jewels. "One thing you were right about," Carnihan said, "is how nervous your hired hands get." He lowered the paper and stared at the old man. "My God, Winston, how do you stand them?"

The old man didn't say anything.

"You should've let him call," I said. "I meant to tell you last night, but with the party going on and all. . . ."

"Yeah, well, we'd heard about it, anyway," Carnihan said. "They were talking about it at Babylon. Or Anita was. Apparently Sorel had told her about this reward for information leading to his whereabouts. A hundred grand, she was saying. She was even planning how to spend it. And there we were, right in front of the whole entire world, chugging g and t's."

"Why don't we just let him call, Jay?"

"Because he hasn't apologized. And it's too late now, anyway." He handed the paper to the old man. "Are you sorry, Winston? Are you sorry for what you've done?"

The old man was quiet. He pulled an arm out from under Beatnik and took the paper, studying the picture, particularly that side with the fuzzy image of his wife.

"When he's sorry he can call," Carnihan said. "As long as he's not sorry nobody knows where he is." He'd resumed his rather studied air and was walking back and forth again, his feet heavy on the wood. "You know what's strange to me, Winston? It's strange to me you're not more concerned about your devoted servants up at HQ. I don't understand how you can let them worry like that when there's not a thing wrong with you."

"I pay them to worry," he said.

"Yeah, but they're losing sleep thinking you're dead or worse, and you're down here drinking gin and sweet-talking young women about one-third your age."

"I'd call, I'd be happy to call. But you're not gonna get an apology out of me."

"All their heartache fretting over you, Winston, it's not worth an apology to some little storekeeper everybody knows ain't worth a damn? You really must help me out with this, partner. I don't get it."

"I shouldn't be blamed for your intellectual inadequacies as well as your business ones. Look to your parents, boy."

Carnihan kept pacing the floor, his eyes tracing the decorative plates of the ceiling. "If I didn't know better," he said, "I'd wonder what's at your heart, Winston. You're always doling out advice, befriending everyone, providing answers to questions no one else has ever had a clue about. And yet, to your own people, you don't have a thing to say—not a word. It doesn't matter to you how scared they are, as long as you don't have to say I'm sorry."

"I owe you nothing. I didn't even know your name until you ran me off the road."

"You knew me, Winston. You knew me and all the others like me, and you knew Smoke and every town like it. You started this—by yourself, you did. . . ."

A dusty, late-morning quiet fell over the room, punctuated every few seconds when Beatnik exhaled in his sleep or grunted at the bite of a flea. We sat watching the light pour through the screen door and waiting for a body to fill it. Finally Bethany Bixler came gliding in, her face and hair aglow with the dappled gold sunlight flooding behind her. She entered with a smile that didn't wear long, that vanished the moment she saw Carnihan and me. "Oh," she said. Nothing else.

The old man, by now, had straggled out to receive her. He held her forearm as you might a rare piece of china. He didn't drop it. And he looked relieved when she reached the counter without falling to the floor and breaking.

She sat down and ordered a cherry Coke. "Isn't that what everybody gets at a soda fountain like this? A cherry Co-Cola?"

"Not really, Bethany," Carnihan replied. "Or at least not in my experience, they don't."

Her head gave a little hitch, as if stung, but she didn't look at him.

"Do you two know each other?" the old man asked. He was staring at Carnihan, a bemused expression on his face. I had to hand it to him: he was on top of his game. "If you two know each other, then how come he just called you Bethany, Miss Lanie?"

"Bethany's another name I sometimes go by, Winston."

"Miss Lanie?" Carnihan asked, offering a bemused expression of his own. "But why would he call you that?"

I was impressed. Carnihan was proving to be as fine an actor as the old man. He stood there waiting for an answer, and in his eyes you could see even more questions than those he'd just posed. The next one was: "Are you and Winston business associates from Babylon?" And after that: "Did you run out on him the way you ran out on me?" And thirdly: "Were your different names part of the package or does a fellow have to pay extra for that?"

"Winston and I met last night," she explained. "He was lost on the road and looking for directions. He came by my door."

"She pointed me toward Smoke," the old man said.

"Earlier you referred to us as a soda fountain," Carnihan said. "But we're not that, Bethany. We're a lunch counter, for your information." This came so unexpectedly that none of us could respond before he started up again. "We don't pretend to be a thing of the past and our meals aren't about nostalgia. They're for hungry people looking to set a spell and enjoy a plate of hot, delicious food." He thought for a moment longer and added, "What we do, we give them good value at a reasonable price."

Not that I'd ever wondered about the aim of Hometown's counter, but I liked Carnihan's description. It was so corny that it reminded me of something Mr. Hank might've come up with.

Bethany, on the other hand, seemed to be straining to make sense of him. "Oh," she said again. Just that: *"Oh."*

"We're fresh out of cherry Coke," the old man suddenly remembered. He pointed to the chalkboard. "We do have plenty of Tang, though. You ever have Tang, my darling?"

She shook her head.

"It's what all the astronauts used to drink," Carnihan explained. "I seem to remember a TV commercial. They're sitting all together in their spacesuits, each of them holding one of those bubble helmets with the vacuum hoses hanging down. And then there's this jar of Tang on a little table in front of them. They're happy about that Tang . . . happy to be alive during a time when such a thing is available."

Bethany said, "Water will be fine, thank you, Winston."

"Born a few years earlier," Carnihan continued, "and they'd be stuck drinking plain old orange juice. What kind of world was it when there wasn't Tang around? I'll tell you what kind, Bethany: a primitive one. A world where no one could get to the moon, that's for sure. A world, better stated, without meaning."

The old man poured her a glass from the sink. She drank it down in a noisy gulp, and I marveled at what an engineering miracle is a neck. It connects the head with the rest of the body and conceals all the unsightly scaffolding, wires, and tubing. On the one hand it is perfectly utilitarian, and on the other so fine and fragile a thing as to take your breath away. Or so was Bethany Bixler's this morning.

"Water's free," Carnihan said. "I mean to say, there's no charge for it." He glanced up at the four giant pictures on the wall. "I'm the last of them, you know?"

Bethany turned briefly to the pictures. Her eyes trembled, and I worried that she was wondering about the profound coincidence of her friend the lost cook working at Carnihan's store. I waited for her to make the connection. But she said, "All right. Give me a Tang, then."

The old man hopped to it, and Bethany swiveled in her seat and glanced up at Carnihan; you could see she had no clue.

"Is there a charge for Tang?" she asked. "Or does it cost the same as your water?"

Carnihan seemed to balloon with confidence: his chest blew up and a satisfied grin fanned across his face. "Winston," he said. "Fix the lady what she wants. And make it a double."

"Right-o," the old man replied, heaping more orange powder into a glass.

In all she must've had a dozen Tangs. She didn't say much, but then she wasn't given a chance to, not with Carnihan detailing the history of Hometown Family Goods. She heard tales which were news to me and which I suspected to be bald-faced lies. The one about Henry Carnihan haunting the place, for example. I knew that was pure baloney. As was the one about the time JFK came in with Marilyn Monroe and had grilled cheese sandwiches at the counter.

"You should write this down," Carnihan told me at one point. "This stuff is priceless."

"Oh," I answered. "Let me run and get a pen."

Word of the new cook had spread around town, and by noon people who usually ate at the Palace and the Little Chef or who brown-bagged lunch were competing with the regulars for seats at the counter. "We remembered you to our friends," a few of them said as they entered the store. And one, a woman I couldn't name, was heard to say, "How could we forget?"

I don't mean to exaggerate the crowd, but it was nearly twice that of any Ruby Dean ever served. By a quarter after all but maybe three seats were taken, and you could see people walking along Market Street, heading our way. "Would you like to eat something?" Carnihan said to Bethany.

"I'm too full of Tang."

"Winston's specialty is pancakes. They come in all shapes and sizes but the normal ones, and they're from a mix. But I promise they won't disappoint."

She shook her head. "No, thanks."

"Then, if you wouldn't mind . . ." He paused and looked out the window. "Me and Winston could use that stool you're on."

He was trying to be polite, but Bethany took it as an invitation to leave. "I was just on my way," she said, reaching for her handbag and keys. "Sorry to have been such a nuisance."

He held a hand up, stopping her. "Please. I didn't mean it like that. Honest I didn't."

From the stove where he was frying eggs, the old man said, "Stick around, Miss Lanie. You might experience something you'll be ashamed of later. Why, the day's still young yet." And he made his eyebrows dance.

"I don't know," she said. "It's my only day off work all week. And I've got some errands to run."

"Stay," Carnihan said. He made a steeple of his hands and held them high as if in prayer. "I'm begging you."

Two city workers in muddy boots came crashing through the door, dictating orders even before they were seated. One wanted coffee, the other a hamburger plate. "Follow me," Carnihan said, then led us to the far side of the store. With his apron he wiped some empty shelf space and told us to wait there until later.

"How long is later?" Bethany asked.

"This long," he answered, and showed her with two fingers, holding them about an inch apart.

I offered Carnihan my help, but he shook his head and explained that he and Winston could handle it. "We're pros," he said. Bethany was studying some odd thing she'd picked up off the shelf, and missed seeing him mouth the words: "Guard her, brother. Don't let her leave."

Although deliveries had started up again, several items on order still wouldn't be available for a few more days. Salad dressing, for example, was in such short supply that Carnihan and the old man had to mix mayonnaise and ketchup; and all sandwiches featured either biscuits or English muffins, since there was no bread. In fact, much of the food they ended up serving barely resembled what had been asked for. No one complained, though. When people weren't reading the *Lip* or gossiping, they were being regaled by the new cook with the matchstick in his mouth.

"You know what love is?" I heard him ask one young lawyer who was being particularly surly.

The fellow answered no, and the old man proceeded to list anything that came to mind, including Tang breakfast drink.

Everyone had a good laugh, but then the lawyer said, "Is love a pain in the ass, mister?"

"There and a few other places," came the reply. "Now get the hell out of my store."

The old man dragged the lawyer by his fancy, striped suspenders all the way to the street, a smattering of cheers and applause lifting in the background.

Genine arrived at twelve-thirty. She was wearing faded, knee-torn jeans and a tie-dyed T-shirt such as the kind favored by hippies twenty years before; her shoes were leather sandals with peace signs on top. Some of the customers were staring at her for how she was dressed, others for what she was, but Genine didn't seem to mind. I, on the other hand, resented their curious gazes, and it was hard to keep from yelling at them. "Leave her alone and eat your stupid food!" I wanted to say, uncertain myself why I should take on the role of her defender.

"Hey, isn't that Genny?" Bethany said. "Genny from Babylon? Wow, isn't she pretty in the daytime?"

Ever mindful of last night, I'd wondered how Genine and the old man would react to each other when they got together again, but except for his booming hello and her slippery little wink there really was nothing for me to get excited about.

"Tang!" Carnihan called to her, pointing at an empty pitcher. "Make some Tang, baby."

"Tang?"

And off he went talking about astronauts and spacesuits and a world without meaning.

Genine gave everyone refills and started moving dirty dishes to the sink. By now the old man had every kind of meat you can imagine frying on the grill, and a cage of french fries sputtering in a vat of grease, and an ice cream shake spinning in the mixer. His performance was both comic and horrendous, and I was only happy that it wasn't my lunch he was serving.

"I've got a few questions for you, Pace," Bethany said. "I was hoping you might answer them, and be honest."

"I'll do my best."

She turned from the old man and settled her eyes on me. "How long has Rayford Holly been working here?" She shot a thumb in his direction. "That is Rayford Holly, isn't it?"

My heart leapt into my throat and lodged there, and for a time I was unable to breathe. I considered exploding with a great storm of laughter and bombarding her with denials; but she had me and she knew she had me. And I had no choice but to confess and get it over with.

"How'd you guess?" I muttered at last.

"No guess. I knew last night when he came to the door."

"You couldn't have."

"Of course I could've. But what I couldn't figure was what he was doing there."

I tried to respond, but she promptly cut me off. "I suppose that's why I called him back in and offered to let him use the phone. You don't think I'd open my door to a total stranger, do you? I was curious, I admit, I couldn't believe it was him." She poked my ribs with a finger. "Did you hear, by chance, all that crap I fed him about reincarnation?"

"I heard it."

"Don't believe a word of it. Or that I believe a word of it. That kind of talk is for suckers, Pace, and a sucker is one thing I ain't. I was just trying to play him along, to find out why in God's creation he picked my door to knock on. And then I saw you and your weird friend at the window." She paused and sighed at length. "I still don't know what he wanted with me, or why on earth he was out running around with the likes of you."

"Is that a question?"

She poked me again. "Just give it to me straight."

"Carnihan kidnapped him," I said. "He blames the old man for the trouble the town's in, and he wanted him to apologize. The old man refused. We offered to let him leave, but then he refused to do that, too."

Her eyes were wide and unblinking, shifting left and right. She seemed to be trying to decide whether to believe me.

"We went to your house because they had a bet. Carnihan said you'd recognize him, and the old man said you wouldn't."

"Well, I did."

"But not in ten minutes, you didn't. The way it worked, if you recognized him by then, Carnihan won five million dollars. If you didn't, the old man got to change the name of the store."

"But I did recognize him, I knew who he was the moment he came on the porch. It wouldn't have been any easier had the president of the United States come asking for directions."

"Well, maybe you did know him, but you didn't say anything. You had ten minutes to put the finger on him." I glanced over at the counter. "Fascinating Hometown Fashions, the old man wants to call it. And I suppose that it will be."

She needed a minute to digest all this. "Now may I ask you a few more questions?"

"Shoot."

"Why does he keep spying on me?" And this time she pointed at Carnihan. My heart began hopping around again and I couldn't answer right away. "Not that it upsets me so much . . . well, let me take that back. I don't particularly enjoy it when he follows me to the bathroom and watches me sitting on the toilet. I can't imagine what pleasure he could possibly get from that."

In that moment I found myself embarrassed to be associated with such a person as Jay Carnihan—a Peeping Tom, no less, and one who . . . well, I didn't want to think about it.

"I'm really sorry, Bethany."

"And that's another thing, Pace. Why do you two insist on calling me Bethany? You know it's not my name. That first night when you and your friend followed me to the house I let you know who Bethany was, and Rupert, too."

"Why do you keep calling him my friend? You've been doing that since we sat down here. Why don't you call him by his name? It's Carnihan, in case you forgot."

"I haven't forgotten," she answered. "And in case you did, I'm the one asking the questions here."

We were engaged in one of those staring contests which pits one person's will against another's, and which a coward like myself could never hope to win without resorting to face-making at his opponent. Not being in the mood for faces, I blinked a few times and cast my eyes downward, ashamed to have been beaten so easily. "Shall we call you Eulaine?" I asked. "Or do you really prefer Lanie?"

"I dislike them both, but I suspect for Rayford Holly's sake I should be one or the other. He might not understand when everyone but him keeps calling me Bethany."

"Yeah, but he won't say anything about it. He's the one who's got everyone calling him Winston, remember?"

This time when she went to poke me I slid back and she stabbed only air. "By the way," she said, "I die in the end. Were you there for that?"

"There for what?"

"Bethany and Rupert. They get shot trying to escape from the police. Everything that can go wrong, does."

"Oh, the book . . . the one you were reading to your mother?"

"It didn't upset me. It was only right they go out that way. They were rebels, and a rebel, if he's true to his guns, expects nothing less."

We stayed there a while longer watching Carnihan spread mustard and ketchup over biscuit halves. I asked myself whether he was a rebel and answered that of course he was. I then wondered whether being true to your guns meant being true to yourself, and I decided that it did. Lastly, I tried to figure why a rebel should expect a violent death, and whether one like Rupert's awaited Carnihan. I thought I knew the answer, but then decided there was no point to living the story when you already knew the ending, especially if it was bad. Also, Bethany Bixler wasn't even twenty years old yet, and what did she know about anything?

"He's in love with you," I said.

She gave a knowing smile. She didn't seem completely enamored of the idea, but neither did it seem to bother her much. "I think he's dangerous," she said.

"Are you going to turn us in?"

She folded her arms and placed them on top of her knees, then rested her head on the bridge. "I suppose I should," she said. "God knows I could use the reward money. But, I tell you, Pace, even more than money I'm in need of a little excitement right about now. My life has become a tragic bore."

This was the last thing I'd expected to hear her say, and I was unable to fashion a response.

"When I'm not at Monster Mart, I'm at home looking after Mama. You saw all those books in the house? The reason I read so much . . . well, cable TV hasn't reached our end of the swamp yet, and the antenna up on the roof's no good. These days a paperback novel is about as close as I ever get to anything halfway warm." She laughed again and strands of hair fell in her face. "I just thought of something. That time I was stacking mouthwash . . ."

"You saw me then, too?"

"How couldn't I? You walked right by my ladder." She straightened up and ran a hand along either side of her face, hooking her hair with her thumbs and pulling it back.

"Why don't we make a deal?" she said. "I'll go ahead and tell them the truth about myself, or as much of the truth as I care to.

What I won't divulge is the fact that I know who the new cook is. In return I expect something from you: you can't tell anyone I know, either . . . you've got to keep it a secret."

I couldn't understand what she stood to gain from such an agreement. Why would she choose to spare the brief and unspectacular relationship she'd built with Carnihan and me and sacrifice the reward money? A hundred grand could take a girl in her situation a long way—off the bayou, to start. I was about to ask her what her intentions were, when Bethany came up with the answer herself: "Maybe it's why I decided to try the go-go back when I did. Maybe I'd like to live dangerous, too. And there's another thing. It's not every day a river rat from Bayou Blanc gets to help kidnap the richest man in America."

I stared at her for a minute, holding her eyes with mine. "You're not like most women, are you, Bethany?"

She pretended to be surprised, and poked me again, this time in the ribs. "No, Pace, I'm not. But that might be due to the fact that I'm still just a girl."

I figured the best way for everyone to catch up was over coffee, and as soon as the lunch crowd cleared I ordered a complimentary round and led Bethany back to the counter. Genine leaned over and kissed her cheek, careful not to leave a print, and just as careful not to show that she was surprised to see her there. "You're looking well, kid."

"You, too, Gen. You're looking divine. Truly."

The word brought a smile to Carnihan's lips, and he placed some cream and packets of Sweet'n Low next to Bethany's cup. "So tell me. How's your friend Rupert? Ever find him?"

Her answer started with a simple "No," then careened into a long essay covering the last several weeks. While failing to mention her job at Monster Mart, she did say that she'd quit the one at Babylon because she'd suddenly been hit with a bout of guilt which she attributed to her strict Roman Catholic upbringing. She lowered her head and gave it a shake. "Now that we're on the subject, I've got a confession to make."

We waited, no one speaking a word. And then she apologized for having misrepresented herself and came clean with details which no one questioned for the solemnity of her delivery. One worth noting involved her father, a womanizing drunkard, who drowned in Bayou Blanc about ten years ago. According to Bethany, he had been diving for a stash of liquor her mother had tossed out in the deep water. "It was Daddy's drowned body that kept me from ever going back for a swim in that bayou again," she said to the old man. "It wasn't just anybody's."

Everyone was too overcome to speak—everyone but Carnihan, that is. He waved me in close and pressed his mouth against my ear. "Why don't you tell her about those floaters you used to see up in Washington, Pace?"

I reeled backward and glared at him.

"Might make her feel better," he said.

Next Bethany talked about her mother, who'd been bedridden for two years now, and who went through nightgowns like babies through diapers. Bethany had come to Smoke today looking for a dress shop she seemed to remember from years ago. She'd wanted to buy her mother something pretty, and to smell what she called the "city air as opposed to what we get down by the water." She'd driven the downtown streets scanning the storefronts, wondering where the place had disappeared to. Just as she was about to call it a day she found an empty building with a family of naked dummies in the show windows. The name of the business had been stripped off the facade, but a grimy shadow could still be seen on the brick. O'HARA'S, it said. She was starting to leave the area when she spotted the sign for Hometown Family Goods and thought she'd come in and wish Winston good luck on his first day at work.

"Know what happened to O'Hara's?" she asked Carnihan now. "Used to be very popular, if I remember right."

"Closed down about four years ago," he said, picking at the remains of one of the old man's mystery sandwiches. "You recall how the Ice Age is supposed to have killed off all the dinosaurs? Well, we got the same thing here . . . right here in Smoke."

"You've got an ice age in Smoke?"

He swallowed hard so as to be more clear this time. "Monster Mart," he said. "It's freezing everybody out."

"And that reminds me of something else I need to confess," Bethany said. She sat up in her chair and started swinging her legs from side to side. "I happen to work there—at Monster Mart. I'm in charge of the Personal Hygiene department."

Carnihan knew this, of course, but it was necessary that he pretend not to. A band of muscles tightened in his jaw, and he put his sandwich down. "Personal Hygiene?" he said. "Now isn't that the perfect place for a filthy little tramp like yourself." His answer sounded so rehearsed that I figured he'd scripted it long before, in anticipation of this moment. "I think the living you might've earned at Babylon," he continued, "was far more honest than the one Rayford Holly pays you."

"Rayford Holly?" she said. "What does Rayford—"

"Rayford Holly, my dear, is a pimp worse than Anita Billedeaux ever was, I tell you that. And sometimes I think he's more corrupting. It might not be young girls he's selling for money, but it's something just as real and just as important to the fabric of this society."

"My God, man," I said. "What kind of crazy talk is that? The fabric of this society? What the hell's the fabric of this society? And what would you know about it?"

"It's the soul of the town," Carnihan answered. "It's the real, invisible, inviolate thing that makes it run—that's what he's selling off, the pimp."

"Best watch your tongue there, boy," the old man said. "After all, this is America's best friend you're talking about. Haven't you ever seen those big balloons out in front of his stores? 'America's best friend.' That's what's written across his chest. They wouldn't go and make that up, would they?"

"Winston," Carnihan said, pointing a finger, "I hired you to cook, all right, not to defend that town-killing S.O.B."

In a moment of shocking clarity it came to me that Carnihan wasn't talking about the Rayford Holly behind the lunch counter, but about the one he'd conjured in his head and turned to whenever he needed to unload his store of righteous fury. The big bad boogeyman was the person he meant, a creature who walked in eternal night, looking for dreams to steal. It also struck me how lucky Carnihan was to have someone like the old man to blame for his failures. We all need enemies, I reckoned, since without them we have no one to dislike but ourselves. Until now I'd never really considered what might happen to Carnihan if ever the old man did apologize. Without Rayford Holly and Monster Mart to hate, would he still love his store and his town? And without that love and hate together, what might his life mean?

"I tried to get on at Monster Mart," Genine said. "But I wasn't as fortunate as you, Bethany."

The old man lifted his face to her, his eyes dark and wounded. He blinked a few times and started making lines on the zinc with a sponge.

"I wore the best clothes in my closet, and I had my hair done. I went down to talk to the manager but his secretary said he was in an important business meeting at the moment. I could see him, though, through a crack in the door. He was making guns of rubber bands and shooting them at a wastebasket. Every time one went in he'd yell 'Twooo!' and throw his arms up high in the air. His secretary gave me a job application and I filled it out. Know what I put for previous employment? I wrote 'hostess,' and then scratched it out. Through the door the man kept shooting rubber bands, and I knew I had no chance at that job. 'Prostitute,' I wrote. And I even spelled it right. For references I listed the names of all the men I'd ever gone to bed with, or at least of those I could remember. Can't tell you how many I had down there. It was a lot, though. I needed a long time to remember them all. When I used that one sheet of paper up, I filled the back side."

"Anyone like some coffee?" asked the old man, his voice tight and brittle. "Coffee?"

No one said anything.

"They didn't hire me. The girl took my application in to the manager and he came out and looked me up and down. 'Oh, I know Wilbur Dejean,' he said, and pointed to a name on my list. 'Trace Wyble, him too.' They'd advertised for positions, but now he was claiming to be overstaffed. Next day they hired a couple of people I know. I think it's what they tell people they don't want—that they're overstaffed. They figure it'll spare your feelings. But it hurt mine. I'd rather have gotten the truth."

The old man's head rocked back as if struck, and then he lowered it to the countertop. "The truth?" he whispered. "What is the truth, Genny?"

She seemed to give it a lot of thought. "The truth? The truth is that no matter how I dress I'm still me underneath. And that while Monster Mart might appreciate my honesty on its application form, no cheap whore name of Monteleone will ever work there as long as that fellow is in charge."

"Hey, Winston," Carnihan said, and slapped him hard on the back. "What do you think of America's best friend now?"

I figured I'd better do something to lighten things up. Included in the morning deliveries were a bottle of Absolut and a basket of hothouse tomatoes, and although it was still early yet, I decided that a round of Bloody Marys was just what we needed to kill the gloom. I lined the ingredients on the countertop and began to hum the melody from "Oklahoma," the title song of the old Shirley Jones musical, and to swing my hips and bob my shoulders in the manner of one of those characters who so enjoys his life he can't help but raise a tune about it. Instead of using the original lyrics, I invented some of my own, and even as I sang I was pulverizing half a dozen tomatoes in a bowl, the juice blood-red against the white ceramic. "Poor old Smokie," I sang, "where mosquitoes come sucking out your brains . . ." My voice was lousy and loud, but my performance succeeded in picking everybody up. Although I'd rarely felt so creative, so engorged with words and ideas, I nonetheless began to peter out after only a few minutes, and to look to the girls for help. Finally Genine came to my rescue, singing, "Poor old Hometown, where the pancakes come cheaper than the shame . . ." Carnihan added a drumbeat, pounding his hands against the counter, and Bethany and the old man started dancing across the floor in the ballroom style for which he claimed to have won a trophy.

"Why don't you join them?" Carnihan asked me above the noise and his own uneven drumming.

"Why don't you?" I shot back.

"That's a good question. Why don't I?" And off he went spinning down an aisle, dancing badly and alone.

I finished mixing the Bloody Marys just as the song-and-dance session was ending. But Bethany turned out to be the only one in the mood for a drink. The others claimed to be hung over from last night and did little more than stare disinterestedly at the line of overflowing tumblers I'd placed on the counter. With the pulp of the fresh tomatoes the drink better resembled an ice cream shake than a cocktail, and since no straws were handy I used a spoon to help get mine down. At first I was disappointed when none but Bethany agreed to join me, but then I was grateful since that meant I could go for seconds.

Bethany seemed to like the stuff as much as I did, attacking it like the defending champion in a chug-a-lug contest, and one determined to keep her crown.

That was the only batch of Bloody Marys I was to make that day, but it provided a buzz unlike any I'd ever enjoyed. For the first time in a long time—since coming back to Smoke, as a matter of fact—I really felt as if the old magic had returned, which is to say I wanted to write. But before retreating to Dr. McDermott's, I decided to try my luck with Genine again. I was uncertain as to how to begin, so I chose to keep it simple. "How are you, Gen?" I asked after too long a time.

"Fine, Pace. How are you?"

"I was thinking we should do something sometime. We should go to a movie or drive to Warren and have dinner."

"What's wrong with here in town?"

"We could do that, but I thought the change of scenery might do us both some good."

She stretched an arm across the counter and leaned her head on it. "I don't think so, Pace."

"Well, let's have dinner here in Smoke, then."

Her eyes were flat and empty, staring off into space. "No, I don't think so," she said again.

"What do you mean by that, Gen? What do you mean, you don't think so?"

"I'll give you a hint. It has nothing to do with driving anywhere or going to a restaurant or eating food."

"So then you're saying it's me . . . that you don't want to go out with me?" When she didn't answer, I said, "Can I come by your house sometime? Would you mind that?"

"I'd prefer you didn't."

"What about the go-go? Can I see you there?"

"No, Pace."

"So it's over between us?"

She raised her hands and reached over and clutched me by the throat, pretending to strangle me. "Quit torturing yourself," she said. "Please. Do us both a favor."

What hurt was that she meant it. Had she been playing coy, teasing me into a plea to spend time with her, I might've thought there was a chance. But it was true: she didn't want me.

"You keep forgetting something, Pace. You keep forgetting who I am, who I was, who I always will be. And as long as you're forgetting I'm remembering, you understand? So stop it. Please."

She pushed by me without another word and walked to the end of the counter. Somebody had turned the radio on, a pretty Cajun ballad called "Jolie Blonde" was playing; and Genine and the old man started dancing across the floor again. He was showing top form, his feet skimming the floor, and she was equal to him, laughing through all the turns. While it was true that the style didn't quite fit the music, it was a beautiful thing to watch.

Once as they whisked by, the old man threw his head back and roared, "Just like at the Satin, Burdette."

I was surprised that I didn't feel worse than I did—about Genine, anyway. I wondered whether it had to do with the words I kept hearing, the ones in my heart and head and arms and fingers. Did I value work above love? Was writing a nice, clean sentence better than being with a woman? Maybe this was a sign of maturity, I thought, of growing up finally. Maybe this was what Pop had meant when, as a coach, he'd told us boys to put our lives in perspective, to "prioritize."

"Jolie Blonde" was almost over when I slipped away and headed for Dr. McDermott's, prioritizing as I went. I walked on tiptoes until I cleared the curtain, then half ran through the stockroom and back to the office. I was in too big a hurry to flip my computer on and wait for the system to boot up, so I sat on the floor with a No. 2 lead pencil and an ancient tablet of Big Chief writing paper. The only light came from the hallway, a cool orange glow. I wet the point of the pencil with my tongue and wrote the first sentence of what I believed would be the best damned story ever told.

"Where I come from," I wrote, "you hear a lot of stories—some of them actually true."

VIII

Pop was famous for his barbecued chicken, or so he liked to tell everyone. While most folks claim that the secret to great grilled meat begins with the sauce, Pop believed it started way before that: with the pit.

His had begun its life as a single-door Amana refrigerator. When, in that form, it had blown a compressor and needed more repair work than was feasible, it was delivered to a salvage yard and dumped atop a pile of similar heavy refuse. That was where Pop, accompanied by a shop teacher from Smoke High, discovered it one fateful day and hauled it to a place which I liked to think rivaled even Dr. Frankenstein's lab. This was the welding room in the basement of our school, and it was where Mr. Ferdie Zerangue and several of his more industrious students converted the thing into a first-class barbecue oven.

This was what they did: they put legs on its back and gave it a pair of wheels and cut a hole in the door for a smokestack and another in its side for a vent. They removed its lifeless mound of electrical hardware and, in its place, fashioned a cabinet for storing charcoal, lighter fluid, and cooking utensils, and then they took out the shelves inside, leaving the body empty except for the braces they'd added to support the grill. Finally they put it in the back of Mr. Ferdie's pickup and drove it to Delmas Street. They rolled it onto the back patio and situated it in the far left corner, where it would not move for twenty years, and where tonight Pop was barbecuing two dozen chicken halves and as many links of smoked pork sausage. He was cooking for his wife, who was stuck in the kitchen making pork 'n' beans and potato salad, and for his two daughters and their families, and for his son and his son's two friends, one of whom happened to be a septuagenarian know-it-all named Winston.

"Why's a refrigerator cook so well?" Pop asked, repeating the question posed by the know-it-all.

He was standing with a long fork in one hand, a bowl of homemade barbecue sauce in the other. Deep lines creased his forehead, a sure sign of his mounting impatience. "The answer," he said at last, "is insulation. Or it is as far as I can tell. The walls are padded with the stuff, about four inches' worth. It traps the heat."

The old man, bent over, was looking at the bed of coals through the side vent. "So the same general principle that kept cold in now keeps the heat? That's ingenious."

"I'd say it's smart, all right," Pop replied.

"This teaches us a lesson," the old man said. He stood erect and waited until he had everyone's attention. "This teaches us that even that which has been discarded still is of some good."

Pop let on an uncertain smile. "I suppose a person, trying hard, could come to that."

"Also, one man's trash is another man's treasure. And this, I just thought of this one . . . our second life is often our most fruitful. While one party finds our productive value diminished, another finds it ready to be explored anew."

Having just met him, Pop wasn't used to the old man's way of crushing you beneath his high-minded notions. "Why, that's really something, Winston," he said, flipping the chicken. "You've gone and found things in a barbecue that most folks don't find looking up at the stars."

"I look, is why. I let myself."

"Then let yourself take a break," Carnihan said. "You've got my head spinning crazy damn wild again."

Pop removed a link of crispy pork sausage from the fire and gave it to Beatnik, who ran off with it to the base of the pecan tree. An electric ridge of hair traced along his back and a growl came from deep in his chest. The barbecue had turned Beatnik into a primal beast, and Pop watched with immense satisfaction. Never had he received a better compliment.

Except for the presence of Hometown's new cook, it was a barbecue like any other our family had enjoyed over the years. Stuart and Jesse, my sisters' husbands, sat nearby on pieces of patio furniture, nursing beers that long ago had turned warm in their hands. Through a back window you could see Abigail and Claire sorting silverware in a big wooden box as they prepared to set the table. The kids were outside playing on a swing set, arguing about whose turn it was on the slide and making faces at poor Mrs. Kuel as she watered her lawn next door. Birds cut lazy circles in the sky overhead, and noisy bumblebees the size of golf balls mined the white ligustrum blossoms.

A week had passed since news of the old man's disappearance had gone public, and no one had come forward with ransom demands or reliable information leading to his recovery. According to reports in the *Lip,* the FBI and local law enforcement agencies were mystified, though no more so than Monster Mart Inc., several of whose higher-ups had appeared on national television news programs, evading almost all questions except those concerning recent company profits. On a radio talk show a terrorism expert theorized that Rayford Holly most likely had been whisked out of Louisiana and into a neighboring state, since the probe which had focused on Acadiana had not borne fruit and it was improbable that even the best-prepared kidnapper could escape such scrutiny. This report had aired just yesterday, as Carnihan, the old man, and I were driving to Bellard's

Poultry & Crawfish to pick up Pop's order for the barbecue. We had listened as attentively as we had to all the other news stories, curious about the many anonymous sources, amused by the hyperbole, and, at times, so caught up in the drama that it seemed to be happening to someone else. Later Sheriff Sorel had been featured on Rachel Wayne's show, detailing how he and his men were busy combing the area. I'd been particularly skeptical of this report since at Babylon two nights before Sorel himself had told Carnihan that the sheriff's department wasn't doing much but patrolling the streets a little slower than usual and checking any abandoned houses within their jurisdiction, and that a pair of special agents with the FBI's New Orleans Division had blown through town so quickly he'd wondered whether he should pull them over for speeding. "All we've uncovered are scads of your so-called homeless people," the sheriff had said. "No billionaires." Like all the other experts, he'd seemed to think that Rayford Holly was long gone from southern Louisiana, if not from this world.

Of all the senses, the old man had said this afternoon, the one of sight was least trustworthy, and he had proved this to be true as soon as we reached Delmas Street, the blind Burnette family serving as an example. I wasn't proud of myself for being talked into getting Miss Betty and Pop to throw the picnic, but of my many sins of late this seemed a lesser one. And, besides, I'd had a craving for Pop's chicken for many weeks now. Obeying the demands of my stomach had always been more compelling than obeying those of my conscience. "Eat first, contemplate life in prison later" now seemed a fairly sensible rule to live by.

The table in the dining room didn't have enough chairs to seat everyone, so Miss Betty asked for volunteers to sit at the dinette set in the kitchen. Those who did would get an extra helping of dessert, she promised, and today that meant strawberry shortcake. The children raised their hands and hollered "Me, me, me!" and ran to claim seats in the other room. Only eight chairs were available, and there were nine adults.

"Pace, baby . . . ?" Miss Betty said.

My feelings were hurt, and I protruded my lower lip to show just how much. I wanted to protest the old man's place at the table, but I reckoned Miss Betty wouldn't permit such bad taste in her home. Kidnapped or not, Winston was her guest, and he would be treated as such.

"Oh, honey . . ." she said to me now, looking wounded herself.

To show my discontent, I served myself more food than I could eat in a week, covering two whole plates and part of a third. I took my assigned seat in the kitchen and noted with a heavy heart that the children were not pleased to see me. They were discussing a Nintendo game called Super Mario Brothers, and paused only to ask why I wasn't with the grown-ups.

"I like it better with you guys," I said, flashing a smile. "You're my favorite people in the whole world. And I'm you're favorite uncle."

"You're our only uncle," Abigail's son Brad said.

Little Jillianne was tapping me on the arm, trying to get my attention. "Hey, Pacie. Hey, Pacie."

"It's Uncle Burnette to you, young lady."

"Hey, Uncle Burnette. Mama says you have a girlfriend. Mama says it's a . . ." Unable to recall the word, she turned to her brother for help. "Ryan? Remember what Mama said?"

Ryan glared at her, his eyes beady saucers of disapproval. Apparently this was one of those family secrets meant to be kept at home. I didn't want to put the boy on the spot, but I was fairly desperate to hear the answer.

"A barmaid? Hey, Jillianne. Is it a barmaid your mother said was my girlfriend? Or did she say 'hostess'?"

Ryan was trying to kick her under the table. His first shot missed and he booted his cousin Marshall. "Stop that!" Marshall cried. "Mama, Ryan's kicking me!"

I put a finger to my lips, then wagged it remonstratively at each of them. "Behave."

"Don't say it," Ryan warned his sister. "Daddy said it's a bad word. It isn't nice to say bad words."

"But we'll forgive her this one," I whispered. "And who has to know anyway? Nobody but us." I patted him on the head to show what a swell kid he was and that we were fellow conspirators, free to speak whatever indecencies we chose. He was not, however, ready to surrender yet.

"For your strawberries," he said. "The shortcake."

"Oh, no. Just wait one second there, buster—"

"Jilly," he said, cutting me off. "Don't tell him, Jilly. You say it and I'll tell Mama."

I knew that Jillianne would rather have died than offend her mother, and I also knew I didn't stand a chance unless I was willing to sacrifice dessert. "This is bloody ridiculous," I said to Ryan, who sat there grinning broadly, certain of his victory. "Okay," I told him, "you get my strawberry shortcake."

"Floozie," he said, kicking his feet again.

"Mama!" Marshall called. "Ryan's doing it again."

"Floozie?" I muttered. "Did you say floozie?"

"Stop it, Ryan," Claire called. "Pace, will you make Ryan stop it, please? If he's kicking . . ."

Ryan and I were staring at each other, in yet another of those contests I could never hope to win. Although he was just a kid, it was obvious from the outset that his will was stronger than mine. "Do you want me to spank him for you, Claire?" I called. She didn't answer, and I whispered to him, "You don't know what a floozie is, little boy. You should never say words unless you know what they mean."

He was holding a drumstick in his fist, gnawing on it. "Floozie means a lady who does nasty things. She doesn't have to be pretty."

"What does being pretty have to do with it?"

He shrugged and Jillianne laughed. "Ryan," she said, her admiration for him so deep that she might've suffocated beneath it. "Ryan said a bad word. Ryan said—" And she clasped her hands over her mouth to keep from uttering the profanity.

"Did your mother say my girlfriend wasn't pretty, Ryan? Is that what she said?" I reached over to pat his head again, but instead I found myself clutching his shoulder, trying to shake the answer out of him. "She said Genine was ugly, didn't she?"

"Mama!" Jillianne called. "Uncle Burnette is being mean to Ryan, Mama! Come make him stop!"

A rinse of tears filled Ryan's eyes and I came to my senses and pulled my hand away. "Sorry, buddy."

He sniffled and rubbed his nose against his shoulder. "Mama said that too . . . that you were wrong."

"Oh, she did, did she?"

Both he and Jillianne nodded. "About the floozie," he said. "She thinks you're making a big mistake."

Marshall and Brad had returned to their discussion about the Super Mario Brothers, and now that I'd been disposed of, Ryan and Jillianne joined them, describing their own difficulties with the game. Above their lively chatter I could hear the adults talking in the next room: Miss Betty was telling the story about the first time Carnihan and I met, and she was stuck on the part about how Darned Dizzy Deenie got her name. She'd exhausted her list of possible medical reasons to explain the fainting spell, when the old man interrupted. "Ever think she was pregnant?"

A long pause ensued, then Carnihan's voice came in a nervous stutter, louder than it had been all night: "Whaddaya mean, maybe she was pregnant? Maybe she was a lot of things, Winston." No one said anything, and his voice came again: "Maybe she hadn't eaten that day. She was a thin girl, you know—skinny, by most standards. Maybe she was bulimic . . . maybe . . ." He fell silent. "Why would she be pregnant, old man?"

"It just popped in my head."

"Well, pop it right out," Carnihan told him. "My father married a virgin, do you understand? A virgin! They consummated their marriage in an infirmary on the beach in Biloxi after she'd been stung by jellyfish." Except for silverware dinking against ceramic plates, the silence was complete now. Someone cleared her throat—Miss Betty, I think it was.

"Plus," Carnihan said, "if she was having her period—"

"Can we move on?" Pop asked. "Winston, you're a cook. What do you think of my barbecue?"

"Well, I can see why you're famous for it."

"Is it even possible, if she was having her period . . . ?"

"No!" Abigail and Claire cried at once.

"Winston," I heard my father say, "pass the barbecue sauce, please. My breast here's in need of a little pick-me-up."

After the tables were cleared we ate dessert in the living room, or, rather, everyone else did. I told Miss Betty that I had no room left for shortcake and promptly turned my share over to Ryan. I was tempted to confront his parents about this floozie business, but Carnihan's outburst had already drawn a cloud over the party and I didn't think it could survive another. On top of that, such an objection was out of line since Genine Monteleone wasn't even my girl to defend. In another hour it would all be over, I told myself, starting to feel pangs of guilt. Miss Betty and Pop had opened their home up to a stranger and prepared a feast in his honor, and although they seemed to like him, I couldn't get past the feeling that I'd pulled a fast one on them. Weeks from now, when this entire kidnapping ordeal was over, I'd confess to them that the barbecue was just another test to see whether Rayford Holly could get away without being recognized, and not one designed to test their patience.

We were all gathered in the living room, watching the kids play Nintendo on the television set, when Miss Betty raised a finger to each of her temples and clamped her eyes shut. "Girls," she said to my sisters, "would it upset you terribly if I asked the children to turn that off?"

"Why, no, Mother," Claire said, flushed with embarrassment.

"It's the noise. We don't want to give Winston a headache."

"Oh, don't worry about me," the old man said. He was still eating strawberries—his third serving.

"Mother, I'm sorry," Claire said. She looked over at the kids. "Okay, gang, that's enough for tonight. You can play when we get home." But this produced hardly a groan.

The four of them, huddled around the TV, were staring up into its colorful blinking face as if at a beatific vision.

"Kids!" Abigail said. "Turn it off, *now*!"

This time when the children failed to respond, Abigail and Claire hurried over to the set and started pulling them away. Miss Betty and Pop, being used to this, looked on with blank faces, while their guest of honor watched with bug-eyed fascination. The old man seemed to be as awed by the picture before him as the children had been by the one of the Super Mario Brothers. "Little ones," he mumbled. "I never had any myself."

"Forgive us," Stuart told the old man.

"Forgive nothing."

"I beg your pardon?"

"Regrets," the old man said. "They deny the moment when we were most ourselves. They seek to make us what we are not." He smiled at Stuart, then, facing Carnihan, turned his mouth into a nasty frown. "Those four kids could kick me in the groin, each of them, and I still wouldn't expect an apology."

By the way everyone was staring at him, the old man might've just confessed a pedophilic passion for new unblemished flesh. The children had stopped fussing, as had their parents, and the only sound came from the television set, an electronic music. "Winston likes to quote from the writings of Walt Whitman," I said. "The poet."

"And from those of himself," he said.

"Oh, was that one of yours?" It was Miss Betty. She went to get his dessert plate. "It sounds so familiar."

"That's the mark of fine writing," the old man declared, choosing to mock me now. "It's the ability to make that which is strange to our experience seem as though we ourselves have actually lived it."

"That's funny," Carnihan said, "I always thought it was never finishing a sentence with a preposition. Just goes to show how much I know."

One of the girls switched the Nintendo game off, and the image of Rachel Wayne flashed on the screen. She was standing in front of the jailhouse in downtown Smoke with a microphone in hand, the graphic at the bottom of the picture pulsing with the words LIVE and EYEWITNESS NEWSCAM. Behind her in the upper distance you could see inmates in orange coveralls staring down through grids of black prison bars. I was trying to hear what she was saying when Carnihan, wheeling around to look at me, said, "I think they got him."

"Who's that?" Pop asked.

Carnihan sucked in a great blast of air, then noisily exhaled it. "The guy who kidnapped Rayford Holly."

Abigail turned the volume up, and we all listened in silence as Rachel Wayne described the arrest of longtime Smoke resident and businessman Silas Poe, who, according to a source close to the investigation, was the mastermind behind a plot to extort ten million dollars from Monster Mart Inc. in exchange for the safe and immediate return of the corporation's billionaire founder, Rayford Holly. As Rachel spoke, providing only sketchy, inconclusive details, Sheriff Sorel and several men could be seen in the background walking toward the entrance, leading Silas in handcuffs. One of the men was wearing a windbreaker with U.S. MARSHAL printed in block letters across the back.

Silas's head was covered with a raincoat, concealing his face from the camera, but you could tell who it was by the way he carried himself. Silas Poe had a way of punching the air with his knees, and of listing off course, rather like a snowy egret trudging through a muddy patch of rousseau grass.

"He was my best customer," the old man said from the couch, his voice thick with sorrow. "He put Tabasco on everything. Just this morning I fed him some pancakes, and before he added butter and syrup he had hot sauce splashed all over them."

Pop kept shaking his head, lost as to a clue. "He's been a friend to all of us for a long time. I've known him practically all my life—since grade school."

"Poor Silas," Miss Betty said. "Poor man."

Rachel Wayne's report ended and Pop walked across the room and turned the set off. "I can't believe she was talking about the same man," he said as he began to pace the floor, eyes focused on the ground. He stopped momentarily, as if remembering something, and searched the room for Carnihan. "This is tragic. This is terrible, isn't it, Jay?"

"Yes sir, it is."

"Why, he was like a brother to your daddy. He loved him." Pop glanced briefly at the dark TV screen. "What on earth could have motivated him to do such a thing?"

"Someone should call Ruby Dean," Carnihan said.

"Did she give any more details?" Jesse asked. "Did Rachel Wayne, I mean?" Abigail had joined him on the BarcaLounger and was sitting on his lap, her arms draped over his shoulders. "I didn't hear whether they recovered Rayford Holly."

"She said they hadn't yet," Stuart said. "But that doesn't surprise me. Rayford Holly . . . well, he's probably—"

"Dead somewhere in a ditch," the old man said, finishing the thought. "Or hanging from a rope in a barn. Tomorrow morning when we wake up it'll be in all the papers, complete with pictures."

"Silas Poe wouldn't hurt a flea," Miss Betty said. "He's as kind and gentle and decent a man as I know. Except for that one right there and Hank Carnihan, and maybe for you, Winston, I can say I never knew a better one."

The old man fitted his gaze on Carnihan and me, although his words were directed elsewhere. "Never let the behavior of even those closest to you surprise you, Miss Betty."

"But Silas . . . Silas Poe? I hardly think—"

"Not even your own children," the old man said. He rose from his seat and gave her his hand. "Thank you for a wonderful dinner. You didn't tell me if you were famous for your potato salad, but God knows you should be."

Shaking my father's hand, he said, "And you, Mike. Had you the inclination to share your secrets, it wouldn't surprise me to see you on your own Saturday afternoon cooking show. 'The Barbecue Hour,' I envision it being called."

" 'The Barbecue Hour'?"

"And today's show features Chef Michael Burdette and his one-of-a-kind Amana oven cooking . . . *brisket*!"

For a moment, at least, Pop seemed to forget the news of Silas's arrest. "We really enjoyed having you in our home, Winston. Please come again."

It was a cloudy night and heavy rains were forecast, but when we got outside Carnihan insisted that we put the Mustang's top down and get some air. He was jumpy and kept running his hands through his hair. Maybe, like me, he was seeing Silas in a suit of orange clothes, his face pressed to a window of iron bars. I knew we had to do something, but I could think of no possibilities that did not include our coming forward about what had really happened.

However much I wished it weren't the case, our adventure seemed to be over.

"I can tell what you're thinking," Carnihan said as we drove across town. "And I admit, I've been thinking the same. But nothing we can do can change what Silas has done. His mistake is separate and apart from ours."

The old man let go a wild, violent shriek of laughter, stopping only when I asked him to. "My head hurts," I said. "Would you mind saving that for later . . . like when Jay and I get arrested and put away?"

"And another thing," Carnihan said. "Silas may've been a loyal customer, but he's turned out to be a looter. He was trying to capitalize on our effort, and for that he should be punished."

"Why would he do it?" I asked.

But neither of them answered. They were staring up at the courthouse square, where television crews were burning portable klieg lights under the trees and reporters were speaking into cameras with views of the Delta and the jailhouse. For every crew there was a van with a station's call lettering scripted across the side and antennae and satellite dishes sticking up from the roof. I didn't count the number of vehicles parked along Market Street, but Smoke's largest automobile dealership didn't keep half as many on its lot.

I drove along without slowing, the air white and hot with electric light, the murmur of all those words being spoken coming like a song. Carnihan sat up on top of his seat and waved at the battery of cameras, and the old man, clutching Beatnik close to his chest, did the same. They waved their arms with the torpid indifference of beauty queens. The smart thing would've been to reach back and pull the old man down to the floor, to hide him from the world, but I no longer cared how many people saw him. The way was clear to me now. Come morning we'd have to help Silas, and that meant turning ourselves in.

The phone was ringing when we got to the store. "Hometown," Carnihan answered at the counter. That single word brought to mind a lifetime of images, starting with my earliest one: Pop buying me a scoop of ice cream there after a haircut at Garbo's Barbershop on the square. Under different circumstances the memory would've been a pleasant one, but now it drew a veil of sadness over me. The old man started a pot of coffee brewing, and I sat waiting on a stool. Carnihan said "Yes sir" a few times, then asked, his voice devoid of emotion, "When are you coming by? Or should I meet you somewhere?"

He got his answer and hung up without saying goodbye.

"An agent Everly," he said, to Beatnik more than the old man and me. "With the FBI. He and his partner are coming over."

"What?" It was the old man, shouting the word. He seemed more upset than I did, if that was possible, since by now I was on the floor, covering my head with my arms as if from attack.

"They want to ask a few questions about Silas," Carnihan said. "Hey, Winston, why don't you and Beatnik go hide somewhere in Dr. McDermott's? Go sit in one of the examination rooms. I'll come get you when the coast is clear."

"But what if they check back there?" I asked, unable to keep from sounding hysterical.

"Then I guess we're a couple of dead Cajuns."

The pot of coffee finished brewing and Carnihan walked behind the counter and poured himself a cup. Hot and black and steaming as it was, he drank it all in a gulp, without spilling a drop. "Pace, brother, if you don't settle down I'm going to have to ask you to go in the back with him. I'd prefer to have you here, on account it looks better . . . but godalmighty, man, if you intend to mess your pants it won't be with those two guys around." He started removing things from the refrigerator, grabbing without really looking, and I knew it was Bloody Mary time. "Get up off that floor," he said. "We'll just be having us a drink, you and me. And we'll ask if they want one, knowing what the answer'll be since they're on duty. But we'll ask anyway, because that's the kind of people we are. We're Smokies born and raised, and you know what that means."

The old man and I waited for an answer, but since none was forthcoming, I rapped the counter to get Carnihan's attention. "What, then? What does it mean?"

He drank another cup of coffee, taking it slow this time. "Not what it used to," he said when he was finished.

The old man laughed, and Beatnik barked. But it was strange, I really think I understood.

Everly was the first through the door, and behind him came the one called Newton, a tall black man with a jaw showing two days' stubble. A simple glance at Everly told you the kind of diet he favored: rice and gravy, bread soaked with butter, anything with a heavy cream base, and anything that had once had warm blood running in it. He looked like a prime candidate for a fat farm where everyone reports drunk with hope and leaves a few days early looking for the nearest Dairy Queen. I didn't like him, not from the second he barreled up to Carnihan and stuck his meaty hand out. "I'm Special Agent Everly of the FBI, Mr. Carnihan, and this is Special Agent Newton. We want to thank you for letting us drop by at such a late hour."

It was a nice introduction, but at the same time so thoroughly rehearsed that it sounded insincere. Also, I couldn't help but wonder how he was able to determine which of us was Carnihan, since neither of us had ever met him before.

"Nice to make your acquaintance," Carnihan said.

Everly threw a suspicious glance my way, a pointed finger with it. "And who are you?" he said.

"He's my brother," Carnihan said from behind the counter. "Pace Burnette. Haven't you ever heard of him?"

Newton removed a notebook from his pocket and wrote on it.

"Since when do you have a brother?" Everly asked.

"We grew up together," Carnihan answered. "I didn't mean it how you're taking it."

Everly still seemed confused.

"We're best friends," I explained. "We're as close as brothers." I was tempted to relate the tale of our first meeting some twenty-eight years before at the edge of my parents' weedy, half-acre lot, but neither Everly nor Newton seemed sensitive enough to appreciate such a story.

"Spell Burnette," Newton said.

As I spoke his lips repeated each letter. He finished and held the notebook at a distance, examining the word. For whatever reason he didn't seem to like the way it looked.

They were both wearing sport coats, poplin slacks, and striped ties held fast to their shirts by gold bars inscribed with their initials. Although they weren't identically dressed, their clothes were a variation of the same theme, and I wondered whether it was their goal to look like ushers at a dinner theater, minus the handy penlights to check for seating assignments. Not that I'd ever been one for fashion, but these two were making a definite statement: it's not the clothes that make the man, but the size of the sidearm on his hip.

"Before we get started," Carnihan said, "can I fix you a drink? My Bloody Marys are legend in these parts."

Everly's eyebrows pinched in close. He started to say something with a nasty bite, then changed his mind. "We don't care for any, Mr. Carnihan. But thanks for asking."

"You're welcome," Carnihan said, squeezing through the gate and taking a seat. "Now how can I help you, gentlemen?"

Newton put his notebook down on the counter and removed a piece of paper from the inner pocket of his coat. It was a Xerox copy of a letter. "Silas Poe, whom I think you know . . ." He slid the paper over to Carnihan and rapped it with his knuckles. "Mr. Poe mailed this note to the company headquarters of Monster Mart in Liberty, Arkansas. Basically, it's a ransom demand for the return of Rayford Holly. Mr. Everly and myself and a few other agents arrested him several hours ago when he went to make the pickup, or what he thought was going to be a pickup. We're holding him in the parish jail just up the street."

"We saw it on the news," Carnihan mumbled.

"I seriously doubt you saw this on the news," Everly said, pointing to the note.

"No, we saw that he'd been arrested . . . we saw it when you took him in." As if to prove that he was telling the truth, Carnihan added, "He had a raincoat over his head."

Carnihan finished reading. "Can Pace see it? We're brothers, after all."

Everly took the letter and handed it to me. Each word had been cut from a newspaper or magazine and taped to the page, and no two were alike. It was the sort of correspondence you'd expect from someone who watched too many old gangster movies, and I wondered whether Silas's purpose in sending it had been to inspire fear or to keep with a tradition that Hollywood had turned into a cliché. In any case, this was what it said: "At 6 P.M. on Friday evening, May 3rd, drop $10,000,000 in small unmarked bills in the Dumpster behind Hometown Family Goods (the old general store at Market and North Streets) in Smoke, Louisiana. Have someone from your Smoke Monster Mart do it. A clerk or lower-level employee would be best. If you call the police, Mr. Holly, whom I am holding, will die. I am not acting alone and I am not afraid to kill. Be warned. You are not dealing with amateurs."

"How well do you know Mr. Poe?" Newton asked.

Carnihan sipped his drink. "He's been a regular customer here at the lunch counter for as long as I can remember. He and my father grew up together. I saw him almost every day of my life, but I can't say I knew him very well at all. He mostly talked about food and horses."

"Horses?"

"He liked to bet the ponies."

"Your father the one with all the goats? Or is that you?" It was Everly, giving away what I'd already suspected: that they'd been to the farm on Worm Road, and probably through the store and Dr. McDermott's.

"How did you know about the goats?" Carnihan said.

"Your father," Everly said, "he's dead, isn't he? Died of a heart attack, is that right?"

"Ask me something you don't know," Carnihan said.

Newton said, "What was his name?"

"You don't know that?"

Newton didn't lift his eyes from the pages of his notebook. "Is this your store? Do you own it?"

"My father was the third-generation Carnihan to run Hometown. I'm the fourth." He took another sip of his drink. "And probably the last."

The men made a quick study of the store's contents. Their eyes roamed from shelf to shelf, stopping finally at the one of feminine napkins. Newton, squinting hard, picked his pen back up and wrote something down.

"I was wondering if you might let Mr. Newton and myself look around the place," Everly said. "In the back, too, if you don't mind?"

He pointed to the curtain leading to the stockroom.

"I think you've already done that," Carnihan said.

For a while the two men didn't speak, and the silence seemed to press against me with a powerful force. I found it difficult to breathe. I kept wondering whether we'd left the rope on the floor of Dr. McDermott's office, and whether the old man's grass-stained clothes were still back there, and whether the sweat on my face would tip them off to the fact that we were kidnappers and deserved life behind bars.

"A fellow named McDermott used to keep a medical office adjacent to the stockroom," Carnihan said. "Mr. Burnette here is renting the space from me now. If you want to see it, you'll have to get permission from him."

"He's your brother and you call him Mr. Burnette?"

Carnihan didn't reply, and I heard myself say, "You can look, but first I'll have to ask to see a search warrant."

"A search warrant?" It was Everly again. His face seemed to brighten. "Why would we need a search warrant?"

Carnihan tapped me on the shoulder, stopping me from answering. "Is there something in particular you were hoping to find, gentlemen? In that letter of yours, the one Mr. Poe sent you . . . do you think when he said he wasn't acting alone that he was referring to Mr. Burnette and me? And, if so, do you think we're keeping a billionaire back there—in a stockroom?"

"It was here," Newton said, "that Silas Poe demanded the money be sent, and it was here that we apprehended him. It wasn't the bank where he works, and it wasn't the church he attends, and it wasn't the Knights of Columbus hall where he meets every Wednesday night or the track he visits on weekends. It was Hometown Family Goods, and that happens to be your store."

"Do you suspect me of something, mister? If you suspect me of something why don't you just come out and say it?"

"Did we say we suspected you?" Everly asked. "I don't recall hearing either of us say that, Mr. Carnihan. Now may we look around?"

"Go ahead."

"Are you giving us permission?"

"I said go ahead."

Newton turned and faced me. "May we look in your apartment, Mr. Burnette? Would you mind?"

"Sure. Look all you want. But you'll only be wasting your time, since it's clear you've both been back there already."

Newton's smile, disingenuous as it was, exposed a mouthful of perfectly white teeth. He ran his tongue over the top row. "Will you come with us somewhere, Mr. Carnihan?"

"I thought you wanted to look around the store."

"We've changed our minds. Now we'd like for you to come with us. There's something we'd like to show you."

"What is it?"

"After you see what we have to show you, I think you'll better understand why we needed to talk to you tonight."

"Do I need a lawyer?" Carnihan said.

"A lawyer?" It was Newton. "Why would you need a lawyer?"

Everly took an after-dinner mint from his pocket, ripped the foil off, and planted the wafer on the middle of his tongue. "Is there anything you'd like to tell us, Mr. Carnihan?"

Carnihan didn't answer right away, and I knew I had to say something. What came out, however, sounded as tired and hackneyed as Silas's ransom note. "Okay, fellas. Cut to the chase, will you? Just cut to the goddamn chase."

The men looked at me, as surprised as I was. "What chase?" Newton said, "What are you talking about? You aren't a lawyer, are you, Burnette?"

I didn't answer and he corrected himself, "Mr. Burnette."

"I'm a novelist," I said. "I write books."

"Oh, yeah?" Everly asked. "Any I would know about?"

"My first should be in the stores any time now. It's called *Strange Weather*."

"Then it must be about this part of the country," Newton said, "if it's about the weather."

I lacked the spirit to explain, and knew that talking about the book would agitate me more. "You're right," I said. "It's a story about hurricanes."

"Are you coming with us?" Everly said to Carnihan.

"Only if my brother can come."

Newton gave a nod and started backpedaling toward the door. "All right, then. Let's get a move on."

Their car was a beat-up clunker with vinyl seats and trash on the floor. The antenna had been ripped off and someone had keyed all four doors, leaving sketches of priapic male genitalia in the paint. It looked like the kind of car you see lined up between a couple of ramps, waiting for a daredevil on a motorcycle to jump, but it started with a roar as soon as Newton turned the key. "We're going to Silas Poe's house," he said, "in case you were wondering."

"Why there?" Carnihan asked. He seemed upset.

"We thought you might like to see something."

Silas lived close enough for us to walk, but when I proposed we do so Everly nixed the idea. He didn't give a reason, except to say, "I don't feel like sweating my clothes all up."

It took us only a few minutes to get there. The ride seemed longer, though, mainly because all I could think about was whether they had spotted the old man's pickup in the trees behind the goat pasture. It made sense to me that they hadn't found it, since they would've arrested us by now; but still, I couldn't shake the feeling that Newton and Everly knew things about Carnihan and me that no one else did. Had they read the reviews of *Strange Weather* in Dr. McDermott's desk drawer? The possibility alone brought a busy pain to my gut.

Better to be thought of as a threat to civilized society, I thought, than as a lousy writer.

The house was hidden behind clusters of mimosas, Japanese magnolias, and Louisiana chicken trees. I'd never been inside before, but I'd always admired its prodigious vegetation, long deep porches, and chimney-studded roof. Painted white and trimmed green, the Poe house had always seemed to me a place where an eccentric artist might live, for the sight of it alone was enough to fill my head with sentences. Under different circumstances I might've been inclined to attempt a little poetry, Cajun style.

I was surprised, then, when Carnihan averted his eyes from the place. He pushed up to the edge of the seat. "Hey, look, fellas, would you mind if Pace stayed out in the car?"

"But I thought he was your brother." Newton glanced at me in the rearview. "Can you believe this guy? Telling us he goes nowhere without his brother, then we get to Poe's and he wants to leave him in the car."

Carnihan stared blankly outside. He didn't say anything.

There was a van parked in the driveway and Newton pulled up behind it. Everly stepped out and opened Carnihan's door, leading him by the arm. "Follow me," he said, and headed toward the rear of the house, his big brogans crunching gravel. As we approached the back door swung open and a young woman stepped up to the threshold. She was almost as tall as me, and she wore her thick black hair pinned in a bun on top of her head. Her glasses were too big for her face, and her navy linen suit hung loose on her lean, quick-angled frame. Unlike Newton and Everly, when she shook your hand she didn't try to atomize the knuckles.

We were standing in a small, immaculately clean kitchen. On the counter an oscillating fan swept currents across the room, and at our feet lay a litter box for a cat. The refrigerator door held dozens of photographs under magnets, but I was too far away to see any of them.

"Angela Brown," Newton said, "this is Mr. Carnihan of Hometown Family Goods, and this is his friend Mr. Burnette, a writer." He checked his notebook to make sure he'd gotten my name right. "Gentlemen, Ms. Brown is with the U.S. Attorney's Office. She's an assistant prosecutor and she comes to us from Warren—she's been assigned to this case. She has a few questions to ask. When she's done, I'm sure she'll be happy to entertain any you may have about what you're doing here."

"Try that one first," Carnihan said. "What are we doing here?" Rather than wait for a reply, however, he added, "And do you intend to harass every one of Silas's acquaintances as you have Pace and me? Or should we feel . . ." He grinned and batted his eyelids. "Special?"

Angela Brown seemed to contemplate the questions. After a minute she said, "While we're at it, is there anything you want to know, Mr. Burnette?"

I gave a stupid shrug. "Just what this is about."

"Shall we have a seat, then?"

She led us from the kitchen and down a hall that emptied into a formal living area. Over in the corner there was a long banker's desk crowded with stacks of newspapers and magazines, some of them scissored to pieces, and behind it sat Sheriff Sorel, his feet kicked up and resting on a trash can. He didn't stand to greet us. He was reading from an ancient copy of *Life* with a black-and-white photo of Elizabeth Taylor on the cover.

"Make yourselves comfortable," Angela Brown said. "You gentlemen are acquainted with Mr. Sorel, I understand?"

"We know him," Carnihan said.

The sheriff nodded and we returned the gesture. "No reason to be afraid, boys," he said, exaggerating his Cajun accent, while still not bothering to look up from the magazine. "No reason long as you ain't done sum'pin that wasn't right." Chuckling, he picked up a pair of scissors and squeezed them open and shut a few times. "Just for your information, boys, I am here as a courtesy to Ms. Brown and my friends with the Federal Bureau of Investigation. I am not a participant in this particular inquiry. They wished to see the home of Mr. Poe, and I volunteered to escort them." He squeezed the scissors again. "Now you just go ahead and forget I'm here."

Newton and Everly walked across the room and stood against a wall of bookshelves. I was still trying to decide what they knew when Carnihan suddenly gasped for air and clutched me hard on the wrist. "Why, that's my mother. Look at there . . . that's her, that's Miss Deenie, Pace."

Since I'd long heard stories about the Poe house being haunted, I half expected to turn and gaze into the face of a ghost, but what I saw, hanging in an elaborate, gilded frame over the fireplace, was a portrait of Deenie Carnihan. Upon entering the room I'd only glimpsed the picture, failing to register its content. But clearly there she was as a bright-eyed girl of no more than eighteen. Her hair was a light wheat brown fanning to bare shoulders. She wore an evening gown which dramatically accentuated the curves of her upper torso.

But what in hell, I asked myself now, was her portrait doing hanging in Silas Poe's house?

I was about to ask that question when Carnihan nudged me on the leg and said, "And that's . . . why, that's me! Look at all those of me!" He was straining to see a collection of photographs covering a small table at the end of the couch. He started to laugh but something made him stop. His face grew red and his hands began to shake. I thought he looked like a man who's just learned something that in one quick stroke challenges everything he had ever believed about himself. "What in the name of . . . ?" Carnihan raised his eyes toward Angela Brown. "What's going on here, lady?"

"That's really what I was hoping to ask you, Mr. Carnihan. We were hoping you might tell us yourself."

Carnihan stood and lifted a picture from the table. It depicted him as a sixteen-year-old shortstop for the Smoke Warriors, our local American Legion baseball team. He was caught in the act of fielding a ground ball, his gloved hand stabbing at the fuzzy white orb spinning toward a bright green expanse of outfield grass. The next picture he showed me was even older. A black-and-white faded to sepia over time, it showed him as a child walking hand-in-hand with Mr. Hank and Miss Deenie in front of the Delta. Above them the marquee said: FRED MACMURRAY STARRING IN THE ABSENT-MINDED PROFESSOR . . . A WALT DISNEY PRODUCTION! Like the baseball photograph, and like all the others on the table, Carnihan was the object of the camera's focus. And except for one showing him in his Hometown uniform standing with Ruby Dean at the lunch counter, he seemed unaware that he was being photographed.

"I remember when this was taken," he said, holding up the one of him and Ruby Dean. "It was a few days after I came home . . . after I got out of the Navy." His voice was so faint that I could barely hear it, and he stared as if for a clue. "Silas came in one day with a camera. He said it was new and that he'd been trying it out and had one shot left." Carnihan was talking directly to me now, and seemed to have forgotten the others in the room. "I thought it was Ruby Dean he wanted . . . I mean, I thought it was her picture he wanted. I was horsing around, trying to get her to laugh."

He put the picture back on the table. "She hadn't wanted to laugh. She said it made her face look fat."

"Jay, come sit down here, brother. Come on, come sit." I stood and tried to lead him to the couch.

"Tell me what this is all about," he said to Angela Brown. "Why in the hell'd you bring me here, lady?"

"Watch yourself there, boy," Sorel growled from across the room. "You don't want to give a bad impression to these fine people, do you, now?"

"There's more," Everly said. "On the refrigerator door in the kitchen. It's full of 'em. I'm surprised you didn't notice when we walked through."

Carnihan didn't say anything.

"To begin," Angela Brown said, "let me just say that it isn't any of my business to learn what these many pictures mean, although I must confess a certain curiosity. We came to this house only this evening, after picking up Mr. Poe. While Agents Newton and Everly were searching the area, other teams of officers were searching your store and home."

"I figured," he said.

"Federal law prohibits me from discussing details of the case, but I can tell you that Mr. Poe is not responsible for abducting Rayford Holly. Mr. Poe, however, has broken the law. He has attempted to extort money from Mr. Holly's company, claiming to hold Mr. Holly against his will and with the intent to kill him if ransom isn't paid."

"I already know that," Carnihan said.

She looked across the room at Newton and Everly. "We showed him a copy of the letter," Everly said.

"This is not uncommon," she said, "what Mr. Poe has done. As a matter of fact, we see it now and then when a person of material consequence is kidnapped. Do you recall a few years ago when an executive with Gulf Oil—a Mr. Bruce Dossett—suddenly disappeared while on his way to work?"

I remembered the name, but Carnihan shook his head.

"Five different parties claimed responsibility, and all but one said it would kill him if so many millions weren't paid. The lone exception was a radical environmentalist who appeared before live television cameras holding what looked to be a detonating device. Connected to the device was a wire which ran from his hand into an adjacent room, the door of which was closed. He announced that Mr. Dossett, wearing a vest of explosives, was attached to the end of this wire, and that he would blow him up if Gulf Oil did not commit two million dollars to build a memorial to all the marine life it had destroyed as a result of an oil spill in the North Sea."

Carnihan had either lost interest in what Angela Brown was saying or he'd decided that she wasn't worth listening to. He sat gazing at the portrait of his mother.

"That man," said Angela Brown, "along with the other four, was convicted of extortion and is now in prison. The FBI investigated each case, and in company with the U.S. Attorney's Office convicted them all."

"This Mr. Dossett," Sorel said, "refresh my memory a second there, darling. Y'all ever find him?"

"We found him all right. He was on a sailboat with a nineteen-year-old girl. He had decided to chuck it all and see the world. Distraught, he telephoned his wife from Belize after his paramour disappeared with a bonefishing guide."

Sorel, looking utterly confused, put his magazine down. "And what is a paramour?"

"His concubine," she answered.

"His . . . ?"

"Dossett was banging her," Everly said with a snort. "She was his . . . well, his stuff."

"So he hadn't been kidnapped, after all?"

"No."

"Well, I'll be," said the sheriff.

I faced Angela Brown. "Are you trying to say you don't think Rayford Holly has been kidnapped?"

She shook her head. "Mr. Dossett was experiencing a mid-life crisis of the sort which compels a man to destroy his life's work, his reputation, his family, himself. In the case of Rayford Holly . . ." She paused and glanced at Newton and Everly, both of whom seemed bored by what they were hearing. "In Mr. Holly's case it appears we have yet another man who has taken a trip. For the last two years, since losing his wife, Mr. Holly has staged a tour of the South with the aim of promoting his business. These trips have found him accompanied by his personal assistant and a bodyguard, although you never would've known that from media reports. They traveled behind him in a limo, in the event he needed them. Mr. Holly acknowledged their presence only occasionally—to threaten to shake loose of their tail and to set off and start a new life. Last year he slipped away for several days before putting in a call to company headquarters from a motor court on the Mississippi Gulf Coast. Mr. Holly, it seemed, had not gotten over the loss of his wife. And to worsen his state of mind, he was beginning to feel that he was no longer of value to his company. Mr. Holly had assembled a top-flight management team which, without his input, was successful in more than tripling sales over the last few years. As a result Mr. Holly's influence had diminished, and increasingly his ideas were met with either skepticism or indifference. He complained almost daily that he was no longer needed, and often threatened to retire, a move that many of his people considered redundant. Last spring when he disappeared and then called in . . . ? They simply told him Monster Mart's latest sales figures and attributed the success to him. His top people got on the phone and pleaded with him to come home. As soon as he hung up the line, he dialed the cellular phone in the limo, reached his assistant, and reported his whereabouts. By morning he was in Liberty."

"What about this year?" I asked.

"This year he convinced everyone he needed neither the bodyguard nor the assistant. Monster Mart had recently purchased kidnap-extortion insurance policies for Mr. Holly and its top executives, and he joked that if anyone abducted him the company had nothing to worry about since any ransom demand would be covered. He called but a few times from the road and didn't seem interested in hearing any news, good or otherwise. He visited only a handful of the stores on his scheduled route. His last was here in Smoke. Then . . ." She snapped her fingers. "He vanished."

From across the room Newton could be heard clearing his throat. "We don't expect foul play," he said. "Monster Mart went public with reports of his disappearance and with appeals for his safe return only after we advised them to do so. We'd hoped to get him back to Liberty before he got into trouble or hurt himself, or before someone really did pick him up. The company even released the latest sales figures a week before schedule hoping he'd call in to make sure what he'd heard was accurate. Needless to say, these efforts have failed."

"I just pinch myself," the sheriff said, "at the thought that this is the richest man in these United States . . . a billionaire, and that he's so insecure with himself he has to pull a stunt of this magnitude."

Everly walked across the room, carrying a small wooden chair with him. He placed the chair a few feet in front of us, turned it around, and sat on it with his arms draped over the back.

"Did Silas Poe ever speak to you of kidnapping Rayford Holly?" he asked.

"Never," I answered. Carnihan shook his head.

"Did he ever say anything about getting money from Monster Mart, or about pretending to have kidnapped Mr. Holly?"

"No, he didn't," I said. And Carnihan shook his head again.

"I was speaking to Mr. Carnihan," Everly said, glaring at me. He leaned forward in the chair. "Mr. Carnihan, would you answer me, please? And Mr. Burnette, would you—"

"Me and Silas hardly ever talked," Carnihan mumbled.

"He ever say anything at all about Rayford Holly . . . anything in passing, say, over breakfast one morning?"

"No."

"Did he say anything to others in the store? Did you overhear any conversations in which Holly's name was invoked?"

"He read the papers a lot," Carnihan said. "But he never talked about any of it."

Everly got up from the chair and walked over to the fireplace. He stood staring at the portrait of Miss Deenie. "Any idea what this is doing here? This is your mother, isn't it?" Carnihan didn't answer, and Everly said, "Why is this house full of pictures of you, Mr. Carnihan? Was he obsessed with you for some reason? Why would he be obsessed with you, Mr. Carnihan?"

I waited for an answer, knowing that at this point they couldn't have beaten a reply out of him. "Why don't you leave him alone?" I said.

"What did you say?"

"I said leave him alone . . . just leave him the hell alone!"

"What I suspect . . ." Sorel said from across the room, raising his voice to let us know we'd just as well take this as fact, "what I suspect is Rayford Holly is relaxing in some cheap hotel not far from here, watching the television coverage of the chaos he's caused and having the time of his life. I wouldn't be surprised if he had his paramour with him." He paused to let us reflect on the word. "If it's attention he was after, it's attention he's got—now with this caper Silas has tried to pull."

Angela Brown was staring at the sheriff, a condescending smile on her face. "Thank you for that, Mr. Sorel."

"Silas never hurt anyone," Carnihan said.

"What's that?" It was Everly.

"Silas is innocent. And you knew all along he was innocent. You should've just ignored him . . . just left him alone."

"He is innocent of kidnapping, it appears," Angela Brown said. "But not of extortion. And the truth is, we didn't know with complete certainty that he wasn't holding Mr. Holly until we picked him up and started gathering evidence. From the beginning we suspected his claim to be no more authentic than that of the environmentalist with the detonator device, but we had to treat it with gravity in the event we were mistaken."

"You boys know Lester Harris?" Sorel asked.

Carnihan dropped his head and closed his eyes. He seemed to anticipate what was coming next.

"Lester Harris is a bookie," Sorel said. "I myself was able to learn that Silas owes him in the neighborhood of ten thousand dollars, and that Lester was threatening to do something to Silas's private parts which at this time I shall not describe for the presence of a lady."

A long silence ensued in which the only sound was of a cat entering the room, its claws catching the rug underfoot. It walked around as if in search of something.

"Can we go now?" I asked.

"We'll probably want to talk to you again at some point in the future," Angela Brown said. She glanced back at Newton. "Mind driving them back?"

She opened a door at the front of the room and led us out onto the veranda. Without any light, and with the dense canopy of trees, it was hard to see much. Carnihan pushed past everyone without speaking, bounded across the lawn, and took off running toward the store, his shoes clopping against the brick.

"I guess he doesn't want a ride," Newton said, once Carnihan had already disappeared from view.

The two agents went back in the house, leaving me alone with Sorel and Angela Brown. "I've got a question," I said. "It's the same one Carnihan asked when we first came into the house. Why'd you bring us here? What was the point?"

Without averting her eyes from mine, she removed a package of cigarettes from her coat pocket and lit one. "We wanted," she said, "to make sure he wasn't involved."

"You mean the extortion thing?"

She nodded. "I knew he didn't know anything the moment he saw the picture over the fireplace. Did you see his face?"

I didn't answer.

"This job isn't always fun." She was trying to sound sympathetic. "Sometimes you have to do things. It might have been a matter of convenience that Silas Poe designated the Dumpster behind Hometown as the drop-off point. But when Sheriff Sorel brought us here to the man's house it just seemed too great a coincidence that his home would be filled with photographs of the same individual who owned the store." She walked to the edge of the porch and leaned against the banister, the head of her cigarette throwing a soft orange light on her face. "You can understand that, can't you, Mr. Burnette?"

When I didn't answer, she said, "Frankly I suspected a conspiracy involving those two. I thought they were working together. That may still turn out to be the case, but I doubt it, especially after what I observed here tonight."

Hands in pockets, Sorel rocked back on his heels. "Your friend seems to be in a state of denial," he said.

"Denial? Denial about what?"

"Come on now, boy. Everyone in Smoke knew about Deenie."

"Well, I didn't know. And he didn't either."

"It's one of those stories you can hardly believe," Sorel said. "Like something in a picture the old Delta used to play."

Angela Brown sidled up next to me. "Why don't you get moving, Burnette? Your friend might need the company."

"And, boy, what a story," the sheriff was saying. "In this one a young man buries his poor daddy one month, then the next finds out that the man he's buried really wasn't his daddy after all. His daddy, as it turns out, is a man he's known all his life, and has even fed twice a day at his counter going back twenty-something years. His daddy, his *real* one . . . he's got a gambling debt that's crossed him with a bookie. If that isn't enough, his daddy pretends to have kidnapped . . ."

Sorel was still talking when I stepped off the porch and started down the street, taking the same path as Carnihan. I might have sprinted the distance, or at least jogged it, but I was in no real hurry to get back to the store.

As much as I would've liked to, I wouldn't be able to change things when I got there anyway.

IX

Carnihan had already left when I got back to the store, sparing me the necessity of having to console him. One moment can erase all the others that have come before it, but how do you tell your best friend that? The delivery truck was gone and the lights were out, and I admit to feeling no small relief. I might've chased after him in the Mustang, but I had no idea where he'd gone. And what would I tell him if I did happen to track him down? That he was a *Carnihan* . . . a Carnihan no matter what?

I could've sat somewhere and wept.

Dr. McDermott's seemed different to me now than the last time I was there. The dirty hands of the FBI had stained everything, and my sense of having been violated was acute. For that reason I determined that a thorough examination was in order before I let myself settle back in. A sharp chill came over me, along with an aching need to relieve myself. I kept imagining the place infested with spooks bearing uncanny likenesses to Newton and Everly, and I stepped quietly lest I alert them to my presence. I saw them hiding in wait, their bad clothes bright in the shadows. Slowly I moved down the hallway, my head aswivel, my hands boxing shadows. "I know you're in there," I cried, then pivoted and entered each room. Five doors down I began to feel foolish and to wonder when I'd become such a shameful yellowbelly. I opened the last few doors without speaking, my vocal cords having frozen solid midway down the hall. If I was to be attacked, I preferred to face my enemy with at least a whit of dignity. "What were his last words?" I could hear Miss Betty asking the police at the city morgue. " 'I know you're in there,' " came the reply. And then the kicker: "We think he meant to be brave, ma'am."

Light shone under the door of the X-ray lab, and I approached it trembling clear down to my toes. The knob felt cold and slippery in my hand; I had trouble grasping it. Only by repeatedly reminding myself that this was my home and my room and my life was I able to summon the courage to enter. "I know you're in there," I muttered before bolting in with fists raised.

"I know I am, too," came a voice—the old man's, as it happened. "I've been here most of the night."

He was sitting on the floor with his legs crossed and my copy of *Strange Weather* propped open on his lap, Beatnik asleep beside him. The ceiling light was on, as was a small gooseneck lamp positioned directly over the book.

"The weary, uninspired, and downright indecent debut of a voice which won't be long among us," I mumbled aloud, recalling one of the kinder comments made by my reviewers.

The old man seemed to remember it himself. He gave a nod and smiled his crooked smile. His eyes were red and glassy—from the reading, I presumed. "But they're wrong, Burdette."

"It's Burnette," I reminded him.

He double-checked the name on the book jacket. "Burdette, Burnette. Whoever you are, son, I've got to give it to you. You tell a story unlike any I've ever encountered."

For a moment I forgave him for being Rayford Holly, and I forgot that he was the town-killer largely responsible for all our troubles. But then it came to me that he might not be heaping praise. How did he mean that, anyway: *unlike any I've ever encountered*? That was a compliment, wasn't it?

He seemed to know what I was thinking, and reached over and lightly touched my leg. "You're on fire, Pace."

"Am I?"

"You're a poet, son. You're a beautiful, young poet on fire. And I just wanted to feel the heat."

He let go of me, and I did indeed feel a flame burn my face: it was the kind that stays with a person forever.

"They've been all through here," he said. "The FBI. They left their muddy tracks everywhere, the bastards."

I sat on the floor next to him. "I kept wondering about the rope Carnihan used to tie you up. I remembered leaving it in the office, I thought for sure they'd find it."

"I took care of that a long time ago—that first morning after he brought me in. Once you two had fallen asleep, I coiled it up and put it back where it belonged. It's still like new, that rope. I hope to sell it."

"And what about the guns?"

He shrugged. "Haven't seen them. Maybe he's got them hidden under the seat of the truck. Isn't that where most rednecks hide their weapons? It's where I always did."

"But he's not a redneck, Winston. He's got a lot of Cajun blood in him, too."

"Aha," the old man said. "That explains it, then. You know what you get when you mix a redneck and a Coonass, don't you?"

I shook my head.

"You get a redass." And he unleashed a storm of laughter that soon turned into a hog call complete with snorts and slobbering.

We talked a few minutes longer. I told him about the meeting with Angela Brown at Silas Poe's house, deliberately failing to mention the pictures and what we'd discovered there. I'm sure he'd have been sympathetic, and better able than I to make sense of it all, but I'd decided that this was a private matter of Carnihan's and not mine to share.

The old man said, "Why didn't he come in afterward? He started his truck and peeled the hell out."

"I guess he just wanted to be alone for a while. It wasn't easy for him, having to answer those questions."

"Well, I suppose you're right. I didn't care, really, that he didn't come in. It gave me more time with your book." He gazed down at the page—a late one. "You wouldn't mind disappearing for about half an hour, would you, son? I'd like to finish."

"Heck, no," I said, pushing myself up from the floor. "You honor me, Winston. And I thank you for that."

"Well, I tell you, it's just one of them stories where somebody's got to die. And I can't wait to find out who."

To my ears this sounded like a hit, and I bristled at the thought of more criticism. I was leaving the room when his voice came up behind me, hardly more than a whisper: "A book without death is as dishonest as a life without it. Just remember I told you that. It'll mean something to you one day."

I went into the store and commenced the near-daily ritual of preparing Bloody Marys. I'd been drinking too much lately, my mood swinging from mordantly depressed to senselessly giddy, and I preferred to keep a cool head tonight, alert in case any more disasters were to come. So I left the vodka out and fixed a deep tumbler of tomato juice over ice, a few pickled string beans as ornaments. Outside a hard rain had begun to fall, beating a sleepy music against the roof, washing the street clean. I watched the lights of downtown Smoke through the window: the winking pinks and greens, the hard, determined whites.

I lay my head on the zinc and napped for a while—time enough, I reckoned, for the old man to have finished the book. Back in Dr. McDermott's I found him where I'd left him: lounging on the floor of the X-ray lab with Beatnik. He started to speak as soon as I stepped through the door. "It's funny, isn't it, how when you read a book the author's voice stays with you for days? If it's a good book, it can stay with you for months. I suspect I'll be hearing you for some time now."

Then, with a voice filled with conviction, he announced: "I rank *Strange Weather* right up there with any novel published in this country since the war."

I tried to take the praise in stride, but it struck me like a hammer blow. I could feel a turbulent swelling at my chest and minor explosions in my head. "Which war do you mean?" I finally thought to ask.

"Well, you just pick a war, Burdette. Pick any war you like. And I'll argue it's as fine as anything since then."

"The Civil War?"

"Okay. Good. The Civil War'll do." I offered my hand and helped him up off the floor, and he stood patting the dust off his seat. "Of course, it's the only novel I've read in several years, but I did enjoy it."

"How long is several, Winston?"

"Oh . . ." For some reason he looked at his watch. "About forty years, give or take a few. Reading books always made me sleepy. I'm a businessman, remember . . . a numbers person. And this is why I always preferred a poem. It's short and to the point and it impresses when you quote from one. Walt Whitman can cover in ten words what it takes ten pages for Herman Melville to do."

I felt the blood drain from my face—not for the slight to Melville, but for the sudden realization that he'd been jerking my chain. As much as it hurt, I knew that I hadn't deserved his praise, and I wasn't happy with myself for having been suckered.

"Maybe I was wrong about you not having lived," he said. "If you're anything like this Peter Burn, you've lived plenty—far past my experience, if the truth be told. It strikes me as funny, but I met your dear mother just tonight, and never in my wildest dreams would I've imagined her stoking such a fire for you. Did Miss Betty really slip into such a depraved state that she attempted, for lack of a better word, to succor you?"

"It's fiction, Winston. I made that part up."

"The milk in the tin pitcher and the bathtub and the soapy water and Miss Louise taking her blouse off . . ." He might've been describing the best meal of his life, what for the way he looked. "It surely doesn't feel made up. Good golly, boy, had I written something like that I imagine my father would've taken a knife to my young manhood and lopped it right off, fried it with garlic, and fed it as a snack to the dogs."

"If there's something you want to tell me, Winston, I'd appreciate it if you just got to the goddamned point."

He gave an unquiet chuckle and said, "How could you do it, boy? Betty Burdette is as fine and gracious an example of Southern womanhood as there ever lived. What you've done in these pages is . . . well, it's unforgivable."

I felt my voice cracking, approaching a scream: "But I thought you said you liked it?"

"I did like it . . . I loved every last perverted little word of it, if you really want to know the truth. But that doesn't alter the fact that you've blasphemed your poor mama. You've set upon her a reputation that will chase her to the grave. She will be the scandal of Smoke, whispered about among her female friends, preyed upon by her male ones. Boys in the street—teenagers!—will covet her. Young girls will follow her example."

"Explain why, Winston? The lady in the book isn't Miss Betty! She's Miss Louise and she's got nothing in common . . ."

The old man put his hands on my shoulders. "We should stop the damage. Nip it in the bud."

"Nip it?"

"Here in Smoke, at least. Where are the bookstores?"

"Only Dunbar's carries this type of stuff. And it's down a few blocks from here—on the other side of the square."

"Would it be open tonight, by chance?"

"Not this late."

"What about weekends? How 'bout tomorrow morning?"

"Tomorrow? Wait a second. She hasn't received copies of the book yet. What are we getting all worked up about? The pub date is still a week or two away."

I thought this would settle the matter, but he was frantic, resolved to spare Miss Betty any humiliation. "We've got a copy of the book, don't we?" And he held it up high over his head, rather in the fashion of a street preacher lifting a Bible for all to see. "If we've got one that means they've been printed. They're shipped right after they're printed—forget what you were told about a pub date." He lowered the book. "This is worse than I thought. Much worse."

"Listen to me, Winston. Just settle down for a second and listen. Even if Miss Dunbar does have the book we can't do anything about it until Monday. Monster Mart's killed her business just as it's killed everybody else's in town."

"Oh, hell. We're not starting on that again, are we?"

"She stopped opening on weekends when people stopped shopping the downtown area, then—"

"Stack it deep, sell it cheap," he said, cutting me off.

I fell silent, unsure as to the point he was trying to make. "What did you just say?"

"Stack it deep, sell it cheap, heap it high and watch it fly. Hear those downtown merchants cry."

"Where the hell did that come from?"

"It's what they chant whenever I stop by for a visit."

"What who chants?"

"My employees . . . no, let me correct myself: my assistants. It's a cheer, is all. It excites them."

I shuffled up next to him and pulled the book from his hands, tearing the cover in the process. He didn't resist but something like a chirp slipped from between his lips. He brought a hand up to his mouth as if to prevent another.

"You've got a lot of nerve, old man, talking to me about right and wrong. You . . ."

"Oh, relax," he said.

"You've encouraged it, haven't you? You've preached it. You really do want to kill everyone off." I raised a finger to his face. "You're the one who should be ashamed, Winston."

I was slightly proud of myself. It was as close to telling someone off as I'd ever gotten, and I rather liked the feeling. Hoping for a dramatic exit, I pivoted sharply and marched from the room, swinging my arms like a soldier on parade. I was halfway down the hall when his voice came roaring behind me: "Stack it deep, sell it cheap, heap it high and watch it fly! Hear those downtown merchants cry!"

He repeated the chant again and again, gaining speed with each utterance so that the words ran together and it was nearly impossible to make them out.

I slipped into an examination room and lay on a table, hoping for sleep; but there was no way with all his heat and noise. I wondered why he'd chosen tonight to come so bloody unwound, and whether Smoke was finally getting to him. Was it possible, I asked myself, that he was beginning to see at what cost he'd earned his twenty-eight billion dollars? The soul of America, you figure it wouldn't have gone for so cheap. And I wondered if perhaps he was beginning to understand that now.

I found him in the bathroom some fifteen minutes later, staring at himself in the mirror above the sink. His lips were still moving, forming the words that made up the chant.

"You oughta fix that," I told him, letting myself in.

"Fix what?"

"That broken record of yours."

He mumbled and groaned a little louder, then moved his face closer to the glass.

"Are we finished yet, Winston? I need to know because I'm heading out to find Carnihan and I'd like you to come. He's probably at Babylon. I'll buy you a g and t. My treat."

I started down the hall, and he followed a short distance behind me, taking baby steps, each a balancing act. He looked like a fellow who'd just had a lobotomy and was teaching himself to walk again. I knew he was joking around, but something about it was painful to watch. I've known people who laugh when they really mean to cry, and who curse with disgust when they'd like to sing with joy, and who can't press their nose into a flower without pretending to have been bee-stung. At this moment, in his own way, the old man was one of these: unable to be true to himself for fear of giving too much away.

"It was just a cheer," he said upon catching up to me. "You understand that, don't you, son?"

Beatnik came scurrying up to join us, barking to make sure we didn't leave without him. I pushed the door open and together the three of us walked out into the rain.

More vehicles crowded the parking lot at Babylon than I'd ever seen there, and I reckoned word had finally gotten around that Anita and the sheriff had patched things up between them and that harlotry, on these premises at any rate, was once again legal in the parish of Saint Landry.

I noted the preponderance of pickup trucks with tool chests in back and imagined a crowd of dirty overalls and steel-toe boots, a stink of sweat and oil and whiskey. Inside they were playing Zachary Richard, his big Cajun voice reaching us when the door swung open and a couple staggered outside for a room. Before the door closed I spotted a lump of red-faced men coagulating at the bar, smoke hanging around them in a cloud. At the center of the group sat the telephone lady, looking bored beyond her capacity to cope.

"Why don't you park?" the old man said with a raw, impatient edge. He was grasping the handle of his door.

"I don't see his truck, I don't think he's even here."

"Maybe he parked up the road somewhere."

"Not in this weather, he wouldn't."

"But you promised me a g and t."

"Don't whine, Winston. Please. With a crowd this size you're likely to be recognized. I'm sorry but I think it's best we just stay put in the car for now."

"And do what? Watch the door?"

"Someone we know'll come out. And when they do we'll ask if they've seen him."

Five minutes passed before anyone appeared, and it was Anita dragging a customer outside. He was yelling and flailing his arms at her, and she was pulling him by the scruff of his neck. Her fat arms rolled in irregular spasms and her chin jiggled and multiplied, but clearly she had everything under control. In the rain her white corona of hair seemed to disintegrate and you could see the pink of her scalp, pink as the calamine salve I recalled Miss Betty having spread on my poison-ivied flesh as a boy. Anita threw the man down on the gravel and when he attempted to stand she drove her knee under his chin and sent him sprawling on his back. He tried to rise again and she waited until he was up on his feet before throwing her knuckled right fist square into his groin and dropping him to his rear, his arms stretched out at his sides. I've seen a few fights in my day but never a fighter so inflamed with bloodlust as Anita, nor one who so plainly relished the activity. Each punch was calculated to achieve maximum results, and none veered off target. To finish the job, she reached up under her long-hanging skirt and wiggled out of her panties, letting them slip past her high heels to the ground. The man was lying supine now, and she squatted over him and urinated an erratic stream, her laughter lifting up above the chatter of the rain. When she was finished, she picked her panties up, held them high above the man's face, and let them drop, a size XXL parachute. They landed on his face, covering it.

"Woman sure can pee, can't she?" the old man said with a note of genuine admiration. "How big do you think her bladder is? You think it's this big?" And he held his hands up about four feet apart, more than the actual width of her body.

I left the Mustang and ran out to help the man, not certain that I wanted to touch him until the rain had time to wash him off. "Damn, Anita," I said, brushing past her, "you didn't have to go and kill the guy."

At the sound of my voice her upper lip started to quiver and her hands tightened into fists again. I'd always known she didn't like me, but until now I had no idea just how much.

"Not you too?" she grumbled, and started toward me, splashing through puddles.

I thought I could take the whipping, it was the other business I wasn't too keen about. I knelt there waiting for her to throw the first punch when the old man's voice came calling above the rain: "Hey there, sweet thing. How're they hangin'?"

She spun around and seemed instantly pacified: the sight of him brought a smile to her face. "Winston? Is that you?" And off she went stumbling toward the Mustang, both hands pressed to her enormous bosom.

Now that she was occupied elsewhere, I knelt beside her victim and lifted the panties from his face. Blood trickled from his nose and mouth, and his hair was plastered to his head and cut shorter than I remembered, and there was a heaviness about his face that might best be described as jowly, but it was still the fellow I'd known back at Smoke High, the one who played with Carnihan and me on Pop's last team, and who went on to marry the girl of my dreams. "Peahead," I whispered, for some reason needing to hear the name spoken aloud.

I didn't expect a reply, but he cracked his eyelids and smiled, not without pain. "Is she gone yet?" He made sure not to move his lips lest he give himself away.

"Not yet," I answered. I could still hear her cutting up with the old man. "Better take it easy."

"I'll play possum a little while longer . . . till she's gone." He clutched my forearm, his stubby nails digging in.

The blood and swelling notwithstanding, Peahead looked just as he had the last time I saw him, some ten years before. His head was too small for his body, hence the nickname, and his body was a large one. When Peahead first started attending Smoke High, Pop had been excited by the prospect of getting him on the football field and molding his extraordinary, muscle-bound form into that of an offensive lineman. He envisioned an All-American tackle leading the student body sweep, single-handedly clearing out entire defenses, forearming his team to the state championship. Peahead, however, turned out to be indifferent to physical contact except that which involved girls. He'd been one of Pop's biggest failures as a coach, and in time people forgot the real reason we called him Peahead and assumed it was because he wasn't very bright in the head.

I myself didn't feel very bright when it occurred to me that I was comforting the same man who'd so deeply hurt Genine. Neither did I like what I reckoned were his reasons for showing up at Babylon tonight: to humiliate her even more, or to try to win her back. I was tempted to report to Anita that he was faking it and to strike him with a few nasty, well-placed punches of my own, when someone stepped up behind me, blocking the beer lights in the windows of the bar.

"Silly fool," Genine said, holding an umbrella high. "That'll teach you to get sassy with Anita. You're lucky she didn't shoot you full of buckshot."

A broad, bloody smile came to his face and when he tried to get up Genine pushed him back down with her foot, driving her stiletto heel into his chest. "Wait till she goes back inside," she whispered, and added another poke. "You don't want her to come pee on you again, do you?"

Genine was smiling herself now—the same smile I'd last seen in her little rented house however long ago. In an evening we'd buried Mr. Hank and made love, and this was how those two events had shown themselves in her face. It upset me to see that look again, because I understood its meaning. "Silly fool," she said. "He paid a thousand dollars to have me for the night—*the entire night, can you believe!* Anita gave him the key to a room but he didn't want to take me anywhere but to a corner of the bar. He was being selfish, and just didn't want to share with anyone else. So guess what we've been doing?"

I didn't attempt to answer, and Peahead kept quiet.

"Well, I've been pumping quarters in the jukebox and drinking g and t's, and he's been trying to convince me to give him a second chance."

Peahead wasn't moving. I watched him for some sign that what she'd said was true, but he gave none.

"He says he's found the Lord, and he wants me back."

"Praise Jesus," Peahead muttered from the ground. "All praise His holy name."

"Only thing," remarked Genine, "I ain't buying it. And even if I was, I wouldn't go back with him anyway. He'd have to spend a thousand dollars a day the rest of my life to have me back, and I know he can't well afford another five minutes."

"I can pay," he said, squeezing the words between his lips. "I got a job now, a good one. And I got a home and a car. I want you back, Genny, I don't care the cost."

"How many days in a life?" Genine said to me.

"What's that?"

"How many days are there in a life? How many days does a person live? You figure there're three hundred and sixty-five days in a year, and you live on the average . . . what, seventy years? I've already covered twenty-eight, so that leaves forty-three to go. Forty-three times three hundred and sixty-five is how many, Pace?" You could see that she was doing the arithmetic herself, and this was a good thing since I'd never been able to count to ten without the aid of a calculator. When she was done she straightened up tall and announced, "That comes to fifteen thousand and six hundred and ninety-five. Add three zeros on to that for the thousand you'd have to pay each day and that makes fifteen million, six hundred and ninety-five thousand. Round that off and you're talking in the neighborhood of sixteen million dollars." She stepped up close to Peahead and nudged his arm with her foot. "Am I worth that much to you, Larry Chowder?"

He blinked a few times. "More."

"More than sixteen million dollars?"

His smile returned, upsetting the wound at the corner of his mouth, letting more blood run. "There's no amount of money I wouldn't pay to have you back, Genny."

In response she lifted her foot and drove the heel back down against his chest. "Why, you really are a fool," she said, then started back toward the door, treading lightly to keep from tripping in the mud.

"She'll give in eventually," Peahead said. "She'll wise up."

"Maybe you should just go home."

"My home is with her, wherever Genny is."

He sat up and warily looked around for Anita. She was still talking to the old man, the top half of her body folded over the door and pressed in through the window. At the sight of her he sank back down to the ground and a violent shudder wracked his body. You could understand his fear, considering the beating he'd just had, but at the same time you never saw such cowardice.

"Why'd she beat you up?" I asked.

"She's greedy, that woman. Plus, I happened to mention the name of Jesus in there."

"Well, Peahead. The second part of that I can understand—no respectable madam wants to compete with God for the souls of men. But the first still escapes me."

"I paid my money and then when all those roughnecks started coming in she saw Genny just sitting there and decided she'd put her to use. She walked over and asked whether she wouldn't help her with a little something, and I said, 'Forget it, lady. I don't see how that's good business considering the thousand dollars I just paid.' Or that's what I began to say. I got only about halfway when she pounced on me."

He'd raised his voice too loud and drawn Anita's attention; she was scrambling toward us with her fists raised and a hot fury coloring her face. I waited for her to tear into us, but her anger was focused elsewhere: a couple of soldiers had just stumbled through the door whooping it up.

Peahead mumbled, "Thank you, Jesus. Oh, thank you, Lord," as Anita beat the two men until they both were lying facedown in the slop.

I helped Peahead to sit up straight and to get the mud and shell out of his hair. The rain had slacked off a bit, but now it started to fall hard again, so I led him to a dry spot against the building, just under the overhang. We stood shoulder-to-shoulder with our backs pressed against the wall.

"Are you coming?" I heard the old man call. "Hey, Burdette. Time to go, boy."

I held a finger up. "One minute, Winston. Hang on."

Peahead was staring at me as if I'd just done some terrible wrong. "You don't think I can do it, do you?"

"What's that?"

"Reclaim my wife."

"It doesn't much matter what I think," I said. "It's Genny who matters, and I think she might object, considering she's no longer your wife."

"No longer my wife?" He whipped his head to the side. "Since when is she no longer my wife? We're separated is all, ever since I came home with that . . . well, if you really have to know . . ." But he stopped himself.

"With that what?" I asked.

"I was lost, Pace, lost without a hope in this world. I'd lay down with anything that'd have me. What really happened . . ." He paused again. "Well, I made her sick is the thing." He raised his right hand in the fashion of one about to be sworn in. "Do you really want to hear it? It isn't easy."

"What isn't?"

"My testimony. How I came to be saved."

The old man blew the horn and waved me over again. He was saying something I couldn't make out for the water beating against the roof of the building. "A few more minutes," I called, holding up three fingers. "Hang on there, Winston." But he pumped the horn a second time and stuck his head through the window, yelling for me to hurry up.

"Wait!" I shouted. "Just wait, goddammit."

He finally rolled the window back up. I could see him take Beatnik in his arms and lower himself in the seat until both of them were hidden from view.

"So you made her sick?" I said, turning back to Peahead. I realized how bizarre it was to be standing in the rain talking about such a thing, but I was fairly desperate to learn the rest. Also, I figured if I didn't get his story now I never would, since it was my plan never to see Peahead Chowder again.

"I tell you how I know she still loves me. I know because she's tried to protect me. She's told her mother she was born with a female problem, something about her uterus. Well, her uterus is fine. It's her tubes that's not, on account they're all scarred up . . . and I can tell you why." He glanced up at the dark, boiling heavens, and took in another breath. "The truth is, Pace, I made us both sick. I caught something not long after we married, must've been . . . or maybe it was before. The symptoms . . . well, there really were none that I could ever tell."

"Symptoms of what?"

He held his hand up, as if to beg my indulgence. "The way it happened, she goes to the doctor to find out why she isn't having babies. They check her all out and give her some tests and a few days later they give her a call." He fell momentarily silent, but not, I knew, because he was reluctant to relate what followed. As part of his testimony, this was where he drew his audience up to the edge of its seat in anticipation of the climax. "Ever hear of chlamydia, Pace?" he asked at last.

I wasn't sure I wanted to hear what came next. I let a moment pass before answering. "I think I've read about it."

"Well, that's what she had."

"Chlamydia? You gave Genine chlamydia?"

While I could barely speak the word, he seemed to accept my question as though it were a medal being bestowed upon him for an act of valor in combat. He was standing at near attention, with his broad, thick shoulders drawn back and his chin held high.

"Then they gave her some X rays, there at the doctor's, and you could see the damage—the scarring and whatnot. Anyway, Genine can't stop crying and I can't find the words to console her. I keep asking her to forgive me but it's not an apology she wants. She says she doesn't feel clean anymore, even after the medicine, and of course

I'm still full of the devil and don't want to hear it. Unlike now, I wasn't responsible enough to accept blame for those many years of womanizing, nor for the condition of her tubes. Things just got out of hand, Pace. I pushed her around a few times, you know . . . I actually aimed to hurt the sweetest, dearest girl that ever was, my wife."

"I think I've heard enough," I said, stepping out from under the overhang. "I'll be going now."

He was still talking as I walked off, his voice reaching me through the rain. "This is it, Pace Burnette! This is my testimony you're lis—!"

"Well, it's a load of shit, Peahead. It's nothing but shit."

"You're a sinner, Burnette. And until you admit that you will never walk clean in the Lord—" He stopped short the moment I spun around and started sprinting toward him, running with my head held down and limbs flailing and an otherworldly roar coming up from my chest. I could no longer feel the rain beating against me, nor did it matter that my traction wasn't any good: I got there fast enough.

"Stop!" he was shouting. "Stop, I say! Stop!"

I struck him exactly as Pop had taught us to strike our opponents back in high school. I led with the skull, using it rather as a spear. "Your optimum point of impact is the center of the chest," came Pop's rich baritone, instructing me from the distance of a decade. "Set your aim just on the other side of your target. That way you'll drive right through it without slowing." I miscalculated by a fraction of an inch and hit Peahead under the chin, driving his teeth together and his head back. Less than an instant after making contact, I added to the force of the blow by thrusting my hips inward and wrapping him up in my arms. It was as fine an open-field tackle as I'd ever made. That I escaped serious personal injury was a miracle considering how much heavier Peahead was than I. Pumping my legs, I pushed him back a couple of yards and slammed him against the building. One of his hands went up and struck a window, rattling the beer light inside. I felt him collapse beneath me, his body suddenly becoming as soft and malleable as bread dough. His breath expired in a loud, beautiful whoosh as I landed squarely on top of him.

Although I was proud of my tackling technique, a wave of regret immediately came over me. I felt shame for having resorted to violence against Peahead when I was perfectly capable of dismantling him in other ways. Determined to still any pain I might've caused him, I knelt beside him and checked to make sure he was okay. "Are you alive?" I asked, suddenly feeling injury to my own neck, a hot twitch of nerves.

As he opened his mouth to speak the door was hurled open and a knot of drunken louts came stumbling into the lot. Sheriff Sorel was leading the group, with agents Newton and Everly following closely behind. Anita and Genine were last to appear.

I glanced back at the Mustang: the old man and Beatnik, to my relief, were still out of sight.

"Now what the hay . . ." It was the sheriff, plodding to Peahead's rescue. He grabbed me by the collar and, before I could protest, threw me against the hood of a car.

"Get her away from me!" Peahead cried, pointing at Anita. "Get her . . . ! Him, too. Get him away from me, too! Get . . . !"

I thought I'd exit quietly. I took a few steps toward the Mustang and Sorel yelled for me to stop. Actually, "Halt!" was the word he used, just like a Nazi before he raises his trusty Luger and fires into your back. I lifted my arms over my head in surrender, inciting a riot of laughter. Keeping my hands up, I turned slowly around and caught Genine's hard, unflinching gaze. She was holding an umbrella over her head, and although I'd hoped to please her by humbling Peahead, her expression seemed to suggest I'd achieved the opposite.

She and Anita escorted the agents back to the lounge, maneuvering past the telephone lady, who mewled, "Ah, boys, ah, babies," as they stumbled through the door.

Peahead was still lying on the ground, curled up like a dried shrimp. The sheriff was scratching air with his index finger, beckoning me to join him. He didn't look happy, and so I took my time, hoping to delay more punishment.

"I want a word with you," he said.

"A word, Sheriff?"

"I just got a call from one of my deputies. Your friend Carnihan, he's been trying to get permission to see Silas."

I could think of no good response. I stepped up closer and gave a nod, and he said, "I just wanted you to know, maybe you can relay a message."

"Sure, Sheriff. I'll tell him."

"Since Silas won't be arraigned until Monday morning, no bail has been set and no one can see him. I'd let the boy visit but with those two FBI dickheads hanging around it don't look like that's possible, they're keeping pretty close tabs." He hooked his thumbs into his belt loops and rocked back on his heels. His voice and manner lacked the belligerence so often ascribed to him, and I wondered the reason.

"Well, thank you, Sheriff. I'll be sure to deliver—"

"And as far as this business about Silas and Deenie is concerned, I don't rightly know what to say. It's been something people've been gossiping about for years."

"Yes sir."

"There are just some of us, Burnette, innocent to the darker, more troubling aspects of human nature, and poor old Hank . . . well, he was one of these." He paused to make sure I was paying attention. "I want you to know something, Burnette. I hated to be among those who had to tell your friend, and I'm sorry for it. Was I a jackass in there tonight?"

"No sir."

Sorel's small, yellow eyes stayed fixed on mine, and I was inclined to believe that he really was contrite.

"I just wanted to tell you that," he said. "Now you tell the boy he's got nothing to be ashamed of. Tell him that for me."

When I reached the car I looked back and saw him standing where I'd left him, watching after me. The rain was falling but he hardly seemed to notice. His clothes clung to his big, thick frame like a second skin, this one as flabby as the first. He gave me a smile and pointed to where Peahead, supporting himself against the building, was struggling to rise to his feet.

"I love Jesus, too," Sorel called out to me. "It's just some people I never could get along with."

I hated to open the car door, knowing a floor light would come on and that any number of people might be watching from the windows of the go-go. The old man had wedged himself between the seat and the dashboard, and he stayed there until, somewhere on the Lewisburg Road, I told him it was safe to sit back up.

"It's why I kept calling you over," he said as I headed in the direction of Bayou Blanc. "Anita told me the place was crawling with FBI."

"Well, she was close. I did see two."

"The sheriff himself brought them by after they complained nothing much seemed to be happening in Smoke. We just missed a fight, I understand." I gave him a look of weary disbelief, and he said, "It was Anita again. She had to beat up the dancing cowboy when he became upset with the sheriff for pushing the telephone lady on those two federal agents. She says she had no choice but to take him outside and let him have it." He was staring out the window, the dreary countryside slipping past. "Says they had to call an ambulance."

"Good God."

"They suspect internal injuries, judging from what he kept spitting up."

I felt a cold shiver, recalling the scenes with Peahead and the servicemen. "Was it blood?"

"Blood, teeth, supper, lunch, *and* breakfast. Plus a few other things they weren't medically qualified to identify. Anita seemed proud. She kept showing me the scrapes on her knuckles."

It had stopped raining by the time we pulled off the highway, but gritty runoff from the twin bridges pelted the car as we followed the old road down near the bayou. I was disappointed upon reaching the summit to see no trace of the Hometown delivery truck. I traveled the muddy stretch in low gear, devising as I drove a list of places where Carnihan might've fled. We were about fifty yards from Bethany's when the old man sat up tall and pointed toward the water. "He's there. Parked under that tree."

That Carnihan had driven down from the levee road told me he planned to visit Bethany in person rather than spy through the windows, and I considered this a remarkable turn considering his history. Only a life-altering event could have driven him from hiding. I was neither disturbed nor jealous that he'd run to a woman in his time of need, choosing her over his best friend in the world, a man. Had I learned a few hours earlier that Pop wasn't my blood father, I probably would've run to Genine before Carnihan. The wise and gentle counsel of an old, bewhiskered pal hardly compares to that of the girl you love.

"We'll stop up here and walk," I said, edging the car onto the grass. "But we'll have to leave the dog."

The old man grumbled a protest, and Beatnik answered with one of his own. He was growling with teeth bared; he seemed prepared to attack rather than be left behind.

"I can't believe this is happening," I said, pocketing the keys. "A blue dog is telling me what to do."

I pushed the door open and stepped out on the road. The old man still hadn't moved, and so I stuck my head back in the car and said, "All right, bring him, then. If that's how you're gonna be about it, then bring him, goddammit."

About three-quarters of the way down the levee I tripped on a muddy divot and went tumbling to the bottom. Since I was already wet the water didn't bother me, but I could've done without the descent through the patch of briars that tore at my clothes and scratched my face and neck and arms. I was on my feet again before the old man and Beatnik caught up to me. They both were eager to make sure I'd avoided injury, but I felt like a fool and didn't want to be made over.

"Just wanted to help," the old man said when I slapped his hand away.

Beatnik was sniffing nervously at my shoes, doing his best Lassie imitation, and I frankly resented it. "Oh, get a life, would you?" As I started forward again, the sting of a thousand scrapes reminded me of how ridiculously uncoordinated I was.

Carnihan wasn't in any of the rooms on the right side of the house. The front parlor was dark and in the second room Mrs. Duvall was lying alone with a patchwork quilt pulled up to her neck, a radio playing to keep her company. The kitchen was empty and Carnihan wasn't on the dock or in the aluminum bateau tethered there. The old man started to say something and I pressed a finger to my lips to shush him; I was about to do the same to Beatnik before it came to me what he was.

We crossed the flagstone patio in back, maneuvering between rows of weather-beaten furniture holding piles of leaves and pine straw and, on one chair, a tangled spool of fishing line.

There was no one in the bathroom, although the ceiling light was on. The old man and I spent a minute observing the sea-green floor and wall tile and the ancient porcelain lavatory with both hot and cold water taps and a Mickey Mouse shower curtain spotted with mildew. The bathroom adjoined her bedroom, which could be viewed from the next window, and which, much to my amazement, held their resplendent naked forms in a bed no wider than their bodies pressed side by side. The head of the bed was just below the window, some three feet from where we stood, and Carnihan and Bethany lay quietly in each other's arms, a plain white sheet covering them to their waists. I couldn't hear much for the monotonous electric purr of a small air-conditioning unit fitted in the window. But I could see Carnihan's mouth moving and Bethany's hand stroking his narrow chest. As we watched Carnihan covered his face with his hands and began to shake with sobs, his muscular belly growing tight and ribbed. Bethany leaned over and briefly kissed him on the mouth, strands of hair connecting them when she pulled away. She sat up and you could see the cool width of her back, on one side the fleshy cup of her breast seeming as soft and pure as a fist of eiderdown. I turned to look at the old man. His face, so worn and mottled, resembled a piece of paper that had been crumpled and flattened out again, smooth now only at the edges. His eyes were full of life, though, and when he blinked a single radiant tear traced down his face.

"We should go," he whispered. "We should leave them."

My intentions might've been worthy, but it was clear to me how mistaken I was to have thought Carnihan needed me at this moment. I left the window and duckwalked toward the back of the house, Beatnik quickly catching up and running ahead. At the patio I paused to see what had become of the old man, and wheeled around to find him still standing at the window, looking in. His head was hanging and his chin touched his chest, and he seemed to be weeping. Watching him there, I felt like breaking down and crying myself. For a man or woman alone, the sight of two people making love is as hard a thing as there is to watch, and nothing is as impossible to listen to as the sound of their pleasure, voices communicating some passion in which you'll never share. Rayford Holly was more than forty years older than me, but he was cursed as I was with that bothersome piece of machinery which made him a man. While I do concede that manliness is inexorably tied to a certain piece of erectile tissue, it is the heart I mean, the heart that yearns to find another. Any journey to self-discovery ends in the arms of another, even for a billionaire.

He was about ten minutes behind me, and entered the car without a word. I'd made a U-turn and was pulling onto the highway before he said anything. "I should be going. It's time."

I was sad to hear it, sad for him and sad for us. I gave him a smile and fixed my stare on the road ahead.

"I'll be gone by Monday. Tomorrow I'll get up early and cook breakfast in the store. Sunday . . . I dunno, I'll rest up, say my goodbyes. I'd like to dance with the girls again, but I suppose that isn't possible." He was looking at me now, his eyes wide and unblinking. "Something happened tonight, didn't it, son? Something happened to that boy."

"I'd say something happened. He wound up in bed with Bethany Bixler." I didn't mean to be flip, but that was how it sounded. I added, hoping to redeem myself, "He's loved her from the moment he first saw her . . . maybe even before he ever saw her."

"I don't mean about Miss Lanie. Something happened earlier, with the FBI, when they took you two away."

I suppose it wouldn't have changed anything had I told him, but I was determined, for no good reason but loyalty, to protect Carnihan's privacy. The business about Silas and Miss Deenie would be his to share. "I'm sorry, Winston. But you won't hear it from me. You should ask Carnihan about it in the morning."

He didn't speak for a while. But then, as we were driving through Port Bess, he reached over and tapped me on the arm. "I need to repay you boys. I need to thank you somehow."

"You can begin by apologizing. I know you don't like to hear that, Winston, but it's all he ever really wanted."

"That won't happen," he said, ending the conversation.

Back at Hometown we drank ice water and ate day-old biscuits before deciding to turn in for the night. Dr. McDermott's was exactly as we'd left it, to my relief free of spooks both living and dead. I went to bed wishing for a dream, and slept pretty hard until dawn, when a colorized film clip of my own imagining, and of the unexpurgated sexual variety, sat me bolt upright and sweating in bed. I'd been making love to Genine Monteleone, unaware that the old man and Carnihan were watching from the window. The setting had been her rented house in Old Smoke, a room dark save a green candle by the bedside.

"Shall I blow it out, darling?"

"No, Gen. Let them see."

I got up, padded down the hall to the bathroom, and splashed some water on my face. And as I was lowering my head under the faucet I heard a sound coming from down the hall: a ghostly moan, it was, like someone crying. I turned the water off and the moan came again and I knew it was the old man. I walked a few doors down and peeked in one of the examination rooms and saw him sitting at a table with his head in his hands. He didn't notice me for his grief, and after a while I went back to the X-ray lab.

Eventually a garbage truck outside replaced the sound of the old man's crying, and in that noisy half minute I was able to sleep again, this time without dreams or the hope of any.

No one came for breakfast in the morning. I was up and dressed by eight o'clock, and when I entered the store I was startled to discover not a seat taken. The sign in the window said OPEN, and smells of fatty cooking wafted on the too-warm air, and by the grill a short-order chef stood with spatula in hand. He was wearing his long white apron and stovepipe hat and spectacles too small for his head, and although he seemed relieved to see me, he didn't say anything in greeting or go for my regular juice and coffee. It was true that this wasn't a weekday, but Saturdays generally attracted a handful of regulars, not to mention one or two strays lost on their way. I looked out at the street and saw no one, not even a car parked nearby, not even a bird making noise.

Even the chalkboard at the end of the counter was clean.

I took the front page of the *Daily Lip* from the stack of papers by the register, claimed my favorite seat at the center of things, and began to read about how the FBI in concert with the local sheriff's department and Smoke and Louisiana state police had arrested Silas Poe and charged him with extortion. According to the story, a spokesperson with the U.S. Attorney's Office refused to comment when questioned whether the area banker faced kidnapping or conspiracy charges, thus suggesting that law enforcement officials investigating the case doubted Poe's actual involvement in the disappearance of billionaire Rayford Holly. In the cloak-and-dagger parlance of journalism "spokesperson" means female, and I gathered this one to be Angela Brown. Skipping to the jump page for the rest, I encountered the now-familiar photograph of Missing One and his late wife, Louella. The piece concluded with a brief profile of Silas, who, it said, lived a quiet, somewhat monastic life, having no known relatives or family members.

"Coffee, please."

"Coffee?" I seemed to have awakened the old man from a slumber. "You want coffee, Pace?"

"Yeah, Winston. The black stuff you have sitting there in that pot. And some juice, too, if you don't mind."

He brought a cup over and placed it in front of me, tipping it slightly and making the coffee slosh over. The liquid puddled under the saucer and ran to the edge of the counter, dripping into my lap. I made a great show of bolting from my seat and wailing in protest, but I really didn't mind because I figured I deserved it. Considering my sarcasm, Ruby Dean would've done the same, or maybe something worse, such as mishandling a plate of eggs. Toting a wad of paper towels, the old man hurried from behind the counter and started sponging the wet spots on my clothes. He was patting the dark cloud on my shirt when suddenly he threw his arms around me and hugged me in a pathetic embrace, pressing his face against mine, his whiskers rough on the flesh of my neck. He was crying as he had during the night, crying with the peculiar violence of one unused to such emotion, and I could do nothing but try to console him, to gently pat him and whisper that everything would be okay, that time would make sure of it.

We broke apart and he went back behind the counter and began whipping eggs in a bowl. I sat on my stool as if nothing had happened. I returned to the paper and tried to read, all the while stirring my coffee with a spoon.

"Scrambled all right?"

"Scrambled's fine, thank you."

Hoping to keep him occupied, I ordered items I knew I wouldn't touch, such as hominy grits and home fries and cottage cheese and pink grapefruit cut in sections, in addition to my usual breakfast of pancakes with cane syrup.

"Did I do something wrong to keep them away?" he asked from the stove, his back turned to me. There was a brittleness to his voice that suggested another bout of tears soon to come.

"It isn't you, Winston."

"Something I said, perhaps?"

"You'll have to trust me. It isn't you."

"Who is it then?"

"It's the town, it's Smoke. It's who we are."

"Who . . . ?"

"It's just what happens to people when they stop thinking good things can happen to them."

You could tell he had no idea what I was getting at, and I wasn't sure I did either. But I did know that in a place that didn't hate itself the customers wouldn't have stayed away on a morning as bright and clear with new summer sunshine as this one. They'd have come and filled the lot and the streets along the square, and they'd have loitered and gossiped about what a scandal it was that one of their own had run afoul of the law and found himself the subject of news reports all across the country. They'd have enjoyed it, too. But this was Smoke and Smoke had an inferiority complex. Silas Poe was just more proof that we were cursed to failure, doomed to shame and turpitude.

"You're not eating much."

"Huh?"

"I'm afraid I'll have to charge you."

"Fine. You're only doing your job, after all."

That famous capacity of mine for pity did not necessarily begin with my fellow man. I could feel as sorry for Pace Burnette as for the families of indigents who twice daily lined up for soup and bread at the Smoke Mission. I was sitting there lost in a gloomy fog, wondering about my future with Genine, when the screen door rattled open and Carnihan stepped in looking as fit and rested as if he'd just returned from an ocean cruise. He was wearing the same clothes he had on yesterday, but his face was cleanly shaven and his hair was combed and there was about his eyes a pearly finish that hinted at a good night's sleep.

He sat next to me and nudged me with a forearm. "So why the long face? Somebody die?"

I didn't answer and he started picking at one of the bowls I'd left untouched, this one of cinnamon oatmeal topped with banana slices. His mouth was full when he said, "How about some coffee, Winston?"

"Coffee?" The old man came alive in a panic. "Coffee, did you say?" He poured Carnihan a cup and dropped a spoon in the saucer and hustled down to the other end of the counter and retrieved the sugar basket with the most packets. "Scrambled okay?" he asked.

"Scrambled? Scrambled what, Winston? Scrambled brains?"

"Scrambled eggs."

"Scrambled nothing," Carnihan said. "Give me a plate of what Burdette has here. If you've got to cook eggs, fry a couple over easy and put them on top of the stack."

"Edges crispy?"

"Yeah, man. Edges crispy."

He nudged my arm again and pressed his mouth against my ear, whispering to keep the old man from hearing. "What you do, you crack the yolks and let them run on into your pancakes."

"Oh, do you?"

"You add some cane syrup and mix everything together and boy do you ever have something else to eat."

I don't know why his behavior infuriated me so. I'd expected him to be upset about Silas and his visit to Old Smoke last night, but that seemed to be the farthest thing from his mind, resolved and forgotten long ago.

He pulled away from me and started nodding his head with the exuberance of one whose truthfulness has just been questioned, and I watched with the eyes of the one casting doubt.

"The thing about food," he said, "it all tastes the same after you've been with a woman."

"Oh? And how is that, Jay?"

"Well, it tastes like her. Like her mouth and other parts . . . the secret ones."

He'd opened the door to questions, but I wasn't asking any—not now, anyway. I was too mad at him.

"I was with Bethany last night, in case you were wondering."

"No. No, I wasn't."

"I spent the night at Bayou Blanc. I actually stayed there." He started nodding his head as if I'd challenged him again. "Go ahead. Give her a call if you don't believe me. She'll tell you."

"Why shouldn't I believe you?"

"Why? Because I live in Smoke—I come from the place. And nothing wonderful's supposed to happen to people like us."

Maybe I was just jealous. He had, after all, won the heart of a girl on the same night I seemed to have lost another's. I picked the *Lip* back up and let him get a look at the front page. As I began to read —or to pretend to—he yanked the section from my hands and tossed it toward the shelves. The pages came apart and scattered across the floor, some skidding as far as the front door.

"Too bad we don't have a cat. I'd tell him to go use the bathroom on that thing and on you, too."

"Beatnik's smart. Get him to do it."

"Beatnik happens to be busy at the moment." He nodded toward where the dog was asleep by the business counter.

He ate a few more spoonfuls of my oatmeal and the old man approached with a rag in hand, making circles. "I thought I'd tell you, Jay, I've decided to leave first thing Monday morning." His voice had a nervous edge, and I wondered whether he was going to start crying again. "I'll be heading back to Liberty. But I just wanted to let you know how much—"

"You're kidnapped, Winston," Carnihan interrupted. "You leave when I tell you to leave. No sooner."

A great smile came to the old man's face, and he began to laugh as tears filled his eyes.

"But Monday," Carnihan said now, seeming to reconsider, "if you really want to go then . . . well, all right."

The old man's smile went away and an urgency came to his cleaning: the lines grew long and crooked. Behind him the eggs had started to burn.

"Not that crispy," Carnihan said.

"I've been lying to myself."

"Yes, you have, Winston."

"I'm no cook." And he removed his stovepipe hat and placed it on the counter. He took his apron off, too.

"I still want my eggs," Carnihan said. "Cook or no cook. Kidnapped or no kidnapped." He sipped his coffee and seemed delighted by it, then he finished off my oatmeal. "Let me tell you something, Winston, and I want you to listen closely. Are you listening?"

The old man waved his spatula.

"A long time ago someone I greatly admire said to me, 'Remember who you are.' But he was mistaken, that man. What he should've said was, 'First find out who you aren't, and then you can begin to remember.' " When the old man didn't speak, Carnihan continued, "It's the key to happiness, Winston. Finding out who you aren't." He was looking for something else of mine to eat; he chose a cup of yogurt. "I bet you feel better now, don't you, Winston . . . admitting you're not a cook?"

"I feel no different."

"Oh. Okay. Then if that's the case, cook me up a new batch of eggs. And tell me: where're those goddamned pancakes?"

The old man turned back to the stove and removed the ruined eggs from the grill and dumped them in the trash. He started over with a new batch, and Carnihan, glancing up suddenly, said, "And while you're at it, Winston, let's just forget about that apology. I don't know why I ever wanted one."

"The apology?"

"Yeah, just forget I ever mentioned it. I can't imagine what I was thinking of."

The old man gave a whimper and leaned against the stove. Never have I seen such pain as was evident in his face. For a full minute he neither moved nor spoke, and another breakfast might've been lost had Carnihan not said something. "God, man, not too crispy again!"

It seemed to take everything in him to get the breakfast together; his spatula alone might've weighed a ton. Finally he put the eggs on top of some pancakes and deposited the plate in front of Carnihan. His eyes were rimmed red and his skin was damp and sallow. His hands were shaking.

"Eggs," Carnihan said, "we don't want to waste too many. It all adds up, you know?"

"I'd buy you more myself," the old man said, "but my wallet, it's still in my truck."

"Not that it matters," Carnihan said. "But you didn't have any cash in it, anyway. I checked. How many eggs can a person buy without cash?" He cut into the eggs and down through the pancakes, soaking them with the bright yellow yolk. "What kind of a billionaire are you, Winston? I thought billionaires blew their noses and wiped their backsides with thousand-dollar bills."

"When I travel I use credit cards, or I just pick things up along the way." The old man's voice sounded as if someone had knocked the wind out of him and he was trying to get it back. "I own a chain of stores, I can take whatever I like." He went back to the stove and started cleaning with a steel brush. The sound of the bristles scraping against steel was so irritating that I thought I'd have to leave the room, but then he stopped suddenly and wheeled back around. "We could do that, you know?"

"We could do what?" It was Carnihan, speaking with his mouth full. "Blow our noses with money?"

"We could go to the one here in town—to Monster Mart. I'd be willing to let you take whatever you need to replenish whatever you think I've taken from you."

"You sell fresh, country eggs there, Winston?"

"No, but take something in exchange—take feminine napkins. I know how much you people like them." The old man's voice had returned, rich and powerful as ever, and it seemed to upset Carnihan, who'd stopped chewing with his cheeks still bulging with food. "The way to get in," the old man was saying now, "there's a computerized lock on the back door, set to open if you punch the right sequence of numbers, and if, at the same time, you've got a key card. The key card you stick in a slot and a little green light comes on and that means you have thirty seconds to go in before an alarm goes off."

"Yeah?" Carnihan wasn't impressed.

"My card was in my wallet, Jay."

"Which means it's in that empty coffee tin." He pointed to a shelf. "Where I put it after I brought you back here."

The old man took the tin down and removed the wallet, wiping it free of the grounds which clung to the sticky eelskin hide. "We'll go late tonight," he said. "After closing."

"Aren't there any security guards or dogs or anything?"

"There's a security system, nothing else. You need a key to cut it off, which I happen to have right here." He took a chain from his pocket and showed us the one he meant. "It's a universal. It works on all five thousand one hundred and ninety-seven of them."

"How much can we take?" Carnihan said. "If it's just enough to cover the cost of a few burnt eggs, then I'm not going. To be quite honest, Winston, I was thinking about taking a riding lawn mower or something."

"What do you need a mower for with all those goats?" I said.

"The only reason we ever got goats in the first place is because Daddy couldn't afford to buy a machine." The memory seemed to depress him. He swallowed hard and shook his head. "Ol' Fontenot gave him a nanny and a billy and that's how we got started. If not for Rayford Holly and Monster Mart we'd've owned a riding mower a long time ago, not to mention a few million other things." Carnihan lifted a forkful of egg and pancake to his mouth, but then he let it drop to his plate. "Did I tell you to forget about that apology?" he asked. "Well, forget that I said to forget it. I want you to remember it, because you owe me, you no-good, town-killing sonofa—"

"Whatever you say, boss." And you could see how hard it was for the old man to keep from smiling. "Whatever on this earth you want. Anything."

"And forget about not being kidnapped." Carnihan's voice was dark with rage now, just like in the old days. "You're not going anywhere I don't want you to go. You're stuck here, Winston—stuck right here in Smoke!"

"Sure, boss. Okay. All right. Whatever you say." He took his hat off the counter and rather ceremoniously put it back on; the apron and glasses followed in order. "You're still the man, boss. You've always been the man and you always will be the man."

"I will, will I?"

"Always . . . always, always, always."

Carnihan started eating his breakfast again, eating with the appetite of one who tastes a pretty new girlfriend in every bite. "Hey, Winston," he said after a while. "Do you even sell riding lawn mowers?" And a big smile of his own came to his face.

X

The morning dragged on, the door staying closed, the phone ringing only once, a wrong number. "No one here named Leo," Carnihan said, then slammed the receiver down.

Tired of seeing newspaper scattered all over the floor, I put the section back together and laid it on top of the others. Carnihan had been waiting for this. As soon as I sat back down, he walked over to the register and started reading out loud from one of the newspaper stories about Silas. His voice was big and showy, and although he pretended to search for a biased editorial slant and other evidence of why we called it the *Lip,* he really was just looking for new information.

"Here's something," he said. "Maybe we should start calling it the *Error.* Why, they've got him living in a Victorian on Court Street. Everybody knows good and well that's a Greek Revival."

Neither the old man nor I said anything.

"The *Daily Lip* strikes again," Carnihan muttered.

At one o'clock the old man turned the stove off and stepped out from behind the counter, signaling his defeat. He flipped the sign over in the front window and said, "I surrender."

"No," Carnihan said from his stool. "You've still got a meal left to cook."

"Oh, do I? And who would that be for?"

"Make a couple of BLTs and wrap them in wax paper, then pour a thermos of Kool-Aid. If there's any coconut pie left give me a piece —no, make that the whole thing, the whole pie, whatever you've got. Take one of those old picnic baskets off the shelf, dust it real good, and put everything in it."

The old man did as he was told and Carnihan stood by the register, recording the charges. "And Winston, add some Tabasco and antacids while you're at it."

A glint of recognition came to the old man's eyes. "Tabasco, you say, boss?"

"Yeah. Make it the biggest bottle you've got."

"But Jay," I said. "We can't see Silas till Monday morning when he's arraigned."

"Yeah, but we can feed him, can't we? Imagine how afraid he must be right now, stuck up there with all those hoodlums. Maybe if we give him heartburn he'll feel more at home."

The old man started cooking and Carnihan and I moved down to the end of the counter and sat watching the street, our feet propped up on the windowsill. It was still quiet in front of the store but you could see down toward the square where a couple of camera crews were trained on the jailhouse.

Carnihan took a notepad and scribbled something in a hurry. "My wish list," he said. "For later tonight." He wrote again and then picked his head up. "Hey, Winston, mind if I bring Bethany Bixler along?"

"Along where?" The old man was turning the bacon with a fork and the question had caught him off guard. "Along to see Silas?"

"No, along to Monster Mart tonight. Isn't it the Bible that says when a man takes a woman two flesh become one?"

"I think it does say that," the old man answered.

"Well, Bethany Bixler and me became one last night and I was wondering if I could bring her along?"

The old man fell silent, watching the grease sputter on the grill. He seemed to be thinking about it. "Sure, boss," he said at last. "You can bring her. That'd be fine."

I glanced over at what Carnihan was writing and made note of the list: *riding lawn mower with grass catcher, motorized weed cutter, gas blower for leaves, radial tires (whitewall), tent, sleeping bag, kerosene lantern, Coleman stove, fishing tackle, boom box, telephone answering machine, television with remote control, microwave ovens, doghouse, dogbones.*

"Why did you make that plural?" I asked, pointing a finger at the entry I meant. "Why would you need more than one?"

"One for you and one for me," he answered, as if the explanation were obvious. "Didn't you want one a while back? We got in a big fight about it."

"Sure, I wanted one. But I also wanted to buy it with my own money, which is how most people come to own things."

"Well, brother, here's your chance to get one without having to raid your piggy bank. If for whatever reason you don't feel right about it, just consider it a gift from me."

"It's got to have a revolving plate," I said. "I don't want one unless it's got that."

Carnihan looked up from his writing and addressed the old man. "We're going to let Pace take whatever he wants, too, all right, Winston? I know he wasn't part of any local business you happened to kill, but he is from Smoke. You owe him, partner."

"That's fine," the old man said, dropping slices of bread into the toaster. "This'll square the score between us."

Numb with excitement, I had to suppress an urge to leap to my feet and uncork a rowdy cheer. Was this how a lottery winner felt just after getting the news?

"You won't have to worry about me taking too much," I told the old man, hoping to show him what a conscientious young thief I planned to be. "You really didn't hurt me all that much. Maybe I'll just take some office supplies . . . paper and whatnot."

"We carry a fine line of computer products," he said, sounding a bit disappointed that I wasn't planning to clean him out. "Don't you need a new monitor or keyboard or something?"

"To tell you the truth, I really could use a printer, but I hardly think—"

"Are you familiar with the laser? It's a sweet piece of machinery, and not at all costly to maintain."

Carnihan handed me a pencil and notepad and tapped his finger against the top page. "Don't forget. I already wrote down microwave, so you won't need to."

"Oh, yes. You did, didn't you?" And I began to write myself.

We had been busy at work for about five minutes when Carnihan lifted his head and cleared his throat to get the old man's attention. "What about Genny, Winston? Can she come, too?"

"Genny?" He was taking the bacon off the grill, laying it on sheets of paper towel. "Sure, you can invite Genny. That'd be nice. Maybe we can introduce her to a new cosmetics line." Before I could ask him what he was trying to say, he came up with an explanation. "Not that she needs it, but she does seem to enjoy makeup and hairspray and whatnot."

"I'll call Bethany," Carnihan said to me, "and you can call Genine. Or would you prefer that I called them both?"

"Better if you called, I think."

He nodded and continued writing.

"But what are you going to tell them?" I said, suddenly feeling panicked. "You can't just say Rayford Holly's taking us on a shopping spree at Monster Mart."

"Heck, no," he said. "I'll tell them it's a surprise party. You know how much those two like to have a good time."

Industrial food processor, was the last thing he put down before getting up to make the calls. While Carnihan was on the phone, the old man fixed the basket. He put the sandwiches and tea in and walked over to the refrigerated pie safe. "I'd bet it's real hot in that jail. So we'd better not send the coconut. We wouldn't want it to spoil. You don't think Silas would object to apple, do you?"

The old man wrapped the pie with aluminum foil and fitted it in the basket. He got some hot sauce and antacids and put them in, too, then he added a few chocolate bars and a box of mint-flavored toothpicks. He was laying red-checked napkins on top when he seemed to remember something. He looked over to make sure Carnihan was still occupied on the phone. "The thing that happened to him? It's about Silas, isn't it?"

"I told you, Winston, I'm not talking."

A few minutes later Carnihan put the receiver down and walked over to us. "Ya got that lunch bucket ready?"

"I got it, boss."

"Remember about the Tabasco?"

"I remembered."

"Hey, Winston?"

"Yeah, boss?"

"They're coming, both of them. I told them it was a party with monster door prizes. They wanted to know where, and I told them a secret place, but to meet us here first and we'd drive them." He laughed and swatted the air. "Maybe I should rent a tractor trailer truck. An eighteen-wheeler."

"Rent two," the old man said. "Rent four."

Carnihan hustled up to the counter with the cockiness of old, his lungs filled to capacity, swaggering so much you wondered how he was able to keep his balance. He grabbed the basket and started for the door, and, as I'd done all my life, and as I figured I'd continue to do for the rest of it, I chased right on after him.

"Winston," he said at the door. "You stay put and guard the fort. We'll catch you on the flip-flop."

"I'll stay, boss."

And together we ran out in the street.

We were standing across from the jailhouse, gazing at the windows upstairs, waiting for a familiar face to appear behind the bars. Ostensibly we wanted to alert Silas that we'd come with food, but if we managed, while playing the roles of Good Samaritans, to be seen on live TV, then that was fine, too. I figured what we were looking at were either rec rooms or bullpens, since so many orange-clothed people passed by, only a few of them restrained with chains or cuffs. Smoke was a small town where you knew everybody, but none of the faces was familiar and after about ten minutes Carnihan started to worry that the mayonnaise and bacon grease on the sandwiches would spoil if we didn't deliver them soon.

We took seats on the stone wall surrounding the square and watched the last of the television crews. It was more than eighty degrees out and humid enough to suffocate a mosquito, but Rachel Wayne stood under a battery of electric lights jawing away about extortion and Silas Poe. You could tell she was concluding her report, because she started looking around for someone to talk to. Her station, as a so-called public service, liked to present a daily "Street-corner Camera," during which Rachel interviewed "ordinary citizens" about whatever happened to dominate the news on that particular day. Generally the ordinary citizens were drunks just leaving a bar or illiterates with neither any knowledge of world events nor the ability to articulate opinions about them. "Well, I think it's awful, just awful," was about as enlightened a response as Rachel ever got, but she always managed to find great meaning in it: more than once she'd been heard to state that there rarely was anything ordinary about the views of ordinary citizens.

Unable to round anyone up today, Rachel started marching toward Carnihan and me with her cameraman in tow. She stopped in front of us and, wheeling around to address the videocam, announced that here were a couple of ordinary citizens she'd known since grade school. "Could you tell us, gentlemen, how you felt upon learning that one of Smoke's most respected city fathers was linked to the Rayford Holly disappearance?"

Carnihan lifted a fist to his mouth and cleared his throat. "I think—" He stopped short and turned to me with upraised hands, offering to let me go first.

I looked into the lens and said, "Well, I think it's awful, Rachel, just awful."

Rachel smiled as if to suggest that these were her sentiments exactly, and proffered the microphone to Carnihan. "I think . . ." he began again, only to stop as before. "Could you repeat the question, please?"

Rachel did as asked, and he said, "Before I answer, Ms. Wayne . . . are we live?"

"Yes, we are, Mr. Carnihan." Rachel sounded as poised as ever. "But don't be nervous. Everything will be fine."

I couldn't tell whether Carnihan was really shaken or just pretending to be. He kept resetting his feet and sniffling, and a nervous twitch had come to his face. "First of all, I'd like to compliment you on how lovely you look today, Ms. Wayne." He bowed at the waist to show he meant it, and the camera held her brightly painted visage, a smile so large that it threatened to carve a fissure in her makeup. Carnihan cleared his throat again. "As I remark to myself every time I tune in to your program, Ms. Wayne, it's truly remarkable what a nose job, a tummy tuck, and a breast enlargement—not to mention cans of hairspray and a tub of wrinkle cream . . . what all these, taken together, can do for a person. You look absolutely smashing."

Rachel spat and stuttered and lunged for the microphone, grasping air as Carnihan stepped back and lightly elbowed her out of the way. One of her heels broke and she went sprawling face-forward in the street, her dress sponging up some of the watery crud standing by the curb.

"And second of all," Carnihan was saying now, facing the camera again, "I'd liked to announce that Hometown Family Goods on the corner of Market and North streets still offers the best for less at prices your family can afford." He seemed to have run two of his most trusty slogans together, but this did not deter him: he threw in a third. "We offer you service with a smile, and the satisfaction of knowing your money is helping to maintain the oldest existing family mercantile in the state of Louisiana. We ask you to come by and see for yourself. And for those of you who do not live in Smoke—yes, we do accept out-of-town checks. . . ."

The cameraman had swung his instrument toward the jailhouse, but Carnihan walked out in the street and stood a few feet in front of him. "Now what was the question?" he said again, looking down at Rachel. "Oh, yes. What do I think of our city father Silas Poe being tossed in the klink?" He seemed hesitant to reply, but finally he said, "Well, I think it's awful, Rachel, just awful."

I went to help the woman back up to her feet, but she took a swipe at me, barely missing, and got up on her own. Carnihan surrendered the microphone with no resistance, and Rachel wheeled around to face the camera with twigs and pea gravel clinging to her face and clothes. "This is Rachel Wayne," she said, "reporting live from the sheriff's department in downtown Smoke. Back to you in the studio, Hoyt."

Carnihan tried to be sympathetic. "Feel free to sue me, Rachel, but I honestly have nothing left to give but debt and heartache. If you need some of that . . . well, come on, then."

The cameraman was one of those sun-deprived ponytail types who, twenty-odd years after the fall of Saigon, still pretended to have fought in Vietnam, an experience which he liked to say informed his life to this day, but which in fact he knew about only from Chuck Norris movies. I'd met hundreds like him, but he was the first I was ever forced to strike in the mouth, the blow being delivered after he took an errant karate chop at Carnihan. The man smashed to the ground and immediately began to yell for help: "You hurt me! My God, my God! You hurt me!"

In seconds Sheriff Sorel and two of his deputies were dragging Carnihan and me across the street, heedless of the traffic filing in both directions. They deposited us in a lobby sparsely furnished with plastic chairs, plastic sofas, and plastic pedestals topped with plastic ferns, then rushed back outside. I watched from the window as Rachel and her cameraman consoled each other under the trees of the square and reenacted the events of a few moments before.

A third deputy walked up, a tall, thin one. "The sheriff," he declared with a lazy drawl, "you picked a really bad day to piss him off." He plugged his thumbs under his waistline and draped his hands over his black leather belt. "Last night there was trouble over at the go-go . . . bad trouble." The man was chewing a plug of tobacco, the juice of which he now sought to purge from his mouth. He walked over to one of the plants and watered it. "Somebody almost got kilt. That close." And he held a hand up, his thumb and forefinger fixed less than an inch apart.

An image of Peahead Chowder immediately came to mind. He was lying in mud, and blood colored his face. This was followed by a vision of the two enlisted men clasping the meat of their groins as though it were their last earthly possessions.

"Old geezer by the name of . . . now what was his name?" The deputy gazed off at the ceiling as if to find the answer there. "Anyway, Anita beat his brains in. He's on life support at the clinic even as we speak, and the old doctor there says he ain't gonna make it."

The deputy needed to spit again, and this time, lacking the energy to walk over to the plants, he let it go on the floor. "You boys got to urinate or anything of that nature?" A brown thread was hanging from the corner of his mouth. "My legs is sore and I'm just gonna mosey over to that couch there and set a spell." He was looking at the place, some twenty feet away. "Y'all keep quiet and keep still. I don't want the sheriff getting no madder than he already is."

He waddled away, his soles squeaking on the yellow-tiled floor which a couple of trustees were in the process of mopping. Before stretching out on the Naugahyde the deputy spit again, flakes of tobacco coming up with it. I supposed that was one of the benefits of running a jail: there was always someone in orange clothes to clean up behind you.

Carnihan said, "I wonder who she beat this time?"

I hadn't told him that we'd gone there looking for him last night, and I still wasn't inclined to. If we checked his favorite watering hole, he was certain to figure we'd checked the house of his favorite girl as well.

"Genny didn't say anything about it when you talked to her on the phone? You'd think she'd've mentioned it."

"Well, she didn't," he said.

"Nothing about the dancing cowboy and calling for an ambulance and blood everywhere?"

"Did this . . . ? How the hell'd you know about that, Pace?"

"You're right," I said. "It could be anyone, I suppose. You know what a bully Anita can be."

He was staring at me, his eyes dark with suspicion, his mouth set in a scowl. Anxious to get him off the subject, I turned around and focused on the activity outside—on Sheriff Sorel holding court with Rachel Wayne and her cameraman. I'd always known him to be a fairly impassive fellow, the sheriff, but he was building pictures with his hands and kicking the heel of his boot against the roots of the crepe myrtles they were standing under. It was clear he was trying to explain something, and that they were receptive to it. They kept nodding and glancing over in our direction, squinting to see past the reflection on the windows. To end the discussion, the cameraman offered his hand and the sheriff shook it, and Rachel did the same. They waved and parted: the crack news team from Channel 10 with their load of equipment, the sheriff with our picnic basket.

As he crossed the street I was reminded of a tired old bull with only one care in the world: where to find some shade.

"Thank you much, there, Lonnie Tom," the sheriff said upon entering the room. The deputy had been napping, and you could tell, coming out of it, he had no idea where he was. He scrambled to get off the couch. "Is this for Silas?" the sheriff asked Carnihan. He held up the basket. Carnihan nodded and the sheriff said, "Lonnie Tom, take this up to Mr. Poe, if that ain't asking too much." He turned to address Carnihan again. "Y'all didn't put no Saturday night special in here, did you, boys?"

"Just a file to saw the bars apart," Carnihan answered.

"Well, if that's the case Silas's liable to be sawing for weeks . . . the size hole he'd need." He laughed for a second then said, "Now, Jay, what is it exactly you got in this basket? Is that bacon I smell?"

The sheriff was checking the contents himself when Carnihan listed them: "Sandwiches, a pie, some candy, a bottle of Tabasco, a roll of Tums, a bunch of napkins . . . what else?"

"Toothpicks and Kool-Aid," I said.

"Toothpicks and Kool-Aid," Carnihan repeated.

"You hear that, Lonnie Tom? Anything missing when I check later I know who to come after, you un'erstand me, boy?"

The deputy's mouth was too full of tobacco and juice for him to speak. He left with the basket, and Sheriff Sorel motioned for Carnihan and me to follow him outside. We walked as far as the curb in front of the Delta and stood looking up at the huge, darkened marquee. "I just did you two a great favor," he said. "Rachel Wayne and her friend have decided not to press charges against you, Mr. Burnette, for your assault on them on the square. And, Mr. Carnihan, you'll be happy to learn that your disorderly conduct, as described to me by Miss Wayne, is forgiven, forgotten, finished. . . ."

"But it was on live TV, Sheriff."

"Well, part of it was. She tells me the engineer in her control room managed to cut you off about midway and break to a commercial." He reached in his pocket and removed the heel of Rachel's pump. "You will have to buy her a new shoe, though."

Carnihan took the thing and sniffed it, then tossed it in the trash littering the entrance to the old picture show. "What'd you have to tell those two to settle them down?" he asked.

"Now don't you worry about that," the sheriff said. "It don't count so much as the fact that I went to war for you two boys." He hesitated to make sure we were listening, and I recalled the fellow in the lot last night at Babylon, the one who'd stood in the rain and informed me that some of us were innocent to the darker, more troubling aspects of human nature, and that I should tell Carnihan not to be ashamed. That man and this one were different people, it seemed, and I wondered what had happened between then and now to produce such a change. "I'll ask you point-blank," the sheriff said. "What did y'all see last night at the go-go . . . out in the lot?"

Carnihan said, "You mean at Babylon? We weren't at Babylon."

The sheriff lifted his face to mine, and after a while so did Carnihan. It was too late for me to do anything but tell the truth. "Anita taking a few swipes at people," I answered.

The sheriff gave a nod. He didn't seem pleased. "You sure it was Anita and not someone else?"

"I'm sure," I said. "And from what I could tell, she went at them unprovoked. I'd even say she was enjoying it."

"How many did you see her with?"

"Three."

"Just three? You sure it wasn't four?"

"Three seemed plenty, considering what she did to them."

The sheriff shuffled over to within inches of where I was standing. He exhaled deeply and I could smell his breath, liver and onions mingled oddly with Mr. Pete's baklava from over at the Palace. "You know what they do to fresh young boys like yourself upstairs in lockup, Burnette?"

"No sir. I'm afraid I don't."

"You want me to tell you what they do?"

"Not really."

"You like to travel, Burnette?"

"Whenever I have the money and get the chance. . . ."

"Ever been down the Hershey highway?"

"No sir."

"Would you like to go?"

"No."

"It's a long, hard trip, if you know what I mean."

I knew what he meant and what I was witnessing: a transformation of the Jekyll-Hyde variety. In the course of about twelve hours he'd gone from being the sensitive, advice-giving patron saint of confused young adults to a snarling, foul-breathed bastard with a penchant for jailhouse buggery. I was slightly nostalgic for the sheriff's other self, and knew better than to challenge this one. When I failed to speak, he said, "The D.A. and I had a meeting a little while ago—right over there in my office." He pointed to the rear of the jailhouse. "Turns out early this morning he got a phone call from a woman who said someone beat her husband half to death."

"What's that got to do with me?"

"Just hang on. I'll tell you." He shoved his hands down in the slits of his back pockets and looked around to make sure we were still alone. "This woman," he said, "she wanted to know why no one had been picked up for attacking her husband. And the D.A., who's just been woken up, you un'erstand . . . the D.A. tells her he'll handle it himself and hangs up and checks the clock. It's five A.M. and he can't get back to sleep and of course he isn't very happy about that. He immediately puts in a call to Smoke police, and guess what they say to him?" He was quiet but you could tell he didn't expect an answer. "They say Babylon is not within their jurisdiction. It's outside the city limits and thus part of Sheriff Sorel's territory. So the D.A. gets dressed and climbs in his car and comes to my house and pulls me out of bed. I get in the car with him and we come here and he wants to know why I haven't made an arrest yet, and I tell him because it was Anita and it was self-defense, she was just protecting herself. But he's afraid this woman, the one who called . . . he's afraid because she's threatened to make a stink with the *Lip.* He reminds me that both his election and mine're coming up in the fall, and wants to know whether I've considered the ramifications of publicity such as that. I'm a law-and-order man, Burnette, always have been. I'm also married with children. You think your mama and daddy would vote for a sheriff who condones harlotry? Or one who steps out on his wife of thirty-four years with a madam who beats up innocent people for no reason but her mood is off?"

"I don't think they would," I said.

"What about their son being arrested on a battery charge? You think they'd un'erstand that?"

"Not that, either."

"Just tell us what you need, Sorel." It was Carnihan, pushing in between us. His hands knuckled up and he squared his feet shoulder-width apart, as if in preparation for a fight. I considered pulling him away, but the sheriff seemed to wither in the face of Carnihan's defiance. He glanced down at the ground and kicked it, then sighed at length.

"What I need is for Burnette here, if ever he was to be asked, and he might not be . . . what I need is for him to remember that he saw Anita fighting, all right, but in each case she was just protecting herself. She was protecting herself against someone making unwelcome advances."

"That's easy," Carnihan said. "What else?"

"Maybe go to the clinic and talk to the one got beat up. Anita says you're friends from nights at the go-go."

"If it's that cowboy you mean," I said, "the one who's always dancing . . . I don't know him at all. I'm surprised to learn he even has a wife."

"The one good thing, from what the D.A. says, is that she doesn't know who did it, the wife doesn't. Apparently he hasn't said who it was yet. But that's likely to get out, eventually, since Anita was bragging so much about how she whipped him. It's motive I'm most concerned about. No one actually saw the man until she was finished with him. If she acted in self-defense then the D.A. has no cause to bring a case against her."

"We'll talk to the guy," Carnihan said. "We'll check in with the wife, too. What else?"

"That's it." Sorel slapped his hands together. He turned to address Carnihan, a sleepy grin on his face. "It's funny, Jay, but when I told Rachel Wayne about how distressed you were over your daddy being incarcerated she really seemed . . . well, *touched*, I guess is the word. Not only how you found out who he was, but how you'd come by this morning with that basket of food to show him just how much you . . . well, just how much you really loved him, is the language I think I used." The sheriff gazed off at the heavens, the pose intended to suggest sympathy. "Rachel said it would make for a nice human interest story, and I agreed. Only thing, I told her this off the record, as background information. And to do that piece she'd have to get permission from me, since I'm her primary source, you un'erstand?" He lowered his eyes and met Carnihan's straightaway.

Carnihan said, "This is sort of like blackmail, isn't it?"

"Sort of."

"Then tell me if I got this right. If Pace doesn't help you out, he takes a trip down the Hershey highway—"

"Up, son. *Up* the Hershey highway."

"Okay. Up, then. He takes it up the damned thing. And if I don't help, everyone finds out who my real father is and that my fake one was married to my real one's girl?"

"I got a little confused at the end there," the sheriff said, "but I think that about covers it."

"What's wrong with you?" I said to the man. I could feel myself losing control. I took a step toward him and tightened my hands into fists. I probably would've hit him had Carnihan not intervened, clutching me by the arm and pulling me away.

"Take it easy, brother. Easy, now."

Laughing from deep in his gut, the sheriff walked a few steps over and picked Rachel's shoe heel out of the trash. "Ever been in love, boys?" he asked, brushing past us on his way up the sidewalk. "There's nothing you won't do for the woman, even when she's . . . well, a fat, ugly whore like Anita Billedeaux."

His back was to us now. He lifted an arm in salute, said "Y'all have a nice day, hear?" and disappeared through the electric doors of the jailhouse.

On the way back to the store I told Carnihan the truth about what I'd seen and done last night at Babylon. I told him about Anita's boasts to the old man, and what the old man had noted about her hands, the scrapes on her knuckles from where she'd clobbered the cowboy. I described my unlikely meeting with Peahead Chowder and detailed the damage Anita had inflicted upon him, and I told him how good it'd felt to drive him into the wall, and how Pop would've been proud of my tackling technique. I was reporting on Anita's encounter with the soldiers from Fort Polk when suddenly I stopped myself and stepped up next to him. "They're still married, you know? Genine and him."

He'd been walking with his head down, but he lifted it back now and stared into my eyes.

"They never even got a divorce, Jay."

"Yeah, man. I knew."

"You knew? You knew and you didn't tell me?" I wasn't quite as upset as I might've seemed, but he needed to think I was. "I can't believe you let me want her when all along you knew she was still married."

"Let you? You don't let a person want another. They let themselves. Where's your head, man?"

"It still isn't right," I complained, "what you did."

"Hey, Pace, let's not talk about what's right, if you don't mind. I forgot to mention it the same way you forgot to mention that you and Winston watched me and Bethany through the window."

"We didn't see anything."

"You saw *everything* . . . all that mattered."

"I was just worried about you, is all. I thought maybe you needed someone to talk to after that business at Silas's. I meant to help."

"Look, brother, just so you'll know, Hank Carnihan, as far as I'm concerned . . ." For some reason he couldn't finish. He lowered his head again and said, "I think of him now and only one word comes to mind."

We took a few more steps and he still hadn't said it, maybe because he wanted me to venture a guess. "What is it? The word you think of?"

" 'Daddy,' " he said quietly, as if speaking to the man himself. "I think of him and my mind says 'Daddy.' "

We were standing under the awning of a defunct car dealership, posters of five-year-old models still hanging on the walls inside, the word AVAILABLE written in white chalk on the giant picture window.

"The truth is," he said, leaning back against the glass, "I'd suspected he wasn't my natural father for years—since puberty, I suppose, which is when you first start to have questions about who you are, where you come from, that sort of shit. You remember, not long before he died, how me and him had that heart-to-heart out at Worm Road, and he pulled out all the old photo albums? Well, he told me then, he told me everything. It really was why I was so insanely happy afterward: because I knew the truth at last. He didn't tell me it was Silas who was my father—I'm not sure whether Daddy even knew that himself—but he did say it wasn't him and that Mama had dated around a lot before he came along. Daddy was the best man I ever knew, Pace. He didn't marry Darned Dizzy Deenie for any reason but he loved her and didn't want to live his life without her."

"Did he know she was going to have a baby? When they got married, I should say."

"He did. She was a few months pregnant when they decided to elope—three at most. All that stuff about going to Biloxi on their honeymoon . . . all that's true, Pace, including the story about the first time they did it in the infirmary. I asked him why he would marry someone who was already knocked up, and he said he'd really wrestled with it until the day I was born and he saw me for the first time. He cried a little when he told me that. 'If you could just find a girl to love as much as I loved your mother . . .' he told me that day at the house. Then he said, 'With the right girl everything makes sense.' "

Carnihan became quiet, and, as usual when I'm called upon to provide clear judgment and pointed advice, I could think of nothing to say. I feigned interest in the showroom, shielding the glare with my hands and standing close to the glass.

He seemed to remember something. "Do you think he married her because he needed an heir to Hometown—another Carnihan whose picture he could hang on the wall and who could keep it going after he was gone?"

"Of course I don't."

"Me neither. Not anymore. I did ask him about it, though—one day at the store when things were especially slow. And he got mad as hell. He threw his duster at me, if you can imagine that."

Carnihan smiled and draped an arm over my shoulder, and together we started on our way toward the store. As boys we'd rambled about the neighborhood in this fashion, daring anybody to try to break us apart, but that was twenty years ago when we were a lot shorter and less likely to attract attention.

"It's not Silas to blame," he said. "I'll help him get out of jail, or try to. And as far as Sorel and Rachel Wayne are concerned, they can go on television and say whatever they want about me. It won't change the truth: I'm a Carnihan, brother. I'll always be a Carnihan."

We strolled past a couple of young boys who looked after us with a mix of caution and curiosity, and who, after tittering noisily between themselves, picked up rocks and made as if they wanted to throw them at us. "Faggots!" one of them shouted. And the other yelled "Homos!" And only then did I realize that Carnihan and I were still hanging on to each other.

I tried to break away but he wouldn't let me. He actually pulled me closer, his arm tightening around my neck.

"So how long did you watch?" he asked as we were crossing North Street. "At Bethany's last night?"

"Not very long. A minute at most."

"Damned Peeping Toms. They drive all the way out to Bayou Blanc and don't even stick around for the good part?"

"What we saw was good enough."

He was staring me in the face, probably to find out whether I was being square with him. "By the way, Pace, I should tell you: they've lived apart so long now all they have to do is sign some crappy papers. That's what she told me, anyway."

"What who told you?"

"Genny, man. Who else? A good lawyer could take care of it in no time."

He pushed through the screen door and let it swing back against me, the frame slapping me in the face. I needed a minute to collect myself before attempting to go back in, and, when I did, he was waiting to slam the door against me again.

"You're a liar," he said. "You did see something when you looked in on us."

"I saw two people under a sheet."

"When we kissed," he continued, "did you notice how pretty that was? You had to."

"I didn't notice anything, I swear."

"You know what's best about a woman, Pace?"

I gave it some thought, pausing to consider. "Her mind?" I said finally. "Her heart? Her generous, loving nature?"

"No, brother. The absolute best thing about a woman, after her smell and the fact that she has parts that we don't, and lacks at least one that we do have . . . the absolute best thing about a woman is the way you can cry in her arms and not feel like you're giving everything away."

He spun around and commenced a solitary dance across the floor, leading his invisible partner through enough dips and turns to make her sick with vertigo. It was the ballroom style of the old man's, and, not to be outdone, the champ himself pressed through the lunch counter gate and joined him.

I hoped they would dance together, but, no, Carnihan went one way and the old man another, both moving to his own unknown music, both seeming to love it.

The clinic where the cowboy was recuperating was only a few blocks from Hometown. Built to provide care for local boys hurt in World War II, it still looked as it had nearly half a century ago when a mayor named Jagneaux pointed to its deco facade and declared it a "sanctuary to the most brave and necessary among us." Of course I was unavailable to attend the building's dedication, but a photographer with a very keen eye had been there, and his perspective of that wintry afternoon still hung on the walls of the lobby: in all some two dozen black-and-whites, the best of them capturing people in attendance.

What struck me hardest about the photos was how the faces of war-torn America were so like those of the lost souls waiting today for medical attention. Pain and grief, I decided, had the same dilating effect on the aperture of a camera as they did on the pupil of a human eyeball.

"Mr. Burnette?" came a voice, a nice one, from directly behind me. "I think I know who it is you were asking about."

Carnihan, the old man, and I had stopped by the clinic less in response to the sheriff's threats than out of curiosity and a desire to burn some time before our shopping spree tonight. I'd told the nurse we were looking for a gentleman of about fifty who'd been badly hurt the day before in a brawl, adding, "The place, I'm afraid, was Babylon." Now that she'd returned, we all huddled close, shielding the nurse from the others in the lobby who'd endured long waits of their own.

"His name is Bernard P. Kuel," she said. "He's in pretty bad shape. Would you like to see him?"

"Bernard Kuel," I repeated, trying to place the name. "Yes, we would, we'd very much like to see him."

"Is he going to make it?" the old man asked.

"He's improving, but he's got a lot of problems and a long way to go. To begin, he's suffered a concussion and multiple contusions. He's broken ribs and torn up a knee. Whoever hit him, they must've used a rock. You'll see the bandages."

"Bernard Kuel," I said again, still unable to recall the name. "Bernard *P.* Kuel."

"We don't want to be a bother," Carnihan said. "But we were driving along the Lewisburg Road last night and happened to have witnessed the incident. My friend Winston here jumped from our car and wrestled the assailant away." He paused and drew glances from both the old man and me. "We were first to call 911. And, well, we were just concerned that he's okay."

Carnihan had told the story with such conviction that I found myself believing it. I stared at him with my mouth ajar, wishing for more. And so did the nurse.

The old man said, "Where is he, miss?"

"He's in what we call the Back Ward. We've kept him there because when he was admitted he had no identification and the night nurses thought, since he was so unkempt, that he might be indigent." She started walking toward a pair of swinging doors with a window at the center of each. "Why don't you follow me? I'll introduce you to his wife."

"His wife?" And it came to me, I knew who he was.

"Mrs. Kuel," the nurse said. "She arrived early this morning. He called her when he came to, I think."

The Back Ward was at the end of the hall, and to get there we had to walk past a nurses' station and two more swinging doors. The room was about half the size of a gymnasium. Rickety fans hung from the ceiling and stirred the torpid air, aggravating the bottle flies that seemed to be everywhere. The floor was asbestos tile, cracked and brittle, and rows of gurneys lay under high banks of windows. Of the two dozen beds only about half were filled, and some of these were cordoned off with curtains.

At the rear of the room Mrs. Kuel occupied a chair next to a bed where the cowboy lay, a gauze sash crossing his chest, casts covering both legs. A turban was fitted on the top of his head and compresses hid his face. Only one eye, his right, was visible, and it was swollen shut and purple with blood.

"Mrs. Kuel?" the nurse said.

She stood and smiled uneasily.

"These gentlemen have come to visit your husband. Is that okay with you?"

"Yes. That's fine."

The nurse left and we were left alone with Mrs. Kuel and the dancing cowboy, who looked no better than a dressed-up cadaver with a little blood still left to be drained.

"Mrs. Kuel? Mrs. Kuel, I'm Pace Burnette, Mike and Betty's boy. From Delmas Street? How are you feeling today?"

"Pace? Is that you, Pace?" She seemed comforted by the fact that I was someone she knew, or was supposed to know, but in an instant her eyes widened, her lips slightly blubbered, and she squeezed her purse even closer to her belly. So worried that she'd identify me as an ally of her no-account whoremongering husband, as she'd long been heard to call him, I'd failed to consider that she too might not want to be associated with him. "He didn't have anyone else," she said, "is why he claims he called me."

"We were there last night," Carnihan told her, "driving around when this one jumped from the car and pulled your husband's assailant away." He shot a thumb at the old man, who was doing his best to seem unworthy of such generous acknowledgment. By the proud glimmer in the old man's eyes, however, you could tell he was beginning to believe it. "My name's Jay," Carnihan said, "and this is Winston. We just wanted to express our sympathies and to let you know what we saw."

"Thank you."

"It was a guy in a ski mask. We couldn't make him out. He was big, though. About two hundred pounds."

"A ski mask?"

"That's right."

I was looking down at the man, wondering why he hadn't attempted to correct Carnihan's story. His mouth wasn't bandaged, and he could've said something had he wanted to. It occurred to me that maybe he didn't recall what had happened last night or who'd saved him or anything of the beating, including who was responsible. And I was suddenly filled with relief, grateful that such a thing as amnesia existed outside the world of daytime TV.

"Bernard, do you remember Coach Burnette? This is his son, Pace, Bernard. Pace was just a little thing when you left home. Say hello to him, Bernard."

Incapable of seeing anything, and for some reason unwilling to speak, the dancing cowboy raised his right hand and fluttered his fingers. I grabbed hold of them and a fragile smile came to his lips. "Nice to see you again, Mr. Kuel. How are you?"

"I'm going to die," he whispered. And it came to me that these were the first words I'd ever heard him speak.

"Oh, listen," Mrs. Kuel said. "Now he says . . . Bernard, why would you say that to this young man? Do you want to scare him?"

But he didn't answer.

Mrs. Kuel blew into a wad of tissue. "Pace, do you remember him at all? From long ago?"

"No ma'am, I don't."

"Nothing at all?"

"No ma'am. Sorry."

"Do you like caladiums, Pace?"

"You mean the plant?"

"Bernard had a way with them. You've never seen anything like it . . . how he made them grow."

She shuffled up close to the bed and reached over and put her hand on the side of his face that wasn't covered. His lips puckered and kissed the old, wrinkled palm and she pulled back as if struck by a current. "My heavens, what's gotten into you?" She started to laugh but at the same time tears were falling from her eyes and she had to use the tissue again. "Bernard, don't . . . don't do that." She put her hand back on his face and this time when he kissed her she left it there. She'd stopped laughing and although her eyes were still wet and glassy she'd stopped crying, too. "You're a sick man, Bernard. I'm sorry, but that's what you are."

Mrs. Kuel faced us, her hand still touching him. Her lips were trembling and a vein, thin and blue, had splintered her forehead in two. She smiled and said, "Bernard's an alcoholic."

We were all staring at him now, his appearance somehow seeming less shocking than when we first entered the Back Ward. I was mad at myself, mad for having been so blind. Ever since I first saw him stumbling about on the floor at Babylon I'd regarded him as a stooge, failing always to look past the comic surface. So it was alcohol that had inspired his solitary dance, and before that there had been a woman, Mrs. Kuel.

"I'm going to die," he said again, louder than before. His right eye twitched as he tried to open it, and his Adam's apple trembled along the bruised length of his throat. He raised his hand again and the old man grabbed it and held it in both of his. "I'm going to die," he repeated.

"Oh, shut your trap," the old man said. "You're not going to die at all. Do you hear me, son? You're not going to do anything of the kind."

Bernard Kuel swallowed and tried to sit up in bed. It seemed he was straining to lift himself so that we might better hear what he had to say. All four of us moved in closer to listen, and he said softly, plaintively: " 'I bequeathe myself to the dirt, to grow from the grass I love. If you want me again, look for me under your boot-soles.' "

That said, a great smile came to his face and he fell back with a wheezy sigh. There was about him a look of sexual gratification, and frankly it spooked me.

"Now isn't that the most awful thing to say?" Mrs. Kuel said. "And this from a man who really and truly hates the grass, and who always had me—"

"It's Whitman," the old man said, interrupting. "That was Whitman you just quoted, wasn't it, Bernard?"

"Why, yes, why, golly." It was Mrs. Kuel again, reeling backward now. She raised the back of her hand to her forehead and began to laugh at an old memory. "Bernard and his poets. I'd almost forgotten." She glanced down at her husband. "You always quoted them better drunk than sober, didn't you, Bernard?"

Once again his eyelids twitched in an effort to open and you could see the blue of the iris in the thin slit. " 'Afoot and light-hearted I take to the open road. Healthy, free, the world before me . . .' " He stopped and a single tear formed at the corner of his eye. The old man reached over and wiped it away, then he finished the verse, whispering: " 'the long brown path before me, leading wherever I choose.' "

Mrs. Kuel was having a hard time breathing. She drifted back into Carnihan's arms, fumbling with her purse. "I think I need some air. I think . . ."

Carnihan led her between the rows of beds toward the front of the clinic, the floor tiles popping under their weight.

"Just come meet us when you're ready," I said to the old man. He was still holding Bernard Kuel's hand.

"You'll be in front?"

"There's no rush."

He took an ink pen from his shirt pocket and started writing on Bernard's cast. His script was rough and looping but I was able to make it out. RAYFORD HOLLY, he'd written, and added the date underneath. He wagged a finger at the man. "You're not going to die, are you, son?"

Bernard didn't say anything and the old man climbed up onto the bed and propped himself on the edge. He leaned on an elbow and positioned his face an inch or so from Bernard's, and when he spoke it was loud enough to draw stares from the patients nearby. "Tell me you're not going to die. Tell me that."

Bernard finally complied but I wasn't sure whether he meant it or just wanted the old man to leave him alone.

"Of course you're not," the richest man in America said. "You're like me, son. You've got far too much left to do."

Mrs. Kuel and Carnihan were sitting on the steps at the front of the building. She had placed a piece of cardboard under her bottom to keep from getting dirty, and she held her knees pressed together, her skirt draped over them and covering her shoes. It didn't seem to trouble her that the hem of her dress picked up dirt and lint from the cement, just as long as her backside didn't. As I stepped outside she was holding her purse up to Carnihan. "My whole, entire life is in this thing." And she opened it and removed more sheets of tissue.

Carnihan took a cigarette from his shirt pocket and was about to light up when he met Mrs. Kuel's glance and thought better of it. He put the cigarette back and tossed the paper match into the ground cover on the side of the building. "I don't mind if you smoke," she said.

"Nah, I need to quit, anyway."

This seemed to please her. She gave him an approving smile.

Carnihan said, "People always say they don't mind if you smoke after you've already put the cigarette away. They never say it while you're in the act of lighting up."

"I guess you've got a point."

"They really don't want you to smoke, but they just don't want to have to ask you not to. I guess they don't want to offend you. Or maybe they don't want you to stop liking them." He shrugged and looked at the match down on the ground.

Mrs. Kuel seemed nervous. The smile had faded from her face.

"I guess what I mean to say," Carnihan continued, "is that sometimes we fudge on the truth so as not to give a bad impression. We don't want to be thought of badly. We'd rather inhale somebody's smoke and feel sick than risk losing a friendship."

Mrs. Kuel was quiet. She stared at Carnihan as if at a puzzle that made no sense. "Are you accusing me of not telling the truth, young man?"

"No, I'm accusing myself of that." He was fidgety and kept running his hands over his pants. He looked up at me and I nodded, knowing now what he intended to say. "Your husband Bernard," he began, "we've been knowing him for a while, me and Pace have. It wasn't how I said it happened."

"You mean about Winston coming to the rescue and the man with the ski mask?"

"Right."

"Well, I'd wondered about that. I really had."

"We used to see your husband at the go-go. He never did much but drink and dance around. He was a good fellow. Everyone liked him." Carnihan reached into his pocket and removed the cigarette again. He lit it and was smoking before he realized what he'd done. "Gosh, I'm sorry, Mrs. Kuel."

He was about to put the thing out, but she said, "No, it's perfectly all right, Jay. I sometimes enjoy a smoke myself."

He laughed and looked at me again. "Did you hear that, Pace? She sometimes enjoys a smoke herself."

He offered her the pack and she took one and he lit it himself, holding a match up to her face. It was a little like watching an old TV commercial for the brand, but at the same time it struck me as one of Carnihan's finest moments. To start, he'd rarely been so generous. And, second, he was showing the kind of courage which turns the most ordinary of us into heroes.

"Her name is Anita Billedeaux, the one who beat up your husband. She runs the place."

"Babylon?"

"She's also the sheriff's girlfriend."

Mrs. Kuel moved her cigarette from one hand to the other and gently tapped him on the shoulder. "You're a good person, Jay. A really good person."

"I know I want to be," he said.

She leaned over and kissed him on the side of his face, and he dragged long and hard on his cigarette, the tip burning red.

. . .

Ace's cab was parked in front of the store when we got back from the clinic. Ace himself sat slumped against the wheel, a green visor shading his eyes. At first I thought he was just taking a break from yet another slow day on the roads of Smoke, but then Genine came walking from the back of the building. I pulled the Mustang into the lot and Carnihan and the old man got out. They entered Dr. McDermott's without telling her anything, not even hello. They seemed to know that she'd come for me, as well as the nature of what she'd come to talk about.

"You can send him away, Genny. I'll give you a lift if you need one."

"Larry took my car to the shop. It needed a tune-up and an oil change . . . a few other things."

"Yeah?"

"He knows a guy in town—a mechanic."

I nodded but didn't say anything. It was too late for that, anyway. She'd already made up her mind.

She walked up to within a few feet of me and stood there with her arms crossed. Her clothes weren't as loud as usual, and her hair was nicely tamed, and for some reason this made me sad. I wanted to send her home and have her return as that other person, the one I had a chance with.

"I just wanted to say, Pace . . ." She paused and I didn't know whether to throw my arms around her and pull her close or to scream for her to get the hell away from me. "I just wanted to say that I'm sorry if I hurt you. I didn't mean to. I never expected what happened, never."

"You mean Peahead coming back?"

"No, what happened with us."

I tried to swallow but could get nothing down. The effort strained my face, and I didn't want her to see it. I smiled to try to keep from showing anything.

"In the long run you'll thank me for it. You're a wonderful person, Pace. You're smart and so talented. You're a writer with this great career." When I didn't respond, she said, "Think of how rich and famous you're going to be. Think of that. Think of all the girls. You'll have your choice, any one you want."

"Yeah," I said with phony enthusiasm. "Won't it be amazing?"

With the flat of her hand she wiped the place where her mascara had run, leaving a smudge. "Plus, and this is really what's most important: you'll have a family. You came from a good family and you deserve the same for yourself. You might not want one now, but in a few years you will. It's only normal and it's right and you'll be great at it, Pace, you'll be a really great father." She inched up even closer. "Trust me, baby. I know what I'm saying. I swear I do."

I wanted to make a case for myself, to draw comparisons between the kind of life I could give her and the one she'd known before with Peahead and surely was returning to. Instead a coward spoke, his voice a whisper: "You're really gonna miss out tonight, Genny."

"That party, you mean?"

"It's more than that. There'll be door prizes."

"What did Jay mean by that, door prizes?"

"Presents, gifts. Free things just for showing up."

This didn't excite her. The stains under her eyes were getting larger and beginning to run. I reached out and put my fingers on them, and she stepped up and filled the space between us. I could feel her trembling and how warm she was. It was true what I often recalled about that night at her house: Genine's body really did burn a few degrees hotter than everybody else's.

"I only decided this morning," she said. "I don't much trust this religious conversion of his, but he seems to still love me. A thousand dollars he blew on me last night, can you believe? And then to let Anita beat him up like that."

"It tells you something, all right."

It told you that he thought she could be bought, and that he had no self-respect, and that he was yellow to the core. But I didn't tell her that. Genine wasn't leaving because she loved him, but because she loved me. "Are you really going, Gen?"

"The car should be ready soon. I'll follow him in his to Houston. I mean, I'll be in mine, and he'll be in his, and I'll follow him there. He's working for something called NuFace."

I shrugged and shook my head.

"It's one of those arrangements where you can make money just recruiting others to sell your product line. He's recruited me already, so there's a few more dollars there."

"So it's one of those pyramid scams?"

"I wouldn't call it a scam, Pace. They actually sell stuff . . . things for the skin, mostly. Last night I tried their liquid body lufra. And it seemed to work all right."

"Liquid body . . . ?"

"Lufra. Don't you know what a lufra is, Pace?"

"Sure. I thought you were saying something else."

She grabbed my hand and lifted it back up to her face. "Feel," she said, and pressed my palm against her cheek. It was a little rough and pitted from the problems she'd had as a kid, but it was nice, too, and I liked it enough to keep my hand there long after she'd moved hers away. "They use a secret walnut formula," she said.

"Who does?"

"NuFace. To make the lufra. They use ground walnut husks. You put it on the skin and it exfoliates the dead cells that cling to your face and clog up your pores."

"It exfoliates them, does it?"

"Walnuts have a cleansing property. They're abrasive, you know? Use this every day and you really do get a new face. There's a money-back guarantee if you don't."

I could feel her tears on my fingertips and smell candy on her breath. The wind blew and her blouse stirred and I could see the swell of her breasts full against the satiny fabric. It was true that Genine Monteleone had never been a terribly pretty girl, but in all my days I'd never wanted one as badly. "I hope you get filthy, stinking rich," I told her.

"Me, too. I hope I make millions."

"If it's a new face you want, I hope you get that, too."

"I'll try some on my hair while I'm at it. Who knows: maybe it'll work there, too. Let's keep our fingers crossed."

I held up mine to show that they were.

She started to move away and I gave her an abbreviated wave which she promptly reciprocated. Ace must've been awake and watching, because I heard him rev his engine.

"Thank God for walnut trees," she said, opening the back door and getting in.

"Yes," I called. "Thank God for them, Genny."

When your girl leaves, you want the moment touched with magic and immortality. You want rain and soft music and the last words to be about love. In other places it might happen that way, but I come from Smoke. Ace proceeded up Market Street and I watched after them. The sun was everywhere, even in the shade. And the only music was the annoying tinkling kind that memory makes, a sloppy rendition of the heart.

I stood there in the heat trying to recall whether I'd ever seen a walnut tree. Upon determining that I had not, I turned around and walked back to the store.

Carnihan brought the Post-it Note along, the one from Bethany he'd discovered stuck to the screen door outside:

> *Came by to say won't make it tonight, Mama's having a bad spell. Dorie can't work so I'll have to stay and sit. I miss out on all the fun, and to think:* monster *door prizes! Behave, please. I know how you boys can get. With love from your,*
>
> *B.B.*

"I let it ring and ring," Carnihan said, "and, still, no answer. You don't think she's stepping out on me already, do you, Pace? This isn't an excuse, is it?"

"No. And don't say anything more about it."

The old man said, "I think it's a cheap alibi, is what I think. She's up to something."

"Like what?"

"She's a pretty girl, after all. She's young."

"This is a joke, right, Winston? You're just playing around with me . . . having a grand old time, aren't you?"

"Right," the old man said, stepping out of the delivery truck with a big, crazy laugh.

"Then how come you're acting like that?" He held the note out for the old man to read. " 'With love from your,' she wrote. This is really how she feels, I'm telling you."

"Right," the old man said again.

Carnihan balled the piece of paper up and threw it at him.

The card and combination got us through the big steel door in back, and the key in the lockbox kept us from tripping an alarm and notifying every law enforcement agency in the area that Monster Mart had just been violated. We walked along a hall that traced through a suite of cheaply constructed offices and emptied into a massive stockroom in which the whole of Hometown Family Goods could've been placed a dozen times. Far away in the darkness you could hear rodents fleeing for safety, their claws scratching the cement floor and inviting chase from Beatnik, who went screaming into the black distance.

Carnihan switched his flashlight on and sprayed its ragged yellow beam over the face of the old man. "Where're the riding lawn mowers?" he asked.

"First we'd better get your dog."

"Oh, so now that he's misbehaving he's mine, is he?"

The old man shone his flashlight toward the place where Beatnik had disappeared and started walking in that direction. He'd covered only a few feet when something crashed and a frantic yelping was heard and Beatnik came running at us with his tail locked between his legs and his black nostrils beating for air. His teeth were bared and a thin streak of blood stained his coat.

"Good God almighty," I groaned, stooping to hold him. "What kind of rats do you people have here, anyway?"

"The monster kind," the old man said with a note of pride. "What did you expect?"

My head was throbbing and my lungs ached from the pressure of having inhaled too much air: it was the excitement, I supposed, of being able to shop without the worry of how to pay. I felt a little dizzy and clumsy of foot, and I kept a hand on the wall to steady myself. I was last in line, behind the charge of Carnihan, the old man, and Beatnik, who seemed to have rallied from his shock. I'd never shopped Monster Mart without hearing elevator music and the phony, redneck words of Rayford Holly pumped in over the intercom, and I delighted now in the silence.

"Stop playing with my butt, Winston."

"Oh, is that what that was?"

The range of our flashlights was limited to about ten feet, at which point the beams seemed to be swallowed by the immense, black void. I worried that we'd be spotted by travelers on the road to Warren, even at this hour when there were few passersby.

"Are we going in the right direction?" It was Carnihan again. "The riding lawn mowers, Winston. Where are they?"

"Don't you want to get a buggy first?"

"Who can put a mower in a buggy? Come on. Use your head."

"The buggy would be for your smaller items—for your bath towels and shampoos and soap cakes and—"

"Soap cakes? To hell with that. I came here for your more pricey items . . . for what you owe me, Winston."

We'd entered a section called Kitchen & Cupboard, and were tramping between shelves crowded with things such as frying pans and ceramic water jugs, wooden chopping blocks and cookie jars. Carnihan said, "Are the microwaves here?"

"That would be Appliances."

"Why Appliances? You use a microwave in the kitchen, right?"

We stopped and Carnihan flashed his light on the old man, who said, "It's a dumb question, boss. I won't dignify it with a response."

"What do you mean . . . dignify? I asked you something that happens to concern me, and I expect a reply." He extended his arm straight out, holding the lens about a foot from the old man's face. "How come the microwaves aren't in Kitchen & Cupboard?"

In the blitz of light the old man's eyes had a luminescent quality both hot and cold at once. I admired him for not blinking or turning away. "I can't give you an answer," he said at last. "I'll have to address that with HQ at some point in the future."

"You fucked up, didn't you, Winston?"

"I don't see how putting microwave ovens . . ." But he didn't finish. He lowered his head and started back up the aisle.

"Hey, Pace, if you came into Hometown looking for a toaster oven, where would I send you?"

"To the wall straight across from the lunch counter."

"You're damned right to the wall straight across from the counter. And what is that section called, Pace?"

I honestly couldn't remember, but it seemed vital that I venture a guess. I bit my lip and said, "Ummm . . ." Then I looked up and gave a smile, prepared to go for broke. "The Kitchen section?"

Carnihan's response let me know that I was more than merely correct. As he ran up and down the aisle in triumphant celebration, shaking his arms up over his head and painting the ceiling with strokes of white light, he let me know that I was also brilliant. "The Kitchen section!" he was shouting. "We call it the Kitchen section because that's what it is! It's the Kitchen section! And what goes in the Kitchen section?" He stopped suddenly and spun around. "Winston Rayford Holly?" he said. "What goes in the Kitchen section?"

"I don't know."

"Of course you don't!" Carnihan erupted. "Why else would you put the microwave ovens in Appliances!"

It was a frightening thing to watch: the sweat dripping down Carnihan's face, the eyes bulging in their sockets.

"Pace Burnette!" he said, taking on the demeanor of the mad professor again. "What goes in the Kitchen section?"

I looked at him and knew I'd better get it right. "Kitchen shit?" I said after a long hesitation.

"Kitchen shit! Kitchen shit! You're damned right it's kitchen shit!" And off he went on another victory lap, sprinting with his flashlight coloring more lines.

No one noticed that Beatnik was missing until Carnihan came back and plopped down on the floor at our feet.

"Little blue-haired demon," Carnihan said. "We should've left him back at Hometown."

"Maybe he figures Winston owes him, too," I said.

"That's true," Carnihan said. "I almost forgot how smart he was. He's probably over in Pets now, rooting around for rawhide bones to load in the truck." I gave Carnihan a hand and helped him back up to his feet. "Hey, Pace," he said, "why don't you go get him? Find him and meet me and Winston where the mowers are."

"By myself? You mean, you want me to go alone?"

"Sure. You're not scared, are you?"

He raised his light to my face. "Scared? Why on earth would I be scared?" I laughed and said, "There's no one here but us, right?" Half a minute passed and the old man still hadn't answered. "Hey, Winston, there's no one here but us, is there?"

"If there is . . ." the old man said finally, "well, it wasn't because I invited him."

The two of them disappeared around the corner before I could protest. I listened to their voices fade as they journeyed deeper into the store. After a while I couldn't hear them at all, and that was when I realized that I had no idea where Pets was.

"Pets? Where the hell is Pets?" They'd already passed from earshot, but I was shouting nonetheless. "Winston? Where is Pets, Winston? Where is Pets?"

Its most likely location, I figured, would be near Hardware, Sporting Goods, and other manly sections, as opposed to those of a decidedly feminine nature such as Bed & Bath and Gift Ideas. By now, though, I'd drifted into Toys with its twenty-foot-high walls, and I was finding it impossible to see much of anything past the bicycles, swing sets, and inflatable swimming pools hanging from the rafters above. And since Toys was both masculine and feminine, I felt more lost than ever.

As I was negotiating a corner to meet yet more shelves of playthings, I spotted a shadow up ahead. It was darting up the aisle just ahead of me, and before I could home in on it with my flashlight, the shadow turned left and vanished behind a display of G.I. Joes. "Beatnik," I said, feeling great relief. "Come here, boy. Come here." Confident that he couldn't have gone very far, I half ran to meet him, and was navigating the end of the aisle when from the corner of my eye the shadow came charging at me with its saber drawn. I took the instrument square in the gut, and dropped to the ground with a shriek. Afraid of being struck again, I turned my light on the shadow with the hope of blinding it, and illuminated the cherubic though somewhat deranged face of a child of no more than ten. He was wearing a Viking helmet and baseball shin guards, a holster packed with a plastic Colt .45, a round of play ammo wrapped around his bony chest. His sword was plastic, explaining why I was still in one piece. "Who are you?" I asked, scrambling to get a better look.

"Monster Boy," he said, then stabbed me again before racing off into the darkness.

Had I not long suspected Monster Mart of harboring homeless waifs, I might've been shocked into wetting my pants, or, worse, fouling them. But my only response was to laugh.

"You're too skinny to be Monster anything," I said.

And suddenly he charged me again, swinging his weapon and missing my head by inches. The blade cracked against the floor and broke from the handle. He reached down for it and I rolled into his path and tripped him up. He fell to his knees and quickly fitted the sword together, whacking me with it when I attempted to grab an elastic strap on his shin guard. In addition to repeatedly stabbing my hands and arms, he clawed and kicked and shouted obscenities. Luckily for me, Monster Boy was puny and not at all hard to restrain.

"Who are you?" I said, giving his shoulders a shake. "Come on, kid. Tell me who you are."

"Monster Boy, I'm Monster Boy. I'm—"

"You're not Monster Boy. There's no such thing. Did your parents forget you here or what?"

But even as I protested he set about to prove me wrong, letting go with the most impressive hog call I'd ever heard, and nearly splitting my eardrums in the process. I reeled back in horror and he was gone again, slipping away from my grasp and motoring around the shelves with his sword high above his head, swatting at the G.I. Joe display.

"He lives," I muttered to myself. "Monster Boy lives. I saw him. It's true. He's real, he's . . ."

"What the hell were you screaming about?" It was Carnihan. I swiveled around and stared into the face of his flashlight.

"Monster Boy," I said. "Hey, Jay. It was him, I swear it was. He came at me with a sword. He struck me here—right here in the stomach. It was him, I tell you. It was—"

"Sit up," he said. "Is this some kind of joke?"

"No, man. I swear. I swear it's true—"

"You saw Monster Boy?" The old man was laughing. "You saw somebody named Monster Boy. How'd you know it was him?"

"He told me his name."

"And he stabbed you with a sword?" The old man placed a hand on my shoulder, as if to reassure. "Okay, then, Burdette. Show me where this Monster Boy stuck it to you."

I pulled my shirt up and pointed to a spot just above my navel. It wasn't cut or marked, in fact, it was like any other patch of flesh I might've pointed to. "How interesting," the old man remarked, although you could tell he didn't mean it. He kept rubbing his jaw in the manner of a detective who'd just uncovered a clue.

We started moving forward again, all together now. In Personal Hygiene, Bethany's department, the old man stopped dead in his tracks and turned to a bin filled with soap. "Look at this," he said. He turned his flashlight on one of the cakes and there in fancy gold script was the name brand, LOUELLA, positioned over the image of a handsome young woman wearing her hair in a pile.

FOR SENSITIVE SKIN was stamped on the paper wrapping, along with NEW AND IMPROVED and the weight in fluid ounces.

"And this," the old man said, taking a bottle of Louella shampoo from a shelf. "It's how she looked when I first knew her: those nights at the Satin, remember?" The old man was looking at the same image on a jar of cold cream. "The way it happened, on her sixtieth birthday I gave her her own line of beauty and health care products. She came up with the scents and textures and so on herself. She had a real fine nose, Louella."

When he thought we'd seen enough, he pulled the items from our hands and put them back where they belonged.

Just as I'd figured, we found Pets next to a couple of departments with masculine themes. It was sandwiched between Sporting Goods and Electric, which was not to be confused with Electronics, a section I'd passed on my way to Toys. Beatnik was sitting quietly before a wall of aquariums burning soft red lights, watching with great interest a tank of goldfish. In particular he seemed to be focused on the dead ones floating in the scum at the top of the pool.

Carnihan asked, "You think he wants to eat them?"

"He'd know not to," I said. "He's not a cat. It's a cat who likes to eat fish."

The old man had drifted over to where scores of fifty-pound sacks of dog food lay stacked on wooden pallets, and he was flashing his light on the center of a bag. OL' RANDY PUPPY CHOW, it said, the words wrapped around an illustration of a bird dog standing in brush, pointing.

"Ol' Randy was as fine an animal as I ever owned. He was strong and fearless and beautiful to behold. I had him ten years before he ran off one hunt chasing a bird and never came back."

"You never found him?"

He shook his head. "We looked everywhere. I had half of HQ out stomping around, some of them in dresses and suits. I like to think he's still out hunting . . . somewhere in the fields, running."

"He must've not been too smart," Carnihan said, "to take off like that. A smart dog would've known to come back."

"A smart dog wouldn't spend half the night so mystified by dead fish, either." The old man gave a laugh to show that he'd intended no harm to Beatnik's reputation. "They'd've gotten along well, those two. Of course Ol' Randy might've been put off by all the blue hair, but I honestly never knew him to be prejudiced."

Carnihan got a big charge out of this. He stood there shaking with laughter, clutching one of the smaller bags of Ol' Randy to his chest. "Who else you name things for?" he asked.

"Well, I could show you the bathroom cleansers. They're named for a maid I liked."

"And the store itself," Carnihan said. "Is it named for you? Are you the monster in Monster Mart?"

"You've got a tin ear, boy," the old man answered, leading the way out of Pets. "Let's go see if we can't get one of them mowers started."

The lawn equipment stood in a far corner of the store like a tank batallion awaiting orders to proceed. In all there must've been a hundred pieces, each painted either red or green, arranged in rows with the smallest push mowers at the fore and the largest riding ones at the rear. Assorted national trade names were represented, but easily the most prominent was the Monster Machine line. It was the house brand, and in every case it was less expensive than the competition's like model. For example, the GrassMuncher fifteen-horsepower industrial/commercial mower with the cast-iron bore cost three hundred dollars more than an identical model with a Monster Machine label, although the Monster Machine had a two-year parts-and-labor repair guarantee which the GrassMuncher did not offer. Or so said the old man. He was making a sales pitch, trying to persuade Carnihan that his Discount City brand was the better of the two.

"You're looking at the finest, most technologically advanced piece of lawn-care hardware on the market today," he said, shining his light on the big red model.

It was easy to see why he'd made billions as a salesman: there was a no-defeat, no-surrender quality to his delivery, as if this were the most important deal he'd ever made in his life.

"I still like the GrassMuncher," Carnihan said.

The old man fell silent, perhaps to devise a new strategy, perhaps to manage his feelings of being rejected. He pinched his lower lip in, folding it. "Speaking as a friend," he said, "I wouldn't decide before first giving each machine a test drive. That's not a lot to ask. You can run each engine and see how it performs. You can test them for comfort and drivability. Motor them up to Garden and back, see how they compare." He let go of his mouth and gave Carnihan a warm, sympathetic smile. "It's not easy being a consumer these days. One thing to consider . . ." And he held both hands up, fingers pointed. "Cost does not always equal value."

He climbed up on the Monster Machine and turned the key. The engine fired right away, the sudden, shocking roar of it filling the store and cutting short my stupor. Carnihan woke up, too, and we cleared a path through the smaller mowers to let the old man through. He inched the Monster Machine up to where we were standing and put it in neutral. "Come on, son. Give it a try." He got down from the machine, nudging Carnihan up into the seat. "It's actually easier to operate than the GrassMuncher—that's another advantage. All you do, you put it in gear and let up slowly on the clutch/brake pedal. The rest is pure mowing pleasure."

He gave the okay sign and another smile intended to show that he and Carnihan were on the same team.

"But it's dark, I can't see anything," Carnihan said.

"Aha," the old man said, rushing up to assist him. He flipped a switch and a pair of headlights flashed on. "Now your Grass-Muncher . . ." And he shook his head to let us know that this was another area where the competition lagged. "Monster Mart is as worried about your safety and well-being as you are," he said. "Take my word for it, son. We love you like family, and we wouldn't—"

"You love me?"

"We love all our shoppers."

Carnihan pitched forward, maneuvering the mower down the aisle. The rumbling diminished as his journey advanced, and eventually you could speak without having to scream. "You're welcome to go next," the old man said. "Test it yourself."

"All I need is a printer," I said, adding after a pause, "and maybe that microwave oven we talked about."

"The one with the plate?"

"The revolving plate," I said.

He was in such good humor that I figured I could've taken anything there I wanted, including ownership. Carnihan made a sharp right in the shelves up ahead, and the old man gripped my forearm and shuffled in close, lifting his face in the misty pose of a lover. "Give it a ride, Burdette. Confirm what he already knows. It'll mean a lot to him."

"I think it'll mean more to you, Winston."

He reeled back in mock horror, his mouth agape. "To me? Did you say to me, son?" And he laughed to let me know just how badly I was deceiving myself. "At Monster Mart the customer is our first priority. I'm the mere instrument to his happiness. I'm the conduit, if you will, between his dreams and reality."

I didn't say anything because I was starting to feel the goose bumps again and the electric numbness at the base of my skull. I slightly hated myself for being such a sucker, but I quickly overcame this feeling by recalling that I wasn't the first to fall for Rayford Holly's sales pitch. As the Monster Machine made its way back toward us, its headlights getting brighter as its roar grew louder, I recalled something Carnihan had told me years ago, shortly after Marla Castle left him and he was a free man again: "Salesman that I am, Pace, I could hustle the panties off the Blessed Virgin Mary. I shouldn't have any problems getting another girl." At the moment

I was just glad the old man hadn't asked for mine—for my drawers, that is. Because gladly I'd've given them: underwear, pants, shirt, you-name-it.

Carnihan brought the mower to a stop and cut the engine off. The old man helped him down and embraced him as if he'd just returned from a long voyage.

"How was it? Was it all you'd hoped it would be?"

"Better," Carnihan answered. "The headlights are what really sold me."

I wanted to tell him that only a fool would consider mowing his lawn at night, and that Smoke had an ordinance against it, besides; but the old man was leading me toward the machine, pushing me up into the seat. "We'll let Burdette here give it a spin, then we'll negotiate terms."

"What do you mean, 'negotiate'?"

And the old man started the engine, preventing me from hearing the response.

I switched the headlights on, depressed the clutch, and put the stick in first gear. I didn't want to drive fast for fear that I'd lose control, tractor over a shelf of something like shotgun shells and blow myself to bits. I motored by Hardware and Shoes 'n' Boots, squeezed through rows of all-season radials in Tires, and was heading into Pool/Patio/BBQ when none other than Monster Boy appeared up ahead in my wash of lights.

He came of a sudden, rather like an image on a projection screen. He was standing in the middle of the aisle, his bearing suggesting that of a warrior prepared to die in battle. I braked and came to a halt, and spent a few seconds trying to determine whether what I was seeing was real or further proof that I'd lost my head. "Move out of the way, kid," I called to him. "Move out of the way or die."

In response he raised his sword and sliced circles in the air.

"You're only a dream," I said, prompting him to charge with a roar of bloodcurdling intensity.

I quickly moved into fifth gear, the highest there was, and deposited planks of rubber as I raced to meet him, screaming myself with a fist clenched over my head.

Monster Boy raced to within a few feet of certain death before pivoting sharply and cutting into an intersecting aisle. I followed him with the hardest left I could manage, and bumped against the base of an overloaded shelving unit, sending dozens of table lamps crashing to the floor. Monster Boy was about thirty feet in front of me now. His helmet was flipped back and dangling from his neck, and his sidearm beat heavily against his hip. He cut right and so did I, taking the corner blind, and thus failing to see him trip and sprawl on the floor. I stopped the moment I realized he was no longer in sight, and I sat waiting for him to reappear, unaware that he was just in front of the machine, mere inches from having been run over.

"Monster Boy?" I mumbled aloud.

I stared down the long aisle, wondering whether he'd darted into one of its many breaks. "Monster Boy? Where are you, you little punk?" Worried that he'd backtracked and was plotting to approach me from the rear, I turned in the seat to check behind me, and stared at nothing but a miserable darkness with no visible end. I swiveled back around and was getting ready to ease off the clutch when he lunged over the front of the machine, yelling in his inimitable way. I took the thrust of his saber square in the neck, and immediately felt grateful that such weaponry was now antiquated. How much better was the prospect of being nuked than being carved to shreds by a sharpened metal shaft. Of course Monster Boy's metal was the plastic kind molded in some toy factory, but it still stung. As before, the blade broke and fell clattering to the floor. But instead of trying to salvage the piece, he dropped the handle and ran straight ahead, sprinting faster than before, and making it virtually impossible to keep up without knocking more shelves down with every turn.

Each time I negotiated a corner it was just in time to see him whip around another, and this continued until I'd driven all the way to the other side of the store from Carnihan and the old man. I was now in Sewing Needs, as feminine a place as there was, and the Monster Machine had begun to cough and knock, and seemed either on the verge of running out of gas or self-destructing.

After a brief search I was able to locate the main corridor. I shifted into first gear and lurched forward again, keeping my head aswivel for fear of attack. I'd covered more than half the length of the store when I saw three people in my headlights up ahead. The two facing me were holding their hands up over their heads in postures of surrender, and the third, whose back was to me, held them at gunpoint, his feet spread apart and firmly planted, both hands gripping his gun. "Monster Boy!" I shouted. "Goddamn you to hell, Monster Boy!" Forgetting about my engine problems, I threw the machine into high gear and raced toward him, aiming to run him over. I could see the frightened white ovals which were the faces of Carnihan and the old man, and hear how frantically they called to me. Then the one who was Monster Boy turned around and began to shout himself.

I suppose he was telling me to stop, because when I kept moving he fired a shot over my head. By now I was close enough to see that Monster Boy was in fact Monster Man, and that Monster Man was Lonnie Tom Long of the Saint Landry Parish Sheriff's Department. His gun was real and so were his bullets, but I realized this only after he'd blown my two front tires out.

XI

We were sitting handcuffed to each other in the back of Lonnie Tom's beat-to-hell cruiser, watching Smoke go by at speeds unsafe for even the Indy 500 crowd. Carnihan had been babbling since we left the store, trying to convince the deputy that you couldn't arrest someone for breaking and entering his own place of business, or for stealing his own property. "This is Rayford Holly, for heaven's sake," he was saying. "This is Mr. Monster Mart himself. Come on, Lonnie Tom, wise up, man!"

It was a good argument, but it was one Carnihan seemed to be conducting only with himself. Lonnie Tom's duties behind the wheel commanded all his thought and energy, and you could see what a fine time he was having. He blew through red lights, took corners on two wheels, and ran over whatever animals were unfortunate enough to get in his way.

Except to blurt out "Oh, wow!" a few times, he didn't speak until we pulled up in front of the jailhouse.

"Now what was that you were saying?" he said to Carnihan, finally daring to glance in the rearview mirror. "Sorry, man. I couldn't hear for the siren."

Carnihan leaned forward and pressed his face against the metal screen that divided the front and back. "This is Rayford Holly, Lonnie Tom. This is the man himself. How could we be burglarizing what's already his?"

Lonnie Tom removed the keys from the ignition and stuffed them among the half-used pouches of chewing tobacco in his front pocket. "He don't look like no billionaire."

Carnihan pushed forward and butted his head against the screen. "Have you ever seen a billionaire, Lonnie Tom? Do you know what one looks like to even make that judgment?"

"I've seen some on TV. They wear suits and neckties and some of them actually shave their faces."

"Well, this is the real thing, Lonnie Tom—a real, live billionaire . . . this fellow sitting right here." Carnihan fell back in the seat and lifted his arm that was attached to the old man's. "Tell him who you are, Winston."

"Winston?" It was Lonnie Tom. "If he's Rayford Holly how come you just called him Winston?"

"Tell him, Winston. Tell him who you are."

Lonnie Tom turned in his seat to get a better look. "Are you Rayford Holly?"

The old man laughed and shook his head, throwing a streak of white hair over his eyes. "In my dreams," he muttered, then bleated in pain when Carnihan elbowed him in the ribs.

We were walking toward the entrance when the old man stopped suddenly and said, "Beatnik. We forgot Beatnik."

"There was four of you?" Lonnie Tom had continued ahead, about ten feet up the sidewalk.

"Beatnik's a dog," Carnihan explained, sounding more irritated than ever. "We left him back at the store."

The deputy waved us forward, hardly seeming concerned. "I've got to call the manager, anyway, to let him know what happened. I'll tell him to run by and check for any dog."

He led us through the lobby and past a door with a small window filled with intersecting bars, then down a long, L-shaped hall with offices on either side. We came to a second door with an Authorized Personnel Only sign and a big double lock; past that were a number of holding cells.

The deputy had used three different keys to get us to this point, and he used a fourth to open the first cage on the right, a bullpen with a wooden bench fixed to the wall. There weren't any toilets, lavatories, or sleeping bunks, and the only light came from down the corridor where a yellow bulb burned in a cone-shaped steel basket. A pair of security windows, both too narrow to crawl through, offered a thin blush of moonlight barely bright enough to illumine our faces.

Although my eyes hadn't adjusted well enough to see who was in the other cells, I could hear snores and coughing, and at least one man engaged in a filthy brand of sleep talk. I also could smell a sweaty liquor stink commingled with the equally dreadful ones of urine and vomit, the combined effect being almost too much to bear.

Lonnie Tom removed the handcuffs before shoving us through the open door and slamming it closed.

"Aren't you gonna book us first?" Carnihan said. "Aren't you gonna take our pictures and fingerprints and read us our rights?" When the deputy didn't answer, he continued, "And what about those orange jumpsuits? How come we don't get to wear any? Everyone else gets one. Give me my orange clothes!"

Had I not known better I might've thought he was genuinely disappointed.

"You just stay put until I can reach the sheriff," Lonnie Tom said. He removed a pouch of tobacco from his pocket and pinched a plug, shoving it way back in his mouth. "When the sheriff comes I'm sure he'll be more than happy to answer any questions you may have."

As the deputy pivoted and started to walk away Carnihan called after him: "Where is Sorel, Lonnie Tom? He's at Babylon, isn't he? He's at the go-go. . . ."

"It's Sat'day night, ain't it?"

"Does he still have those FBI boys with him? Tell him to bring those FBI boys back here, Lonnie Tom. Tell him I've got someone they'd like to meet. Tell him . . ."

Lonnie Tom opened the door and was about to leave when Carnihan said, "Won't you give us our phone call? We're supposed to get a phone call."

The deputy spat on the concrete floor, the sound like a face being slapped. He was standing in a bolt of fluorescent light, his puckered skin giving off a woolly iridescence.

"Who tipped you off that we were at Monster Mart?" It was Carnihan again, screaming. "Did someone see us through the window? How'd you know we were there, Lonnie Tom?"

"That'll all be revealed in time. Just wait till I get the sheriff." And he spat again before proceeding through the door.

The old man and I sat on the bench and leaned back against the reinforced cement wall. The seat was damp and greasy and I hated to put my hands on it for fear of what I'd pick up. I wondered why Carnihan had pushed for a telephone. The last thing in the world I wanted was to let Miss Betty and Pop know where I was and why and the names of my compatriots. It made sense why jailbirds so often hanged themselves: they didn't want their decent, law-abiding parents to learn that their children had grown up to be hoodlums.

Carnihan paced the length of the cell slapping his hands together and spitting one foul word after another under his breath. After some two dozen trips he finally stopped and faced the old man. "What about an I.D.? You've still got your wallet, don't you, Winston? Maybe if you showed Lonnie Tom—"

"I left it in the delivery truck."

"Why would you do that?"

The old man shrugged and looked at me, and I mimicked the gesture. Who could say why the old man did anything?

"I took the key card out and stuck the wallet in the glove compartment. It was as simple as that. Had I known this was going to happen, I'd've brought it along."

"But why'd you put it there?" Carnihan asked. "That's the question I want answered. What impulse made you put that wallet in the glove compartment?"

"What do you mean, 'what impulse'? There wasn't any impulse—I just did it, is all."

"I mean, what were you trying to protect? Could it be you didn't want anyone to be able to identify you?" He paused and let a knowing grin come to his face. "You were the one who called Lonnie Tom, weren't you, Winston? You've deceived us. Here I am worrying about a burglary charge when what they'll get us on is kidnapping."

He drew his hands into fists and batted them against the iron bars. "Why? Why did I ever have to run him off the road that day? Why did I need to hear him say it?"

"You're going to give yourself a coronary," I said, falling back on one of Miss Betty's favorite sayings. "And you're not making sense, besides."

"Tell me what doesn't."

"The business about the wallet, to start. Lonnie Tom's calling the store manager now. Don't you think he'll be able to identify his own boss? And, second, what about Newton and Everly? They'll be coming over and surely they'll know who he is. Listen to me, Jay. It's only a matter of time before we're out of here. You're taking this all too hard. Just give it a rest, okay?"

"I'll give it a rest, I'll give it a rest. . . ." But off he went pacing across the cell again.

I was wondering how to settle him down when something came to mind which for the past week I'd seemed to have forgotten. "Hey, brother." I walked over and stood next to him. "Hey, listen, you need to focus on the bright side of this. You're almost off the hook. They'll recognize him and you win your bet."

He stopped pacing and wheeled around to face me.

"The store," I said. "You don't have to change it to Fascinating Hometown Fashions."

"I'm afraid you're mistaken, Burdette," the old man said. "Your friend lost the wager the moment he told the deputy who I was. He violated our covenant, so to speak. And, if I recall, the conditions of his losing weren't that he change the store's name. It was that I get whatever I want . . . anything."

"Not anything," Carnihan protested.

"Yes, anything." And the old man jumped to his feet.

Carnihan swept past him and plopped down on the bench, his back thudding against the wall. I sat next to him and gave him a pat on the leg. "Trust me. It's gonna be all right."

He shoved my hand away and slid farther down the bench. "You should've kept your mouth shut about the bet."

"He's rich. He won't ask for anything."

"You don't know him. He'd take my last dime. He'd take my life."

The old man had resumed Carnihan's former job of pacing the floor. He held his hands behind his back, and he kept his head down as if in deep thought. It was the pose of someone trying to make sense of life's great mysteries, and it must've helped because after about ten trips the old man stopped and stood straight and tall, his shoulders drawn back. "When I was a youngster," he began, "before Louella entered the picture, I'd've asked for a night with your girlfriend." He held a finger up. "Just one night with Miss Lanie. That would've been enough."

"And I'd've told you two things," Carnihan said, showing a couple of fingers of his own. "Number one, her nights aren't mine to give away. They're hers, Winston, all of them. And number two, go to hell. Some things Jay Carnihan don't share."

My eyes were growing accustomed to the yellow-tinted darkness and I could make out about half a dozen figures, all but one of them in the cell directly across the hall. This was a bullpen which seemed to be identical to ours, and everyone there was sprawled on the benches and floor, appearing to sleep. To the right of the pen was a much smaller cell holding a single inmate who at the moment was hidden in shadow back against the wall. But as I watched he struck a match and brought the flame to the cigarette at his lips, shining light on his face. Carnihan rose from the bench and shuffled up to the bars, clutching a couple. You could smell the smoke now and see the cherry, the sudden brightening when the man took a drag.

I knew who it was before Carnihan said the name, but I was still surprised to hear it spoken: "Silas, is that you?"

The man struck a second match and let us get another look. "How are you, boys?" he asked quietly, then whipped his hand against the air, extinguishing the flame.

"I've been better," Carnihan said. "I'm a little upset that they haven't given us our orange jumpsuits, but I suppose you can't expect to have everything the first hour they throw you in the slammer, can you now?"

"You're absolutely right," Silas said with a laugh. "It was a dumb question. I take it back." The tip of his cigarette flared again, momentarily coloring his face. "So is that *the* Pace Burnette in there with you?"

"It's him, all right. And Winston from the store. You remember our new cook, don't you?"

A few seconds went by before he answered. "I remember." And something about the reply let me know that there was no point in continuing the subterfuge: he'd heard everything.

"Well, as it so happens," Carnihan said, "Winston is really Winston Rayford Holly. You know him, don't you, Silas?"

"I do. Yes. Yes, of course."

The old man and I were sitting about a foot apart on the bench. I said, "How are you tonight, Mr. Poe?"

But once again he was slow to answer, so slow that I wondered whether I'd offended him with the greeting. "I'm fine, Pace," he said at last. "I thought I'd get beat up and sodomized in here the first night, but everyone's been real nice and congenial. The food's good, too. You'll like it."

"The food . . . ?" It was the old man.

"Hey, there," Silas said, seeming to perk up. "You should've told me who you were, Mr. Holly, back when you first started at the counter. I wouldn't've squealed to anyone. And I wouldn't've given you such big tips, either. America's richest man, and I'm leaving five bucks behind on a two-fifty breakfast."

"You were very generous. And I thank you."

Silas said, "I could kick myself for not recognizing you. I suppose you just don't expect to see a person like yourself flipping pancakes in a town like Smoke, not to mention a store as old and whatnot as Hometown."

"What do you mean by that?" Carnihan said. " 'A store as old and *whatnot* as Hometown'?"

"It's the last place you'd expect to see a billionaire. Let's be honest with each other here, Jay."

"I bet we've served lots of billionaires over the years."

"Oh, come on, now, boy."

"No, I mean it. The thing about billionaires, they don't want anyone to know how much money they have so they act worse off than your average person. They dress down and don't say anything worth listening to. They don't wash as often as they should, they don't shave or comb their hair. They wear funny glasses: Co-Cola-type glasses. They do just what Winston did, and they get away with it."

"Then I guess I'll know who to hit on for money next time," Silas said. "You just described everyone to ever set foot in Hometown—the regulars, the irregulars, even yourself." He flipped his cigarette onto the floor and I watched the burning tip roll all the way to the front of the cell. "Another thing I'd like to tell you, Mr. Holly. I don't think, had I known who you were . . . I don't think I'd've leaned on your people for quite so much money. You'll forgive me for that, I hope."

"You're forgiven, Silas. Of course you're forgiven. Think nothing of it."

"From what I understand," Carnihan said, "you owe Lester Harris in the neighborhood of ten grand. Now what you were asking from Monster Mart, that's a thousand percent markup."

"Well, yes it is. But for extorting ten grand you spend the same amount of time in prison as you do for ten million. I thought if I was going to break the law, I might as well break it all the hell to pieces, know what I mean?"

"Did you ever get that picnic basket full of food we sent you?" the old man asked.

"Picnic basket? Nah, nothing like that. Lonnie Tom or one of the others must've gotten to it. Lonnie Tom . . . last night I caught him eating chewed-up gristle off a trustee's tray."

Silas stood and shambled over to the front of the cell, finally showing himself in the yellow light. It was strange to see him behind bars, dressed in orange, a seven-digit number painted in stencil on his left breast. He must've found it just as strange to see us in the cell, because he started to laugh and shake his head. "I know it's none of my business," he said, "but why'd Lonnie Tom bring you in here? They didn't raid the go-go again, did they?"

Carnihan said, "Somebody called and ratted that we'd broken into Monster Mart, when in fact we were just enjoying a shopping spree courtesy of Winston here. It's like I was asking the deputy: How can you steal something you already own?"

"They won't keep you long. Where you are and the big one next to me . . . those are the drunk tanks. They put people there to sleep off the booze and wait till their wives can come get them in the morning." This made sense to me, since as of yet no one had complained about our talking back and forth, or about Carnihan's noisy outbursts. The stench was another giveaway.

"Upstairs," Silas was saying, "that's where they usually put people who've really done something. I stayed there part of last night, then they moved me here. They said I was bad for morale, but the real reason . . . it's easier for Sorel to show me off from down here. He keeps bringing people in and letting them have a look. The city council and the police jury have already been through, as has every church pastor and school board member in the parish. I think it's his first step toward reelection: to show what a law-and-order man he is, protecting Smoke from outlaws like myself."

Carnihan wheeled around and glared at the old man. "Yet another shining example of what you've gone and done to the people of Smoke. How's that make you feel, Winston?"

Silas said, "Now hold on a minute, Jay. There's no need for any of that. It's not Winston's fault. He didn't put me up to writing that ransom letter. I did it myself." He tapped his chest. "I take sole responsibility."

But Carnihan wasn't listening. "Winston's had himself a big old time in Smoke. He's cooked for everybody and danced with pretty girls and he's given a lot of advice, mostly about love. Now he's put three good people in jail, not to mention himself: a bad one. Only thing he hasn't done is apologize, which is why we went and took him in the first place."

For some reason this struck Silas as wildly funny: he erupted with a howl of laughter loud enough to draw complaints from the drunks in the cell next to him. It was shocking to finally hear their voices, and to get a whiff of their collective breath. Silas lit another cigarette, the brief life of the match showing a generous smile on his face. "You never told me. What was it you wanted him to apologize for?"

"For what he's done to Smoke, for killing it."

"Oh? When did Smoke die? Must've been after they brought me here, because otherwise I'd've noticed."

"My father, too," Carnihan said. "I want him to apologize for what he did to Daddy."

"You've got to be kidding." Silas let go with more laughter. "You blame Rayford Holly for your daddy, too? You really think he had something to do with that?" Carnihan didn't answer, and Silas said, "Let me ask you a question, Jay. You think Hank Carnihan ever for a minute held Rayford Holly responsible for what happened to his store? Your father wasn't that kind of man. There was only one person to blame for the troubles at Hometown, and that was him and he'd be the first to admit it. He let it run down and he didn't put up the first dime to modernize. He didn't advertise. He was content to keep it looking like a museum for as long as he lived."

"Well, that's your opinion—"

"No, Jay, it's the truth, it's how it was. It was always fine with him if people came by to see Ruby Dean and to sit sipping coffee at the counter, just so you let him alone with his memories of Deenie." Silas laughed again, but this time with a sadness. "Your father was living in the past, Jay, waiting for something that wasn't coming back. You can't find again what's already been lost no matter how bad you try. It doesn't ever come back . . . it can't."

"Yeah?" Carnihan said. "And what would you know about it?"

Silas went back and sat on the bunk. He leaned forward with his elbows propped on his knees. "I know about it," he answered finally, "because I've been there myself—hoping for something that I knew wasn't mine anymore. . . ." The red light flared at the center of his face, shedding sparks. "And as far as Hank's heart is concerned, Rayford Holly, I can assure you . . . Rayford Holly had nothing to do with it. He'd had problems for years, your dad."

"Those were just gas pains."

"So you knew about them yourself, did you, son?"

Carnihan dropped his hands from the bars and walked over to the bench. He sat on the opposite end from the old man and me. "Don't call me son," he said quietly—too quietly, I thought, for Silas to hear.

But Silas stood again and crossed to the front of the cell, his form once again bathed in yellow. "What's the matter? Can't anybody call you by anything but your name?"

"Which is Jay," Carnihan said. "Short for Henry Jackson Carnihan IV. The third Carnihan had permission to call me son. No one else." He flashed a smile manufactured just for the occasion. "I'm glad we have that all cleared up now."

"Me, too," came the response, Silas's voice a whisper. You could see a trace of understanding in his face, or maybe it was one of regret. "Who told you?" he said.

"Nobody told me, exactly. But I'd've been a fool not to know after what Angela Brown showed me in your house." Carnihan glanced at the old man and me as if in apology for what he was about to say. When his voice came it was with an impassioned quiver. "You loved my mother and you think I'm your kid. Why else would you keep all those pictures around?"

"I had them . . ." Silas paused, unable to finish. "Why don't we talk about this later? It's not the right time."

"The right time? When will that be? When you're in a federal pen somewhere serving twenty years to life, and I'm in another serving twice that?" Carnihan got up and lay his head against the bars. "Tell me everything."

Silas eased down to the floor and sat with his legs pulled up to his chest, his back against the side wall. A problem with the soles of his slip-ons kept him occupied for a while, and then a stray thread on the seam of his pants needed attention. Done with that, he rubbed his hands over his face and hair, a gesture which struck me as oddly familiar: it was something I'd seen Carnihan do all his life, ever since he was a kid.

"We dated, me and your mother . . . it was during the summer after our senior year in high school." He stopped and looked up. "Is that what you want to know?"

"Is that it . . . the whole story? I want the whole story."

"I was one of those people"—and he laughed—"I was one who couldn't commit to anything. You remember the old Waldorf-Astoria on Landry Street? I used to play dominoes there, dominoes and cards. I played for what you call the house, and the manager—I was making money for him . . . well, he liked me and let me have a room whenever I wanted one. I'd take girls up there. Believe it or not, people were having sex back then, too."

"So you got her pregnant at the Waldorf? Well, that's good to know. At least I started out with a little class."

"No," Silas said. "I never brought her upstairs, not your mother. I was just trying to make a point about the kind of riffraff I was. I think, if I had to tell you honestly . . . I think I thought I was going to die. My dad was a grunt in World War II who got killed somewhere in the South Pacific, and my brother was lost in Korea, and it was just me and my mother in that big house on Court Street. We were both sort of biding our time, I suppose: Mom for the day when she got to be with my father and brother again, me for the next war to come along and take me with it. So, what I'm trying to say . . . I was sort of between things when your mama came into my life. I met her on the square, by that old statue to the Confederate dead. I was in the hotel and went out for some air—we'd been playing in a room off the lobby all night . . . and I saw her sitting against the stone eating a sandwich. Maybe I'd been drinking, or maybe I just felt like I had to know her, but something made me cross the street and introduce myself, although you'd think in a town our size everybody knew everybody else. She'd gone to Smoke High, and I was a Catholic school boy. But, anyway, that's how I met her. It went on for about three months, all through the summer, 1957. She wanted to get married and I suppose I did, too. But what you had to take into account were my feelings about how I wasn't going to be around very long. You boys're lucky, you didn't grow up in times like that. It was all we knew, it was sort of who we were."

"I can speak to that," the old man said, interrupting.

"No, you can't," Carnihan said. "Finish the story, Silas. And if she was cheap, just come out and say it. I don't want a whitewash—you're giving me a whitewash."

"Cheap? Your mother was anything but cheap, Jay. But I will tell you what she was. She was one of these girls everyone seems to think he has a right to. She was uncommon for Smoke insofar as her beauty was concerned, and she had the kind of spirit . . . well, I've often said this: it was a wonder her body could hold it, big as it was. When I was dating her I'd hear stories from other boys, I heard them in the hotel from fellows at the table. I knew they were lies but they still weren't easy to listen to. After a while I used them to justify my own running around. I'd go to the Elbow Room, for instance, and see who was there, and if who was there knew your mother then so much the better. I'd pick her up and take her back to the Waldorf or to my own house if my mother happened to be away. I suppose I wanted Deenie to hear about it. In a way I thought I was being noble, sparing her the pain of having to hear how I'd died somewhere fighting. That's actually how I justified it all: by telling myself that it would be easier on her in the long run. We just finally had a big blowout, accusing each other of this and that. It was out on the square, too, under the trees with everybody watching. But I can tell you, she really hadn't done anything. Then one day I see her with your father. It's lunchtime again and they're sitting by that same monument. It had become a daily thing with us, to have a sandwich there, and I guess this was her way of telling me it was over between us. Or maybe she was trying to make me jealous. Or maybe . . . heck, maybe she was just being friendly. In any case, I didn't do anything about it. I went back to the hotel and played blackjack until about four o'clock, and then, when I left the place, I marched down to the recruiter's office on Main Street and enlisted."

"Tragic," the old man muttered.

"No, not tragic," Silas said from across the hall. "It was stupid and cowardly, was what it was. But, anyway, it's several weeks later now and I'm in boot camp at Parris Island, South Carolina, and my mother writes to say that Deenie's gone and married Hank Carnihan and that they're expecting. Well, about six months after that I'm stationed at a base in Puerto Rico and get another letter saying the baby's a healthy boy. My mother doesn't say anything more except that it weighs eight pounds, which to me is her way of letting me know that the baby wasn't premature. And so I automatically figure it's mine. For weeks I thought about going AWOL and heading back to Smoke and just confronting them about it, but something always stopped me. I think what it was, was that I was still waiting to die, I really believed it would happen any day now. We'd bomb Russia or somebody and there'd be a fight on some beach and it'd happen in the sand. On top of that, and maybe this was even more important: it came to me that Deenie would be happier with Hank, and that so would you, Jay. He had Hometown and it was still a big business back then, and I figured he could give you a better life than I ever could."

Silas stopped and got up off the floor. He seemed to be finished, but then, sticking another cigarette in his mouth, he said, "Just one more thing and I'm done, okay?"

Carnihan nodded. "Say it."

"That picture you saw, the one over the fireplace . . . that was actually done when we were dating, Deenie and me. I hope you don't think I had some weird fixation on your mother, because I didn't. That painting was up in the attic, and on the day she died I climbed up there and took it down and hung it on the wall. I suppose it was a moment of weakness and regret, together, but at the time it was my way of reaching out to her again. Until her dying day my poor old mama would ask me when it was coming down, and I'd say, 'Soon, Mama. Soon.' I think after a while it just stayed up as a reminder of how lucky I'd been, and how blind I was not to have recognized it. I was nineteen and believed that I was going to die, when the truth was, I was nineteen and just starting to live."

Carnihan seemed to be trying to decide whether to accept or reject the story, or perhaps whether to embrace or rebuff Silas. "And what about those pictures of me?"

"Yeah, those."

"They gave me the creeps, I gotta tell you, man."

"As well they should. I can understand it."

"It's like you'd been stalking me all those years."

"Yes. I do see how that could be the impression they gave. But you need to remember something. Those pictures and the end of Ruby Dean's lunch counter were as close as I could ever get to you, and I wanted a record of the good . . ." His voice broke and he dropped back down to his haunches. He'd moved out of the light and if not for the burning end of his cigarette you wouldn't've been able to see his face, the tears starting to run down his cheeks. "I wanted," he began again, "an accounting of the one good thing in my life I'd ever done. And that was you, son."

Carnihan turned to me with a look of such utter confusion that I thought he, too, might break down in tears. Silas had dared to call him "son" again. But Carnihan brought his hands up to his face and it was a laugh he ended up muffling—a rich, happy laugh coming from deep within. "If I'm the good, Silas, I must tell you, partner, I do pity you for all the bad."

Silas took his time to reply, and when he did it was something I most certainly could relate to. "Pity," he said, "is a favor I could use a little of right now, thank you very much."

As I stated at the outset, Carnihan had always been reticent when dealing with the subject of his mother, but this night he couldn't say or hear enough about her. Now that the hard truths had finally been aired, he quizzed Silas about the small things. What did she smell like? he wanted to know. And how did she walk: did she strut and swing her hips, or was she more deliberate and boyish in her step? And the kind of clothes she favored: did she sew them herself or buy them in Smoke or Warren or where? And what about makeup and perfume: were there brands or colors she particularly liked?

Silas dispensed with each inquiry as best he could, straining to answer some of the more specific ones such as whether she painted her nails. And then, as Carnihan was introducing a round of questions about Miss Deenie's switch from a dark to a light hair coloring, Lonnie Tom burst through the door followed by Sorel, Newton, and Everly. The manager of the Smoke Monster Mart came in about half a minute behind them, still dressed for bed, sprinting with a face as yellow as corn. As it happened, he was the same fellow we'd encountered in the Personal Hygiene section some weeks before, the one whose pen Carnihan had crushed underfoot. His reaction upon seeing the old man was immediate and terrifying, for he commenced to scream loud enough to shake all the drunks from their sleep.

"If you don't shut up and keep still," the old man said, "I'll stick you behind the snack bar frying corn dogs for the rest of your living life."

The manager's robe had come open to reveal a T-shirt and pajama bottoms, and he seemed to wither now. The door swung open and he stood at the threshold, begging permission to enter. "May I, Mr. Holly, sir?"

"You want to help?" the old man said. "Go home to your wife and kids. Get away from me. I'll crown you if you don't."

Despite the warning, the manager attempted to make himself useful by helping the old man off the bench, and the old man was forced to slap him across the face. "I'm telling you to leave me alone. Get away from here!"

Carnihan seemed highly amused by it all. "How come my employees don't get this excited when they spring me from jail?"

"You have no employees," I answered.

"Oh, yeah. I guess that's true."

The manager backed away, shuffling in his little leather slippers, his face all yellow again, and the two FBI agents replaced him in the cell. They were smart enough not to try to assist the old man, but when one attempted to interrogate him, the old man reared back and struck him just below the eye. The punch came at the instant some of Lonnie Tom's spit made contact with the cement floor, giving the blow the resonance of a well-timed combination.

" 'I celebrate and sing myself,' " the old man announced. " 'And what I assume you shall assume.' "

The old man's choice of words seemed even more difficult for Everly to understand than the hand to his face. "I beg your pardon, Mr. Holly. Would you mind repeating that?"

" 'I loafe,' " the old man continued, " 'and invite my soul.' "

"You loafe?" It was Newton, standing by the door. "What do you mean, you loafe, Mr. Holly?"

"Dumb sonsabitches," Carnihan said. "Don't you know Walt Whitman when you hear it?"

The FBI men were confused and curious at once; without saying anything, they begged for clarification, which the old man was only happy to provide.

"Go fuck yourself, boys, is basically the point I'm trying to make. This is a free country and I'm a free man—free to go wherever I want, and to be whomever I like, and to answer only to myself. Right now I'm on vacation and you're cutting into the party. So if you don't mind . . ."

He got up from the bench, pushed past Everly, and stood in front of Newton, who was still blocking the door. "You want me to quote Whitman to you, too?" the old man said. "Or would you prefer I slapped your goddamned face?"

Newton backed away, and so did the sheriff and Lonnie Tom, when their turns came.

As we were walking toward the entrance to the L-shaped hall Carnihan suddenly stopped and spun around to get a last look at Silas, who was still standing there holding the bars, staring after us with a wearisome look on his face.

"Open the door," the old man said to Lonnie Tom.

"Whah . . . ?"

"Open the door. Open Mr. Poe's door."

"But I can't."

"Not to let him go," the old man said. "You can keep him. I'm just commanding you to open his door for a second."

"But . . ." Lonnie Tom looked over at the sheriff for authorization, and the sheriff, in turn, consulted the two FBI men. While no one was willing to give the okay, no one had the balls to deny it, either.

"Open the door, Lonnie Tom."

"Here," the deputy said, fumbling with the knot of metal at his hip. "You do it." And he handed the old man the key.

When the door was opened Carnihan walked into the cell and threw his arms around Silas. They held each other and broke apart, only to embrace again.

In the bullpen next door some of the drunks started to whistle and applaud, and after a while the old man and I joined them, the noise echoing against the ceiling and coming back down. For the size of that echo, and for the strength and beauty of it, you might've thought that all of Smoke approved.

He made breakfast the next day, starting at around 6 A.M. It was the first time in history Hometown had ever opened for business on a Sunday, and people stopped by before church and lined up outside the door to wait their turn at the counter. On this the Lord's day Smoke had always been a doughnut town, and I felt a trifle sorry for poor Ernie Mason, the baker, who by now was probably trying to make sense of why nobody was coming by to order their usual dozen glazed and half-dozen chocolate-iced.

The reason for the crowd wasn't hard to figure. This morning's *Lip* had run a long but sketchy front-page article about Rayford Holly's last two weeks in Smoke, the source of which was the same anonymous informant who'd tipped off authorities to his whereabouts, and who, the paper said, stood to receive a hundred thousand dollars in reward money. The story, which appeared under the heading MONSTER BILLIONAIRE NOT MISSING, AFTER ALL, was no doubt the biggest scoop in the paper's history, and each paragraph, while bemoaning something or other, included a boast of exclusive authorship.

Rayford Holly, it said, had chosen Smoke as his summer vacation spot because he was a close personal friend of Henry Jackson Carnihan IV, owner of Hometown Family Goods at North and Market streets, and because there he could escape the rigors of his "jet-setting corporate lifestyle" and "get back to the basics which have helped to make him America's best friend." Holly's last day as substitute chef at the Hometown lunch counter was scheduled for today, the story correctly reported, and everyone was invited to come by and try his famous pancakes, a recipe of which was printed at the bottom of the story. "Winston's Flapjacks," they were called. Among the ingredients listed was a pinch of cayenne pepper, which I found curious beyond telling. There was no mention of a mix.

How had the paper obtained this information? I wondered. Some of the details were too particular to have come from anyone but an insider. And why did the story read like an advertisement for the store and an endorsement of Carnihan as the town's favorite son? After reading the piece a few times, I shuffled over to the person who I reckoned was its source and spread the paper out in front of him. "How could you do it?" I said. "It wasn't the old man who ratted on us. It was you."

Carnihan was busy with a can of biscuits. He hardly looked up. "Now why would I go and do that, Pace?"

"To collect the reward. And to get this story in the *Lip*. You knew it would attract a crowd. You sold out for the money."

"I'm telling you I didn't," he said. "Now put an apron on and get over there and start cracking eggs."

"It breaks my heart, Jay. I'd really believed you wanted that apology. I thought you were acting on conviction. But all you really cared about was making a buck."

"I swear to you, Pace, it wasn't me. Now let's get to work." I didn't do as ordered or say anything more, and he said, "I really don't know what else to tell you, brother. Do you think I like the way it makes me look? Hell, man, Winston might think I've gone soft on him or something."

I flipped to the jump page and took another look at the recipe. "Who'd put cayenne pepper in pancakes?"

"What's that?"

"These flapjacks call for a pinch of red pepper. Who on earth would use that in pancakes?"

"Only person I know . . ." And he stopped himself. He didn't have to say the name, and I didn't need to hear it. He started tearing off small hunks of dough from the can and placing them on a buttered cookie sheet. "God knows she can use the help. With her mama like that. Maybe she can put her in a home now. I don't feel betrayed. I'm glad it was her."

"I bet you're glad."

"No, I am, Pace, I really am. Last night I called her when we got back from the jail and she'd been changing sheets. Her mama just goes to the bathroom right there in the bed . . . doesn't even know she's doing it." His hands were shaking and blood had begun to pool in his face, and his defense of Bethany didn't seem to be convincing either of us. "She did what she had to," he said, his voice just a whisper now. "Better her than someone else, better her . . ." You could see the pain in his eyes and hear it in his shallow breathing. He took another piece of dough, rolled it into a ball, and threw it the length of the counter. He missed the trash can and the dough smacked against the register.

"You weren't aiming to hit me, were you?" the old man said. He was over by the stove, mixing a bowl of pancake batter.

Carnihan didn't answer. "Let me go open that goddamned door." And he shuffled off.

Even with all the people who came to the store that morning, it seemed something was missing, and only after about an hour did I recall that Beatnik still hadn't been returned. I started collecting leftover pancakes in a giant bowl heretofore used only for soup, and Carnihan put what rims he could scavenge together on a serving platter. For his part the old man spooned uneaten cane syrup into an empty peach tin.

Carnihan said, "I just hope he didn't mess on the floor."

"Nah," the old man replied, "he's too smart for that."

"You think he's all right?"

"Having the time of his life, I'd bet. Don't worry, boy. He's probably full of malted milk balls by now." Unlike Carnihan and me, the old man didn't seem concerned. "I'll call the manager at home a little later on, once this crowd starts to fizzle. I'll tell him to bring him over."

"And don't forget my mower," Carnihan said. "The big red one with the lights. The Monster Machine."

At around seven I spotted Miss Betty and Pop waiting in line outside. Had I not feared a riot, I would've let them cut ahead and given them the best seats at the counter. As glad as I was to see them, I wasn't very keen about having to address their certain charges that I hadn't been very honest with them lately. All told they had to wait about half an hour, not long if you considered the size of the crowd and the lack of experience of the three cooks. Pop led Miss Betty to a couple of stools and draped his handkerchief over one of them. He was covering it to make sure Miss Betty's backside didn't pick up anything—and to remind everyone how a gentleman treated his wife.

Miss Betty lifted her eyes to the chalkboard and studied today's specials listed in a crazy chalk scrawl. There were only a couple of items to choose from, but she was pretending to have a hard time deciding. "Before I order," she said directly, "I have a question."

I gave a quiet nod.

"Why didn't you tell us who he was?"

"I was afraid you'd treat him differently."

"Well, you were wrong."

"No, Miss Betty, I wasn't wrong. Had you known who he was, you'd've taped welcome posters to the walls and hung bunting from the ceiling, and you'd've had the whole neighborhood over to surprise him. Confetti, champagne, popguns, the works."

"Listen to him, listen to how your son is talking to me." Pop knew better than to say anything, so Miss Betty continued, "So what if Rayford Holly's worth twenty-eight billion dollars, he still has to go to the toilet just like everybody else, doesn't he? Now doesn't he?" Miss Betty stopped suddenly because the old man, making his way along the counter, had spotted her and lifted a wave. "Why, if it isn't our Winston," she said, swooning as if before a movie star.

"Just like anyone else," I reminded her. But she was too busy climbing up over the top of the counter and squeezing next to him. Pop fished his Instamatic from the inner pocket of his suitcoat and promptly filled the room with a cold white flash. "I'll frame it and put it on my nightstand with the ones of my grandbabies," Miss Betty said. "You're just like an uncle to me, Winston. And my home will always be open to you."

"Why, thank you, Betty."

He and Pop shook hands for a longer period of time than I would've found comfortable. At first I thought it was a spontaneous show of mutual affection, but then I noticed that Miss Betty had taken hold of the camera and was struggling to get them in frame. Pop's smile grew anxious and crooked, and the old man seemed worried about his batch of pancakes cooking on the grill. "Mama?" It was Pop, clenching his teeth to keep the grin. "You wanna hurry it up there?"

At last the flash came, and they were free to part.

"Is Winston like an uncle to you, too, Pop?" I said.

But he, like Miss Betty, was too excited to register the barb. "What were the words you used to describe my barbecue?" he asked the old man.

"That it was the absolute best thing I ever put in my mouth," came the reply.

Pop sat back down and nudged Miss Betty. "Did you hear that, honey? Rayford Holly just said my barbecue was the absolute best thing he ever put in his mouth."

"Didn't mean as much when he was a short-order chef, did it, Pop? You should've brought a tape recorder along."

"What?"

"You could play it back over and over: the richest man in America praising your barbecue."

Once again I went ignored. "It all starts with the pit," Pop said to the old man, then proceeded to tell the story about how his had begun its life as an Amana refrigerator.

Miss Betty and Pop weren't the only ones who treated the old man differently than before. The lady bank tellers, to name another pair, asked for his autograph and kisses on the lips, and they even sat right next to each other, no more than a few inches apart, hardly seeming to care that they shared the same glass booth eight hours a day, five days a week. Some regulars even exaggerated their memories of things that had happened during the last fortnight. To Ol' Fontenot, for instance, a glass of spilled milk became a testament to the goodness of the human heart. The old man had cleaned the mess without a fuss, and this had struck Ol' as proof that there indeed was hope for mankind. To show what pals they'd been, Ol' had the old man sign his name on a brand-new dollar bill, which Ol' planned to seal in Lucite and place on a pedestal in the lobby of the Homestead Bank.

Another thing that struck me as odd was the fact that no one called him Winston anymore. He was Mr. Holly or Rayford Holly. And when they asked him a question it had nothing to do with food or the day's special. It was about money. "What's it like having all those billions?" was most often asked. Second was, "I bet you could buy anything in the world you wanted, couldn't you?"

It wasn't just the diners who'd changed: the old man, too, was different. His step was slower than usual, and he didn't dance around at either the sink or the stove. Before he'd asked personal questions of the people at the counter and counseled them when they related their troubles. Today the effort of having to acknowledge everyone made him distant and aloof, and he tended to lose focus when anybody tried to engage in anything more than small talk. He didn't laugh and he didn't hum old show tunes and not once did he mention love.

"Hey, Winston," I said at one point, shortly after he'd escaped the clutches of another woman who wanted a kiss. "Tell me about love. Talk to me about it."

"Love?" But as quickly he was swallowed up by a local insurance salesman who wanted to know if the old man would consider one of the whole-life policies his firm had to offer.

By nine o'clock the crowd outside, having grown impatient with the wait, stormed the door and made itself at home among the shelves. I heard somebody say that church started in half an hour and that they didn't want to miss the opportunity of seeing America's richest man. Even though the store was filled to capacity, no one seemed to have an appetite for anything but the old man. I spotted the mayor, standing with his wife over by the feminine napkins. I'd never been formally introduced to the man, but you'd never know that by the way he greeted me. He hustled over and gave me a hug and a painfully strong hand to shake. "Two weeks from today," he whispered with a hint of confidentiality. "Mark it on your calendar, Burnette."

"Two weeks . . . ?"

"A parade." He seemed surprised that I hadn't been able to figure as much. "If you could get Mr. Holly to ride—"

"But he's not even from here," I said, interrupting.

"He lived here for two weeks, didn't he? I'd say that qualifies."

"Two weeks? Is that all it takes? What a time you must have keeping up with your census rolls."

The mayor didn't respond. He was watching the old man flip pancakes at the stove. Every time one landed without the batter spreading he gave a quiet round of applause. It was as though he was watching an animal perform a complicated human trick, and he just couldn't get over it. Whole minutes had passed before he remembered that he'd come to see me about something. "Anyway, Burnette, the township of Smoke would be eternally grateful if you could convince him to make an appearance. As a token of our appreciation, we'd even let you ride in the same car as him."

"That's generous of you."

"Or maybe we could build a float and put you two on it?"

"What about Carnihan? Why isn't he part of the equation?"

"He hasn't done anything famous. At least you've written a book about your mother. Or so I hear."

"Thank you, Mr. Mayor, but I'd rather not commit to anything just yet."

"All you have to do is ask him—Rayford Holly, I mean."

"Why don't you ask him yourself?"

"I thought we'd have a better shot if you approached him. You're his friend, aren't you?"

"All right, Spitty. I'll ask him, but I can't guarantee anything."

The mayor's real name was Manny Peete, but behind his back everyone called him Spitty because he tended to expectorate whenever engaged in debate with rival politicians. To avoid being doused, I tramped over to the other end of the counter and settled in behind the gate. The stool nearest me was where Silas had always sat, and I regretted that he wasn't with us this morning, reading about the ponies in the *Lip* sports page. At the moment his seat was occupied by someone who had no more loyalty to Hometown Family Goods than to the plate of food which had gone untouched in front of him for the last half hour.

"You gonna eat that?" I asked the diner.

His eyes, focused on the old man, were glazed over with a film as thick as cheesecloth.

"You gonna eat those pancakes or let them go to waste?" I tried again. "If you're not gonna eat then why don't you make room for somebody else?"

When he failed to respond, I reached over and gave him a nudge, and he tottered in his seat as if awakened from a trance.

"I don't mean to be rude, but there are a lot of people here who'd love some breakfast."

"Yeah, yeah, yeah," he grumbled, and proceeded to cut into his stack. You could tell he had no appetite for the food; each forkful seemed to take forever to get down. As he ate his stare remained fixed on the old man, who seemed to be the one thing in the place he truly wanted to devour.

"The mayor wants you to ride in a parade," I told the old man sometime later. "Two weeks from now."

He was whisking eggs in a bowl, working extra hard since all eyes were on him.

"It's to boost Smoke's morale. They have one every now and then celebrating any local folk who happen to distinguish themselves. It's mostly new farm tractors, old convertibles with their tops down, horses shitting in the street, and skinny teenaged girls twirling silver batons."

"Are you gonna be in it?"

"They invited me because I'm the only Smokie ever to have read a book, much less written one."

"And what about Jay? He gonna be in it?"

"The mayor says absolutely not, since he hasn't done anything famous yet."

"He kidnapped me, didn't he?"

"That's true, Winston, but no one's supposed to know that."

"Then the answer is no." The old man ladled the eggs onto the grill, producing a great cloud of smoke which went rushing up into the vent, and which inspired a roar of approval from the crowd. "Tell the mayor it's a security risk. Someone might attempt to kidnap me, and I'm only good for one of those a year."

The mayor took the news better than I'd expected. He seemed to understand the old man's concerns. And his only question was of a personal nature: "You didn't tell him my nickname's Spitty, did you, Burnette?"

"No. I referred to you as Mr. Mayor the entire time."

"We just might have to go ahead and build that float for you anyway." And he gave me a happy slap on the shoulder.

An hour or so later I stood at the window and watched the activity starting to brew across the street. I could see Rachel Wayne and her cameraman filing what I presumed to be a live report, and beside them a few dozen other newspeople scattered along the sidewalk, several of them waiting with Minicams poised on their shoulders. Recalling my own days in the news-gathering trade, I wondered why no one had attempted to enter the store for an interview, but then I spotted Newton and Everly standing among the group, their eyes hidden behind mirrored sunglasses. Newton was speaking into a walkie-talkie, Everly into what looked like a microphone on his lapel. When one of the cameramen ventured out into the street, the two FBI agents chased after him, grabbed him by the collar, and led him back to where he belonged.

As Newton and Everly were returning to their posts a general excitement swept over the crowd of reporters. As if on cue they wheeled around and faced in the direction of the square, watching for something in the distance. They reminded me of blackbirds on a telephone wire, turned to greet an unexpected wind. In seconds a small limousine pulled up to the curb and two people emerged from the backseat: the first, a young fellow about my age, seeming in a great hurry, and the second, an older man who was dressed in the fashion favored by Newton and Everly, and who, I noted with some curiosity, some alarm, packed a pistol in a leather shoulder holster.

The men crossed the street without looking for cars. They brushed by the cameramen who'd started their instruments rolling and ignored the FBI agents who converged on them to serve as escorts. The younger of the two was carrying a briefcase in one hand, a big appointment book in the other: he lugged them like someone struggling under the load of pails filled with too much water. He was wearing a plain brown suit a size too large for his narrow frame, and a fancy striped tie which had blown over his shoulder and was being whipped by the wind. The older man opened the front door and let the other through, then, still outside, he turned his back to the screen and crossed his meaty arms. The younger one pushed into the crowd without minding the knot of delicately put-together old ladies standing by the stomach medicines, and eventually worked his way to the center of things. By now Carnihan had noticed him, as had the old man, who, lifting his spatula in greeting, said, "Why if it isn't Benny Ben Benson, come to the rescue."

"Good to see you again, Mr. Holly."

"Benny Ben Benbo, here to take me home."

"Just Ben, Mr. Holly. Thank you, sir."

"Benny Ben Benbo Benedictine Bengali Ben Benson."

Some of the customers started to laugh nervously, others to attempt to repeat the name. The young man smiled and rocked back on his heels. "Whatever you say, Mr. Holly."

"Ben."

"That's it. *Ben.* Just Ben, sir. I appreciate that, sir."

He seemed like a decent fellow, did Ben Benson, though one more accustomed to electric lamplight than what the sun gives, and to talking to people on the telephone than in person, and to being treated with at least a small measure of respect than without any. Pop, ever the gentleman, offered him his stool and relieved him of his book and briefcase. Benson sat down with a noisy sigh and showed his gratitude with a big-lipped smile. He was about to say something when one of the ladies standing behind him flicked his tie off his shoulder, letting it fall in place. He swiveled around to get a look at her, and another woman, this one just over his left shoulder, ran a hand through his hair, trying to repair what looked like one of those chronic cowlicks that even a liberal dab of grease can't tame.

"Coffee, Benny Ben?" the old man asked, placing a cup in front of him.

Benson said thanks and the old man filled it to the brim, leaving little room for error. Benson's hands were shaking and, as he sipped, some of the coffee spilled down his chin and muddied his pretty white shirt. Benson's face filled with pain, and he let out a chirp no louder than a baby bird's.

I was impressed when he didn't scream and curse, knowing I would've. Miss Betty leaned forward on her stool, yanked the hanky out from under her, and went about trying to clean him up.

Carnihan said, "Tell us who are you, Ben," and walked over from the sink, wiping his hands on a rag.

Benson was slow to speak, either because he wasn't sure about Carnihan or because his throat burned. "I'm Mr. Holly's assistant. I just flew in to Warren and met a car there. I'm here to escort Mr. Holly back to Liberty."

"But I can get back on my own," the old man said. "I drove down in the truck, remember?" He raised an eyebrow at Benson. "You come in the jet?"

"Yes sir."

"You come alone?"

"Just me and Terrence and Collie, sir."

"Collie's my pilot," the old man explained. "And Terrence . . . I'm not rightly sure what Terrence is."

"Terrence is in charge of security, Mr. Holly. He's waiting just outside the door, sir."

I glanced through the glass at Terrence's big broad back held tight by a sheet of blue polyester.

"Now Collie," the old man was saying, "you should see this Collie." He didn't seem to be talking to anyone in particular, just talking to talk. "Flew combat missions in Vietnam, Collie did. Knocked Soviet-built MiGs out of the sky like he was out target shooting. His eyes . . ." The old man paused and looked around the room. I figured he was searching for a pair that matched Collie's. "In the sun you can't tell the irises from the whites, *that*'s how clear they are."

"Collie asked me to tell you how much he's missed you, sir."

"Huh?"

"Collie, sir. He said he's missed you."

"A good boy, Collie. A damned good boy."

The old man took his apron off and hung it on a nail. You'd think hanging a piece of cloth on the wall wouldn't take much effort, but it seemed to sap the old man. His arm went up light and came down heavy, and the blood drained from his face. He suddenly seemed a lot older and more frail than before, and when his voice came it was like that of someone who'd just been punched in the gut. "Who'd you say was with you?" He was staring at the ground, his eyes loose and unfocused.

"Collie, sir. And Terrence."

"Terrence? Oh, yeah. Right. Terrence."

"Shall we be going home, sir?"

Ben Benson stood up and Pop handed him his book and briefcase. The crowd cleared a narrow path and Benson followed it to the door, occasionally glancing back to make sure the old man hadn't strayed off. "A short trip, sir. Only ninety minutes. Even less if we get a strong tailwind."

The old man opened the gate and shuffled through. He had plenty of room but for some reason he seemed crowded, as if he wasn't getting enough air. "The truck, I drove down in it."

"We'll worry about that later, sir. We'll have someone take it back up for you." Benson opened his appointment book and made a note of this. "We'll see to it first thing tomorrow morning. You know how I am about your scheduling, Mr. Holly."

"If it's written in that book it's gonna happen."

"That's exactly what I mean, sir."

Carnihan was over by the register, watching the old man in utter bewilderment. It occurred to me that he looked even more confused now than he had the other day at Silas's house. His lower lip was quivering and he didn't seem to know what to do with his hands. "Hey, Winston?"

The old man didn't hear.

"Hey, Winston. You can't go yet. I still owe you, remember?"

"What . . . ?"

"You can't go. I lost the bet and now I owe you."

The old man seemed to understand something. He smiled at Carnihan and tapped him on the shoulder. "But it is I who owe you," he said. Did he mean the sort of debt only their time together had been able to give him, something bound to his experience at Hometown and Smoke? No. He staggered back over to the register and started removing the tips he'd stuffed into his pockets. In all he added almost a hundred dollars to the till, most of the cash so crumpled that it didn't lie flat in the drawer. "I told you I owed you. And now I don't."

"The bet, Winston." Carnihan sounded scared and desperate. "I owe you for the bet. Anything in this world you want. You can't go until I pay up."

The old man started toward the door again, ignoring Carnihan, who'd stepped out from behind the counter now. About halfway through the crowd the old man stopped and turned and looked long and hard all around him. You could almost tell what he was thinking: that he'd danced on this floor, that he'd kissed a girl on that slab of zinc, that he'd fed a lot of people, nearly an entire town, in fact. He seemed more happy than sad, and that was what made it so impossible to look at him. He staggered back through the crowd and his legs wobbled and his head pitched forward. As he headed toward the door people reached out to touch him and some whispered goodbye. "God bless you, Winston," Miss Betty said. "God bless . . ." And Manny Peete's voice came calling above the others: "Shall we reserve a seat for you in the famous parade, Mr. Holly? Shall we reserve a seat?"

The screen door creaked open and the old man stumbled past Terrence without saying anything. "You're looking good, Mr. Holly. Yes sir. You're looking mighty good."

Terrence ran out in the street and held a hand up to stop a couple of kids on bikes, then he motioned to the old man that the way was clear. "My God, you are, Mr. Holly. You're looking ten years younger, if I do say so myself."

The driver opened the back door. He tipped his hat as the old man approached. "How are you, Mr. Holly? My name is Rodney, sir. So nice to be your chauffeur today."

The old man didn't speak.

"Tonight you'll get to sleep in your own bed. I bet you've missed that, haven't you, Mr. Holly?"

Newton and Everly were struggling to keep the reporters and cameramen from storming the car.

"A seat, Mr. Holly? Shall we reserve a seat . . . ?"

Some of the reporters, perhaps inspired by the mayor, started shouting questions of their own, the chorus of voices coming loud and garbled and difficult to make out. They seemed to want to know what the old man thought of Smoke, and why he'd chosen to come there, and what other towns he might visit next year on his journey to self-discovery.

Did he like the Cajun cooking? somebody wanted to know. And what was it like having all that money? Actually, that one was asked about a dozen times, and in every way imaginable.

"It's a lovely parade, Mr. Holly. Everyone turns out. . . ."

Why didn't the old man start on the subject of women or bird dogs or ballroom dancing? I wondered. And what about love? Was there nothing worth mentioning? Whitman: I thought of Whitman. Didn't something of his suit the occasion? Something about the road, perhaps? The long, brown path?

"Yes," the driver said. "There's no bed like your own bed, no pillow like your own pillow."

The old man stood at the open door and lifted a high-handed wave, his fingers moving as if on a plain of piano keys. The hand came down and he blew a kiss which some of the unattached women in the crowd pretended to catch.

"I owe you, goddammit, Winston. Tell me. You can't just leave like this. Tell me what I owe you."

The old man went to get in the car, but then changed his mind and stepped back out. He was looking at Carnihan and past him at the store, seeming to take in both at once.

"For you to apologize to yourself," he said.

"Is that . . . ? What did you say?"

"Right here in front of everybody. That's what I want. For you to apologize to yourself."

"What kind of a silly, god—"

"I want you to tell yourself you're sorry."

"To apologize to myself? To forgive myself? For what?"

"For living with regret," the old man said.

"For living . . . ?"

"And for wanting when you already have. And for a million other things you need to get off your sad, young soul. Go ahead. Do it, son. Apologize."

"I won't." Carnihan backed up a step. "Please don't make me, Winston. It isn't right."

The old man faced the driver and smiled. "What did you say your name was?"

"Rodney, sir."

The old man bent over and got in the car. "Let's get a move on, Rodney. I'd like to see Liberty before dark."

"But I won't," Carnihan said. "Why should I be the one to apologize when it's you who killed the town?"

The driver got behind the wheel and started the engine, and the old man lowered his window about halfway, just enough to see his eyes. "Hey, Burdette . . ." He motioned me over.

"Yes sir?"

"Burdette, you need to teach that hardheaded fool brother of yours the difference between what is killed and what isn't." He pointed to the mass of people, the faces that were so alive and familiar to me I could've named every one.

"It's Burnette, Mr. Holly. And I've tried to for years."

"Don't stop trying. And don't let him, either."

The driver revved the engine and started to nudge his way through the crowd, taking it slow for the stubborn throng of reporters who were still determined to find out whether the old man preferred seafood gumbo or crawfish bisque, baked or candied yams. The old man had put his window back up, and now you could only see the shape of his body through the tinted glass. His head was lowered to his chest and his shoulders sagged and he seemed to be crying. Everyone was waving and the cameras rolled and as the car pushed into the clear a pack of stray mutts ran after it, barking fiercely and snapping at the back tires.

"Why should I apologize?" Carnihan said, more to himself than anyone else. "And why to myself? He's the town-killer, after all. Not me."

I turned to answer but by then he was already gone, chasing after the limo as he'd chased after Ruby Dean, running with his elbows pressed close to his sides and his knees kicking high.

"I'm sorry! I'm sorry, Winston! I'm sorry!"

He never quite caught up to the car or the dogs, and although I gave it my best effort, I never quite caught up to him, either. I ran in a straight path behind him, taking the faded lane marker that bisected Market Street. I got only as far as the jailhouse before calling it quits; Carnihan continued way past the Palace Cafe and the Smoke Mission and the old Pavy mansion burning a thousand lights. I sat on the curb panting to cool the fire in my lungs, and I listened to his words beating down the poor, undying streets of Smoke, beating like a song. "I'm sorry, Winston! My God, man, I'm sorry!"

XII

"First the bad stuff," Carnihan said, depositing the Bloody Mary on the counter in front of me. He crossed his arms and leaned back against a stool. A clock just above his head said it was a few minutes past one o'clock in the morning. "We'll get rid of the bad, then graduate to the good."

"Fine, Jay. But what do you mean by stuff?"

"News, brother. What else?"

I'd been away for almost two weeks, hiding in a place called Dew River, where Miss Betty and Pop had rented a cabin as a gift for my twenty-ninth birthday. They'd hoped that the change of scenery would inspire me to work more and play less, and I'd managed to knock out two whole chapters of my new book, neither of which included a character named Saleena or a cup of iron-black coffee. Tonight I was tired and bleary-eyed from the drive home, but at the same time I was excited about being back in Smoke, though not nearly as much as Carnihan was about having me back. He was breathing as if he'd just had a long run, and his eyes were unable to focus, moving from this to that, trembling.

"Is there more bad than good stuff to hear about?" I asked.

"I honestly couldn't say, brother, I've been too busy to keep score." He paused before adding, "No one's died, at least."

He began with a report about Beatnik, who was still missing, he said, despite continuing searches of Monster Mart by the store's entire staff. The dog's disappearance had been a great source of distress for Carnihan, and one for the old man, as well. Just yesterday word had reached Carnihan that Monster Mart was planning to launch a new line of dog food.

" 'Smart Boy,' Winston wants to call it. That's what the manager here said on the phone, anyway. 'Smart Boy Hi-Pro,' with a picture of Beatnik on each bag."

"That would be quite a tribute."

"Don't worry," Carnihan said, refilling my tumbler. "All the rest of the stuff is good, or pretty good. You ready?"

"Tell me."

"The real good or the pretty good?"

"Start with the pretty good," I said. "And end with the real. By then we'll be tipsy and it'll sound even better."

The pretty good stuff was that the dancing cowboy and Mrs. Kuel had decided to reunite as husband and wife. Bernard, as Carnihan referred to him, was now attending nightly AA meetings and had agreed to commit himself to a chemical dependency unit if the twelve famous steps to recovery failed to help him. Tangential to that, none other than Sheriff Sorel had replaced Bernard in the Back Ward of the parish clinic, his convalescence having begun on the same day the old man left town. "It's why he wasn't there that morning," Carnihan explained. "While we were serving the last breakfast, Anita was trying to kill him in her room next to the go-go."

According to Carnihan, Sorel had given his lovey too much lip about her recent rash of assaults, and consequently had become the victim of one himself. While he lay unconscious, a cut on his forehead pouring blood, Anita had emptied a jug of Tom Moore on his face. The whiskey had worked as a corrosive agent and aggravated the wound, which doctors said would need months to heal. "It'll leave a scar in the shape of a question mark." Carnihan traced the design on my forehead, adding a point between my eyes. "Since some bad did come out of it, I've chosen to classify this only as pretty good stuff."

"You were right to do so," I said. "Sorel might be a terrible human being, but you don't want to wish that kind of harm on anyone."

"I didn't mean about Sorel. His getting brained was real good stuff, perhaps even great. The bad is this: Babylon's been chain-locked again, this time by the D.A.'s office." He gave a sigh and shook his head. "I'm afraid it's permanent."

Anita was in the jailhouse, up in a solitary cell set some distance from the rest of the female population. Apparently she'd been trying to recruit girls to work, and when any refused she raised fists against them. Lonnie Tom Long was acting sheriff.

"And how does that rate?" I asked.

"You mean about Lonnie Tom? That would be real good stuff for thieves, rapists, killers, and the like, but just pretty good for people like us."

"What about for law-abiding citizens like Miss Betty and Pop? How good is it for them?"

"Oh, it's bad for them, it's worse than bad. No one is safe in this town but the anarchists."

I sighed at length, pretending to feel great relief. "Looks like we've been spared again," I said.

"Yes. It does, doesn't it?"

The real good stuff, or the first of it, was that soon after I left for Dew River he'd invited Bethany to dinner at a restaurant in Warren, with the aim of setting the record straight. And there, over plates of barbecued ribs and creamed potatoes, he'd asked her directly whether she was the one who'd reported seeing Rayford Holly in our presence. In response she'd been up front and steadfast, answering without embarrassment that yes, she had phoned the sheriff's department and spoken to a deputy, provided her name, and reported what'd she called "strong female suspicions" about the new cook at Hometown Family Goods. She wasn't certain that we'd planned a shopping spree at Monster Mart, but she'd had a pretty fair idea when Carnihan offered "monster door prizes." The reason she turned us in, he said, was simple: she needed the reward money to put her mother in a nursing home and to move away herself from Bayou Blanc. She hated to end our adventure, but it was coming to a close anyway and she didn't want to see the money go unclaimed.

"She said it was like holding a winning lottery ticket and not cashing it in."

"What did you say?"

"I didn't agree with her. I told her she'd betrayed us. But then I came around."

"Yeah?"

"She kissed me, Pace, right there in front of everybody. And she had all this sauce on her mouth . . ."

The reward money had been wired to her bank account, and on the same day her house went up for sale Ol' Fontenot bought it for fifteen thousand dollars, paying with a certified check from the Homestead Bank. Ol' had given her an additional two grand for the furniture, minus the hospital bed, and for the pledge that she would move out by the weekend, when he hoped to entertain a friend, a woman, who he claimed had a "thing" for big-bellied Cajuns. Twenty-four hours later an ambulance had come for Mrs. Duvall and driven her to Smoke, and Carnihan had followed in the delivery truck, delirious with happiness for having helped to make this day possible. Carnihan had been able to see Bethany sitting at the rear of the ambulance. As they slowed to pass through Port Bess, he'd pulled up close enough to watch her press her lips against the glass and to leave a smooth red print. They had brought Mrs. Duvall to the convalescent home just around the corner from the store, and she'd been given a private room with a view of Dr. McDermott's.

"Which brings me to the last of the real good stuff." He paused to catch his breath and to let me catch mine.

"Say it."

"Well, we flew to Las Vegas the next day and got married. Stayed overnight at Caesar's and flew back in the morning. It's official: Bethany Bixler's my wife now."

I was too stunned to respond. I lay my forehead on the counter and closed my eyes.

"We've been staying here, brother—back in one of the examination rooms. She's there now, as a matter of fact."

"You've been staying in Dr. McDermott's?"

He nodded. "I didn't think you'd mind."

I picked my head up and raised the tumbler to my mouth, but I found that I couldn't drink. "I'm really happy for you, Jay—about getting married. But Dr. McDermott's . . . that's my apartment, that's where I live, man. In case you forgot, I'm renting it from you—*paying* for the right to stay there."

"It's only for the time being," he said. "And if it's money you're worried about you can forget about next month's rent. Bethany'll pay for it, she's got plenty of cash now."

"I don't like it."

"What's there not to like?"

"A writer needs privacy, for one. How can I stir up any magic with a girl living down the hall?"

"How can you stir up any without one?" he asked, starting to sound irritated himself. "Look, man, she's more than a girl now, she's my wife. I offered her the place at Worm Road but her car couldn't take the beating the road gave and she didn't like the goats or the isolation. Plus, something happened to her out there." He stopped and looked away, back toward the curtain as if to make sure she hadn't entered the room.

"What happened?"

For some reason he looked up at the clock. It now was 2 A.M. "I'll tell you this only if you promise never to repeat it, especially to Bethany."

"You got it."

"You won't bring it up? Swear you won't bring it up. She's really sensitive about it. It makes her cry."

I lifted my right hand and lay my left flat against the zinc. "Okay, man, I swear. Now tell me."

He started shaking his head. "You'll think this is crazy, brother, but Bethany . . ." He paused and looked at the curtain again. "She says she saw a ghost in the house."

"A ghost, did she?"

"It was Daddy. Up on the second floor landing between his bedroom and mine. It was about this time of night and she'd gone down for a glass of water. When she came back up he was standing there wearing his old clothes from the store—the tie and coat and the apron all starched. He was even holding his feather duster. She claims he spoke to her."

"He talked . . . ?"

Carnihan managed a timid nod. "He told her to take good care of me, that I needed taking care of. Can you believe he said that? It spooked her pretty bad, as you might expect, and she took off running. She ran down the stairs and out of the house and into the goat pasture. She ran through the trees to where I'd left Winston's truck, which no one's bothered to come back for, by the way. When she opened the door to get inside—she said she was looking for a place to hide . . . when she opened the door Daddy was sitting there behind the wheel. It was dark but she could see his face. She said it seemed to be lit from the inside. He smiled at her and said, 'I don't mean to frighten you, Bethany. But I want you to encourage him to close Hometown. It's time.' "

"He wouldn't've said that, not Mr. Hank . . . not a Carnihan."

"That's exactly what I said, but she swears it. She says she put up an argument, I think she shouted at him, and he said, 'That's nice. You're brave and you're strong. You'll be a good wife to him, he needs a good wife. But encourage him to close the store, Bethany. It's time.' She told him she wouldn't, and he just laughed. Then what was the light in him went away and everything turned dark. She said she looked all around the truck, inside and out, but that he was gone."

"He just disappeared, right?"

Carnihan sipped his drink. "Yeah. He just vanished. She woke me up a few minutes later and told me what had happened, and that she wanted me to walk out to the truck with her. I didn't want to go, I thought she'd had a nightmare or something, but she insisted and I finally got out of bed. I put on a robe and some slippers and I walked with her across the pasture. I remember wondering where the goats were, and then I saw them up ahead through the trees. They'd surrounded the truck, all of them just sort of standing there looking at it. So me and Bethany push through them and I look inside, I look in the truck, but nothing's there. 'What do they see?' I say. 'Why do they stay here?' And in that instant it comes to me that they weren't seeing anything, but smelling something. As you know, Pace, goats can raise a helluva stink, but tonight the air was different. It was sweet, like roses. Bethany smelled it, too. And she was the one who named what it was. 'Flowers,' I say. 'It smells like flowers out here.'

She takes my hand and squeezes it and I can see tears come to her eyes. 'No, baby. That's not flowers. It's something else.' She waits a minute and the smell seems to intensify. You can actually feel it now, pressing like a wind. 'It's the divine essence,' she says. 'It's God, it smells like God here, Jay.' And then she lifts her face up to kiss me."

A lamp behind the counter had been our only defense against the gloom, but suddenly the overhead lights flashed on and I swiveled to see Bethany standing by the curtain at the back of the store. My heart thudded against my ribs and tiny explosions seemed to be igniting in my head. I was spooked to the core, but at the same time I was relieved to know that it was Bethany who'd switched on the lights and not the ghost of Hank Carnihan.

She'd been standing there all along, listening to every word. "You're a snake," she said to Carnihan, and crossed her arms at her chest. She didn't sound as angry as the charge might suggest, but rather as if she'd just been tipped off to one of her new husband's character flaws: he could not keep a secret. "No one was supposed to know. You swore to me."

"It's just Pace. You won't tell anyone, will you, brother?"

I shook my head.

"Come have a nightcap," he told her. "I was filling him in on all that happened while he was away."

"I think I'll go back to bed."

Only now did I notice that she was wearing one of my dress shirts, and a favorite at that. The tail hung down to her knees and the tiny buttons at the collar had been undone. I'd bought it some years ago at a men's shop in Washington, and it remained one of the few I had professionally laundered. You could see the web of creases on the front, from where she'd lain on it. "You'll forgive me, won't you?" she said.

Carnihan erupted with a nervous laugh. "I was just going to ask *you* that," he said.

"I was talking to Pace. I meant about his shirt." She held an arm up to show a stain on the sleeve. It was a pool of black ink, marking a spot near the elbow. "I'll pay you for it—out of my reward money. And I'll buy you a new suit to go with it. We can drive to Warren first thing in the morning."

"I don't want a new suit. Just forget about it. Or, better yet, keep it as a wedding gift." She smiled and I said, "Congratulations, B.B. I wish you every happiness."

"That suit," Carnihan said, "you really should let her buy you one. You could wear it to the parade on Sunday."

"On Sunday, now, is it?"

"That's more real good stuff," he said. "They're running it now to accommodate Hayward's schedule. He starts training camp and wouldn't've been able to come down any later. Let Bethany buy you a suit. I let her buy me one."

I was confused and he could see that. The parade was about as attractive a proposition to me as an enema; at least during the enema you didn't have to smile and wave, and you knew what to wear. I said, "I'll tell you why I don't want a new suit. A writer doesn't work in a suit. He works in house clothes—in whatever's comfortable."

"You're not riding in the parade as a writer. You're riding as a close, personal friend of Rayford Holly's."

"Oh, am I? When did I agree to that?"

"When Spitty called and spoke to me personally. He said he'd given it a lot of thought and wanted to see us recognized—you and me, brother, together. He's having some of his maintenance people build a Rayford Holly float for the occasion. Sometime down the road, you can ride in a famous parade as a writer. But I need you next to me in this one."

"Why is it what's real good to you feels real bad to me?"

"Oh, and Miss Dunbar called last night. I was wondering if you'd notice, especially after Bethany turned on the lights."

He faced the business counter and the portraits of the four Carnihans hanging in dreary sepia tone. At the center of the group, now, was one of Ruby Dean, and she smiled down on the store with warm, bright-eyed gaiety. Unlike the other pictures, Ruby Dean's was in color, so vivid as to seem surreal. It looked to have been taken about twenty years ago, when there were a few more things in this world to be cheerful about, namely customers with money to spend. The sight of her brought a fat lump to my throat, and I lifted my Bloody Mary in salute. "Welcome back. Nothing's been the same at Hometown since you left."

"Daddy was the one who'd arranged to have it made—only a few days before he died, as a matter of fact. It took them long enough to get it done, but get it done they did. Isn't she perfect, Pace?"

"She's the most perfect thing I ever saw," I answered.

"Oh, and there was one other reason Miss Dunbar called . . ." Carnihan tugged at my shirtsleeve. "It's in, brother. Your book."

"My book? Which book is that?"

"Remember the strange one you wrote about meteorology? She got her first shipment in yesterday afternoon."

Over the last two weeks I'd conveniently managed to forget about *Strange Weather*. Or maybe some survival instinct had forced its pending launch date from my mind. In any case, learning that it had made its way to Smoke was so shocking that I grabbed a stool before the ground rushed up to meet me.

"I went by to see it," Carnihan was saying. "And as I walked up they were just finishing the display in the window. There must've been a hundred of 'em, Pace, stacked like a pyramid." He spread his arms out wide, to demonstrate. "Behind them there's a bulletin board like you'd see in a classroom. It's got copies of that same picture on the back of the book jacket, and your name in cutout letters. 'Pace Burnette,' it says." He looked at Bethany. "You remember what else was on that board?"

From the corner of my eye I saw her shuffle toward me on bare feet. She put her hands on my shoulders and kissed me on the cheek, a little thing you could barely feel. "I'm so proud of you." And she took the chair next to me.

"What did it say, Beth? Next to his name?"

"I don't remember it saying anything."

Carnihan looked at the clock. It now was closer to three than to two o'clock, by a minute or so. I probably would've excused myself and trudged off to bed had he not grabbed me by the arm and started pulling me toward the door. He opened it and we were out in the street, heading in the direction of the square and Dunbar's Camera & Books.

The store occupied a corner building two stories high and half a block wide. It was flanked by a bail bondsman's and a defunct guitar store with cardboard pictures of dancing musical instruments taped to the facade. Every window in the entire block was dark tonight except for one of Dunbar's—the one showcasing a first novel by a young author named Pace Burnette. Carnihan threw an arm around me, and I threw one around him, and then Bethany wedged herself between us.

"There it is," he said, pressing a finger against the glass. "What we couldn't remember back at the store."

He was pointing to the bulletin board behind the stack of books, the words forming a rainbow under my name.

"Well, I'll be damned," Bethany muttered. "That's you, all right. That's Pace Burnette."

I felt a pride unlike any I'd ever known. And in that moment and on that little piece of earth I knew I'd do great things with my life, the very least of them literary.

SMOKE'S OWN, the sign said, the *O*'s in the two words decorated as happy, smiling faces.

We gathered in the parking lot of the football stadium and took our assigned places. At the head of the parade were a couple of Boy Scouts who'd killed a giant timber rattler in the Thistlethwaite Reserve, earning them a place in state record books. They came wearing uniforms, looking freshly scrubbed, with perfect parts in their hair. Behind them was another record holder: a fellow named Joe Angelle, who'd grown a Best Boy tomato as big as a pumpkin. Everybody in Smoke knew Joe to be a drunk and wondered whether it wasn't moonshine whiskey he'd used to fertilize his plants. The Boy Scouts and Joe rode in open convertibles, as did the young woman who occupied the third place in line. She was the nineteen-year-old unmarried mother of quintuplets who hadn't realized she was pregnant until late in her second trimester. She'd always been a hefty girl, and she'd assumed the rumblings to be indigestion. That she'd delivered five babies in a bathtub without a doctor's assistance or the use of drugs made her famous by Smoke's definition of the word, and negated the issue of the children's illegitimacy. At the moment her kids were sick with colic and being cared for by her mother, which proved to be a great disappointment to the mayor and his assistant. They'd hoped to show everybody just how fertile a place Smoke was, the land as well as the people.

The Smoke High band trailed the teenage mother, and then came the Rayford Holly float. It was really just a flatbed trailer with ribbons of crepe paper hanging from the sides and a couple of church pews to sit on in the event we got tired of standing. I'd thought that only Carnihan and I would ride on the thing, but as it turned out many others were included, among them the telephone lady, Ol' Fontenot, the two bank tellers, and an elderly woman who claimed to have eaten lunch at the local Monster Mart snack bar every day for the last ten years. In recognition of this achievement, the store had once named her employee of the month, even though she did nothing but take a daily bowl of soup there, her lack of teeth making it difficult to handle much else. I thought Carnihan might object to the woman's presence on the float, as well as that of the others, but he seemed delighted to have her. Back in a stadium bathroom he and Joe Angelle had gotten together for a nip, and I figured this contributed to his willingness to bring her along.

I was wearing the sand-colored business suit Bethany Bixler had bought me the day before, tolerating the outfit as you did a gun pointed at your head. Had I worn anything else I'd have risked losing her as a friend, and that was a greater concern than looking foolish in new clothes. The pants were blousy at the waist, but I wore my belt tight; to keep the legs from dragging the ground, I'd hemmed them with safety pins, the metallic arms of the clasps forming shiny bands around my ankles. I looked as clean and polished as the Boy Scouts up front, and nothing like the wildly creative bohemian artist I fancied myself.

I doubt that I'd have given my clothes much thought had Hayward Clark not arrived looking like a fabulous prince, his dark linen suit, Italian loafers, and hundred-dollar necktie immediately placing him in a realm where only the truly famous dwelled. Next to him the rest of us were mere impostors: cheap pretenders at the heavenly gates of celebrity. LaShonda pulled up in a rental car and dropped him off, then colored the asphalt with parallel rubber strips. Hayward was to occupy the last vehicle in the parade: my own Mustang convertible, which I'd volunteered for the occasion, and which Lonnie

Tom Long, himself famous for that night at Monster Mart, was enlisted to drive.

Hayward ran by us in a lazy sprint, a hand held over his necktie to keep it in place.

"You're late, little brother," I heard Carnihan say.

"Yes, I am. And it's your fault."

He didn't bother opening the door. In one clean, athletic stride he bounded into the open carriage, hopping from the front to the back seat. Along the line drivers were starting their engines, and when Lonnie Tom followed suit Hayward had to shout to be heard. "We just flew in at noon. I'm late because of Mama."

"Yeah?" It was Carnihan. "What's wrong with her?"

"Soon as we get to the house one of the neighbors comes over and tells us about Silas. She's been upset, just about hysterical ever since." He wrapped his hands around his mouth to make certain we didn't miss what he had to say. "What's the matter with you two? How come you can't pick up the telephone?"

"We didn't want to worry you," Carnihan said.

"I'd rather you worried than ignored us. Mama's so upset she won't be able to leave the house. Her blood pressure's sky-high—it's clear up through the roof."

"She'll miss the parade?"

Hayward attempted to respond, but his words were drowned out by the band, which had kicked off a rendition of the Smoke High alma mater, or what I thought was the alma mater. Loudest of the instruments were the drums, beating with no more rhythm than a screen door in a rainstorm. The cymbals crashed, frightening everyone, and when the brass section joined in the driver of our tractor answered with a blurt from his diesel horn.

"God, they're awful," Carnihan said.

"Yes," I told him. "It's what they're famous for."

After about a hundred yards the band quit playing altogether and chose, instead, to concentrate on marching in step, which proved as difficult an assignment as the one of making music. They looked, I thought, like workers in a giant office building at quitting time. No two seemed to be going in the same direction, and there were so many collisions that you wondered how they hoped to survive the three-mile-long trek to the other side of town. "Were we ever that goofy?" Carnihan asked.

"We lost every football game we played but one. We couldn't run, if I recall."

"Yeah, but at least we could walk. These poor dimwits can't even do that."

Although I'd been selected to ride in the parade as a close, personal friend of Rayford Holly's and not as the brilliant new voice of my generation, I was still pretty excited about being included—so excited, in fact, that I was disappointed when the crowd turned out to be a dud. So few people were on hand for the first leg of the route that Carnihan and I resorted to waving at trees, signs, and buildings, and to shouting pleasantries at any other inanimate object that happened to catch our eye. Carnihan seemed particularly pleased to see parking meters along the roadside, and I was delighted by the sight of mailboxes, especially those with red flags standing at attention.

Offended by Carnihan's and my cynicism, Monster Mart's former employee of the month lost her composure and hissed at us with her toothless mouth. We smiled and blew kisses.

Carnihan said, "If this doesn't get any better, I might have to run up ahead and ride with Joe."

Every fifty yards or so we encountered a group who knew someone in the parade and who cried with arms upraised for candy and doubloons. These people seemed to have forgetten that Mardi Gras was eight months away and that this was an event honoring famous local people whose contributions to society, in general, and to the town of Smoke, in particular, were of such magnitude as to inspire others to reach for similarly bright, high-hanging stars. It struck me, of course, that a couple of snake killers, a besotted grower of monster vegetables, and an unwed mother of five, not to mention a bunch of badly dressed misfits whose only claim to fame was having met a certain man . . . that these weren't the sorts of role models most towns would choose to recognize, but this was Smoke and allowances were to be made.

The only person anyone got excited about was Hayward, but his extraordinary good looks and dignified manner, taken together, were intimidating to those unaccustomed to seeing their heroes anywhere but on a TV screen. A few star-struck children, dressed in Miami Dolphin jerseys bearing his familiar number 27, chased after him for his autograph, but the adults were more restrained. With the exception of a couple of rough-looking women who shouted declarations of love, they stared after him with the sort of wide-eyed wonder generally reserved for weeping religious icons, UFOs, and Elvis look-alikes.

About a mile into our trip we finally passed a clutch of familiar faces. Miss Betty and Pop were sitting on a picnic blanket in the shade of a pecan tree, and fanned out on the ground around them were my sisters and their families. Pop had brought his cards along and was engaged in a game of solitaire, and Miss Betty was crocheting a sweater for one of the grandchildren. They all stood when they saw us coming, and like everybody else along the parade route my family seemed confused as to the purpose of the event. "Throw us some beads, mister!" the kids were saying, shaking their arms up in the air. "Hey, mister, throw us some beads!"

Having nothing else to give, Carnihan and I removed the boutonnieres the mayor's assistant had pinned to our lapels and tossed them in high, shivering arcs toward the children. The flowers dropped through a tangle of leafy branches and landed on the picnic blanket, upsetting Pop's game. The children scrambled to claim the things and sent cards flying everywhere. To show who was in charge, Abigail and Claire pounced on the leaders of the riot, led them off to the side, and gave them the spankings they'd asked for. Through all the commotion Stuart and Jesse remained standing in the shade, their hands fiddling with the change in their pockets. By the passivity of their expressions you figured they were discussing the will of a God who would saddle them with such domineering wives, lawless young'uns, and a brother-in-law whose renown had robbed them of their Sunday afternoon naps.

Pop moseyed over to the curb and started running with the float, and Miss Betty, shouting that he'd have a heart attack, chased a few feet behind him, her needles and fuzzy ball of string still in hand.

"What did you two do to get so famous?" Pop called.

"It isn't because we know you," Carnihan answered.

"You're just jealous," I yelled to Pop. "No one in town's recognized you for your barbecue yet."

"Will you be coming by the house when this is done?" Miss Betty asked. Poor woman, she'd only covered half a block and already her tongue was hanging from her mouth.

"Depends on whether you're cooking," Carnihan said.

"I'll have something, you know I always have something."

"Then we'll be there," he said.

"Will you be coming, too, Hayward?" It was Pop, lagging back to run with the Mustang. "Bring your wife and mother along."

"I'll sure tell them, Coach Burnette. Thank you, sir."

Hayward held his hand out to shake, and Pop had to pick his pace up to reach it. For more than a block he ran clasping the hand of the finest player he'd ever coached, and the only one to make a professional career of the game. Hayward's success as an athlete meant little to Pop, however. As he jogged along with the Mustang, wearing a proud smile, you could tell that Pop's joy came from having been a part of molding Hayward Jeffrey's life and from seeing what a fine man he turned out to be.

Eventually my parents quit their chase and walked back to the pecan tree. Carnihan and I stood at the rear of the float and watched them recede to small dark lines, then a number of smaller dark lines —their children and grandchildren—converged on them from all directions. They were a unit now, a single thing, moving toward the dense blanket of the grass.

For whatever reason I expected to see the old man at some point along the parade route, standing at the roadside. In everyone who greeted us with a wave I searched for his face and whenever someone hollered for beads I listened for the accent that was uniquely his. People roared and made their peculiar human noises, but not one of them called like a hog.

A figure leaning against a light standard was Winston; another dressed all in white; another with a dog at his heels.

"Wonder what happened to him," I said to Carnihan as we motored past the Abdalla building in the heart of downtown.

"Me, too. I wonder the same." He scanned the crowd for a face. "You mean Winston, right?"

"We'll see him, he'll surprise us."

"He'll be just around the next bend." Carnihan pointed to the place. "He'll come running and jump up here on the float."

We moved past where the road turned, but the old man wasn't to be found there, either.

"Maybe he plans to drop from the sky," Carnihan said. "He has a plane, remember? It wouldn't surprise me to see him parachute and land right here . . . right where we're standing."

How many different versions of his arrival were Carnihan and I able to imagine? A score, at least. We saw him turning into our path from a side road and assuming the lead, racing past the Smoke High band and the motorcycle cops, blazing toward the finish; we saw him ascending from a manhole cover and climbing onto the float, throwing everyone off but Carnihan and me.

"I know he's here," Carnihan said. "I can feel him."

And then there he was, already among us, driving the tractor that pulled our float. He had the narrow shoulders and feathery white hair; the back of his neck was as tough and wrinkled as an elephant's hide; the ears were red. He wore a straw hat and simple clothes, and, most telling of all, he'd managed to go unnoticed since the parade began.

"I spotted him earlier," Carnihan said, "just before we got under way. I think he winked at me."

"He winked, did he?"

"Maybe he wanted to keep it a secret—to surprise everyone. Winston's full of surprises, remember?"

I shuffled past him to the front of the float. I was close enough to catch a whiff of the driver's fruity cologne and to see that he was in fact some years younger than the old man and more sturdily built, with muscle in his upper arms. I knew who he wasn't now, but nevertheless I spoke to him. "You couldn't keep away, could you?"

The driver, deaf to anything but the roar of his engine, didn't give me a look. His sole focus seemed to be on the band members up ahead, many of whom were lagging behind and endangering themselves—it was a tractor, after all.

"I knew it." I stepped out onto the steel tongue that connected us.

"Hey, Winston, you couldn't keep away, could you? You had to come back."

The others on the float were laughing now, but Carnihan watched with great expectation. The fantasy had overpowered him: he was willing it to come true. "Winston," I heard him say, and then I moved a step closer.

The driver swiveled in his seat and faced me. You fool, I told myself. You poor, sentimental fool.

"Sit down." He waved me back. "It isn't safe. It isn't—"

"The heat," I told him. "It's starting to get to me. For a second I thought you were someone else."

"We're almost there." He waved again, this time more emphatically. I saw the muscles in his arms tighten. "You've been drinking," he said to me, then, muttering to himself: "They're famous, they think they can drink."

We were wrong about the old man, he never did show up. But toward the end of the run—when our disappointment was such that we'd stopped waving and responding to those who called to us, and it was beginning to feel as if our entire adventure with Rayford Holly had been nothing more than fantasy—we did see Silas Poe and he wasn't in the window of the jailhouse. He was standing in street clothes next to a tomb in the parish churchyard, looking twenty pounds lighter than when we saw him last. He'd been leaning against the granite but stood up straight and tall as we came into view. He seemed to have trouble deciding what to do with his hands: whether to hide them in his pockets or behind his back He'd grown a mustache that tended to dress his face up while at the same time making the bald spot on top of his head seem more barren than ever, and his eyes were as clear as those of someone who'd just awakened from a long sleep.

Carnihan spotted him before I did. "Why, look who's there?"

"Winston? Is it . . . ?" I'd been dozing on a church pew, and sat up now with a start. When I saw who it was I wished I hadn't thrown my boutonniere to the kids. "Well, I'll be damned."

"They let me out," Silas called. "They let me . . ." He ran up to the iron fence and stood looking over the barbed arrows on top. "They let me out," he said again.

"But how in the world?" Carnihan said. "How . . . ?"

"They didn't say. They just opened the door and told me I was free to go. The charges have been dropped."

I suddenly remembered Lonnie Tom, driving the Mustang behind us. I wheeled around and eyed his big, goofy face. He tipped his hat and waved. "Angela Brown," he said. "She came in at noon with the papers. Orders from Washington."

"From Washington?"

"I called to verify it. I guess he must know somebody."

"Who . . . Silas? Silas doesn't know anyone in Washington."

The deputy shook his head. "I didn't mean him."

The old church was just ahead: a redbricked structure with a steeple and windows of stained glass and the Stations of the Cross posted under trees in the back parking lot.

"How are you there, Mr. Poe?" It was Hayward, standing up in the back seat of the Mustang. I wanted to tell him to watch it, but it came to me that his shoes alone were probably worth more than the entire car.

"Well, look at you," Silas said. "How are you, son?"

"Feeling better, sir, now that I see you're doing the same. I'll have to hurry and give Mama a call. You had us worried."

"Your Mama's back in Smoke, is she?"

"Back at the house."

"You'll tell her how much I've missed her, won't you, Hayward?"

"I will, sir. Thank you."

"And that nothing's been the same around here since she left?"

"Maybe not that, Mr. Poe, figuring how much crying she's done already. But I will send your regards."

The parade filed into the church lot and swung around to the front of the building. I looked up at the summer sky and saw Christ and a lamb, windows great with color. The band was loading into a yellow school bus, and Joe Angelle was attempting to charm the teenage mother in the first of the cars up front. The girl showed no interest until Joe disclosed his whiskey flask, and then they slipped off together toward the Grotto of the Blessed Virgin Mary. I had hoped to see them embrace in the vine-dense shadows, but a young deacon dressed all in black ran them off, shooing them away like dogs. How unfortunate, I thought. He seemed entirely ignorant of their fame.

"Will you sign your name?" It was the employee of the month, offering me an autograph book.

"I beg your pardon?"

"Your name. I'd like to have it."

I felt ashamed of myself for having wanted to boot this lady from our float. You couldn't help but pity a person without teeth, not to mention one who took soup daily at a place like Monster Mart. "Sure, I'll sign." And I applied my signature to the blank page. I added more loops than usual, and there was a flair about the general construction that came, I presumed, from my having been recognized.

She grinned hugely as I gave her the book back. I saw her diseased gums the color of gunmetal, her tongue like an enormous parasite fixed to the back of her throat. "Is that who you are?" She was studying my name.

"Pace Burnette," I answered.

She nodded, closed the book, and shuffled away, toward a filthy clunker parked under the trees. I'd just signed my first autograph, and I wanted to share this bit of history with someone close to me. I looked for Carnihan, but he seemed to have disappeared. And then I spotted the toothless woman. She tore a page out of the book, squeezed it into a ball, and tossed it on the ground. Had she read the reviews? I wondered.

I waited until she was gone before running over to retrieve the thing. The day was coming to a close, but there still was light to see by. "Winston Rayford Holly," someone had written—Carnihan, it came to me, his penmanship, like his charity, leaving much to be desired.

My heart felt light and strong. And how relieved I was to learn that it wasn't my name she'd discarded.

A magnum bottle of champagne awaited us on Delmas Street, as did a foot-deep pot of crawfish etouffee, a Hitachi steamer bubbling over with spicy brown rice, loaves of buttered French bread, a tossed green salad, and sheets of chocolate cake still warm from the oven. Carnihan and I had spotted the cars parked up the road, in front of a house we knew to be uninhabited. "Act surprised," I told him, and that he did, clutching his chest as we opened the door to their raucous battery of cheers. Miss Betty was in her glory, buzzing about like a bee; Pop was in his recliner, pretending to sleep. The usual spirals of bunting hung from the ceiling, and banners and poster boards still wet with paint congratulated me on the publication of *Strange Weather*. They actually said that: CONGRADS, PACE, ON THE PUBLICATION OF STRANGE WEATHER. They seemed an awful mouthful, even for a mouth as busy as Miss Betty's; and then she'd gone and misspelled "congrats." A clumsier sentence I'd never known, but to my ears it sounded damned near symphonic. I kept repeating it, feeling better with each utterance, gaining confidence. My sisters kissed me and sniffled at the thought that they had such a brother, and Ruby Dean got mad at herself for failing to maintain control. "What's wrong with you?" she grumbled as tears began to well in her eyes. "My lord, R.D. What's wrong?"

"Will you sign my book?" LaShonda asked. And I did.

"What about mine?" Hayward said, implanting a playful forearm in my ribs and frightening me more than I can say.

"Pace," Mrs. Kuel said, stepping through the crowd gathered around me. "I'd like you to meet my husband Bernard."

I raised my head and gazed upon a man both strange and familiar at once. Shed now of jeans, western shirt, and muddy boots, he wore a suit as new and ill-fitting as my own. Except for an eye patch, his face showed no sign of the beating, and his smile was relaxed and steady. I liked him immediately.

"Bernard, is it?"

He gave a solemn nod. "I left home before you were this high." And he showed me with his hand.

"You're back now?"

"Yes. Forever this time."

The party lasted a little more than two hours; Pop stirred only after the last of the guests were leaving the house. He staggered into the kitchen like a beaten prizefighter looking for a corner in which to collapse, and deposited himself on a chair at the dinette table. "Pace," he whispered, removing a letter from his shirt pocket. "This came for you."

"You can stop faking now," Miss Betty told him. "It's only us."

"Jay's still here," he mumbled.

"Yeah," Carnihan said, "but I'm one of you, remember?"

Pop did remember. He hopped from the chair and raced over to the stove, frantic to see whether there was any food left. "God, I thought they'd never leave." And he loaded a plate.

The letter was a mailgram sent late yesterday afternoon from New York City: "Happy to inform you that 50,000 copies of *SW* have been purchased for sale by Monster Mart Inc., of Liberty, Ark. Publisher very happy, as am I.

"XXOO, Cinda Lovey."

"Bad, pretty good, or real good?" Carnihan asked, stepping up to have a look for himself.

I stood and put my arms around him, and I felt his warm face against mine. And of course by then he had his answer.

XIII

If this weren't a true story I'd end it differently. My aptitude for pity has made me such a sucker for sad endings that I've grown distrustful of the warm, happy goodbye. Give me the implausible: a man and a woman parting in the fog, colliding passenger trains, a rare terminal disease with a difficult name to pronounce. I've decided that it's when I grieve that I most trust myself, that I most believe.

Here's something else I can tell you: when I'm moved to tears the world holds its brightest promise, and when I am socked in the chest I most appreciate the big bad beating of my heart.

Just don't give me anything to cheer about. Not the check in the mail, or the battered underdog with the miraculous right hand, or the reunion on the pretty park lawn. And especially not Ruby Dean Clark standing in the X-ray lab at 7 A.M. on a sunny August morning, a Monday of all days. Take her spatula and her apron and hair net, and take her voice telling me to rise and shine, to get up, and to eat, hotdamnit, my biscuits are getting cold. Even more than that, take the permanent thing within her that I always knew would bring her back.

Was I dreaming this horribly contrived finish? I thought so until she reared back and slapped my bare bottom, producing a sound only half as loud as the pain that accompanied it. "Five minutes, boy! And don't think I don't mean it!"

And Silas Poe, take him too with his eyes fixed on the morning *Lip,* trying to determine which pony or team or race car to drop a day's wages on. "You're wrong about that," he said as I stumbled through the curtain and entered the store. I didn't have to speak; this man Silas could read my mind. "These are the Classifieds, for your information, not the sports page. I'm looking for work, not a flutter."

I took a seat and sipped black coffee. The bank tellers on either side of me smelled softly perfumed—like magazines, I thought, with rub-on samples stapled to the page. Ruby Dean approached with a plate and a pile of yellow receipts, both of which she unburdened on the counter in front of me. "You haven't paid your bill—not a penny since I left."

"No, I haven't. But I'm not sure why that should be any of your concern."

"I'm back is why."

"You don't live in Miami anymore?"

"Hayward says he's going to retire. They're coming back to Smoke to live." She smiled and said, "After this season, Pace."

"Yes, well, I'm sure the mayor will be happy. Now he can throw a famous parade every other weekend."

Ruby Dean didn't appreciate my brittle attempt at humor. She balled her hands into fists and rested them on her hips. She said, "I just thought I'd help prepare their way. That's why I'm back so early."

"Why don't you just admit it, Ruby Dean? You missed the store and the town and the people. You missed the life."

"I missed . . ." But she didn't let herself finish. She'd rather have fought than admit such a sentiment. "This new cook," she said at last, "how come he never made you pay?"

"He didn't have time, he was too busy talking."

She started scrubbing the counter as if to show that she still had her priorities in order: you could visit, but it was critical to work while doing so. "So he talked, did he? And what was it he said exactly?"

I examined a slice of perfectly cooked bacon and recalled what a burnt, gnarled mess the old man's had been. "He thought he knew something about love," I finally answered.

She laughed and said, "Love? Who knows anything about that?"

"Did you see this?" It was Silas, rising now to bring me the *Lip*. He laid the paper out on the counter and gave it a pop with his middle finger. LOCAL MONSTER MART TO CLOSE, said the headline, the banner as big and bold as any ever given to war coverage. Suddenly my feelings of sleep deprivation vanished, my headache with them. I felt a hot, electric shudder race through me, wondering if this could be true. Take it, I told myself. Take this too . . . the paper with its news. Take it away from me.

"Let me read it to you," Silas said. Then he cleared his throat and began. *"The Smoke Monster Mart, the most profitable business in parish history, will close its doors in six months, according to Nathan Perl, spokesman for the Arkansas-based discount chain. 'We just couldn't turn a profit,' said Perl last night in an exclusive telephone interview. 'These things happen in a free-market system. We had many good years in Smoke. We'd like to say thanks.'*

"The store, which opened in 1972, employs four hundred and eleven full-time workers, but it also is an enemy of downtown merchants who complain they can't fairly compete with the chain of almost two thousand stores.

" 'For the record,' added Perl, 'we'd like to publicly thank our Smoke employees for their devoted service, and to reassure them that we have no intention of laying them off their jobs. Some will be transferred to our Warren store, and others will be hired at our wholesale club soon to open in Bayou Loup.'

"Rayford Holly, founder of the chain, was not available for comment. Said Perl, 'Mr. Holly has informed me to say that he has no regrets—none. He has close, personal friends in Smoke, and recently visited there. This decision was based on economics alone. While feeling disappointment that this had to happen, he is excited and optimistic about the more than two hundred new Monster Marts presently in construction across the country.' "

The story continued on a jump page, but Silas decided I'd heard enough, as indeed I had. He folded the paper and laid it on the pile by the register.

"Does Carnihan know about this?" I asked, struggling to restrain my excitement.

"Ruby Dean woke him up first," he answered. "He was like you, too sleepy to read. So I did my part and guess what?"

"He didn't take off running again?"

Silas sighed at length and then started to rumble with laughter. "He ran toward the square, screaming, his arms up in the air. We all got a little worried because all he had on was his birthday suit."

"The suit he wore to the parade, you mean?"

"No, the one he wore when poor Deenie brought him into this world . . . the fleshy colored one."

"Has he come back?"

"Bethany just ran after him. She was screaming herself. They shouldn't be long."

"I hope to God she was wearing something?"

"Besides a pretty smile, no, not much. A brassiere and panties, maybe. I saw two streaking bands of black wrapped around a bundle of brown."

Lonnie Tom Long brought them back about half an hour later. He'd spotted Carnihan running toward the home where Mrs. Duvall was staying, with Bethany fast on his heels, and covered them with a couple of Army blankets. Since he was new to the sheriff's badge, and filled with the bravado that generally accompanies such a responsibility, Lonnie Tom threatened to arrest them and throw them behind bars, but then in the car on the way to the jailhouse Carnihan told him the news about Monster Mart and Bethany accidentally let the blanket fall from her shoulders, exposing a few secret parts of herself. Lonnie Tom nearly veered into a telephone pole. Reaching Market Street, he changed his mind about putting them in jail. "Well," he said, still eyeing Bethany, "if your business has been spared . . ."

I would learn all this later, but you could almost figure as much when Lonnie Tom escorted them into the store. He tailed after Bethany the way Beatnik used to follow Mr. Hank and the old man: his tongue loose and his tail swishing, eyes clouded over with what resembled isinglass.

"How 'bout Winston?" I yelled to Carnihan. "Hey, Jay!"

But, holding the blanket tight, he marched straight past me to the business register and pressed the No Sale button. The money tray slid out and knocked musically against his hip. Everybody at the counter swiveled on their stools to watch, and in the air in front of him he drew something with his finger. At first I thought he was making an *S* such as what the comic book hero Superman wears on his chest, but then he slashed two vertical lines through the letter to complete the picture.

"Smoke lives," he declared, then went behind the counter and started mixing Bloody Marys.

I glanced over at Ruby Dean standing by the stove. Although she now was facing Carnihan, what she really was looking at was the picture of herself among the four Carnihans. She was fairly successful at keeping her lips from drawing up in a smile, but the tears in her eyes were something she could neither manage nor disguise. She noticed my stare and I gave her a quiet smile. When she wiped her eyes I felt as if I'd just opened a door marked PRIVATE and encountered someone's most stubbornly held secret. She wasn't pleased.

"Pace?"

"Yes ma'am?"

"You just be a good boy and drink the rest of your milk." And then she went back to her duties at the stove.

A few weeks after Monster Mart announced its plans to leave Smoke, another discount chain store reported its intentions to lease the building which Monster Mart had occupied and to establish a business there: Value Savings USA, the outfit was called. "With a name like that," Carnihan said, "it's unlikely they'll do much business here."

"How do you mean?"

He smiled but you could tell he wasn't amused. "Where the hell's the poetry?"

The *Daily Lip* kept us abreast of any and all developments, and sometimes in the afternoon we drove out to see for ourselves. Carnihan liked to park in the middle of the lot and watch the Monster Mart trucks roll out as the ones from Value Savings USA rolled in. Then over a period of three days we watched as the Monster Mart and Rayford Holly signs came down and the Value Savings USA one went up in their place. The new sign was bigger and brighter than the others—big enough, in fact, to cover most of the shadow of the old Monster Mart lettering on the facade, and bright enough to cause electrical problems for the entire south end of Smoke when they finally put it on. I didn't say anything, but I couldn't help remembering the day Carnihan stabbed the balloon and the night we went there with the old man. At the time neither event seemed like the sort of thing I'd ever look upon fondly, but in memory they were adventures of heroic proportions, they were mythic.

"I just wish someone would tell me who owns this sonofabitch," Carnihan said once as we sat there watching. And I was able to do so, having recently read about the man in one of Miss Betty's celebrity magazines.

"His name is Linton Greenspan, and he's a billionaire from a small town somewhere out west—Bird, Utah, I think it's called. He was an orphan who grew up on a sheep farm and didn't speak until he was ten years old. Guess what his first words were?"

Carnihan seemed to think about it. His old fury was back, and, strangely, I was heartened to see it. "Something about Mama?" he said at last.

I shook my head. " 'Close the gate before the ewes get out.' "

" 'Close the gate before the ewes get out'?" he repeated, biting each word. "What kind of person says a thing like that?"

"They say he's pretty eccentric."

Carnihan's eyes tightened to a squint. He was staring at the building as if it were the thing to hate, and I could hear his breathing grow strained and heavy. A nasty red sore of a smile occupied his mouth, and he mumbled, "I wonder if Mr. Greenspan's ever been on a journey to self-discovery."

We were also there the day Value Savings USA officially began accepting job applications in a circus tent set up in the middle of the parking lot. You might've thought the store was enjoying its grand opening, so many people turned out. The applicants formed a line that stretched from the mouth of the tent all the way to the service road some two hundred yards away. A young, frenzied voice in a megaphone thanked everybody for coming out and instructed them to raise their hands if they felt faint and needed medical attention. The day was hot and no wind stirred, but in all the time we watched not a person raised his hand—in fear, I supposed, that doing so would hurt his chances of landing a job. People fanned themselves with copies of birth certificates and letters of reference and what scrap paper they could find on the pavement. Carnihan and I were parked a few car lengths from the tent, and when I became weary of gazing upon the crush of desperate human traffic I closed my eyes and tried to identify the various smells wafting on the air: tobacco fresh and tobacco chewed, coffee boiled too long and new leather shoes, talcum and baby and bathroom powder, sweat and hair oil and peppermint, drugstore perfume, wine, something fried in hog lard and something in vegetable, fresh-cut grass, the dark green sap of pine. The dark green sap of . . . *Genny!*

This last smell forced my eyes open and made me see. I sat up and there she stood in a pretty pink dress, waiting for her turn in the tent. A purse was hanging from her padded shoulder and she wore sunglasses and sandals and shiny new stockings. Her hair was in pigtails, just as she'd worn it twenty-some years before in Miss Irene's kindergarten class.

I turned to tell Carnihan that Genine had come home, but he was asleep with his head rocked back and his mouth open. He was snoring a noisy clip, but even that was drowned out by the clatter of my own heart.

I left the Mustang and walked toward the tent, shoring myself against the sides of parked cars for balance. Earlier I'd seen men fighting over a place in line, and I knew better than to give the impression that I was trying to cut in. One lady in particular seemed suspicious of my intentions. She seemed pretty common: the type who thrashes the umpire when her son loses a baseball game, who beats him mercilessly until he relents and agrees to alter the score.

"I only want to say hello to someone," I told the woman, flashing a smile that she didn't seem to appreciate. "To that girl . . . to the one there in front of you."

Genine turned at the sound of my voice. I'd wanted to greet her as she'd greeted me that first night at Babylon: "You 'member me?" And then, when she pretended not to, I'd hoped to wave a knuckled fist in front of her face.

"Pace, what are you doing here?"

"I'm not sure," I replied, certain that this was the truth.

We had an audience of no less than fifty, but it deterred neither of us. "I left him again," she announced in a bright, winning voice. "Larry. I couldn't take it anymore."

"I'm sorry, Gen."

"There was a story in the paper . . . about this laser surgery girls like me're having. You can get pregnant, is basically what it said. The laser . . ." She stopped and hugged the purse even closer. She'd recalled something else, I supposed. "Larry told me, by the way, that he told you the truth that night—about my uterus really being normal and all."

"Yeah, he did, Gen."

"To be honest, I'd rather have an undeveloped uterus than the thing he gave me. What I told you, you're born with—it's none of your doing. But what he gave me, it's the choice you make when you agree to lie down with a person like Larry Chowder."

"Why don't we talk about it later?" I smiled at the line of applicants to show that I, like them, knew a thing or two about discretion. No one smiled back, however.

"I didn't have to go with him," she continued. "I could've said no, from the beginning I could have . . ."

"Hey, Genny? Hey, Genny, why don't we talk about all this later, okay?"

"Larry thought I was protecting him, but that wasn't it at all. I didn't want people to think things, is the reason."

Everyone was watching her now. The men looked confused, the women sympathetic. "Jay fell asleep in the car," I said. "Hot as it is and he's in there snoring."

"It cuts the scar tissue away somehow," she said, "so the egg can travel along the tube and go into the womb."

"What does?"

"That laser I was telling you about."

The woman who'd glared at me earlier tapped Genine on the shoulder. "My sister had that. They had to take out a second mortgage on their mobile home." She turned back to me now. "It isn't cheap, that surgery, I'll have you know."

"Let's go get a cup of coffee at Hometown," I said to Genine. "Ruby Dean's back. It'll be like old times."

She shook her head. "I just want new, Pace."

"You want new, Genny? New what?"

"I just want new times. I don't want any old . . . I'm through with old."

I nodded and tried to smile. I couldn't get over the pigtails, how young and innocent they made her look. This was the Genny from Miss Irene's who went home at the end of the day with a lunch pail filled with paper hearts.

"I'll just wait in the car," I said, thumbing where I meant.

"New tubes, new job, new attitude, new life." She stood straight and tall to let me get a good look at her, to let everyone. "Do I seem as new as I feel?"

The crowd leaned in close, and I could tell she wanted an honest answer. "You seem new to me, Genny. You seem brand-new."

"I'm not anybody's whore anymore," she announced. "Not Anita's, not Larry's. You can tell everybody I said that, too. Tell the whole town."

I walked back to the car and got behind the wheel, wondering why some people couldn't start their lives anew in private. Carnihan mumbled something when I shut the door, but then he went back to sleep and started snoring again. I watched as the line shortened and Genine moved closer to the mouth of the tent. Every now and then she'd look at me and wave. Her mouth would say, "Hi, Pace," and she'd give her purse a hug. She also talked to the lady standing behind her in line, you knew what about. The woman liked to draw pictures with her hands, and you could see her performing the laser surgery herself, correcting the damage to the fallopian tubes she'd drawn in the air, directing the egg to the place where the sperm awaited.

Carnihan woke up finally and sat up in the seat. He yawned and rubbed his eyes, and when he spotted her up ahead he said, "Hey, man, that's Genny."

I didn't say anything. She looked our way and saw that he was awake, and she gave him a wave. "Hi, baby," her mouth said.

"Hey," he said in response. He waited until she'd turned away before saying to me, "She looks different, doesn't she?"

I nodded and our eyes met, Genine's and mine. I was seeing her as she was, as she'd always been to me.

"She's new," I told him.

Everything ends, I often remind myself: the lives of stores and people and towns, the book you thought would be the best damned story ever told.

Early on the morning of the old man's death someone stopped by Hometown and tacked a wreath to the front door. Purple and black were the predominant colors; a sash across it said, in scarlet glitter: "IN MEMORY OF A GOOD LIFE, AND IN GRATITUDE."

There wasn't a note, but everyone had an idea about who'd sent it. Ruby Dean said it was Hayward and LaShonda. Carnihan wondered if it wasn't from Linton Greenspan and Value Savings USA, a cynical message. My own guess was Miss Betty and Pop, knowing how thoughtful they were on occasions such as this.

"I'd bet it was somebody you'd never imagine," Silas Poe said in a smug way that was peculiar to him. "Well, maybe I wouldn't bet, but that's who it was."

At nine o'clock when the breakfast regulars finished checking out Ruby Dean called Durio's flower shop and spoke to one of the clerks. I could see a spark of surprise come to her face and hot tears dampen her eyes. She lowered the receiver, pressed it against her breast, and said, "Silas was the one. It was meant for the store, not for Mr. Holly."

"Oh, for the store," someone said.

"He wanted to pay his respects."

Some of us walked up to the window and watched him hobble down the street, his hat pulled low over his eyes. I couldn't recall ever seeing a more desolate picture in all my life, and yet it didn't sadden or disturb me. Silas was headed toward Old Smoke, toward the small studio apartment he'd rented there after selling his house and paying his debt to Lester Harris.

"He ordered it last week," Ruby Dean said after putting the phone down, "as soon as Jay made up his mind. The girl said they delivered it to him yesterday afternoon." She shrugged her heavy shoulders. "You know how funny he can be. Maybe he was just embarrassed by the coincidence: both the store and Mr. Holly having to pass at the same time."

"Poor Silas," I muttered, although in fact I was happy for him. He'd finally settled the last of what he owed, it seemed to me. Now he could have some peace.

"You wouldn't believe what I heard the other day," Carnihan said. He was still standing at the front of the store, gazing outside. "I heard he had a date. You remember Daddy's friend, the one he kept all those boxes of deals for . . . those napkin deals?"

"We know what you mean and we know the lady," Ruby Dean said. "Don't be getting too descriptive now."

"He took her to a movie. They held hands." Carnihan stepped back from the window and looked at me. "Hey, Pace, wake me up when it's all over, will you, pal?"

"When what's all over?"

"This dream that has become my life."

I sat at the counter and read the *Lip*'s lead story for the third time today. It was an AP account with a Liberty, Arkansas, dateline and a montage of file photos. One paragraph in particular stood out, and I returned to it yet again.

Rayford Holly, it said, had known about the cancer for more than a year but had chosen to keep it a secret, fearing that people would treat him differently. Even his closest friends and business associates didn't know of the illness, a melanoma. "We would've acted the same," I said aloud.

"What's that?" It was Carnihan.

"Winston. He knew he was dying when he was here in Smoke. I don't know why he didn't tell us anything."

Carnihan took the paper from my hands and folded it in half. "None of it would've happened," he said. "That's why." He placed the section with the others by the register. "He may have seemed full of it sometimes, but let me tell you something, brother: Winston was right, Winston was always right."

Few people turned out for lunch that day. Ruby Dean's chalkboard said ANYTHING YOU WANT . . . but she served only two cold ham plates, a tomato sandwich, some french fries, and a chocolate malt. I wasn't hungry but I sat at the counter anyway and had a bag of potato chips and a lemonade. As sad and hard a time as this was I figured I'd be cheating myself if I spent the day anywhere but in the store. The handful who did come had nice things to say to Ruby Dean and Carnihan. They all commented as to how they were going to miss Hometown and how like the death of a friend it was. Ol' Fontenot took pictures and the two bank tellers wept and left tips three times as much as the cost of the food they'd ordered. When they left they didn't turn back around, and that was how you could tell how true their feelings were: when the goodbye is final you can never look back, it's too painful to.

Miss Betty called to find out if everything was okay, and Pop got on the phone and said, "Hang in there, son."

By half past one Silas still hadn't shown up, and we decided he was just sparing himself the agony of a last meal. Feeling sentimental, I asked Ruby Dean if I could have a bottle of Tabasco as a souvenir. She took the one by the place where Silas always sat and emptied it down the drain, then she rinsed it out and put the cap back on. "He never really liked it, you know?" she said, handing me the bottle. "He told me the other day. He only put it on his food to aggravate me."

"But he wrecked his insides over it!"

"That's what I'm telling you," she said, and went about her cleaning, drawing circles one after the other.

What we put ourselves through, I thought. What miseries. And then the end comes, anyway.

"Silly man," Ruby Dean said. "He deserves what he got. I wouldn't've liked him no matter how much sauce he used."

At three o'clock Carnihan left his stool at the business counter and walked the length of the store. The floor creaked underfoot and everywhere glass shook and for a second all the old, familiar smells came up and teased your nostrils. He reached the front and flipped the sign over in the window, and from where I sat you could see the word OPEN in big red letters, while everyone outside had to contend with CLOSED in black.

A few days later a man named Red Burgess called and identified himself as chief counsel for Monster Mart Inc. He was looking for

Carnihan, and when I told him who I was he said, "Yes, of course. You're the novelist."

Burgess said the old man had brought a hundred stories back home with him to Liberty and often mentioned us in conversation, even toward the end. "We've never met," Burgess continued, "but it seems as if I know you."

"That's interesting," I said, "because after he left we never talked to him again. We tried calling but his secretary wouldn't put us through and he didn't return messages. I sent him a letter and he didn't reply."

"You shouldn't take it personally," Burgess said. "Mr. Holly, as you well know, was famous for his disappearing acts. It didn't mean he wasn't thinking about you. I can tell you from firsthand experience that he often talked about returning to Smoke. He seems to have had an inspired time there."

"Sometimes I think we just imagined it all."

"Did he talk about his bird dogs?"

"Yes, he did. He talked about them a lot."

"Then you didn't imagine it. If an old fellow with a country accent was down there talking about bird dogs, then chances are it really happened. I'll tell you something kind of strange, Burnette. Those dogs of his have been real quiet since he died—they seem to know something's wrong."

I had no reason to think that this wasn't true. I kept picturing the old man with Beatnik, stroking the dog's long blue face, the joy he seemed to get from such an idle exercise.

"And what about Whitman? Did he talk about him, too?"

"All the time. He quoted him every chance he got."

"And love? I bet he had plenty to say about love."

"Oh, yes. Love seemed to be his favorite subject."

There was a silence during which the only sound was of papers rustling on the other end. "Mr. Carnihan hasn't returned, has he? I thought I'd run something by him."

"No sir, he's still out." It was late afternoon: he and Bethany had gone to visit Mrs. Duvall at the home.

"Then I'll tell you, Burnette, and you can relay the information. Is that all right?"

"Yes sir, that's fine."

"Mr. Holly has included you and Mr. Carnihan in his will."

I could feel the heat rise in my face; a bright pain came to my chest and my hands started to shake. It hardly seemed possible, and yet I knew what we were in for. The old man had no survivors, after all. And hadn't everyone referred to us as his close, personal friends?

"In his will, Mr. Burgess?"

The man chuckled softly. He sensed my excitement and wanted me to relax, I reckoned. "He left a riding lawn mower to Mr. Carnihan and, to you, a box of typing paper."

"Typing paper?"

"Well, let me check that . . . no, computer paper." He rustled the papers again. "A box of computer paper, says here. Two thousand nine hundred continuous sheets. Blank white twenty-pound computer bond." He laughed a little louder now. "That's the biggest box we carry."

"That's a lot of paper."

"Yes, it is," Burgess said. "That's a lot for anyone." And I wondered what he meant . . . *a lot for anyone.*

"What about a microwave oven?" I asked, immediately feeling ashamed of myself for having brought it up. "Anything in the will about one with a turntable, Mr. Burgess?"

The papers again. "No, nothing. But that doesn't surprise me. Mr. Holly never liked them. He said they took the flavor out of food." He gave another laugh and said, "Of course we'll have them delivered—the mower and the paper. To Hometown, is it?"

"That's right, Mr. Burgess. To Hometown."

After the call I left the store and went for a walk through town. I still had the shakes and I wanted to exorcise them, and I was tired of feeling down about the old man and the store. I passed by the jailhouse and the Delta and the Palace Cafe. I couldn't say how long I was gone, but when I returned it was dark and someone had turned the lights on inside the store. From the street I could see the rows of green shades and the red wood floor and the zinc countertop, and for a moment my heart soared at the notion that it wasn't all lost and gone after all. But then, getting closer now, I saw the black word

CLOSED and Carnihan sitting by himself at the business counter. He was leaning forward fiddling with something, and when I reached the front door the better I could see with what.

Beatnik was at his feet, lying on his side with his ugly tongue hanging out. I pushed the door open and both of them ran to meet me, Carnihan lagging a step or two behind.

"What in heaven's . . ." I said, and took the dog in my arms. He licked my neck and face, sprayed a measure of urine on my shirt, and generally did his best to show how delighted he was to make my acquaintance again.

"They found him this afternoon at Value Savings USA," Carnihan said. "They were cleaning out some air-conditioning ducts and there he was, asleep on a pillow." Carnihan smiled. "They also found a little kid."

"A little kid?"

"Eleven years old. He kept poking everyone with a dagger and calling like a hog. Remember how Winston used to do?"

"Monster Boy," I said, unable to restrain myself. "That was Monster Boy they found!"

"Well, that's who he claimed he was. But then Lonnie Tom spanked him good and he finally came clean. You remember the Trussell clan lives just across the tracks?"

"The ones with lice in their hair?"

"That's them. There were so many kids the father had to borrow a neighbor's school bus to take them to church on Sunday morning. Well, he was one of them—Simon's his name. He'd been missing for almost three years."

"Three years, my God."

"I rode out with Lonnie Tom when he brought him home. Know what his mama did? She got up out of her chair, met him on their old sagging porch, and bopped him hard on the ear."

"How terrible."

"But nothing compared to the father. He just stayed on the couch in the living room, watching a wrestling match on TV. He didn't even get up. The boy went in, wading through about two dozen other kids, and the father told him to move out of the way, he was blocking the goddamned set."

Beatnik jumped from my arms and scurried, sniffing, along the length of the counter. When he reached the end he noticed the pictures hanging overhead and barked a few times. He seemed disturbed by the one of Ruby Dean, or perhaps he was just fussing in honor of it. He stopped after I reproached him, and Carnihan said, "When I have my son I'll never treat him like Trussell did young Simon, I can guarantee you that much."

I faced him and his lips curled into a smile. "We actually found out the day Winston died. Doctor over at the clinic called with her test results." He paused and looked back at the pictures on the wall. "A fifth Carnihan, can you believe that, brother? Poor Smoke, having to put up with another one."

"Poor Bethany," I said.

"Yeah." He wrapped an arm around my neck. "Poor everyone."

After Ruby Dean retired the second time I went nearly three months without seeing her. She was supervising the construction of an addition to her house, I'd heard, and had time for little else. But it was my theory that she didn't come around because she didn't like to see the store as it was. Carnihan had painted the words HOMETOWN FOR SALE: INQUIRE WITHIN across the window in front, and the old cypress shelves and most of the stock had been sold to a Warren flea market. The only real life that remained was the movement of the electric clock behind the counter and the steady humming of the refrigerator, which Carnihan still used to store his Bloody Mary ingredients.

I found Ruby Dean in her thoroughly modern kitchen preparing what she called a "snack" for the team of builders. She had heaping platters of hot-cooked food laid out on the kitchen table, and she insisted I eat a plate. I obeyed and soon enough found myself trying to engage her in a conversation about the old days at Hometown, a conversation in which she seemed determined to have no part. "Don't make me go back," she said. "A person can't live there." Instead she talked about how disheartened Hayward had been sitting the bench during his last year as a pro, and what a turnaround she figured Carnihan would make now that he was going to be a father, and why she thought Genine Monteleone was a right fine choice for a fellow like me. "Genny's brave, and, let's be honest, Pace, you're a bit of a coward. She'll help you when times get hard."

I didn't argue because I knew she was right. And because you just didn't argue with Ruby Dean.

After the meal she gave me a tour of the construction site, pointing out where she planned to put this and that. "Did you know Jay let me have both registers? They'll go there—under glass, of course." She pointed to the place. "You know the No Sale button on the one we kept on the business counter? The word *Sale* is rubbed completely off. *No* is all it says. Wonder how many times in his life Jay pressed that thing?"

The addition would include three bedrooms, two bathrooms, and a library, and although only a few more games remained in the NFL season, the completion date was still a few months away. "I guess until then we'll just be climbing all over each other," she said, seeming overjoyed by the prospect.

She walked me out to the car and stood by the open door with her arms crossed. "Do you ever run into him around town?" she asked, her voice suddenly sounding as soft and dreamy as a young girl's recalling a first love.

"Run into who, Ruby Dean?"

I immediately regretted the question, seeing the blush at her cheeks. I cleared my throat and attempted to cover up my error. "Oh, sure, I see him. He walks around a lot. I hear he takes his meals at the Palace now." When she failed to say anything, I added, "He looks real thin, though. I bet he misses your cooking."

"Is he still going out with that lady?" The question was hard for her to ask. She kept her eyes on the ground. "That one who used to come in and ask for—"

"I don't think it amounted to much," I answered. "They only went to the movies a few times—for the company, more than anything. I think he's on the loose again."

This seemed to perk her up. She let her arms drop. "Well, you just go and tell him not to bother coming around Ruby Dean Clark, do you hear?" Her voice was full of fire now, and her eyes were big and wide and fixed on mine.

"Silas Poe," she said at last, spitting the name as if it had brought a bitter taste to her tongue.

After the Smoke Monster Mart closed, Bethany was transferred to the company's store in Warren. Shortly thereafter, however, she went on maternity leave under orders from her doctor, who thought keeping up with her own personal hygiene was more important than keeping up with that of shoppers looking for bargains on toothpaste and mouthwash.

Carnihan sold the place at Worm Road to an adventurous young couple who promised to keep and care for the goats, and he moved what furniture and farm equipment they didn't want to the store. He and I spent the better part of a day hauling the stuff in the Hometown delivery truck, and when we were done we returned to the farm and drove through the pasture to where he'd hidden the old man's pickup truck. He added a can of fresh gas and changed the battery and spark plugs; and the engine, to my surprise, turned over on only the second try.

"What are you gonna do with this old thing?" I asked.

"Drive it," he replied. And then he did just that, leaving me to follow him in the other vehicle.

Now that three of us shared Dr. McDermott's, my rent was reduced to a hundred dollars a month. This agreed with me because I was running desperately low on cash, and I still had the lunch counter tab, about a thousand dollars' worth. Although Carnihan didn't seem concerned that I pay him, he liked to remind me every now and then just how much I was indebted to him. I think he enjoyed the role of literary patron, and some days he locked my office door from the outside, leaving me alone inside for stretches of twenty hours at a time. But then there was the other Carnihan, the one who often made it impossible for me to work when I was feeling most inspired.

"Let's go play," he often said, bursting into the office while I was in the middle of writing. He had a knack of intruding when the magic was starting to come.

"Let's go play" meant a game of basketball. So, more often than not, I put on some gym clothes and sneakers and drove with him to Delmas Street, where Pop invariably joined us on the court outside and, with more trick shots than seemed fair, beat us into the ground. Afterward Miss Betty served refreshments on the patio, and we sat on the hard, wrought-iron furniture and watched the birds swirling overhead and Bernard and Mrs. Kuel toiling in their backyard garden. It often occurred to me that as a boy I'd dreamed of being the sort of writer who traveled the world and encountered more adventures and women than he could ever hope to put down on paper, and that as a man I was the sort who settled for one girl and saw the great cities of the world only on cable TV. This probably would've bothered a lot of folks in my line of work, but I can honestly say I never feel as if I'm missing out. In Smoke I've discovered everything I ever need of happiness, for the town holds my heart.

"How do you like my do?" Genine asked me one night at Dr. McDermott's. She'd spent the better part of the afternoon with Claire and Abigail, and now she seemed to resemble them. She wore their clothes and their shoes and their makeup and, yes, their too-precious haircut, which I'd thought last seen in this country sometime during the Great Depression. She also carried herself as they did, which is to say with the supreme confidence of an absolute worldbeater.

"My sisters," I said, "have snatched your soul and now they want your body. I'm not sure I like that very much."

We were in the X-ray lab, sitting on the edge of the bed. "I'll take something else of theirs soon enough," she said, "and you'll give it to me." Her voice was full of the promise of sex; it was the one I was lucky enough to hear now and again, sometimes as often as twice a day. I reached out and touched her hair, the place in front where it curled cleverly upward.

"Would you mind," she said, "if I took your name when we finally do it? That's another thing: I'd like a new name."

My sigh of reluctance was designed to spur her on, but she merely glared at me as if I were a turd; and I was forced to try something else. "The divorce from Peahead isn't even final yet," I protested halfheartedly, "and already you're calling yourself a Burnette."

"You will marry me, won't you?"

"Do I really have a choice?"

She shook her head. "Love doesn't allow for choices. It makes your mind up for you."

I drew back to let her see my face. "Why is everybody always quoting Winston about love?"

"Winston? I came up with that myself, I'll have you know."

I knew better than to say anything more. Her voice wasn't as ripe with promise as it had been earlier, and I didn't want to risk ruining my chances.

Later, after we'd closed and locked the door and turned out the light, and did what we always seemed to do when the door was closed and locked and the light was out, she pressed her mouth against my ear and whispered, "I love you, Pace Burnette."

I smiled and swallowed hard. And she did the same, falling back on her pillow. "I love you, too, Genny Burnette."

But the words had hardly left my mouth before we'd both fallen asleep.

Unable to find a job in Smoke, Carnihan applied for an entry-level position at the Rayford Holly Wholesale Club near Bayou Loup and was hired after passing a drug test and memorizing a chant of which the store's late founder was particularly fond. Standing with his hand over his heart in the manager's office, he fixed a jingoistic gaze on a glossy color picture of the old man and said: "Stack it deep, sell it cheap, heap it high and watch it fly! Hear those downtown merchants cry!" Of the twenty new employees, Carnihan would tell me later, his voice had been the loudest, an irony which seemed to escape him but which always sent something like a dagger through my heart.

His work consisted of unloading trucks, stocking shelves and pallets, and retrieving shopping buggies in the parking lot. The store had opened only recently so there was plenty of opportunity for advancement, and he liked to boast that he'd make assistant manager before his thirtieth birthday. To work each day he drove the old man's pickup, and wore a white shirt with a Rayford Holly patch on the breast, a jumble of Rayford Holly ink pens poking up from the front pocket. Needless to say, it was hard for me to square my image of him as a romantic rebel ranting against the monopolization of the mercantile trade with the fellow who swore his undivided loyalty to a subsidiary of Monster Mart Inc. If I forgave him it was because I knew that principles mean little when a man's got a pregnant wife and there's no other living to make, and also because I still glimpsed some of the old Carnihan fire whenever Linton Greenspan's name came up. I glimpsed it in the way his eyes fogged over and his body stiffened and his lips grew pale and twisted. Carnihan now seemed to enjoy hating the owner of Value Savings USA as much as he'd once hated the old man. "They're trying to cut into our customer base! We need to stop this Greenspan character . . . we need to—"

"Two things," I said, flashing the appropriate number of fingers. "First off, watch your mouth, brother, there's a woman who happens to be your wife in the next room. And, second, you might want to think about what you just said, kemosabe."

He'd been pacing the floor and pummeling the air with his fists, but presently he sat down and seemed to regain his composure. If nothing else his voice was back to normal. "You know, Pace, I figured something out when Winston was here. I figured out that it's not a sin to hate a person as long as you leave the door open to love him."

Not love again, I told myself. Not that.

But there he went, his voice rising as he made the declaration: "Love is the last, best thing. It's what you find after you've lost everything else."

I didn't speak for a minute. I kept thinking about what Genine had said in bed a few weeks before and wondering why suddenly everyone felt compelled to talk this way. I let on a weary smile. "Winston told you that, didn't he, Jay?"

"No, brother. It just came to me."

"Say it again, if you don't mind."

He repeated the thing and I sat staring at him, waiting for him to crack up. Had Genine put him up to this? I wondered. His expression gave nothing away, and I couldn't decide whether to take him seriously.

"You don't mind if I write what you just said in my new book, do you, brother?"

It was a test: if he broke down and laughed or punched me on the arm I'd know he was only having fun; anything else and he really meant what he'd said.

It was anything else. "You can write it," he said, "but just remember you heard it here first. And spell my name right."

He started pacing the floor again, and cursing Linton Greenspan a thousand times. Last I heard, he was trying to figure out how to make the man apologize for the evil he'd done.

"Who does he think he is, anyway? Will you tell me that, Pace? Just who?"

If not for the old man *Strange Weather* would not have sold enough copies to fill a No. 3 washtub, but Cinda Lovey chose to ignore that when she pitched my second novel to a select group of New York publishing houses. I'd sent her the first few chapters and a story outline, and from this she'd been able to determine that *Remember Who You Are*, as I was calling it, was an "exciting, fast-paced caper in the tradition of R. Chandler and D. Hammett. And with the promising figures of Mr. Burnette's debut offering," she continued in her cover letter, "I don't see how his follow-up can fail to be a runaway international bestseller."

When I told Cinda that I'd read neither Chandler nor Hammett, she laughed her quixotic Manhattan laugh and said, "Neither have I, honey, but what, pray tell, has that got to do with anything?"

I was delighted with the twelve-thousand-dollar advance. It was enough to help pay for Genine's microsurgery, to replace the Mustang's tattered ragtop, and to cover my account with Carnihan. The money arrived in a Federal Express letter one day and was spent as soon as the check cleared seven working days later. I was nearly broke again but Pop had spoken to the principal at Smoke High and the man had agreed to let me substitute-teach whenever I needed "a little *lagniappe*," as Miss Betty put it. Fall was upon us but in South Louisiana the grass was still growing, and I accepted a number of jobs mowing lawns, Ruby Dean's among them. Carnihan had no use for his new riding mower, and offered to let me use it in return for my keeping the weeds down in the parking areas at Dr. McDermott's and the store. He also let me haul the Monster Machine from site to site in the back of the Hometown delivery truck, just as long as I kept the magnetic signs on the doors.

Every now and then in the early evening after a day of writing hard or trimming grass or teaching Louisiana history to terminally bored sixteen-year-olds, I invite Bethany and Genine for a drive in the Mustang, and, together with Beatnik, we cruise the forgotten streets of downtown Smoke. The fading light colors the facades of the dusty storefronts, and I watch our reflection in the show windows that remain empty except for undressed mannequins and an occasional poster featuring fashions from two decades ago. No matter where we start out going, the road always leads us to Bayou Loup and the Rayford Holly Wholesale Club, and we park in a field of asphalt and wait for Carnihan to appear.

Sometimes he comes to collect the buggies left standing in the lot, to gather them one after another until he must have fifty and it takes all that's in him to push them back to where they belong.

"Why does he have to do them all at once?" Bethany asks. "Wouldn't it be easier if he made a few trips? What's he trying to prove?"

"If he keeps this up," Genine answers, "he's sure to get a hernia. And then he'll be no good for anyone."

We watch in silence and I recall Sisyphus and his rock and hill and his head like something you could break down doors with. "He's showing off," I say after a while. But I know as soon as the words leave my mouth that that isn't it at all.

Other times it's an hour or more before we see him and by then it's closing time and the electric sign out front has gone dark and the lights inside have blinked three times just like the ones at Babylon used to do when morning was about to break and it was time for everyone to go home. He comes walking straight down the middle aisle on legs that wobble under his weight and the wind catches his hair and you can see him remove his snap-on tie and unbutton the top few buttons of his shirt. His lips are moving and he might be singing or he might be talking to himself. In any case, I'm really incredibly proud of him and although I feel like saying as much something always stops me. Maybe I'm thinking of what might have been, or maybe I'm remembering what was, but almost always I laugh to myself a little sadly and say, "One thing I've learned about living is that if you planned on things going one way, count on them going the other."

He reaches the old man's pickup and joins the long line of traffic leaving the store. We get in somewhere behind him and follow him out to the interstate where too many commuters are heading home at once and cars are backed up for miles, moving one-third the posted speed limit.

Finally, near Smoke, the congestion thins and opens up and we find that we're the only cars left on the road. I flash my brights a few times to let him know we're the ones riding hard on his tail, and in reply he gives me a turn signal. Sometimes we pump horns at each other, and sometimes we race. But always, together, we drive into town.